AT THE EDGE

of the

OTHERWORLD

Rise of the Celtic Gods
Book 3

Kristin Gleeson

Published by An Tig Beag Press

Cover design by JD Smith Designs

ISBN: 978-0-9956281-8-2

OTHER WORKS BY KRISTIN GLEESON

In Praise of the Bees

CELTIC KNOT SERIES

Selkie Dreams

Along the Far Shores

Raven Brought the Light

A Treasure Beyond Worth (novella)

RENAISSANCE SOJOURNER SERIES

The Imp of Eye (with Moonyeen Blakey)

The Sea of Travail

The Quest of Hope

The Pursuit of the Unicorn

HIGHLAND BALLAD SERIES

The Hostage of Glenorchy

The Mists of Glen Strae

The Braes of Huntly

Highland Lioness

Highland Yuletide

RISE OF THE CELTIC GODS SERIES

Awakening the Gods

In Search of the Hero God

At the Edge of the Otherworld

NON FICTION

Anahareo, A Wilderness Spirit

LISTEN TO THE MUSIC CONNECTED TO THE BOOKS

Go to www.krisgleeson.com/music

Receive a FREE novelette prequel, *A Treasure Beyond Worth,* and
Along the Far Shores

When you sign up for my mailing list www.krisgleeson.com

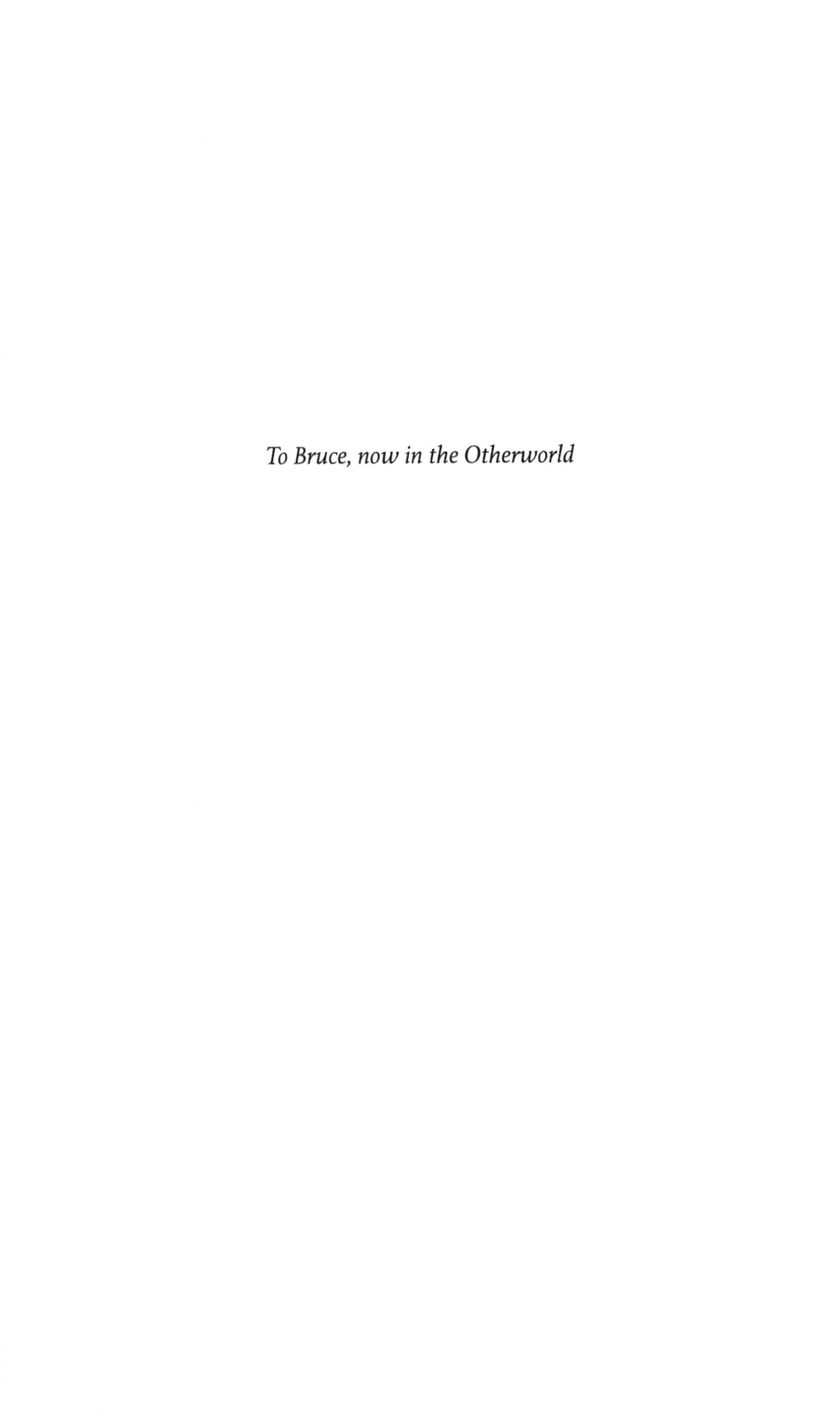

To Bruce, now in the Otherworld

PART I

A TRICKSTER LIFE

1

MAURA

The caws and cackles set me on edge. It was my lads, the crows, perched up in the tall conifers outside my house, having their own little giggle gossip, thinking it would get me going. I wouldn't let them, the feckers, I stretched my mouth, my muscles taking the shape of the cheeky grin, the "I don't give a toss" and "feck off" to you expression I had cultivated for so long, and beamed it through the window up to the trees at them. It was me, so it was. It was me. The lips stretched wider and I felt my cheek twitch. There was a steely glint in my eyes, I knew that, and I widened them just so they'd see. Just so they'd know who was in charge.

I pulled away from the window and shook out my black hair, enjoying the feel of it spreading out wild. That was me, so. Wild, wicked, wrathful and wearing all those "Ws" like a goddess breastplate. Because that's what I was, the most fearsome "w" of them all. War.

I would own that, so I would. Own it now and forever because there was no escaping that "w". Cut out any of that oh so soft flute solo, that winsome fiddle tune that would make me smile, and especially that sultry, siren guitar that slowly riffed its way into the belief that all things were possible. They weren't.

I opened the front door, letting it slam hard against the wall with the force of my pull. Outside, the caws and chitter slowed and the birds eyed me curiously from their branches. The conifers were as old as this farmhouse, which was slowly sinking into the mountain it resided on and was folded in a little at the edges, along with an outbuilding long past its milking date. The cows and sheep that had once dotted this farm, too, were only echoes in the grass, gorse and brambles. But for all its outmoded and tired state, this farm had suited me, appealed to a perverse quirk I couldn't quite put my finger on, but then my fingers were busy doing other things, elsewhere.

Now, I stood and looked up at the lads, my head tilted to the side. "Anything you care to share?" I asked, a slight edge to my voice.

Rook, his perch on the large branch just above me, looked me straight in the eye and shook his head. It wasn't a "no" type of shake. It was a "you right pitiful dab" kind of shake. As in "look at the state of you".

The state of me. "Ah, go on, so," I said irritably. "Get out of my sight, the lot of you."

They flew off, a wave so large and Mexican, it could have been started there, rippling wide and heavy. "What are you, star-lings?" I shouted after them. Rook screeched back in protest and I laughed. I knew that would get him.

I chuckled for a few moments, watching them disappear into the sky, letting the humour of it all settle on me and in me. Build me up. The state of me. The humour seeped out, taking good will and any kindness that was left. State of me indeed. Feck off to all of them.

I caught sight of the axe that was embedded in the block of wood over by the shed and stomped off to it. Oh I was having a proper rant. A paddy. Though this was a paddy with power – and wasn't I just so clever with that little play on words of the famous chain of betting shops? Would wager my life it would make someone laugh.

I drew the axe from the wood block, positioned a bit of wood on the block and drew the axe back for a swing. It fell hard and heavy, the great "thwack" sounding satisfying to my ears and my heart as the wood sprung apart. I swung again, not caring that the wood didn't need it, and the pieces were small enough for the stove. I kept swinging, losing sight of the target, my mind filling with images and people. Swing and splat, I thought. Swing and chop. The smell of blood was nearly tangible. Yes.

I wouldn't think of Anu, our mother, the earth's mother. Our goddess. No, I wouldn't picture her, ill and failing because that Fomorian fecker Balor, the poison of all poisonous beings, was doing his best to kill her off. To kill us all off. Me included. No, I wasn't included, that was the whole point. But my heart stopped just for a moment at the thought of Anu dying and the deaths that would follow her own. No, no, and no.

I kept swinging, pausing for only a few seconds to place a new piece of wood on the block. My leather jacket strained and creaked a little with the effort and my jeans stretched at the seams against my flexing thigh muscles. It felt good. I could feel my body sing with the effort. I could of course. It was almost as good as battle practice, I told myself, even though my opponent was a block of wood. And some of my opponents in the past had just as little skill. And some of them had as much in their heads as well. Those who fought at my side, I could honestly say were far from that. All so skilled, so filled with ideas and wit and courage...I caught my thoughts before they could go further and gave them a good old flogging before they could get any more ideas. Yeah, they were grand fighters, and thinkers, but what of it? It was the fight, the battle, the war that counted. I would fight no matter what. I didn't fight alongside the Tuatha de Danann because I wanted to defeat the Fomorians. I just liked to be on their side because it was great craic. Such fun to share the parry, toss the look, know that they would get in on the jab and thrust and turn the sword in a just so manner, with style, with grace, and oh it would fly. I would fly.

There, that was it, so. The reason why. The story of Daghda and helping. Of fighting on their side and not against them. The craic of it all. I held the axe at my side, my breathing heavy with the exertion of chopping. Around me, the wood pieces lay tumbled about in disorderly order. A house of wood collapsed, all splayed out in every direction. A leaf floated by, from a tree that looked like ash, but shed like beech. Ash trees don't shed yet, I thought. It must be beech, but where are the nuts? Is it a year for beech nuts? I giggled a little at the word play, the notion of nuts and craic and my fierce little outburst, that thanking all that was, the lads hadn't seen it. But still, I felt a little better. Just, what to do? And that was the nub, the nut, if you will, of the issue. The "what to do" of where I found myself. Because the "self" I found at the moment felt off and wrong and completely out of sorts. Because my ire, my fire, my ire fire was the wrong sort. It didn't fill me, it didn't sing in my blood or beat my bodhran with a soul beguiling rhythm that no mortal could refuse. No, it made me hack at a piece of wood with an axe.

I had the sudden notion to swing the axe around my head and hurl it off into the field below me. I started to move for the trees when I heard my gate creak. I turned and spied Finn entering the path to the house, shutting the gate behind him. I stiffened. He walked slowly towards me, a tentative smile on his face, his eyes luminous and filled with doubt, anger and... something else. The sun shone on his hair, making the copper shiny and bright. I hated that I noticed that. All of it.

"Go away, Finn," I said darkly. "There's nothing to say."

"Ah, now, Maura, I've only come to have an old banter, nothing more."

His arms were down at his sides, his expression now assembled into studied neutral.

I crossed my arms, frowned, and started to open my mouth to tell him and the rest of them to feck off out of it, but he interrupted me.

"You've got the 'feck off' look, so you don't need to say it."

I shut my mouth and narrowed my eyes. "And so why won't you?"

"I told you, I just wanted a chat. A 'how's things' kind of chat."

"Things are fine. You can go now."

"Fine? Are you sure?"

"Certain."

"Certain as you'll ever be?"

I sighed. "I'm not playing games with you Finn."

"But I like our games."

I frowned again. "What's that supposed to mean?"

"Maura, will you get it through your head that I enjoy hanging around with you. Chilling."

I raised my brows at him mockingly. "Chill? Netflix and chill, babe, you mean? Who are you and what have you done with Finn? With the god of wordsmithing, Ogma, oh master of diplomacy and orator extraordinaire?"

Finn laughed, the glee in his eyes and all over his expression. Such joy. I'd always envied him that. Such joy.

"See now," he said. "There it is. What I love so much. The craic. The way it is with you."

"There is no 'way it is with me'," I said, holding up my fingers to form quotation marks. "I am who I am. I am not responsible for craic of any sort. I mock, I jeer, I condescend, but I do not do anything else."

Finn giggled, the fecker. He actually giggled at me. My eyes narrowed automatically as I studied him carefully. I'd known him so long, sometimes I forgot how well I knew him. Something was off, something wasn't right.

"What is it?" I said flatly. I didn't want him getting any ideas I was that interested. Not at all. Never, no never no more. The song of that name flashed through my mind, mocking me. "What's got the wind up you?"

Finn's giggling halted, disappearing like some flighty swallow with one fell swoop and "you're off, boys". He was off, definitely.

"Nothing," he said flatly. He turned his head away, looking over to the trees. He indicated to the conifers. "Lads not here? That's not like them. It's not like them to miss a jeering, leering, caw caw or two."

"You don't miss a trick, do you? It took you until now to notice they aren't here? Tsk tsk, Finn. But that's beside the point. They're not here, so now you can tell me what it is without their jeering, leering, caw caws."

"Ah, no, you can feck off with that yourself," he said, a slight twist in his mouth. "You haven't told me what's going on with you, so don't try the distraction ploy."

"What's going on with me?" I said. Why did I pick at his scab, because I knew he would pick at mine? And mine was a big scab. It wouldn't enjoy being picked at. I wouldn't be responsible for what would happen if just a tiny particle of that scab was picked at. It was a "not to be picked at ever in this lifetime" scab.

"Nothing is going on with me," I said, matching his flat tone.

"Nothing is going on with you, in my eye," said Finn, the flat tone turning hard.

Ah, feck, a tiny prick, just a little fraction that could hardly be called picking at the scab. So I told myself. I thought of the tipper. The one for the bodhran, how it felt in my hand, the different shapes and patterns it could make. The pattern for "this beat is flying" for the old polkas, and the one for "my blood is singing" for the mad reels and the shape for "lazy old slidy, slidy get your body swaying" I used for slip jigs. It was the slip jig shape now. I would be the slip jig beat. Lazy, slidy. Dum de dum de dum. So chill. So chill.

I looked over at Finn now, ready and able to give him the answer. His eyes were on me, the trees having lost his interest, the distraction strategy having collapsed. But my strategy wouldn't collapse. I was chill, without the Netflix. Shaping that pattern in my head, hearing it there, feeling it.

"Everything is going on with you, Maura," said Finn.

His voice was even, but I could hear something in the back of it. No. . . . Slidy, slidy. I started to tap my foot, drown out the effort of the words, the "what's at the heart of them", but he wouldn't stop.

"Ever since you negotiated that deal with the Hunters in the forest, you've been increasingly angry. Shoving everyone away. Shoving me away. And now you decide you're going to leave. Just when we are about to go after the two things that will help kill Balor. But you can only say 'feck on out of it'. I want to know why. You didn't say why, Maura. Not really. I want to know why. I want to understand. Maybe I can help. We're friends, Maura. Friends help each other."

He stopped, oh feck me, finally, he stopped. I could hear his breathing, almost panting with the emotion, the effort of the words. And those words. Pick, pick, pick. Picks so loud, fierce and deadly and determined to mine the nuggets beneath the scabs they stabbed and dug at. This was more than a prick. The scab was open, apart, bloody.

"We are not friends!" I shouted. The rage, dark and terrible, was rising up and I hugged my body, not wanting it, fighting it, trying to squeeze it back down. "I don't have friends," I said, my voice choked with this massive effort of pressing down.

He gave me a stunned look. Pain washed through him, followed by anger and then – yes, there – it was a look of pity. But it was all I needed. I could press down now. Not a bother. I drew myself up. "I am Morrigan. I don't require friends, Ogma. There is no place for friends for a GODDESS OF WAR." I made sure he knew that the last three words were all in capitals, the size, the emphasis necessary, because that's who I was. I was big, large, unpredictable, inevitable, unavoidable.

He shook his head. "You're more than that, Maura."

I snorted. "You don't know me. No one knows me. And it's best that way. I'm dark, Finn. What you see...what you saw was only surface."

"No."

I frowned at him. He gave me a fierce look. "Tell me what's wrong."

The fury rose again and this time there was no pressing, no squeezing back. I opened my mouth to scream, shut it at the last moment and did the only thing I could do at that point. Take flight and feck off myself.

2

SMITHY

He prowled his sitting room, in part because he wanted to keep his leg moving. Test it. Ensure its strength. No sudden collapse yet. Reassuring, that. His wound from the battle at the Beara was a little sore, but nothing more. If he didn't have to go to Anu's in a short while he'd bring in a few logs and light the stove. He could chip a few sticks. That would test it. Bending, twisting and all that. He glanced at the huge pile of sticks in the basket by the stove. No accusation, just a smug statement sitting quietly in a corner. A "you old fool" smugness. Yes, okay.

He turned away from the stove and eyed the fiddle. Yes, the T-shirt to that was well and truly got and worn. But maybe a little spin on it wouldn't hurt. He knew his limitations now and it wouldn't take him by surprise this time. He felt the draw of the music, though its magic might be gone. The draw was there, the hum, its pure sweetness and depth still an invitation. A tune rattled around his head suddenly and he grinned in surprise. The surprise felt good. The surprise and the lightness that came with it. He grabbed on to it because he was sick of himself, so he was. Sick of the pitiful gobshite he'd become. Sure, who could stand that? Not him, that was certain.

He went over to the fiddle case, opened it, grabbed the fiddle and manhandled the bow like it was a sword. The little idea in his head that flitted in, like an annoying fly, suddenly seemed hilarious. Perfect. No tuning, no, not at all. Not what he had in mind. He'd call it the cat's meow, and the meow would hang awful and piercing. Him the pitiful old fool.

He ran the bow across the string, no rosin preventing a skip, smoothing the way. Not at all. The "yeow meow eow" the fiddle emitted was worse than any beginner. And yet. And yet. He ran the bow back across, the other direction getting the harmony, the double double stopping of the strings all at once his only goal. He could hear something in that. Was it good, was it bad? Or was the cat in heat? Who the feck knew. All he understood at that moment was that the fiddle was speaking to him in a way it had never done before. Some might say, thank feck for that. But he was saying nothing for now. Just listening.

SMITHY SWUNG his leg across the motorcycle and surprised himself by forgetting to be aware of the supporting leg, to be constantly on the alert for it to collapse in the midst of any kind of use that might test its strength. He'd been too busy thinking about his little cat diddly tune. The worst and best tune he'd ever created, or so he imagined, because he still couldn't feel his old tunes and bring them up like he used to, before. Yeah that "before" time. He shoved that "before time" out of his mind with a big old cat swipe, claws out and drawing blood. Shove that feckin' "before" down the Well of Slane where the "before" and "after" had met. He was living with "after" now and it was all he had. Meow. Swipe.

Meow Yeow (what other title could it be?) was firmly back in his head by the time he flipped out the kick-start, pushed it through and started up the bike. He liked the motion of the kick-start, none of this press ignition electronic shite for him. It all went with the *Meow Yeow* sort that he was.

He opened the throttle and took off up the hill, the breeze catching his face under the helmet. He gave little thought to what Anu wanted this time. Getting back the slingshot and the sacred spear. Feck's sake. Let Luke do it all. He was the hero boy, wasn't he? Well, have at it, me lad, thought Smithy. He would just be laid back, *Meow Yeow*, ready to swipe if need be, but let Luke take the lead, take the hits. Yeah, he liked that tune, liked that idea. So feckin' what if he couldn't make any swords? They had some of the old ones. It would be enough. And of course, there was Hero Boy and his sword.

He pulled into the area beside Anu's house. The small white house was in full sun, the field in front of it alive with the buzz of flies on the blackberries, a September promise that made you forget all the broken ones of the days and years before. Finn's car was there, and he was just getting out of it. His wiry curls were wilder than usual, his broad shoulders slightly hunched as he unfolded himself from the car's interior. He saw Smithy and gave him a chin nod but little more. It was then Smithy noticed Finn's eyes. No humour, no mischief, no "I'm ready to banter" was there. Nothing. Flatness. Jaysus, aren't we a pair, thought Smithy.

"How's things?" asked Smithy, giving his shoulder a punch.

Finn grunted. "Ah, you know."

Smithy grunted back. "I do. Any word on Maura? She still in a strop?"

Finn stopped and stared at Smithy, his face a stone. Or a slab of concrete, thought Smithy. Set, unmoveable.

"She's not here then, I take it." Smithy couldn't resist the words. Waited for the banter, the flippant remark to bring Finn back to life. But nothing. Not even a "feck off" look.

Finally, after some very long moments, Finn shook his head. "I don't think so. She left this morning."

"Left? Where did she go?" This unsettled Smithy for some reason. Reasons he probably should just give that swipe gesture. Meow Cat's signature move. He rolled his shoulders, prepared the shrug and executed it. Perfection. Meow.

"It'll be grand, Finn. It's probably nothing, and she'll be back soon, in her usual terrible form."

A flash of hope flew across Finn's face, but then it became neutral. He shrugged. "It'll be grand, yeah. Of course."

Saoirse came out to them as they headed towards the door, a look of relief and delight on her face when she saw Smithy. She greeted them both. Finn gave her a nod and walked past her, his face once again that concrete slab, a motorway barrier.

She frowned and looked at Smithy, raised her brows. Smithy shrugged and started to walk past her too, but Saoirse grabbed his arm. He stopped, giving her a puzzled look.

"How are you?" she asked.

Smithy sighed, repressing the surge of anger at her mother henning him. She meant well, he knew. She cared, he knew. Cared too much. It didn't help, her caring. Nothing could come of it. No, he was better figuring this out on his own. Hadn't the pompous old healer Diancecht told him that it wasn't his body that was the reason he could remember feck all about his own ancient language, about the details and people of the Other-world? The "before". No, for now, "after" was all he had. That and Meow Cat. And he was cool. Smithy was cool. Off key, howl. Yes.

"Ah, you know yourself," he managed to say to her.

"No, Smithy, I don't," she said, her tone a little terse. "I know only my own experience. Sure, I can't remember the Bríd I was, that goddess with all that she was. But I have my own self, the Saoirse self and that's good. In fact it's grand in all the grandest possible ways."

It was a lecture, a reprimand delivered with a firm "slap and don't be bold" kind of way that all the best mammies have. Ah, feck me, he thought. Well, good. She's had enough and so maybe we can all get on with it, he thought.

He cleared his throat. Gave her a big grin. "Ah, sorry now. Didn't mean it like that. Sure you are grand, Saoirse. We all think you are."

Saoirse gave him a glare and shook her head. "Oh, feck off, Smithy." She turned and walked to the door, opened it and disappeared inside.

"Yeah, yeah, if only," he said softly to the air. "If only Anu would let me."

There was no reply. Just the hum and the buzz amidst the brightly shining sun that still gave out promises Smithy knew would never be kept.

3

———

LUKE

Luke parked his SUV next to Finn's car and watched Smithy disappear into the house. The man was mad, he concluded. He was nothing like the Smithy he remembered, or the one whose talent with the fiddle was now making itself known to Luke from a whisper here and a whisper there back in Dublin and later in Allihies in this very short lane of whispering that was Ireland. From what Luke had observed, Smithy was still decent in a fight, his sword skills obvious, his athletic grace and strength undoubted. But the surly was new and it was all there, mostly focused on Luke. For feck's sake. He must know that it had all been a mistake with Saoirse. A mistake on so many fronts that it was nearly embarrassing to talk about. And it was between himself and Saoirse, really, no one else, and they'd made their peace. Hello, goodbye and thank you.

He absentmindedly rubbed the scar-come-tattoo on his upper left arm. It was all Kayla, now, in any case, and Smithy would have to be blind not to see that. Blind, deaf and dumb, because he was certain that his body played and danced a Kayla tune every waking moment. Kayla, his heart, his love and the land she was woven into – *An Cailleach*, the Wise Woman of

Beara. The Beara Peninsula, as much a part of him now as she was. The mother of that land. Her tune was his tune. He could feel it humming in him now, down deep, as if the earth was rising up and using him as its mouthpiece. All the ties that were connecting him to her were pulling him at the moment, an elastic band that was determined to send him back where he came from this morning. And even now, though the tune was there, he could feel her illness, the poison that Balor had leached into her through the land, poisoning it and her.

And as much as he wanted to allow that band to pull him, to spin him as fast as the wind would carry him, he knew he had to get out of this SUV and go into this meeting with Anu and the others because of that pull. For Kayla. He'd promised her and he wouldn't break that promise. He'd kill that fecker, Balor. Bedamned to Anu's reasons or the others' reasons. For her. He'd do it for her.

With that resolve he got out of the SUV and strode to the house. No matter the promise, he would prefer to get this done quickly. To announce his intentions. Find Balor, kill him. And ensure he and his company were no longer able to poison the Beara Peninsula or any other place their chemicals and petroleum ships could reach. Kill Balor, kill the company.

Once inside, he took the short left to the old slab floored kitchen, the sun pouring in the south-facing window lighting up the interior. Smithy was standing next to Anu trying to coax her into a chair while Saoirse saw to the obligatory refreshments. Tea of course. Slabs of cake, wrapped best company biscuits and meat sandwiches. Luke raised his brows in surprise. This was rural hospitality normal, but was it normal for here?

"*Conas atá tú*?" he said, without thinking, looking at Anu. It seemed natural to use the local Irish "how are you" in this house, with the table laid out as if for a seating for a wake.

Anu lifted her head and smiled at him. Luke stilled. Sure, it had only been a few days since he'd last seen her, hadn't it? But in those days her pallor had become worse, her skin dry and her eyes, well the pale eyes were clouded, bleary. A sheen of sweat lay across her forehead. He knew that look, that pallor, that sheen of sweat. Kayla had it, and though she was marginally improved from the days just before he'd gone with the others to the ancient fort at Tuireann and killed Balor's men to stop them poisoning the mines, Kayla was still ill. He knew what it meant with Kayla and he knew what it meant now, with Anu. He tightened his hands into a fist.

"What's happened?" he asked. "What's that fecker after doing now?"

Finn, Saoirse and Smithy all turned to stare at him.

"What do you mean?" asked Finn.

Luke nodded over to Anu. "You're ill. Worse than before. It can only mean that Balor has done something. Something more harmful, because I've never seen you like this, Anu. Never."

"Never is a long time," said Anu calmly. But her voice was weak enough, thready.

The other three exchanged glances. Saoirse sneaked a look at Anu, her eyes filled with concern. She turned to Luke, worry and fear written all over her face.

"Do you have any news?" asked Smithy, looking at Luke.

"Me?" said Luke. "Nothing new, why?"

He shrugged. "Just thought. Well, you just came from the Beara. How's Kayla?"

Luke shrugged. "The same. Maybe a little better."

"And Bláthín, Nana?"

Luke bit his lip. "No real change."

"Well, they're not worse," said Saoirse. "And there's some comfort in that."

"Yes," said Luke. "Some comfort."

Screams filled his head, now. "Let's get on with it" shouting with "will they give over with the opening pleasantries" all taking up the chorus of frustration that played tug of war with the elastic band drawing him out the door and back into the SUV.

He grabbed a chair, pulled it out and sat down. Get them seated, moving. Feckin' forget the cup of tea pouring shite and just start talking. But no. But feckin' no. The milk was set out, the tea poured and plates offered round and the feckin' war anthem in his head was reaching fever pitch.

"Where's Balor, now, then?" he asked. Let's get to the point.

Anu took her cup and drank slowly from it while the other three glanced, looked down and then avoided glances. Did they know something? Were they deferring to her?

"Do you know where he is?" Luke asked Finn. Finn was reasonable. Finn was a warrior. He knew tactics, he knew killing enemies.

Finn gave him a startled look. "What? No. Why would I know?" His tone was curt, whip sharp.

Was anyone thinking straight? It appeared not. Luke looked over at Anu. "Do you know where he is now?"

She took a deep breath, gathering her strength in such an obvious manner that Luke was reminded once again that it wasn't only Kayla who was seriously affected by the situation.

"We know where he's been and the likely places he is now. But not precisely where he is, no. And that's part of what I wanted to discuss with all of you." She glanced around the table. The empty chair where Maura would have sat spoke volumes. She frowned. "While it's important to know where he is at all times, he isn't our first priority, retrieving the spear and slingshot are."

Smithy sighed, caught himself and turned it into a throat clearing. Luke gave him a disdainful look. It was no good acting like some whiny child who was tired of an adult repeating himself, this was serious and important. But still. But still and all. He found himself squirming a little.

"Why?" asked Luke

Anu blinked, her thoughts interrupted. "Why what?"

"Why are they the first priority? Are they really necessary? We have three of the treasures still. Retaliator, the magic sword, is mine once more. I'm here. If you tell me where he is, I'll go after him and finish it. Now."

Luke could feel the others' glances. Felt the mental eye rolling, the "will you look at the one", and "never backward about being forward" thoughts, along with an added curiosity. Somehow, he knew that Saoirse's was more curiosity. That she understood him, the "why" of their past and how it now was permanently separated from "not" and "not" being what was left.

"As much as I'm gratified to hear you say those words, finally," Anu paused a little to give the last word emphasis, "we have to wait until we have the remaining treasure and the slingshot in our possession. They are key to drawing Balor out and finally ensuring his death. A death from which he can't return."

"And how is that?" asked Luke. "You think by stealing the spear and slingshot back from him, he'll come after us?"

"To some degree, yes," said Anu.

"He might just send someone else to do his dirty work," said Luke.

Finn and Smithy exchanged glances, but Luke could tell that they agreed it was a possibility.

"I doubt it," said Anu. "For one, it would be a point of honour for him, but also he'll be angry, furious, in fact. Especially if he knows that it's you who's taken the slingshot and the spear."

Luke considered the sense of her words. "Right, so. Fine. He comes after me and I slay him. Do we need all that subterfuge? I'm still not clear about why I can't kill him outright."

"The theft is just part of it. We need the slingshot and the spear, as well as the sword as part of the ritual that's necessary to finish him permanently. And we need his army and all his followers there when he dies. So that there is no question, no opportunity for deception or anything else to counter the fact of his death. And there he can't bring modern weapons, let alone use them."

Luke stiffened. "I killed him before in front of his army, what will change if it's the same this time?"

"It won't be the same," said Anu. Her face was unnaturally flushed and her chest rose erratically. The plait that rested on her shoulders seemed almost too heavy for her. She took another deep breath. "This time it will be a death he can't escape. Everyone will see that, everyone will know that."

The others were silent and Luke understood suddenly what she meant. "A threefold death?" he said, his voice nearly a whisper. "But how?"

Or was it "how" that he meant? Really it was more "what" or, something in between. Because there was so much in that statement. The implications. Or clarifications.

"Sacrifice?" said Finn softly.

Saoirse, whose bewilderment had become increasingly apparent, finally voiced it. "A threefold death? What does that mean?"

"A death, three times," said Finn, darkly. He looked down at his hands when Luke glanced at him.

Luke sighed, noticing for the first time that Smithy was saying very little. That had been grand, perfect in fact, up to now. Now it just seemed off, unnatural. He was staring out of the window, his expression bland. Unengaged?

"A death three times?" asked Saoirse. She bit her lip. "Is that possible?"

Luke frowned. "Yes, in some ways. In this case, I suppose it's the only way. Maybe." He looked at Anu. "Spear, sword and slingshot? But you can't be certain..." Anu stared at him and he let the words trail off. "Right, fine. Of course I can do that. It's what I am."

"You are Lugh of the Long Arm," Anu said, a steely firmness present in her voice.

"Lugh of the Long Arm," Luke echoed with a sigh. He stretched his right arm, flexed his fingers and rested it on the table. He did the same with the other arm. "Slingshot first? Or spear? Or maybe even sword? A sword won't draw too much attention in the middle of a Cork office building. But hey, I'll give it the old go."

His attempt at humour drew a slight smile from Finn and a small giggle from Saoirse. Smithy managed to turn his head towards the group as though he might be wondering what all the fuss was about. But Anu just looked at Luke, her eyes sad, her head shaking in silent protest at his humour.

"Not here, Lugh," she said gently. "Across the water, as I said. It will be in the presence of his army, his men and all his people to witness his final end."

"Across the water?" Luke said.

It wasn't a question really. He'd heard. He'd heard and felt the terrible gut wrenching punch inside him. It had been so long since he'd been across the water and he'd no desire to go there now. The self-sworn oath was still strong and it had been made for a reason. The "getting on with things" reason that coupled so nicely with the "not looking back" reason and made a whole that was so strong it was unbreakable.

"Ah, no," he said. "I don't think so. Sorry now, but it isn't something I can consider. I'll do it here. Sure, we can arrange to do it on the Beara. Fitting, that. The Beara, the perfect place. We'll draw his men there, his family, all of them. And I'll do it then. Not a bother."

He'd said the words with conviction, a loud firm voice, certain that it would do the job. Convince himself and the others that this was the plan and best be getting on it with it, now it was settled. The voice was right, he was certain. The tone, the words. All of it.

Finn opened his mouth, shut it and glanced at Anu. Smithy had returned his gaze to the window and beyond and it was fixed there.

"Do you think it would work?" asked Saoirse, her voice small and soft.

The sympathy was there in the voice and in the words which hinted at "you don't really think this would work do you", and all the other little inferences of his avoidance and denial that were said in a kindly manner to help him realise this idea was too silly to even countenance a remark from the others. It not only wasn't going to fly, it was being strangled before it even opened wings to take flight. Which brought him in mind of Morrigan. Maura.

"Maura can help," said Luke. "She can retrieve the spear and slingshot. And when the time comes, she can throw the spear, because," he took a deep breath—

"No," said Finn.

Luke looked at him, mouth open, startled out of his "make it fly" narrative.

"What do you mean, no?" said Luke.

Finn's face darkened. "I mean no. Not at all. It will not happen. No."

"She's not here," said Saoirse. "She can't say yes or no."

"I'm saying the no for her," said Finn. He looked away. "She'd say the same, if she were here, but she isn't and won't be."

"How do you know that?" asked Luke. Under the table, Smithy kicked him, suddenly attentive. Luke frowned at him and turned his gaze back to Finn. "Where is she anyway?"

"Gone," said Finn.

Finn's face was set. Hard. Luke couldn't remember a time when Finn had been like this. Well, except the once. The once and first, or nearly first time they'd met. Surly, he'd been then, though. Getting over it, getting over himself as well and who he was and still had to become. No honey tongued Ogma then. He was all "king's champion" battle fierce, except that he wasn't. Not after Luke arrived. And wasn't that the problem? The problem then, but surely not now. Luke thought back to their recent exchanges. Sure, they'd been grand enough, no agro, nothing to bother about.

"Gone where?" asked Luke.

"Gone. There's no 'where' or 'why' to answer. But the how is on wings. And that's your answer."

His voice had raised, become sharp, as sharp as any spear or sword. And it was cryptic Finn. Wordsmithing Finn, but the meaning was clear after a moment, both overtly and subversively. She'd shape shifted into a crow and flown off.

Saoirse reached over and squeezed Luke's arm, a kind warning in her eyes. Smithy's eyes whipped to Saoirse's hand, still resting on Luke's arm. Luke withdrew his arm quietly.

"I see," said Luke.

The "gones" he thought of included "gone back across the water, gone to Balor" or even "gone to find a war". He had an inkling which was most likely, but he wasn't going to say it to Finn. Besides, there would be other options.

He looked at Smithy. Sure, he was a fine enough warrior. But Smithy was frowning, a barely contained glare directed towards Luke. Luke scrubbed his hair. Though it had grown out some since he'd first chopped those deadly plaits from his head, he still hadn't become used to the stubbly length after years of the shaggy surfer look he'd adopted. Surfing was the last thing on his mind.

"Well, we can come to the details later," Luke said finally. He turned to Anu. "You want the spear and slingshot. Do you know where they're kept yet?"

Anu considered his words and seemed to accept that they wouldn't resolve the issue of the battle's location. Or was it an assassination? Or something more, because of the threefold death. Sacrifice? Sacred killing? For didn't the word "sacrifice" derive from the concept of making it sacred, holy?

"We don't know exactly where they are, except that they're in Balor's possession and not across the water."

"Oh, perfect," said Luke.

"Perfect," said Finn, his tone flat.

"It's all perfect," said Smithy, sitting back in his chair, arms crossed over his chest. "'Mister I am Good at Everything' will soon sort out the where, we have no doubt about that."

Luke was about to retort with his own cut but Saoirse interrupted him. "Get over yourself, Smithy."

Luke could almost feel the elbow jab the words delivered. Smithy looked over at her, startled. He opened his mouth, caught himself and took a deep breath. After a few moments his gaze returned to the window, his lips moved slightly and Luke swore he could hear a foot tapping lightly under the table.

Saoirse sighed. "Sorry, Anu. Do you have an idea or thought where the spear and slingshot are likely to be?"

Anu allowed her a smile and a pat on the hand. "It's fine. We're all a bit on edge. But we'll be grand. We have so much on our side. As to ideas, I think it's likely they would be where Balor could keep a personal eye on them."

"And to view them and gloat," said Luke. "Somewhere like his home."

"Or his office," said Finn.

"Both are good possibilities," said Anu.

"So where is his home?" asked Saoirse. "Surely it would be near his headquarters here in Cork."

"He does have a home near Kinsale," said Anu. "But he also has another home in America. In Oklahoma, close to his other headquarters."

"Two headquarters," said Luke. "He would of course, the fecker. But Oklahoma?"

Finn shrugged. "Oil country. So I guess it makes sense."

"Two homes, so," said Luke.

"There are a few others, but it's less likely the spear and slingshot would be there," said Anu.

"Let's hope," said Luke. "Right, fine. Where exactly is his home?"

Anu looked at him. "I'll tell you. And I was also hoping you could use your great computer skills and discover the blueprints, the location of cameras and anything else that you can think might be helpful to plan the retrieval of the slingshot and spear."

Luke raised his brows. "I'm skilful in design on computers, but I'm not sure I'm expert enough for that." He looked at Finn.

"Not at all," said Finn, shaking his head. "Maura does my website. Did my website. I'm a poet, a storyteller, not a software engineer. I answer emails, manage my Facebook account, but that's my sum total."

"Ah, not dancing on TikTok?" asked Luke.

Saoirse laughed and Luke smiled at her, glad at least someone still had the humour.

"Only when reciting poems," said Saoirse. "#rappingcelt."

"Celt Rap," said Luke, delighted. The tightness in his chest eased just a little. "I have my sword, to kill the hoard," he began, beating out the rhythm on the table for a few moments.

"Make that a wrap," said Finn, a slight twist on his mouth.

"Oh, he's a one," said Smithy, rolling his eyes. "So clever."

"Computer skills," said Anu, her voice firm. "You have them, yes?"

Luke shrugged, looked over at Saoirse. "You?"

"Me? I've a degree in English Literature from Trinity and experience as a barista. I can recite Keats, make coffee and work a till."

"And play the flute," said Smithy. His eyes suddenly clouded and filled, emotions all over the place.

Saoirse caught the look and her eyes reflected his. "Yes. I play the flute."

"And sing," said Smithy.

"And sing," she said and sighed. She turned and looked at Luke. "But no special powers with the computer."

"That would have been Maura," said Finn, his tone flat once again.

"Yes," said Anu. "But as you clearly pointed out, she isn't here and isn't likely to be. So Luke, we have you."

Luke took a deep breath. It was done, he was done. For now. "Right, so. Me it is, then seeing as Herself has flown the coop. I'll try my best." He rose. "I'll let you know when I have results. For now, I'm off back to the Beara."

4

MAURA

I brushed the hair out of my face. It was a tangled mess, just like I felt. I blinked against the blinding light of the sun and put my hand up to block it from my eyes. There was no wind at all, the brown, parched grass that surrounded me was still. I craned my neck, trying to see further, though the flat horizon stretched endlessly. End with no end. Grass.

Sweat beaded on my forehead and I felt drips gathering between my breasts and dripping down my back. Feck it, my leather jacket was like an oven and I was the chicken cooking. I stripped it off and resisted the impulse to strip to my underwear. Though it was nearly September the heat was like an unbelievable, never in a thousand centuries, hot day, no, moment, in Ireland. Or never in Ireland. Sure, I was never in Ireland. Not now, not in this moment. The truth of the statement hit me. Janey Mac, where the feck was I?

I walked a few steps and stopped, shoved the sleeves of my black T-shirt up my arms and continued. My legs felt like lead weights and my arms even heavier, but I pressed on. More grass greeted my gaze. I turned slowly, surveying the area, looking for some clue. I could see a distant scrubby tree or two, but little more. I sighed, squinting against the light, hand over my eyes, aware of the sweat dripping down into them. I brushed the drips off, but one escaped and I could taste the salt of it on my lips. Would I take flight again, see where I was? Keep my crow shape until I found something that would give me a clue? Surely that would be cooler than cooking in my black jeans, T-shirt and boots and a heavy leather jacket draped over my shoulder.

This was my punishment for taking off in such a mad flurry of temper. Rage. I said the word, trying to convince myself that it could only be the rage that would take me this far. I knew it was far by the time that had passed in flight, though I'd scarcely noticed and had flapped my wings, flying into the winds with fierce power. I'd loved the resistance, matching the wind's strength and then some, until I was so tired that I'd had to land and transform. But in the short while I had been here, I surely had enough strength to fly just enough to find something. I flexed my arms and felt my muscles scream. That was my answer, so.

A stream of "if onlys" ran through my head. I tried to shove them aside, along with the thought of Finn, who had those "if onlys" attached to him like barnacles. Ogma. Not Finn, because Finn made things so much fun, made it seem possible with his auburn hair, curled tight and long. His piercing eyes, his words. "Honey tongued" all right. It's what they called him, even as Ogma. Like some feckin' Aisling poem. "Honey tongued, his auburn tresses long and curled". Tresses. It had to be tresses of course. The absurdity called for a cackle, but I just hadn't it in me.

I sighed and looked at the distant tree. Resigned, I headed towards it, acknowledging that if I had to rest it would have to be under a tree. I couldn't survive otherwise. A fly buzzed around my head and I swatted it. It became part of my rhythm. Walk, buzz, swat. Not particularly foot tapping but it was the best I had. The fly didn't understand the slip jig, reel, or polka beat, just its own thing. An improv at best. A feckin' annoyance at worst.

I was so wrapped up in the annoyance beat, soon threatening to be a "beat the fly to death" beat, I didn't see the road ahead that suddenly appeared in the shimmery distance. I perked up. A road meant something. It had a direction. It came from something and went to something. Another something. It held promise.

I made my way to the promise, not quite a land, but a strip, a winding strip that didn't disappear as I neared it and my walk, buzz, swat took on a faster speed that, despite my leaden legs and sweat soaked body, I forced myself to continue, until I reached the road.

When I hit the road I walked along it, heading east, because west was what had got me into this bother. A bother that was so far from "not a bother" that I needed some time to think. So, east it was. Well, as east as this road made it possible. I walked for a bit, the heat from the tarmac radiating up and cooking the soles of my boots. The joy at finding the road and the promise that went with it, soon melting away, just as I was. If I kept this up I was going to die here. Shade. I needed to find it. Water seemed a stranger, so shade it would have to be, until I could recover and take flight.

I sighed, looking at the scrubby tree up ahead. Sure, that would hardly shade this feckin' fly that had insisted on taking the road with me like some kind of witch's familiar. A boon companion. Still, tiny shade was better than none and it took me off this sizzling road.

I reached the tree and lowered myself down beside it. The branches were stumpy and few, and looked like they belonged in a black and white horror film. I sighed, staring at the few leaves that clung to the branches, already brown and shrivelled in warning.

"Yes, I hear you," I said.

I turned around leaned back against the trunk. I tried putting my leather jacket over my head to shield me from the sun, but that lasted only a few minutes before the weight and heat of it became oppressive. Eventually, I settled for my arm propped on my bent knee, allowing my hand to shield my eyes. I closed them and tried to find my inner coolness, or whatever it was the latest gurus advised. Glaciers, icebergs, frozen lakes. But they all morphed into molten lava. Just a little while, I told myself. Just a little while and I'll take to the skies. Deep breath.

A few deep breaths later and I heard something. The something shimmered in the distance and came over a small rise in the road. A car. Or rather truck. I stood up. A potential spin to the next town. A natural thing in Ireland. Or it was, mostly. Always someone to give you a spin. Here though? But where was here? I gave the truck a wave and drew my breath in as the dusty dark red truck slowed, nearing me. It was then I noticed the number plate. It read "Oklahoma".

Stunned, I stood there as stiff and still as the tree behind me as the truck pulled up beside me and the window drifted down. A man with shaggy black hair, dark T-shirt and mirrored sunglasses leaned over.

"It looks as though you might be lost," he said and turned off the engine.

I looked at him and a moment later the laughter came. High pitched, a giggle, at a stretch, but that stretch would be long and heavily elasticated as it would touch the edges of hysteria with no problem. Feck and all the rest of it, piling those fecks higher than any pile before it.

"Is that a yes?" said the man.

"Oh, I think so," I said.

"You'd best get in then. I'll see if I can help."

I cocked my head, considering, the laughter gone. "A spin it is." I glanced around. "Since I presume the bus isn't coming soon, and the taxis are busy."

"Good assumption," said the man.

His accent was there and it wasn't. American of no description and every description. But different. Different to me who knew nothing about this country or its people, so maybe no different.

"Grand, so."

I plastered a smile on my face. A "no bother to me and thanks for all this". I opened the passenger door and slid in.

He reached for a bottle of water from the back. "You'll be needing this."

I took it gratefully, nearly fainting at the sight of it. I swept my tongue along the dry, chapped desert that was my lips in anticipation. The grin on his face meant nothing to me, he could mock all he wanted – the water was going nowhere but down my throat.

"Careful now. Drink slowly."

I nodded, the bottle already at my mouth and the first slug of water hitting my tongue. Slow was difficult. But eventually, I had my fill and handed it sheepishly back to him. There was hardly any left.

He shook his head at me and grinned. Again. "Keep it. I have more."

I managed a smile this time without effort and nodded. "Thanks a million."

"That many?"

"Of course," I said.

He nodded thoughtfully. "I'm glad to hear you appreciate something that precious."

I opened my mouth to explain that it was just an expression

we used in Ireland. As natural as "your one" and "Himself," maybe even more so. But I stopped myself and I looked over at him, instead, studying him. He'd made no move to turn the engine back on. The coolness from the air conditioning inside the truck was beginning to fade, but it didn't seem to bother him. I noticed then his copper skin, the high cheekbones barely visible under the cover of his mirrored aviator frames. As if he could sense my question, he took off his sunglasses and I saw the dark, almond shaped eyes. Their black colour was more ebony than sepia and my own reflection stared back at me, as if the sunglasses were still in place. There was something about him, something more than his race. A something that was more. I felt something stir at the back of me, behind, or backwards, or something. There was that something again. I tried to shake it off.

"Are you an Indian?" I corrected myself, remembering the term thrown out loosely in Ireland wasn't the right one for here. "I mean Native American."

"We are on a reservation," he said. "So odds are in favour of it."

I looked out on the flat landscape. "No tipis?"

He looked over at me, amusement in his eyes. "No. They're all on a Hollywood backlot owned by MGM."

He nodded, his manner sage and all knowing. Mocking me, the fecker. He cocked his head, studying me. "Are you Irish?"

"Good guess," I said, laughing. "What gave it away?"

He surveyed me slowly and raised his brows at me. "The red skin?"

I gave a full laugh, filled with humour. "Oh, you are good."

"Am I? Some would say not."

"Even better," I said. A man of my own kind, I thought. From his black clothes to his dark dry humour, he was an "ah, yes". I held out my hand. "I'm Maura."

He nodded. "Raven."

My eyes widened. "Feck me, really?"

Amusement crossed his face. "Really."

"Oh, right. Well how perfect is that?" I said.

"Is it perfect?"

"Oh, it is," I said. "You have no idea."

He nodded slowly. "Let's hope that proves the truth." He turned back and grasped the steering wheel in one hand, turned on the engine and placed it into gear. "Where were you going?"

"A town?" I said.

"Is that a question? Because if so, only you can answer that."

"A town."

"Would that town have a name?"

"The next town?"

"Again, the question only you can answer."

I snorted. In some situations his banter might prove irritating but not now, not here in this situation. It was part of the perfect.

"The next town, whatever that might be."

"Well, I was heading to Bartlesville, but I can take you to the next town, if that would be better for you."

"What's Bartlesville?"

"A city."

"Oh, that sounds perfect," I said.

"Another perfect. I'm becoming impressed with your perceptions of perfection."

"I'm glad."

He nodded and pulled out into the road, driving at a speed that left dust circles behind the truck. But I suspected it would take little for that to happen.

I relaxed back into the seat and closed my eyes a minute, taking in the cooling air. Oh, this was good, He was grand, perfect and I was enjoying this so much. The freshness, the novelty.

"What brings you to Oklahoma?" he asked after a while.

"An impulse and an east wind?"

"Another question?"

I smothered a laugh. "Well, probably, since I'm not sure and it wasn't planned."

"So definitely an impulse. Odd place to choose on impulse."

"I'm not sure there was choice involved. It just seemed as though I ended up here, rather than chose to come."

"I suppose you'll find out in time if it was a good wind and a good impulse."

"I hope so." I pondered our conversation for a moment. "You don't seem like an Indian—I mean Native American."

"What does a Native American seem like?" he asked. The dryness was in the tone, just a shade to the side of sarcasm.

I paused. What had I meant? I certainly didn't expect war paint and feather bonnets. Well, not really. "Sorry, I don't know what I meant."

"Am I your first?" he asked.

"My first?"

"Your first Indian."

"What?" I said, startled. I gaped at him and burst out laughing. "Sorry," I said after it subsided. "It struck me funny, as if you were asking me...something else."

He looked over at me, and though the sunglasses were back in place, the smile was there and the laughter in the twitch of his cheek.

"You want to go to Bartlesville, then," he said. "Anywhere in particular?"

"Well, somewhere I could stay? Near potential jobs?"

"A job? What kind of job?"

I shrugged. "Do you live in Bartlesville? Do you know

anyone who's got a job on offer? Say...," I thought about what my strengths might be but he cut in before I could say anything more.

"Bartending?"

I gave him a smirk. "Now who's stereotyping?"

He laughed. "Point taken."

"But all the same, if you know someone who is looking for a bartender, I'm game."

He laughed again. "Oh, I think I know the place for you."

"Oh, I hope it's a place for you, too," I said.

He shrugged. "On occasion."

I grinned, looking at him. "Good. What's this place called, then that needs a bartender?"

"Murphy's," he said.

I roared. "Perfect."

"I think so."

I had no idea the why or who reason that I'd ended up here in Oklahoma, but Murphy's seemed a good place to be until I figured it out.

5

SAOIRSE

Saoirse entered the small yard hesitantly, trying to see if Smithy was in the forge or inside the house. She was half hoping the door to the shed that housed the forge would be open, because that would mean he was doing something. That he was creating and working at what he did best and loved best. She felt the itch herself, to create something with metal, to create with Smithy.

She sighed. He was such a feckin' arse about it all, sometimes. Did he think she didn't understand? She understood some of it, if not all. She understood that she had pieces of her own life missing and a bewildering amount to learn. And if she truly thought about it, she had no idea who she was. It certainly wasn't the girl she'd grown up with. Or been in school with. Her father wasn't the man who'd she'd seen little of while at boarding school, the man now dead. No, he was someone else entirely – and who would understand that, besides the few people who surrounded her now? Her grandmother, Anu? Hah. The others? Were they people she could count as her friends, or were they forced upon each other's company by virtue of being gods? And what virtue was that?

She thought of Jilly, her friend from Dublin. And the others she'd played music with in those sessions at The Mangle Pit. Those days were gone and so were the people. She could hardly rock up to Jilly's and tell her all that was going on in her life. The only person from those days who knew, who understood, was Luke. And what a joke that was on her. But she was thankful that, though their past together was filled with miscues and misunderstandings, at least they were on even footing now. He had Kayla and he seemed better for it. She had Smithy. The sigh came again. Did she have Smithy?

She saw that the door to the forge was shut and the sigh was joined by a bit of annoyance. Joining annoyance was a flicker of anger shaped around the words, "get over yourself, for feck's sake" that was so close to it becoming welded to the annoyance.

She went through the yard and up to the back door. After giving it a slight tap she opened it and entered. She could hear movement in the sitting room, so she made her way through the kitchen, pausing to note the sink cluttered with dishes, the half-filled Power's Whiskey bottle on the table and the greasy frying pan on the cooker. It broke her heart and made her angry all at once for what it told her. She didn't get back Smithy from the Well of Slane. She got back a shell.

She took a deep breath. Enough was enough. She was annoyed with herself for the moment's pity. A pity that had been as much for herself as it was for Smithy and it did neither of them any good. Not facing this task, no – she told herself – not task, but battle. A real battle and the journey that took them there would be no less dangerous. Smithy needed to be a man on the top of his game, fit, strong, not wallowing in the bottom of a whiskey bottle full of the woes. She straightened and moved to the sitting room.

What she found there didn't reassure her. The stove wasn't lit, the curtains were half adrift, shirts and jackets were strewn around the floor or across chairs, as if Smithy had tossed them and not always succeeded in reaching his goal. A few issues of *The Irish Examiner* and an *Irish Independent* were tossed into one of the chairs. Smithy himself was lounging on the sofa, a leg crossed over his knee, plucking the strings of his fiddle and repeating the word "meow" in varying dissonant tones.

"What the feck is going on, Smithy?" asked Saoirse in a stern voice.

Smithy looked up at her and grinned. "Hey Saoirse Bríd. Bríd Saoirse. What's going on?" The words were spoken in the most ridiculous American accent she'd ever heard.

"Are you high?"

Smithy started to laugh. The laughing continued as she watched him, hands on her hips.

"Ah, I'm just a cool cat," he said finally. "The coolest."

"For feck's sake, Smithy, the state of you. You're making such a show of yourself not even your mammy would like it."

Smithy began to laugh harder at those words. She knew as soon as the words were out of her mouth that it was ridiculous to bring his mother in, especially as she didn't even know who his mother was. Another gap to be filled at a later time. For now, besides a good whack to pull him out of whatever world he was in that had kept him captive and created this twat that was barely tolerable now, it was important to get him on track.

The meows were starting to irritate her. "Smithy, will you give that shite a rest and listen to me? I have some important things to tell you."

Maybe it was the words or the loud severe voice she used, or both, she didn't care. All she cared about that he stopped with the feckin' meows. There was a sigh that came after, a heavy world weary type, but she'd enough of that as well.

"Anu has heard from Luke."

"Oh, Hero Boy. What's he got to say for himself?"

She gave a mental eye roll but ploughed on, determined to ignore the remark. "He's looked at Balor's Kinsale property. He's found out the type of security system there and the location of the cameras around the property. He thinks he can work out how to hack it and turn off the system and cameras so he can get in there and look for the spear and slingshot."

Smithy shrugged. "Of course he can. So?"

"So, he plans on going there tonight."

"Again, so?"

She took a deep breath. Another one. It was becoming a regular event when she was around Smithy.

"We're going along, too, to help out. So you need to pull yourself together." She waved her hand around the room. "You could start by tidying up a bit. Finish with the cat gut noises, as well."

"Why do I have to go? I've got nothing to offer in the way of helping someone break into a house. And I'm sure Hero Boy would rather do it all on his own."

"Stop calling him that. It sounds pathetic."

"Well isn't that the point?"

Saoirse gave an impatient snort. "Will you just make sure you're ready to go tonight when we pick you up? Ready and sober."

"*We* pick you up? I can go under my own steam, so."

"Don't be stupid. We'll go in Luke's SUV."

"Ah, you can go, I'll stay here. Three's a crowd and all that."

"Smithy will you stop acting like a twat? There are far more important things to do than sitting and creating scenarios that aren't the least bit true."

Smithy shook his head, suddenly deflated. He sighed. "Ah you're right, so. I just can't seem to get my head out of my arse. I'm sick of meself, so I am."

Saoirse laughed. "Ah, I know."

He frowned at her. "Yeah, well."

"Just put it aside for now. All of it. There's things to do."

"Yeah, things."

"Come on, now. Tonight. We go with Luke to search for the spear and slingshot at Balor's house."

"Right, so. Do we know for certain that he's in the country? Or in Cork?"

"From what Luke can tell he doesn't seem to be in Ireland at the moment. So we have that in our favour. But Eithne is here and she uses the house often. So we need to be careful."

Smithy gave a wry grin. "Eithne, eh? How does Luke feel about being this close to his mother?"

Saoirse looked at him, surprised. "Oh, feck. I didn't realise that. But of course, being Balor's daughter, who else could she be?"

"So I take it he said nothing when he was updating you."

"It was an instant message, you plonker. So no, he didn't say anything and since I couldn't see his face, I can't tell you about that either."

Smithy nodded. "Another complication for Hero Boy."

"Will you ever stop with the 'Hero Boy?'"

Smithy shrugged. "Ah, probably not." He turned away from her. "I've been thinking, Saoirse Bríd."

Saoirse rolled her eyes. "Dangerous stuff, that."

He looked back at her and frowned, his eyes distant. "I've been thinking about us. And I feel it's best that our relationship should be on a friends basis only."

Saoirse's breath caught, too stunned to reply. When she did recover, she managed to fling out a retort. "Ah, so this is the 'it's not you it's me' speech? Well, newsflash, fecker. It is you. You breaking it off. You being ungrateful for my support. You being a wanker."

She turned around and strode away, through the kitchen and

out the door to the yard before he could see the tears that had flooded her eyes and now poured down her face.

ANU WAS THERE when she arrived back at the house. She was sitting at the table in the kitchen, staring at a small plate of sandwiches and a full cup of milk. When Saoirse entered the room she looked up and smiled weakly.

"The sandwiches seemed a good notion when I began to make them, but somehow, they've lost their appeal now."

Saoirse frowned at her. Luke had been right when he expressed his concerns to her privately after their meeting a few days ago. Anu was ill and her colour at this moment seemed even paler than it had been the day before, if that were possible.

"Will I make you some broth? Would that appeal to you?"

"Ah, you don't have to bother, it's grand."

Saoirse nearly smiled at the classic mammy response. But classic or no, it was Anu. She wanted to be the one to do the looking after. It was who she was.

"No, no," said Saoirse. "You know it's not a bother. I'll make it and there's no argument."

She busied herself making the broth, pouring it from the small tub that she'd made the day before into a pot and slinging the pot on the hook that hung from the crane. She was glad for something to do to shift the turmoil of her thoughts into something more calming.

"What's wrong, Bríd?"

Saoirse halted her stirring and turned to look at Anu. "Nothing, I'm fine."

"Ah, you're not. Your face is still red and it's clear you've been crying."

Saoirse forced a smile on her face. "I'm fine now, though. Don't worry about me."

"Is it about Smithy?"

"Why would you say that?"

Anu gave a small laugh. "Because Smithy's demons are running amok and it's natural that they would catch you up in the process."

Saoirse snorted. "Oh, so it's his demons, then, who make him act like a first class eejit and not him?"

"His demons are him, at the moment. I'm sure you can see that."

"Oh, I can see that fine. And I suppose it's his demons who told me we should just be friends and forget all that's gone between us? To forget all that we've been through together. That means nothing, I guess."

She knew her tone was angry, bitter, but she couldn't help it. Just for five minutes, so, she would give into it. And then she would be all business. She promised herself.

Anu leaned across to her and took her hand. Saoirse nearly snatched it away, because she knew what Anu was going to say. Blah, blah, blah. Give him time. Keep being there for him. Blah, blah, blah and all the rest that went with the "give him time" speech. Save your breath please. He'd had her time and slapped it across the face. Punched it really. Punched it hard. No, she'd give herself over to this task and then move on. Move on properly. Go find Jilly and her life in Dublin again. Find another barista job if she had to. It hadn't been too bad, really.

"I think he's right, Saoirse," said Anu.

Saoirse's thoughts halted mid-stream. "What?"

"I think he's right. You should put aside your relationship. It's obviously putting pressure on him, making it tougher to deal with all that is going on inside of him. Diancecht did say there was nothing physically wrong with him, so we know that the only cure for his problems is himself. And it's becoming increasingly clear that he doesn't want your help to solve them. Nor anyone else that has offered. Perhaps it's because we know him and his past too well. He feels we judge him, whether we do or not, and it affects how he reacts to everyone and events that have occurred. Let him find his own way, in his own time."

Saoirse had no idea what to say to Anu's words. She sensed a deep truth there, although part of her rebelled at the idea of abandoning Smithy, even though moments before she'd been contemplating that very idea.

"So you think we should just be friends?"

Anu cocked her head. "I'm sorry, but yes, I do. For now, at least. I think it's best for the both of you. Otherwise you two may ruin what you have."

"We don't have anything," Saoirse said morosely.

"You, do, Bríd. You do. And the two of you have been through so much. You are a pair. Friends or lovers. You are a pair. Twined together."

A laugh came out of Saoirse and it surprised her, because it hardly seemed part of her. That laugh held some biteen part of her that found all of this so absurd it could hardly be taken seriously. A "come on you must be joking" part that stood back and enjoyed all the craic a tale like this one gave. Ah yeah. She was full of the craic. But at the moment she wished this tale would feck off out of here and leave her alone.

"Friends it is," she said dully.

Hah. He would have a friendship from her that he wouldn't know how to define. It would be "friends without benefits" all right. It wouldn't even be "frenemies". No, she would find a new kind of friendship for him. An "all work and no play" friends. The kind that stayed away from each other.

6

LUKE

Luke stood outside, staring at the hills in the distance that comprised part of the ridge of mountains that ran along the Beara Peninsula. He could make out a few sheep dotted along their sides, like little white specks with an occasional darker spot marking those that weren't white. The black sheep. Like he felt now. Certainly the black sheep of his own family, if you were to ask Balor and his mother. But he refused to count them, because they didn't count – as he'd never counted with them. Not really. He was his father's son, a Tuatha de Danann, though he knew little enough about Cían. Only that he was a strong warrior. Proud and true and cut down in his prime by those less than him in a fool's trick that had turned sour.

Luke shook his head now, trying to push those thoughts away. He heaved a sigh and made his way back into the kitchen. He was surprised to find Kayla, dressed and sitting at the small table.

"Kayla," he said. "Should you be down from your bed?"

She gave him a wan smile. "Ah, no. I'm fine, really. Better for being up and about."

He noted her pale haggard face, the dark recessed eyes and her frame, gone thin in the past few weeks since she, her daughter and her mother had fallen ill. Had it only been that long? It seemed longer in some ways, because it made their own acquaintance only a few days more. And that most certainly didn't seem right, since he felt in his bones there wasn't a time when he hadn't known her. And despite all her suffering, she was still so beautiful to him. As she ever had been.

He made his way to her and stroked her head. Still so beautiful. She turned his face up to him.

"And what are you about, my lad?"

He snorted at her reference. "Hardly a lad."

"But you are my lad. My glorious surfer lad."

"Not so much the surfer now. Not for weeks."

Her eyes glimmered with humour. "And that's an eternity for any surfer. Not a surfer indeed."

He smiled at her. "Not a surfer. I leave that to Mon now. I'll keep the music, but the surfing..."

"Oh, you couldn't get rid of the music in you if you wanted to," said Kayla.

He leaned down and kissed her lips. "You're my music, Kayla."

She laughed, but the laugh turned to a cough, reminding him of the present and all that was at stake.

"How's your mother and Bláthín?"

Kayla's eyes clouded at the mention of her daughter. "About the same, I suppose. They're both eating a little. Enough to keep going. Bláthín asked if you could come up and see her."

He nodded. "Of course. I'll read her a story."

"Tell her a story, you mean. You know she won't let you get away with some stuffy old book."

"A story?" He frowned. The last time he'd started a story, he'd ended up telling her a thoroughly sanitised tale about himself. "I've not many stories. At least one that's suitable for Bláthín."

"You have plenty of stories in you, Luke. And plenty more to spin."

He looked at her carefully. It was remarks like these that reminded him the depth of her knowledge, her power, to see in him and through him. And why there could be no other woman but her.

"A story, so. Well I'll tell her one that even Finn couldn't best."

"You will, of course, *mo chroí.*"

He took her hand, so small and delicate seeming compared to his big hams and squeezed it, willing his strength into hers. But as usual, it was her strength, so ill spared, that poured into him, keeping him whole.

LUKE PULLED up outside Smithy's house and kept the engine running as Saoirse exited the SUV to fetch Smithy. Luke could only hope that Smithy was in better form than he'd been the last time he'd seen him. Otherwise he would prefer to take his chances with Finn who had, it seemed, discovered it was more amusing to be a difficult fecker as well. At least he understood Finn's issues. Or he thought he did. Or their direction. Maura. And well, the past. The past. The warrior past between himself and Finn.

Finn could have the hero role and so he'd tell him when he saw him, if he was set to "difficult fecker" mode. Luke just wanted to get on with it, get this task over with, get the battle finished, so that he could put it away in that overstuffed locked press with all the other shite that was his own past.

He tapped the steering wheel, beating out the rhythm that

was his and Kayla's tune, the hum and call of the Beara, the place that was him and all that was good. Where that locked press didn't matter and the key could go feck itself because the press really never needed opening, until it was all rotted into nothing.

Saoirse finally appeared, Smithy trailing in her wake. On the short spin down from Anu's place to Smithy's, Saoirse had been full of banter. Not so now. Tense shoulders, set expression were anything but hidden clues, and her Doc Marten clad feet said it even louder. Stomp was one word that came to mind, but to Luke it had a better rhythm than stomp. It was aggravated, full of bounce and sung its own tune. The "I am pissed" tune.

The thought made him laugh, and feck knows he should savour it all he could because he knew in the mood they were in and what was ahead of them that night, it would be the last amusing thing for a while.

Saoirse slipped into the front passenger seat, leaving Smithy to slink into the back. He was attempting the "I am cool with the world" look, but he hadn't achieved it by a short mile, let alone a long one. Luke could hear some kind of weird tune coming from him, sung softly, but not so softly that Luke couldn't hear it. Feck me, it was going to be a long night.

They drove towards Kinsale with relatively little issue, Saoirse chatting to him in seeming but unconvincing light heartedness, while Smithy got it on with his weird tune, staring out of the window. He'd already briefed them about the plan once they got to the house. It was simple, nothing complex. He didn't think they could handle complex, but also simple meant there was less room for things to go wrong. He had his laptop with him to use to disable the security system once they arrived, and he would make his way inside the house while Smithy and Saoirse kept watch. Saoirse would remain in the car down the road from the house set in three acres, Smithy hidden outside the house, in case anyone approached on foot inside the wall that surrounded the property. Luke would do the rest, leaving any complexities to him.

As they came to the outskirts of Kinsale and made the turnoff towards Balor's property Saoirse fell silent. Behind them Smithy's tune kept on, seeming louder now that Saoirse had stopped talking. She sighed and Luke glanced over. Her face was set once again, her mouth in a tight line. Jaysus feck, he wished Smithy would sort himself out and the two of them would resolve this shite. He shook his head and tried to focus on the task at hand.

A few minutes later Luke pulled up the SUV at a small layby just down from the house. It provided good cover and it didn't make it look too strange to any passers-by that might wonder what a SUV was doing parked outside Balor's house when he wasn't there, a likelihood in the countryside, even in this day and age of anonymous neighbours.

He switched off the engine. "Smithy, could you go and check that there aren't any cars parked in the drive at the house? Text me when you've checked. If all is fine, stay there. I'll come after I disable the security."

Smithy nodded, got out of the car and began to jog down the road. It was nearly dark by now, the sun having been swallowed by the horizon during the journey. He watched Smithy disappear into the dusk.

"Are you okay?" asked Luke after a few moments.

Saoirse took a deep breath. "Yeah. I'm grand."

"Are you sure?"

She laughed. "Yes, Luke. Really."

"Good. Don't worry, it'll all be over soon. Just a nip in and out. There are only so many places you can store a spear."

She laughed again, this time the humour was evident. "The hall press? Under the sofa?"

"The bathtub? The bed?" He could sense her smile, even though he could hardly make it out in the dim light.

A ping sounded on his phone. It was from Smithy. He opened it: *All clear.*

"Everything good?" asked Saoirse.

"Yep," he said, reaching for his laptop in the well of the passenger seat. He fired it up and after a few moments brought up the screens he needed and set to work. It took a little while, but finally he was done. A discreet phone call to a friend who had a little more knowledge in this area had made it simpler than he thought it would be.

He pulled up the hood of his dark hoodie. "We'll be back before you know it."

"Right. Be careful, though. Don't take any risks you don't need to."

"Yeah, of course," he said and got out of the SUV.

Luke jogged down the road and climbed the wall that surrounded the property. He moved towards the house and saw Smithy's dark figure making its way to the shrubbery at the side of the house. From there he would have a good view of most of the property.

It was a statement house with glass, wood and cut stone that everywhere said, "the big I am" and for Luke, though he could admit to the beauty of some of it, to him it said, "I am a big prick".

He made his way stealthily to the wood covered modern door, careful of the crunch the gravel made, though he knew no one but Smithy would hear him. Still, it felt better to take that precaution. He found the lock, inserted the little pick Smithy had sullenly explained how to use and waited for the satisfying snick of it opening. When he heard it, he opened the door slowly, alert to any untoward sound.

The dim interior yawned in front of him. He moved inside,

noting the faint grey light in the back where the patio door from the kitchen was located. It provided enough illumination to the interior to allow him to make out the open staircase that led to the next floor. He moved towards it, deciding to check the bedrooms first.

Once upstairs, he turned right and headed for the far bedroom. The door was closed and he opened it slowly, again, just to be cautious. It was dark, but the long curtain was pulled back, allowing the grey light from outside to pour in the large floor-to-ceiling window. In the light everything seemed neutral in colour, including the bed linen, though Luke suspected that even in bright sunlight the decor would be no less neutral. It wasn't a guest bedroom, though, the personal items and photos hanging on the wall made that clear. A brush, a laptop, a photo of Balor shaking hands with some feckin' celebrity with gelled hair hung on the wall close to Luke. It didn't seem quite large enough to be his grandfather's room, a thought he shoved aside with a mighty force that would have made The Hulk envious. Balor. The man was called Balor and he would be nothing more to him. It didn't matter whose room it was, it needed to be searched.

He made his way quietly around the room, focused on the task. First, he checked the walk-in wardrobe, avoiding acknowledging the dresses and other women's clothing it contained as he systematically pulled aside all items necessary in the search to locate either the spear or slingshot. When he was satisfied there was nothing, he exited the wardrobe and gave a cursory look under the bed, using the torch of his phone to provide light. Nothing again. Another quick glance around the room and he spotted another door. Probably the ensuite. Should he check it? He decided against wasting the time. Time that was silently ticking by in his head. Really, he told himself, there was no point in checking that, since there was little chance the bathroom would hide the spear and the slingshot, it really was a joke to think that. Balor would never do that, he knew. He had too much pride. Balor would lock it somewhere secure, he was certain. But it would be somewhere he could view it, take satisfaction from outwitting the Tuatha de Danann. Outwitting Daghda.

That thought led him out of the bedroom to the next. It was smaller and clearly a guest room. He made short work of that bedroom where every wardrobe and drawer were empty and the bed free of bed linen. The next one was the same. The far bedroom was so large and stamped with the "I am a big prick" decor that no one could mistake it for anything but the master suite. Balor's bedroom. The huge, custom built bed had a headboard of leather padding matching the large leather chairs and sofa that were at the opposite end. Sheepskin rugs covered the wood floors in the seating area and a modern fireplace became its focal point. A large modern monstrosity of a chandelier hung from the ceiling and modern paintings were hung along the walls.

Luke shook his head and wondered that there weren't mirrors on the ceiling, since it fitted with the image he had of Balor in his head. Maybe in America. Sure, those things were always in America.

He headed for the walk-in wardrobe and searched through the clothes, presses and drawers that lined it, having the thought "yeah that's more what I expected" at the sight of the several sets of leather trousers that hung among the slick expensive Italian suits, though it still made him shake his head. "Oh I Am the Man" (capitals please) became a tune in his head and it found a beat and melody that carried him through to the sight of the ensuite, viewed more out of curiosity than any expectations. It was a "this I have to see" moment that reaped its own reward when he burst out laughing. The sunken tub was huge, of course, yes of course it was, and obviously sported more functions than any home entertainment centre. It was the mirrored ceiling that provoked the laughter and the "well feck me" that came out of his mouth. Too funny. Too, too funny. It made the whole "Oh I Am the Man" tune take on more life and meaning, a sure hit thing kind of tune that Luke knew he'd never let go. It was just too, too funny.

Still chuckling, he made a sweep of the rest of the bedroom, confirming what he now knew to be true, the spear and sling-shots weren't here. Something inside him told him that they weren't anywhere in the house, but still he would look.

He made his way quietly down the stairs and began a search first through the living room which definitely had nothing approaching the common term of sitting room, in its slick design of marble, glass and wood, with a touch of wall here and there. There was hardly any furniture or storage to provide any place to house something like a slingshot, let alone a spear. This was minimalist at its designer best. Not a house to live in, but one to splash across the pages of *Irish Homes Quarterly*, or whatever it was called.

From there he moved through the dining area, past a large glass table with contorted chairs that looked like you wouldn't lament the fact you were served a lone artfully carved potato and two bits of celery with some jus swirled dramatically over top, because it meant that you spent as little time as possible in them. His own house may be modern, but at least you could sit in a chair without wanting to move to the floor. But, fine, so. It all added to the tune. The "Oh I Am the Man" was already climbing the charts.

There was a door off to the side and he had a peek inside. It was moderate sized and furnished with little but a huge screen on one wall and plush moulded oversized chairs and a leather sofa facing the screen. Built in presses and a counter containing a sink lined the back wall, with a bar at the side of it. "Oh I Am

The Man's" chill room, Luke thought. A quick search came up empty, except for the ever expanding tune, that he now thought might have some lyrics by the time he left.

The lyrics were trickling through as he took in the kitchen, searching all likely places with no result. Wit was shaping the lyrics and making him smile when he made his way to the entrance and the front door. A sound stopped him just before he reached for the handle and he turned.

A figure stood at the top of the stairs, shadowy, the flowing dressing gown marking her as a woman.

"Who are you? What do you want?"

Luke stood frozen to the spot. His breath caught, heart rose to his throat. The voice was all too familiar.

"Lugh, is that you?" the woman's voice was filled with disbelief.

Luke turned around, grabbed the door handle, turned it, opened the door and flung out into the night, running from the house and the demons that chased after him.

7

MAURA

"I 'll have a beer, darlin'."

I gave the burly man a nod from over my shoulder as I filled the whiskey glass from the optics. A week in and I was getting good at this.

"I'll be with you in a second, so," I said and handed the whiskey to the thin as a rail man with a shaven head who was propped up at the far end. I told him the price, but he already had a grubby twenty in his hand ready for me. I went to the till, no, sorry, the *cash register,* keyed in the code, and made the change, closing the drawer with a flick of my hip.

When I'd finished with the thin man I turned to the one who'd ordered the beer. He was the polar opposite to my previous customer with his heavy beard and long hair pulled back into a ponytail. His eyes glittered at me.

"That was one sexy long second," he said.

I shrugged. "It's the only kind of second I do."

He licked his upper lip. "I'd like to have more of those kind of seconds."

If it had been a text or instant message I would have sent him several eye roll emojis.

"What kind of beer can I get you?" I asked in a flat tone. Time to cut him off, feck the tip.

He leaned forward. "I just love your accent," he said.

Here we go, I thought. "What accent?" I said in a deadpan tone.

"That accent. You know what I mean. You're Irish, right? Or maybe Scottish?"

Oh, feck, this man had so many silent eye roll emojis crowding that message it would cover the screen.

"Irish," I said with a sigh. "Scots sound a wee bit different, ye ken?" I brought out the broadest Scots accent I could muster. For my own amusement, because this fella wasn't getting any of it.

"Irish, yeah, of course. Cool." He beamed a smile at her. "Ya know I'm part Irish."

"Which part? Certainly not your third leg."

The man beside him gave a soft snicker, but continued to stare into his drink. Vodka, I thought. He was a regular, nice smile, always polite, something past forty in age.

Over to the side I heard a burst of laughter. I looked over at one of the booths nearby and saw Raven sitting with two people and they were all looking at me. When did they get here? I glanced at Raven's friend, Lenny, the other barman and owner (Leonard Murphy—I ask you), who was at the far end talking to thin as a rail man.

"You haven't seen my third leg, doll," said the bearded man. "But I'm happy to show it to you."

I looked at the bearded man up and down. "Ah, no, you're grand. You keep that third leg to yourself, Irish or no."

I moved away from him, came from behind the bar and over to the booth where Raven and his companions sat. The light was on the dim side in this bar, or excuse me, "tavern", a detail Lenny had pointed out to me when I'd first started. I liked Lenny. He was easy-going, but tough when it called for it. The scar across his brow told that story well, as did the tattoos that covered his light brown arms and more than likely lurked under this T-shirt. I wasn't certain if he was mixed race or what the nature of his background was, and unlike bearded man, I wasn't going to ask. I'd learned that much, and also that it mattered little in this place where all shades of colour seemed to take up roost. Those that didn't like it found a different place. An odd place in an odd city, or so it seemed to me, but it was the only American city that I'd experienced. It was all straight lines and right angles with solid buildings fashioned in 1950s architecture and Wide. That "w" had to be large, because it's what it felt to me when I walked to the supermarket, or anywhere else, following the grid layout of the streets. It was a difference that was new. A difference that made me grin and feel the "I'll bide here for a while" vibe.

I stood at the booth that held Raven and his companions, noticing that he and the woman each had a beer. She smiled at me, her dark eyes inquiring. She was the Pocahontas the Disney Corporation wished they had, with her black hair, velvet rich, falling loose down her back, her dark eyes and perfect skin. The term "stately beauty" echoed through my head. I glanced at Raven, who looked at me speculatively, a hint of amusement in his eyes. I surveyed him closely, hoping for an annoying flaw there, at least. But my memory of him hadn't become a victim of enhanced reality. He was really chiselled body and face, a golden boy with copper skin. And the tattoo. All yum, or was it nom, nom? Pity, because it seemed like Stately Beauty was paired with him and, sure, didn't they make a perfect couple?

Still, I suddenly wished my black T-shirt was a sheer blouse, or at least something low cut so I could show him all my advantages.

"Hey," I said. "Will you have anything more?"

Raven grinned. "Hmm. There's plenty we might want, but what will we have, when it all comes down to it?"

Stately Beauty gave a small laugh. Delicate, short of tinkly, because that would be feckin' annoying. Suddenly I wanted just short of tinkly.

"Oh, Raven, don't be irritating," she said.

Tinkly sounded even better now that I'd heard her voice and the first thing that came to mind was "mellifluous" and the next thought was, where the feck did that come from? Who even said mellifluous when they were out and about?

I glanced at the lad with a laptop open in front of him, seated across from Raven and Stately Beauty, hoping for a distraction. Sure, wasn't he a study with a long black plait hanging down from his forehead and along his cheek? A matching plait hung down his back, making the whole a shade past the border of trendy to weird. The weird style he was working extended to a hooded sweatshirt that he wore backwards and inside out, the hood bunched up under his chin.

"Goodbye," he said in a pleasant voice and went back to studying his laptop.

I gave him a puzzled look. "What?"

"Don't mind him, he's just contrary," said Raven.

"Your friend has a very unique dress sense," I said.

Raven laughed. "He's his very own person."

"I don't know what that means, but it's probably right," I said.

"It's who he is," said Stately Beauty.

"I have no doubt," I said.

I still had no understanding what they meant. Vague allusions to a story, to which I had definitely missed part one. This sounded like part three or even four, but somewhere near the rising action. And it unsettled me. They all unsettled me. More of that something, that at the back and behind feeling just niggling at me, a faint scritch scritch.

Raven laughed again and Stately Beauty smiled. The smile

lit her face in a manner that made you want to ensure it wouldn't ever disappear.

"Sorry, I should introduce you," said Raven. He nudged Stately Beauty. "This is Skye."

I nodded. Her name fitted, somehow. Though her hair and eyes were black, her skin copper, she seemed to fill the air, expansive, like the sky.

"And this is Sherman," said Raven, nodding to the lad with the peculiar plaits.

"Sherman," I said, looking at him. Sherman looked up and grinned. What a name. But still, somehow it fitted. And better than that sweatshirt he was sporting that looked ready to swallow him whole.

Behind me, I heard Lenny clear his throat. I glanced over and saw that there were a few more people at the bar, waiting to be served. Lenny was himself grabbing a bottle of beer and a glass for one of the customers.

"Sorry, now. I'll just serve those people a minute and be back to check on you."

"Take your time," said Raven. "We're just hanging out until you get off."

I blinked in surprise, then grinned. "Really?"

"Yeah, we thought you could take us back to your place for coffee?"

Surprise took me again. I looked at the three of them curiously. "Why the feck not?"

"Isn't she cute?" Raven said to Skye. He gave me a wink. Again, that something, this time laden with twinkles over a layer of take care.

I ONLY HAD A ROOM. No apartment, not yet, at any rate. This place was my "at the moment place" and it provided me with all the necessities anyone who only needed an "at the moment place" could want. It had a small hotplate, coffee maker and press – excuse me, *cabinet* – where I could store food. The rest of the moderate sized room was taken up by my bed, a small cabinet beside it, a small table and two chairs, as well as a couple of upholstered chairs that had seen better days. It was above a florist's shop and not too far from the bar, or rather, tavern. Murphy's, so perfect for me, really.

Nevertheless I felt a little nervous leading the three into it, even though I'd already warned them it wasn't going to make a huge impression, except for what it lacked.

Raven took a seat in one of the upholstered chairs and Skye took the other. Sherman sat on the floor, spreading out the long beribboned skirts he was wearing over his knees, his laptop perched on top of them. Colourful wasn't the word. There was a word, it just wasn't coming to me in the face of the overwhelming picture Sherman presented.

"Coffee?"

It was all I had, except for a small bottle of whiskey and some cans of Coke. And a large bag of crisps which I discovered were called potato chips here. I'd become a Yank before I knew it.

"Sure," said Raven. "I take mine black."

"A little milk for me," said Skye. She pushed her long black hair over her shoulder with fluid grace. Raven's wing, was what you'd say if you were describing her hair, I thought. The woman was poetry.

"Hot chocolate?" asked Sherman looking up from tapping away on his laptop. He'd wasted no time there.

"I have hot, but it's coffee hot," I said.

Sherman shrugged and shook his head.

"He'll have the coffee," said Raven.

Raven gave me a wink. It was a wink that said "you're in on the joke," only I had no idea what the joke was. They were a peculiar threesome. But entertaining, there was no doubt about that.

I made the coffee, thankful that I had enough mugs left behind by a previous tenant to be the hostess tonight. I should have been tired after a full shift at work, and the coffee would do me no amount of good, but I was no stranger to late nights that became early mornings, and tonight there was a hint of mischief and good craic to be had. While I made the drinks I could hear Sherman murmuring to the other two, shaking his head. I strained to listen, that scritch scritch made me do it, but it was if they were speaking a language I didn't know.

I handed out the coffees in my nothing fancy mugs and took a seat on the bed, my own coffee in hand.

"So," I said. "Are you three from Bartlesville?" An innocent probe, hardly a nudge and surely innocent.

Ordinarily I wouldn't have asked questions like that. It wasn't me, really, and often it was a question you didn't need to ask in Ireland. For the most part accent, manner and a lot of other subtle things told you all you needed to know. The most subtle of course, was that they mostly knew you or they didn't. Or they knew someone you knew. But it was different here, now. Different country, different customs and judging from Sherman, different in a way I didn't altogether understand but certainly was interesting.

Sherman with his plaits, his backwards, inside out hoodie and ribboned skirt, had the features of a Sioux brave straight out of the cowboy films – hawk nose, high cheekbones and staring black eyes. He looked different from Raven, whose face and eyes had more of an Asian quality to them, his eyes more almond shaped and tilted. Eyes that seemed to be perpetually amused, as if everything was a constant joke to him. At the moment the amused eyes were fixed on me and laughter was spilling from him like water. But still.

"None of us are from Bartlesville," he said.

I shrugged, trying to feign casual, because that scritch scritch was adding another scritch, increasing the rhythm. "Fine, so. I just wondered. You seem to know the place well enough. Are you all from the reservation where you picked me up?"

"The Osage Reservation?" said Raven. He shook his head. "No, but we have friends there."

Skye smiled. "Many good friends."

"Oh, right," I said.

"Are you from Ireland?" asked Sherman. He looked up from the laptop, cocked his head studied me.

I nodded. "Yes."

"What brought you here?" asked Skye. I looked at her, detecting mild curiosity, but maybe something more.

"A stiff wind," I said.

Raven laughed. Sherman blinked and Skye smiled.

"That's quite a wind, then, to come all the way here from Ireland," said Raven. "And passing so many other places on the way."

"I didn't really notice, to be honest," I said with a small laugh.

"Sometimes you have to leave a place to appreciate it," said Skye.

It seemed the banter was leaving the room, taking its promise of craic and good times along with it, leaving only the scritch scritch scritch. I wished for a fiddle, a banjo, or something with tunes and rhythm to drag the old banter back in and kick up its heels.

"What brought you to Bartlesville?" I asked, finding wit had slipped out the door the same time as banter.

"A wind of another sort," said Raven.

Feck, there was that triple scritch again. I gave a little smile. It was a good one that was determined to quiet the scritch.

"What wind would that be? South wind of the odorous kind?" I had tried for the banter but that was poor, very poor. Wit wasn't cooperating.

"An ill wind," said Skye.

"Oh. I'm sorry." I had nothing more. What could you say? I looked at Sherman, who was tapping away. It wasn't online gaming he was at. Obviously. I looked at Raven. He chuckled and shook his head.

"Am I missing something?" I asked.

"No," said Raven. "Not at all. Skye was just being enigmatic." Skye frowned.

"Enigmatic?" I said.

"She likes to speak in a mysterious code," said Raven.

"Right. Is it a special Skye code or is it known to all of you?" Skye started to speak but Sherman cut in. "All of who?"

I gestured to them. "You three. Or is it your tribe thing."

"Tribe thing?" said Raven.

"Oh, feck me," I said. "I feel like I'm walking through a maze and the signs are in Urdu."

"Urdu?" asked Sherman. "We're not that kind of Indian."

I gave a frustrated laugh. "I know. It was the first thing that came to mind."

Clearly the kind of Indian they were had a different type of banter than the type I was used to. Theirs tied me in knots. Or was it more? There it was again. That more.

"Don't mind us," said Raven. "There's not much to know or tell about us. We're part of the fabric here. But you," he said, and there it, was that feckin' wink again, "you're the interesting one. We don't often get to meet a real Irish person."

"As opposed to a fake one? You get many of those?" I forced

the banter here, because there was something about the way he'd said "interesting one". Like he knew my own "something".

Raven lifted his brows. "Not fake, no, but there's plenty of part Irish here."

I grinned then. Okay, this I could understand. "Oh, right. I can imagine which parts."

"Best not to imagine," said Raven.

Skye looked between us both, raised her brows. Was I crossing a boundary? Moving in on her territory? I glanced at Sherman but he was still grinning and so no help at all.

"And you're not considered interesting?" I said to Sherman.

Sherman looked up. "I'm contrary, not interesting."

"Interesting and contrary," I said. "Why are you contrary? Did something happen?"

"I have seen the thunder beings. It's who I am."

"He's Heyoka," said Skye.

"Hey, who?" I asked.

Raven laughed and Sherman joined him, both emitting a big belly laugh that had me grinning, even though, again, I didn't understand the joke.

"He's a fool," said Raven, grinning.

"Is 'Heyoka' Indian for fool, then?" I asked. I felt I was getting part of the "something" here, but the nub of it was eluding me.

"Heyoka," said Skye, kindly. "Heyoka are fools." Raven snickered and Skye frowned at him.

"He challenges people's weaknesses, speaks truths in ways others won't," said Skye. "He helps those in pain, brings laughter when it's needed."

I looked over at Sherman. Sacred? But the more I looked at him, as he laughed away, seemingly unaffected by the solemn words Skye had spoken, I could see hints of it. Feel hints of it. Was that the only "more" that "something" that was doing the triple "scritch"?

I looked at Raven. He'd stopped laughing, his eyes on me, a knowing glint there. I raised my brows.

"You wouldn't call that interesting?" I said.

"Interesting isn't what I'd call it, no," said Raven.

"No," I said.

This wasn't a night of music, laughter and all things fun. This was a night for all that was eerie, strange and... I wouldn't let that word in. Would I feck. Not here. That "something" that triple "scritch" meaning. There would be no room in my mind, here in feckin' Bartlesville, Oklahoma, for anything not of that world.

MAURA

The bar was crowded when we entered, the musicians playing enthusiastically at one end and cowboy hatted and western shirted dancers at the other, hustling along in a line, moving in unison. I smiled at the sight of this real thing in front of me. Cowgirl happy, I turned to Raven and dug my elbow in his side.

"You didn't tell me this was a real country and western bar," I said.

Raven tipped his cowboy hat back and grinned. "It's very real. A taste of Oklahoma. I thought you might like it."

I suddenly wanted cowboy boots, hat and all the rest that went with this cowgirl happy I felt. Be that girl, a "lasso me a man" girl. Behind me, Skye laughed. It was knowing. Again. A "knowing me" kind of laugh that left me surprised and for an instant foolish. I cast her a sideways glance but there was nothing teasing in her eyes. It was all merriment and joy. She smiled. No cowgirl dream concession for her, she wore her black hair long and free, no hat, and a simple pair of jeans topped with a short sleeved shirt and ballet flats. Sherman was equally rocking his own style – the backwards inside out statement that included the plaits. His expression was unperturbed, though he scanned the crowd, his eyes taking in everything. He caught my look and grinned. I smiled back. This would be fun.

The beat caught hold of me, an "I'm so country" kind of beat with a "dosey doh" flung in, except the "dosey dohing" was all footwork done in a line. I'd never really tried country and western line dancing before, though there was a strong Irish country scene back home that was certain to have opportunities. Irish trad had been my thing. It was who I was. But maybe, this was what I came for. A new music. This could be my new music.

I moved past Raven and into the bar, seizing this new opportunity that was presenting itself with enthusiasm. The place was busy and there were few tables to be had in the section to the far side of the band and the dance floor. Stand it would be, until I'd dance, because I knew I would be on that dance floor soon enough, thumbs in pockets, elbows out, legs moving. It didn't look that difficult, sure it didn't. I'd be grand, sliding, crossing and shimmying my legs. Cowgirl *Sean Nós* dancing.

I moved towards the bar, Raven close behind me. I could hear his laugh, strong and full of amusement with a hint of mockery. Yeah, I was looking at everyone with stereotype glasses, my eyes large, conscious that I was bordering on "where are the leprechauns" side of gawping that made most Irish shudder.

"Did you bring me here to tease me?" I asked, leaning into him to be heard. We'd arrived at the bar, but there were several ahead of us.

"Never," he said, his eyes twinkling.

"I'm glad I can provide you with so much entertainment."

"Oh you do. You really do. It's part of your charm."

I snorted. No one would have used "charm" or "entertaining" in a sentence describing me. Finn maybe, but that had been banter. I shoved that thought aside, as I'd done every other time he'd entered my thoughts. I was still annoyed at him, the reasons fading into the general reason of "he's annoying". Annoying Finn. Finn and annoying, a pairing I would imprint in my mind and push it into the lake of "no more". The new me didn't need any of that. Or him. I was "cowgirl happy", now. Dancing to the country beat. Dancing a line full of slick moves, twists and turns, thumbs tucked happily.

"Where'd you get your hat?" I asked Raven.

"This hat?" he said, poking at the brim. "Picked it up along the way."

"Along the way where?" I was leaning in close – so close I could smell his scent. It was pine and wood with an undertone of sea air. It made me think of somewhere that felt sun, wind and rain differently. I inhaled deeply and suddenly I wanted to be in that place, with him. Dizziness came over me for a moment and I tottered a little, uncertain of my bearings.

Raven put a steadying hand on my shoulder. "Are you sure you want a drink? Maybe have a soft drink. Or water."

"No, I'm grand. A drink will help."

He raised his brow but said nothing. The barman came up and Raven ordered a couple of beers and I asked for a whiskey.

"Jack?" asked the bartender.

I gave him a quizzical look. Oh, right. "Yes, Jack, so."

"Jack so?" he asked. "We only have Jack Daniels."

Raven laughed.

"That'll do," I said. "Jack Daniels is fine."

The bartender got our drinks while Raven continued to chuckle. I turned to look towards the dancers, ignoring his open amusement. The music washed over me, a wave of rhythm that moved my toe to tap and my head to bob. The steps had patterns and a bit of style to the shimmy and slide that drew me in.

A few moments later I had my whiskey in one hand and a water for Sherman in the other hand, while Raven had his drink and Skye's. We made our way towards the back, where we could see Sherman and Skye propped up against the wall, watching the dancers. A couple of men were talking to Skye, their light coloured T-shirts bright against the dim light of the back of the bar. One wore a cowboy hat, his brown hair peeking from under it. The other one's head was bare, his short black hair curled tightly to his head, his brown skin dark against his white T-shirt. Both of them were well built and approaching their thirties and were in the midst of a lively conversation with Skye. Sherman just studied the men, his eyes full of question. He elbowed Raven and mouthed "he's one".

I could feel Raven stiffen beside me. I didn't need to hear the conversation, but I could imagine it. The postures, the gestures, the expressions all told the "cock of the walk" story. Rooster strutting, peacock flashing. Hilarious. But Raven clearly thought the opposite and I wondered if he was going to spread his feathers in display.

But he didn't and that made me wonder more. He went up alongside Skye and grinned at the two men.

"Hey," he said to them. He handed Skye her beer and I moved over to Sherman who took the glass of water from me.

The two men looked at Raven, gave a small nod and turned back to Skye. She was looking them both over placidly as if she couldn't decide whether she liked them or not.

"What's with the kid?" said your man with the cowboy hat.

"What do you mean?" asked Raven.

"You know, the way he's dressed, man. Doesn't he know his sweatshirt is on wrong?"

"And the skirt," said the bare-headed man.

Raven shrugged.

"It's who he is," said Skye.

"Is that right, babe?" said cowboy hat. "He wears dresses does he?"

Another man in a dark T-shirt and jeans and perfect tousled hair came alongside cowboy hat and grabbed his arm. "Come on, Clyde, you don't wanna hang out with these people."

"I don't know," said Clyde. "Jeb and me, we were kinda enjoying talking to this babe, here. What did you say your name was?"

"I didn't," said Skye.

Clyde's friend frowned at Skye. "Come on Clyde. These people aren't worth your time."

The bare-headed man looked at Clyde's friend. "What do you mean 'these people'?

Clyde's friend indicated Sherman. "Well him, for a start. Stupid Indian doesn't even know back from his front."

"It's who he is," I said, repeating Skye's words. I'd had enough of Clyde's friend and I wasn't feeling especially kind feelings towards Clyde either.

Clyde's friend glanced over at me. "Don't be offended, babe. I didn't mean you. You're not strange at all."

"Oh, you don't know me," I said.

He gave me a smile that defined salacious, leering and all things that provoked "feck off away from me" thoughts.

"I'm happy to get to know you right now," he said.

"And I'm happy not to," I said.

He frowned. "Come on, babe, you know you don't mean that."

"Oh, I do." My war grin was forming. I could feel the loosening, bouncing feeling of an impending argument-come-fight. Oh, yes, the rhythm of it all was starting to hum. I struck a pose. My provocative "do not mess with me" hand on one jutting hip, fire in the eyes kind of pose.

Clyde's friend's eyes narrowed. "Come on, Clyde. Let's get away from this Indian trash. It's beginning to smell here."

I started to step forward, issue a challenge, the music beating a rhythm that seemed in opposition to my current focus. On impulse, I looked at Raven instead. He was smiling, almost laughing, while Skye tilted her head, still regarding the two original men placidly, ignoring Clyde's friend.

"Come dance with me, sugar," said Clyde, holding out his hand to Skye.

"I don't think so, thanks," said Skye. She turned to the bare-headed, brown skinned man. "Maybe you though, if you want to."

The man straightened, licked his full lips and smiled. "Yes ma'am." He took her hand and led her to the dance floor.

Raven held out his hand to me. "Come on, Maura." He turned to the two men. "Sherman and I have a few steps I've learned that you two might not know."

Raven nodded to Sherman to follow and he led us across the room to the dancers who were just forming up for another dance. Sherman tagged along, humming a little tune, his steps bouncing.

The steps were quick. They slid, they turned, they sidled and shimmied and I loved the steps for their slyness, their almost bend and down, the nod to here and a nod to there. It was grand and full of fun. It took me a few moments to get them, but the rhythm entered me, and the steps took hold, I was laughing, I was stepping. I was cowgirl happy.

Clyde and his friend watched us sourly. They saw Raven with his lightning quick steps, showy and improvised, adding his own little bob and rooster stomping moves. It was oh yes, oh yeah, and I wanted to give my own little whoop, like a session going regular, giving the praise that was due. Sherman moved backward on the forward dipped on the rise, doing his own little "it's who he is" dance that somehow found the rhythm.

Clyde wouldn't be outdone and neither would his friend. The two fanned their feathers, elbows out dipping and swaying a double swirl and then three, leg raised a little higher and higher. Raven threw his head back and laughed. It was a laugh that caught up my own and there we were the two of us, meshed in that line, turning, dipping, kicking and sliding – my rooster and those two peacocks. The two peacocks worked to keep up, until Clyde's legs become tangled in his own vanity and his little higher step became too high and he found his next step had his arse planted hard on the floor, bringing the other peacock with him.

The dancers stepped around the two without missing a beat, myself included and Raven too. It was icing on the cake, craic of the best sort, because, sure you couldn't have planned it if you wanted to. It was all perfect karma and "who's the fool now" occurrence that you'd be telling at parties for years. A "remember when". I looked at Raven and the answering twinkle in his eyes made me wonder if I would be remembering when with him in years to come. If I could be "cowgirl happy" with him.

Later, when I was breathless and sitting down at the back with Raven, Skye and Sherman. I heard Skye lean over to Raven and say in a low voice, "He was asking me about the land."

Sherman turned at her words, his brow furrowed. "Told you, man," he said to Raven.

9

SAOIRSE

Saoirse knew Anu was speaking, but she wasn't really listening to the words, let alone their meaning, as Anu sat beside her, staring into the computer screen that held three separate images and their own up in the corner. A Zoom meeting. Saoirse's eyes kept going to one image, as much as she didn't want it to. An image that she studied carefully, trying to pick up any hints or clues about what Smithy was thinking or feeling. If there was any change. If there was anything. But there was nothing. He just stared at the screen's middle distance. Or far distance, or anything that had the least possible chance of catching her eye. And any eye that might be caught would most certainly be a blind eye. An eye blind to her, refusing to see her in any way but a person, sitting next to Anu.

This was the first time she'd seen him since they'd been to Balor's house. An almost disastrous experience that had sent her heart racing when she saw the two men come haring down the road, Luke's eyes filled with horror and panic. Smithy had just looked bewildered. It wasn't until they were well clear of the house and on another road that Luke slowed down and was able to explain what had happened. A JaneyMacHolyMaryMotherofGod moment that he could only translate into a feckityfeckfeck oh feck. His mother. After all this time he'd encountered his mother. After the words tumbled out with all their emotional toxic spillage of fecks, Luke shut down. Shut his mouth, shut his expression and all trace of emotion.

Anu hadn't made too much of it when Saoirse had relayed what had happened. Luke hadn't even stopped to explain any of the night's activities. He'd dropped off Smithy first and then Saoirse and said she could tell the story and the results herself. On hearing it, Anu had focused on the disappointing absence of the slingshot and spear.

Looking at Luke now, a small image on the computer screen, Saoirse could see in his paleness and the occasional lip worrying that he was still rattled by the incident, though it was clear the emotional "shop shut" was in full swing. The "I am a cool surfer dude" stance he'd had when Saoirse had first met him was in play. Still, he had more life in him than Smithy's apocalyptic zombie stare, or Finn's thin lipped detachment.

Another life and soul of the party was Finn. Possibly the zombie party Smithy was currently throwing. The two of them. The state of them. She missed Finn's banter, his lovely manner, his stories and his kindness. He was missing Maura, she knew, but wore a "not in a million years will I admit it" expression on his face whenever she brought up Maura's name. Some group of top notch secret mission warriors, special hit squad, fearsome foursome they were. The state of all of them.

Anu's reedy voice soldiered on, explaining their situation and Saoirse tried to focus, knowing it was important. The state of all of them, she thought again. Anu's state wasn't much better, though thankfully it didn't seem markedly worse in the past few days. Saoirse wanted to hug her, put her arm around this woman who was her grandmother, but somehow she couldn't manage to do it. It wasn't that Anu wouldn't want it, or would she? Or that Anu didn't need it, because every impulse Saoirse had regarding Anu said that she did. It just somehow seemed that Saoirse's embrace wouldn't be wide enough, her arms, secure enough, her hug would do nothing but make Anu understand her frailty in a way that would paralyse Saoirse. And bring home to Saoirse that there was nothing she could do to fix it.

Saoirse understood now, how frail Anu was and how much frailer she could be. That she might die, and Saoirse didn't want to even think about what it would mean if Anu died. And as she peered at Luke on the computer screen, she could see he understood it, that his "shop shut" face was just as much about his understanding and fear of its implications, as it was that he'd encountered his mother. Kayla, Anu. They were linked, entwined. Woven into the fabric of this world. They were this world. Just as she and Smithy were twined and woven. It was a thought that gladdened her, scared her and filled her with so much confusion.

"Right, so," said Anu. "Given that we have ruled out the presence of either the spear or slingshot here in Ireland, we'll have to focus on America."

"America?" Saoirse said, stunned.

"Yes," said Anu. "Finn and Luke both feel there's no other place here that he'd have it. It's not in a bank, or Cork headquarters, or any other possibilities here, and we know it isn't across the water, so that's the only remaining possibility."

"How do you propose we do that?" said Finn.

"You'll have to go to America," said Anu.

"We can't do it remotely?" asked Saoirse. "Can't Luke do a search, or hack into his computers and see what he comes up with?"

"Luke has done as much as he can remotely. The only way to determine if they're in America is to physically search Balor's American headquarters and his home there."

"Really?" said Saoirse, weakly. The thought of going all the way to the US held little appeal. She'd never been there and had never really felt the inclination to go, unlike a lot of her friends. All she'd ever wanted had been here, in Ireland. And if she was honest with herself, she was reluctant to leave Anu.

She looked at the screen and wondered if Smithy had registered Anu's words. Luke was frowning and Finn seemed politely quizzical.

"Do you want all of us to go?" asked Finn.

"Yes," said Anu. "Of course."

Why "of course" thought Saoirse. "Surely Luke and Finn would be able to do this without myself and Smithy?"

"No, all of you have to go. It's about a lot more than searching the two sites. And that will take a bit of planning and teamwork. Think about it."

"There's really no reason for me to go," said Luke darkly. "And there's much to keep me here."

The "I am a cool surfer dude" had vanished and now Luke was hardened stone, immovable. Saoirse could understand it, now more than ever, all that tied him here.

"You will go," said Anu, her voice the firmest it had been in a while. "I've explained it all before and I won't waste my breath explaining again. All of you will go. There is a difficult task ahead and it will take all of you to succeed."

"We're not prepared for anything dangerous," said Luke tightly. "We aren't in top form, we lack some of the abilities required. We aren't a crack team. The only crack thing about us is possibly the great music we can make together."

At that moment Smithy blinked, as if Anu's words were just

beginning to register. Saoirse could see the moment their full meaning took hold.

"You want us all to go to America?" he said.

Finn sighed and shook his head. Luke frowned.

"I rest my case," Luke muttered.

Anu brightened. "Exactly. All of you together, playing music, what better craic than that?"

The "what" that came out of Smithy's mouth was echoed by the expressions on Finn and Luke's face and undoubtedly Saoirse's.

"You'll travel there as an Irish traditional music band. It will be the perfect cover," said Anu.

"She's watched too much crime channel," muttered Finn.

"Scandi noir," said Luke, still frowning.

"Irish noir," said Finn.

Saoirse snorted. Smithy rolled his eyes.

"We'll have to think up a name for you," said Anu.

"The Irish Mugs," said Finn.

"Oh, no, something clever," said Anu. She was smiling now. "You'll think of it, Finn. In the meantime, we'll outline a plan."

Saoirse stared at the empty suitcase on her bed, a bundle of clothes in her hands. She wasn't certain what to pack. She didn't want to pack. Below her, she could hear Anu's heavy breathing, the effort of making a meal almost too much for her. Saoirse had tried to coax her to bed, but she wasn't having any of it. The "I'm grand" statements were always at the ready, each time Saoirse suggested anything that approached resting or letting Saoirse take over. All the worry this caused her made the packing process anything but appealing. The only thing that held promise for the journey was the possibility of playing music with the lads at some venue. But all her other concerns outweighed that thought.

Her main worry was Anu's frailty and the thought of leaving her on her own. She knew neighbours could be counted on to help her to some extent, but they had no idea what was the real cause of her illness. And, Saoirse knew, it was that very cause that meant she had to go to America. She wasn't certain what kind of help she would be, but she would be there nonetheless, to do the best she could. She only wished that she wasn't so useless. Her sword skills were improving, but would that count for anything in this task? She doubted it. But her other abilities, the abilities she had as Bríd, would have counted for much. She only wished she had them now. More and more she felt frustrated by her lack. And why was it she had lost all of those abilities from before, when she was fully Bríd and no one else? Was it really because Anu had ensured that all her memories were wiped clean, removed, for Saoirse's own protection? But did that mean she'd lost her abilities along with her memory, or did she still have abilities, her powers, lying innate within her?

Saoirse put down the bundle of clothes, caught up by this thought. If it was true that her abilities were innate, how could she access them? Was it a case of waking them up, triggering them in some manner? Or was it a case of learning them again, or to harness them, as though they were some raw power within her?

It was an exciting thought but one that she had no idea how to take forward. It couldn't be a case of just laying her hands on someone and wishing them healed, because she'd done that with Smithy and all the wishing in the world hadn't helped him. But then his wasn't a physical ailment and maybe she was only capable of assisting physical healing.

On the other hand, she wasn't spouting poetry, but she'd managed to practice smithcraft with Smithy's help. Deep inside her she felt certain that, given the chance again, with Smithy present, she would be able to create something. But getting Smithy to agree to that was as remote as spouting poetry at will. Still, it was something to think about. Maybe talk to Diancecht about when she returned. Or perhaps not. Maybe it was something she could figure out herself.

10

SMITHY

Smithy stuffed clothes absentmindedly into his duffel bag. He'd no suitcase, sure, why would he? He'd never had the desire to go on a plane or leave Ireland for that matter. A duffel bag, worn and with the zipper rusting, was enough for him. Besides, wouldn't it fit the remit for the ragged at the edges Irish trad band funding their little American tour by playing gigs at every "all things Irish" pub?

Remit. He had to laugh at that. It suggested big and clever plans. The last thing he was capable of was big and clever plans, no matter what Anu thought. But still and all, he'd go. Try and stir up his "yeow meow eow" again to meet the challenge. Or was it "meow yeow"? The feeling and the idea had been fading over the last few days, along with the energy and chilled quality that had come with it. Or had it really? Was it just the "old fool" feeling he'd felt before, only in a new tune?

Everyone was sick of him, himself included, so the best thought was to live with the "old fool" feeling and stop trying to make it what it wasn't. He was old. Old by any standards in this world and in this life, so why not. "Old fool", emphasis on "fool", and this old fool needed to pack his old fool of a fiddle and everything else that would make up his great innovative disguise of "Irish trad musician on tour" look.

There was a knock on the door, halting Smithy's musings. Knocking? Few would bother. Not around here, in any case. He made his way from the bedroom to the sitting room and then to the kitchen. He could see the shadow through the frosted glass and it made him pause. When he opened it, Finn stood there, hands in jeans pockets, shoulders hunched, and a frown on his face. The red wiry curls on his head were tangled and knotted, obvious strangers to any kind of comb or brush.

"Smithy," said Finn. "How are things?"

Smithy shrugged. "Grand, so."

He opened the door, allowing Finn to pass through, curiosity growing about this sudden appearance. He headed over to the kettle. "You want tea?" The nod came but Smithy already had the kettle filled. He needed the routine, the form to get his head going and in a mode where he might be able to make sense of Finn being here, now, with that look on his face that wasn't Finn.

The tea was made, during which all things weather related were discussed and when it was finished Smithy gestured to one of the chairs at the small table. It seemed like it would be a kitchen kind of talk, not a sitting room, relax on the sofa kind of talk. And he needed a chair. And a table to rest his arms and a cup to grasp. All these things could orient him, help him face all this swishing, swirling that "meow yeow" let loose inside him but left him nearly frozen half the time, instead of laid back cool cat. What a load of shite.

"You ready for America?" asked Finn, when the weather had been put to bed, tucked in fine and even given a lullaby.

Smithy blinked, opened his mouth, shut it and shook his head. "No."

Finn gave him a sympathetic look. "No, I don't want to go either."

Smithy grunted. He didn't know how to explain it, except to state the obvious. He didn't feel ready.

"Are any of us ready for this?" said Smithy, following on from the thoughts in his head.

Finn snorted. "Ready for what? That's what I ask myself. This is a journey that seems to involve more than just stealing two items."

"To be fair, they're a bit more than just items."

Finn conceded the point with a nod. "Maybe. And maybe that's part of my point. It doesn't feel right. Something about all this is off."

"Off in what way?"

Finn shrugged. "I'm not sure. I've been trying to put my finger on it."

Smithy paused before he spoke his thoughts, wondering if he dared. Oh what the feck. "Do you think you might be feeling that way because Maura isn't going with us?"

Something sparked in Finn's eyes. "Do you think she's betrayed us? Gone over to Balor?"

Smithy looked at him, stunned. "What? You think that's where's she's gone?"

"No!" He gave an anguished laugh. "Maybe. Do you?"

"Hadn't thought about it. Yes? Maybe?"

"I know Luke thinks that."

"How do you know that? Has he said anything?"

Finn gave him a dark look. "He doesn't have to. I can tell he thinks that."

Smithy nodded. "Well, that's Luke. He's not well disposed towards many of us. Well," Smithy added, frowning, "except Saoirse. He seems to like her fine."

"Ah, right. Yeah, I'd noticed that, all right. But then it seemed just as friends. He and Kayla, well, it seems like Kayla has all his focus, really."

"So he's just a flirt?"

Finn grinned. "It's the hero syndrome. Or magnet."

"Maura never seemed to bother with his magnet."

Finn laughed hard at that. "No, Maura requires a different magnet altogether." He fell silent again, his expression sobering. "I wish I knew where she went."

"If she wanted to let you know, she would. You'll have to let her be."

"But she wasn't in a good frame of mind. I'm worried she might do something stupid."

"Maura can take care of herself if it's stupid."

Finn snorted. "Her stupid isn't someone's average stupid. It has the potential to be huge."

"True. But huge Maura stupid may not be something you can do anything about, Finn."

"Maybe not, but I would still feel better if I could remain here, in case she does need me."

Smithy thought about his words. "And that's why you don't want to go to America?"

Finn shook his head. "No, that's another reason. Or maybe a little part of why it doesn't feel right. The balance is off."

"The balance?"

"Feck me, I don't know how to explain it."

"You, the wordsmith doesn't know how to explain something?"

It was a gentle tease and Smithy was glad to see that it brought a hint of a smile to Finn's face.

"We're a group. We function best when there's a balance between us all. At the moment, it seems off."

"Everything about us is off," said Smithy drily.

Finn gave a small laugh. "It was there, believe me. But it became worse after Luke."

"You think Luke is the reason for the imbalance?"

Finn paused then shook his head. "As much as he might paint himself as the lone hero god, and as much as I might have had some issue with that at one time, I don't think he's the cause. I think all of us are unbalanced, on the back foot, something."

"And what caused that do you think?"

"I don't know."

"Do you think Balor has something to do with it?"

Finn considered that idea a moment. "I'm not sure how he could, but possibly."

"And you think Maura's behaviour is caused by this imbalance?"

The idea was dubious to Smithy at best, but he couldn't argue with Finn's observation about imbalance. At least when it applied to him. There was no question that he was off balance, but he knew the cause, no matter what Diancecht said. Diancecht's dismissal of Smithy's weak leg, lack of memory and any other failing he had, really irked him. Irked larger than life, irked so big it would slap the life out of Diancecht and see how Diancecht felt when he was dipped in the Well of Slane and brought back to life. Let him find all his faculties intact. Find his normal, living his best life, with or without the hashtag.

"Maura's behaviour is caused by many things," said Finn. "She's angry about many things."

"Ah, now. Sure, Maura is always angry. It's who she is. It's what she is. Anger is her thing. She thrives on it."

Finn shook his head. "No, she's conflict. A coming together of two opposing forces. That doesn't always need anger."

Smithy gave a faint smile. "I see the wordsmith is back."

"A weak moment."

"You're right," said Smithy. "But that doesn't mean that Maura doesn't like anger or that she doesn't function best when there is anger in the midst."

"Exactly," said Finn.

Smithy knitted his brow. "What?"

"She isn't functioning at her best, yet she's angry. There's something more."

"Fine, so. Does that change anything?"

"No, it only helps me explain to you why I'm worried."

"And there's nothing you can do. She could be anywhere."

"She's not across the water."

"Right. She could be anywhere except across the water."

Finn sighed. "Yes."

"But there's nothing you can do. So why not go to America?"

"Why don't you want to go to America?" Finn countered.

Smithy stared at him, at a loss for a moment. "Er, ah, you know yourself. The whole balance thing."

"You feel it too?"

"I suppose. Yeah."

"How does it feel to you, then?" asked Finn.

Smithy paused, collecting his thoughts. "Off. Not right."

"Like your sudden lack of the old language?"

Smithy blinked, his expression darkening. "Did Maura tell you?"

"Smithy, I've noticed. Your little dramatic performance at the hall was good, but it seemed to conveniently avoid a situation. And then there was the meeting with the Hunters, in the forest." He studied Smithy. "And your leg, I've noticed you favour one leg sometimes. Is that part of it?"

Smithy looked down at his mug, the milk sitting there quietly, providing no answers. "Yes, no." He sighed. "Yes. I-I've not been right since the battle."

"Since you died."

"Yes."

"Ah, no, Smithy. It was a lot. But you can still fight well. We've seen you. You're grand, once the battle begins."

Smithy considered that. "Maybe. It's just that, it might not always happen that way. And what if when it happens, it's the worse time possible?"

"There's always a lot of mights and might nots."

"I'd rather they'd be definitelys. I like definitelys."

"Don't we all. But they don't usually keep us company."

"No, they haven't liked my company at all. Especially lately."

"Ah, they've gone off with the Sure Thing."

"Oh, the Sure Thing is an elusive old fecker."

"He is indeed."

"Snobby fecker."

"Not friendly at all."

"Maybe we should improve our hospitality?" said Finn.

"More than just a cup of tea?"

"A right old spread."

"A Mammy spread."

They grinned at each other. Some balance restored. They just needed to get their Mammy style hospitality sorted. If only. If only. But those "if onlys" were as elusive as "Sure Thing" and "Definitelys."

11

______

LUKE

L uke sighed as he sat at the kitchen table staring at his laptop. He couldn't add "ninja web stalker" to his string of "good at everything" talents. He'd been at this for several hours and still he had little to tell him about Balor and his exact location. How did Anu know Balor was in America? He couldn't find anything that confirmed it beyond a doubt. There was no meeting schedule shared with his staff, let alone where they were held. At least Luke had managed to find a copy of the blueprints to Balor's headquarters and his home.

He paused a moment, considering other angles. If he couldn't track Balor's movements, would it help to track Eithne's? Luke had deliberately put the thought of his mother aside since that night at Balor's house. The shock of seeing her had stayed with him and he'd found it difficult to shake. That feckityfeck moment. The thought might be aside, but the feeling kept nudging him like an annoying sibling who didn't know when to stop. He gave over to it now and all the dark thoughts that came with it.

His mother. He thought about her expression when she'd seen him at the top of the stairs. The light had been dim, but he hadn't mistaken the shock. That was something. Something that counted in favour of their task ahead. Though Balor would now know that they were looking for the spear and the slingshot. He would take extra precautions. Anu seemed to have made little of it when Luke had told her, something that had surprised him. Yet another piece that was missing from this puzzle. A puzzle that was so filled with gaps that he could hardly make out the design, let alone the finished whole. Didn't the others notice this? Or were they too wrapped up in their concerns to understand the implications of it? Either way, it didn't reflect well on the group and their capabilities, or their chances for success.

All of it felt off balance. He felt off balance. A hand rested on his shoulder. He looked up at Kayla, her hair loose about her shoulders, the watery sun from the window behind her limning her in light. He reached up and covered her hand with his. An unspoken communication, he could feel some of his disquiet easing with her presence, her touch.

"How are you feeling?" he asked.

She shrugged. "Grand enough. Nana and Bláthín are no different. How are you, though? I didn't hear you return last night."

He shook his head. "I stayed in the caravan. I didn't want to disturb you."

She frowned at him, knowing that he wasn't telling the complete truth. And what was his real truth? The shock of seeing his mother had left him rattled, so rattled he didn't want Kayla to see? Did he know the real truth? His real truth – the truth that ran deep inside him, that shaped him, that guided him? Right now the only real truth he had was the desire to punch something. Sword bedamned. Retaliator could feck off on its own. Though, chopping might not be bad. Chopping wood, chopping heads? "Truth," that one that was his, and was large and big, and every other adjective that meant big and large was trickling in, swelling the biteen one that was in the desire to punch, with an insistent persistence. Not so long ago, Mon would have helped. No words would have been needed, but that was gone now. And that was part of the desire to punch, as well as possibly part of his real "Truth" he didn't want taking shape. He sighed.

"What's wrong, Luke?"

He shook his head. Could he even articulate what it was? Did he know, beyond the desire to punch?

"What happened last night? You went to Balor's house."

He glanced up at Kayla, took her hand and swung her around to pull her on his lap. He buried his head into her neck and sighed. She wrapped her arms around him and he revelled in the warmth and comfort it brought.

"How did you know?" he asked.

She gave a small laugh. "I'm ill, Luke, not deaf."

"The phone calls?"

She shrugged. "And it was an expected task." She rested her hand on his cheek. "What happened?"

He looked into her eyes, saw the depths of her compassion and love and, for the moment, felt an easing inside of him. The ever present tune in his head lost some its frantic beat that held hardly any trace of diddly idly, slowly shifted into their tune. The tune of Beara, with all the sea, skies, valleys and mountains it spoke of.

He stroked her arm, felt the tune's hum vibrating through him to her. The connection. Their connection.

"I saw my mother."

Kayla leaned her head against his. "Your mother?"

"Yes. At the house." He told her the facts, an accounting that gave no details, gave no emotions, though he knew she could sense the feelings that swirled underneath.

"What will it mean for you?" she asked.

He paused, looking at her. "She knows that I'm looking for the spear and slingshot. So that means Balor knows, too. He'll be extra careful, maybe change the location of the spear and slingshot."

"You mean it might have more risk," she said.

He shrugged. "Most likely. But it's grand. I can handle it."

She gave him a warm smile. "I know, Luke." She stroked his cheek. "You haven't answered the question I asked. What will it mean for you after seeing your mother?"

The words were subtle and they settled in on him, sinking slowly, seeping in. It wasn't a question he could answer promptly, or use any "I'm grand, it'll be grand" or any of that laid back positivity that made everyone all right with the world and smiles all round. It required deep thought that nudged and poked at his "Truth", the one that was slopping all around inside of him now, ready to rise up into its true shape to be "True Truth".

"Feck me if I know," he said, resisting and hoping that a bit of the old cajoling and a laugh or two might keep it all down, because he certainly wasn't ready for it.

"Oh, Luke," she said, sadness in the words and in her smile.

"Ah, sure, it's all grand."

She shook her head. "If only." She kissed him. It was the kiss of blessing. A kiss that showed him the beauty of life and all strength that came with it.

"I know you have to go, Luke," she said quietly.

His breath hitched. "Go?"

"To America."

"No, no, I don't. I've told them they can do it without me."

"You have to go, Luke."

He shook his head, his lips pursed. "I don't want to leave you," he whispered.

"It'll be grand, Luke. We'll be grand."

He sighed. Oh, feck me, he thought.

LUKE STARED through the window of the SUV. Around him, parked cars extended outwards in rows, poles with lettered signs to guide those returning from their destinations to seek their cars. In the distance he could see the huddled figures of Saoirse, Smithy and Finn making their way towards the Shannon Airport Terminal. Finn carried his guitar and pulled a small suitcase, Saoirse mirrored him, only she carried a flute instead, while Smithy trailed behind with a duffel bag in hand and his fiddle case slung across his back. There it was. The four of them. They were the Four Musketeers, the Fantastic Four, without the muskets, or anything of the fantastic about them, their godlike powers skewed by their fractured "Big Truths". The state of them, now, heading west along the road. Westward ho, with all the emphasis on the ho and a ho,ho,ho.

PART II

THE WILD WEST

12

———

MAURA

I kept nodding, like a bird pecking at bugs in a tree, but there were no crow instincts in play, I just couldn't help it. It was the drums, the singers, vibrating through me, setting me alive in ways I didn't know were possible. I'd never seen anything like it on this side, in this time, it harkened back to the "time before time" that called up words like "ancient" and "mysterious".

The colour I saw all around me seemed to vibrate with just as much energy. People, hair and clothes befeathered and beribboned, swished and swayed, feeling the beat of the drums pounded on with padded sticks by a circle of men who sang chant-like in that key called "ancient". It wasn't anything like I'd imagined when Raven had asked me if I wanted to go to an Osage powwow the day before. I'd bartered with Lenny to give me the day off. It had been an opportunity that was high up on the "not to be missed" list and I was definitely not missing it. But once here, after a long and dusty ride in Raven's SUV, the experience moved off some trivial list into something much more. That "much more" was in my bones, shouting at me, shaking me, telling me over and over to pay attention.

We were at the Osage County fairgrounds, in a large building that squatted among other buildings on the grounds. It was all flat. As if these feet I was hearing had been pounding this area for so long the earth had flattened with the effort. But not so, according to Raven, for the Osage had only arrived here in the nineteenth century after being shoved from one place to another on a trail of death that had lasted decades. The history, according to Raven, was as complex as the intricate beadwork adorning heads, sashes, moccasins and shirts – and most of it was full of tears and blood.

Now, I saw a pride in their heritage, so evident in the bearing of the dancers who stepped solemnly in front of me, a mixture of men and women, some women carrying shawls, others carrying feathered fans, and some with long fringes on their dresses that swayed to their movements. The bells that jingled on ankles, legs and even dresses sounded like a soft and soothing summer rain, a calming juxtaposition against the thrum of the drum. The men's dress was no less colourful and was marked by feathers, bells, fringes and even ribbons. All together it was a celebration and marking of who they were, no apologies. Osage people. The Wahzhazhe. And Wahzhazhe people were short, tall, broad and slim. Some wore glasses, some were pale, some bald. It was "Osage now". Osage that had survived and was still surviving all the onslaught of disease, alcohol, drugs and poverty that had tried to negate them in so many different ways over the centuries. But here they were, celebrating in a manner that said "the best craic is had here" and I wasn't going anywhere.

My fingers itched for a bodhran, a way to salute and acknowledge who they were with the who I was. My *"fadó, fadó, fadó"* salute to their ceremonial "ho". But I didn't want to do the "where's the leprechaun" thing equivalent for them, so I stayed quiet and watched. First standing and then sitting. And then standing. It was when I stood again that I realised Raven was gone. That I hadn't really felt him by my side for a long time. He'd said little to me since we'd arrived. All his explanations had been given on the journey. It was as if the moment he arrived at the fairgrounds he became a shadow, slipping in beside me, only to disappear once I was in the hall.

I rose and headed to the exit, my curiosity aroused along with a tiny bit of unease. A few people nodded to me on the way out, but no one took any real notice of me. From the back of the hall I scanned the seated crowds and those who lined the walls, but I couldn't see him. The fairgrounds were extensive and for a moment I wondered if I'd find him. Until I heard a voice behind me.

"I'm right here."

I turned and saw Raven hovering at the door, his hat pulled low across his face.

"Are you wanted by the Osage or something?" I asked.

He paused, then laughed, tipping up his hat a fraction with his finger. "No, I've just been outside in the bright sun."

I raised my brow. "Still cooler inside?" The weather had taken a little break from the heat in the past few days but the fairgrounds could be hot if the sun was out and the sky cloudless.

"Still cooler inside. Though I thought you might want to take a break and have a little walk around."

I nodded. "Sure". I'd noticed a few areas had crafts and other artwork that attracted me. I wouldn't be averse to having an old mooch.

He took my hand and led me outside, where people milled around or ambled in different directions.

We were walking towards the next building when I saw two familiar figures flanked by two strangers.

"Look, Sherman and Skye," I said.

Raven nodded. "Yes. I need a word with them."

"Who's that with them?"

He looked over at me, but he had his sunglasses on now, so I couldn't read his expression. "Just some more friends."

"Your friends that could be my friends?"

He laughed then shrugged. "Maybe. That's up to you."

As they neared I could see that the two strangers were clearly Indian. Native American, I corrected myself. Or was I right the first time? The more time I spent in Raven's company, not to mention Sherman and Skye's, the more I realised that I didn't know what was right. Or when it was right. Or what term to say to any group that had been called myriad names and descriptions. I'd learned much about my ignorance of all things race, and in my desire not to leprechaun any people who passed my way, in a country that contained so many different kinds of people, I was becoming tongue tied. Raven was Tlingit, he'd told me one time, but at other times he'd called himself Tsimshian, then Haida and more recently, Kwakiutl. When I'd challenged him on it, he finally pronounced that he was all those things. Elusive. Elusive like Sherman, whose backwards forwards inside out styling was hip and cool in a way that was beyond anyone else being hip and cool. He was the Rainbow Warrior in Indian form, making statements and fighting his fight with a bold naiveté that would surely get him into serious trouble. But, as Raven would say, "it's who he is" and the tone would infer that there was no possible way to change it or safeguard him.

Sherman's origins were Lakota and Dakota, though that didn't pin him down in anything but the languages he could speak, since his litany of home places covered Pine Ridge, Rosebud, Wounded Knee and several others that rang bells that meant strong history and hard experiences.

Skye was the most elusive of those elusive three and even before she spoke or explained anything there was an echo of the ancient about her. "Haudenosaunee" was how Raven described her when I'd asked her origins. "But," he'd added, "she is everything and anything to all beyond them". That was as clear as the mud he'd said she represented. The metaphors and cryptic mysteriousness stretched even beyond what I could imagine. When I'd asked who the Haudensaunee were, he'd laughed and told me "Iroquois". Right, so. Everything was clear, now.

Sherman, Skye and the other two came up to us and I gave them a nod and Raven greeted them all.

"How's things?" I asked.

Sherman looked at Skye and the two men. "What things?"

I wanted to laugh, but I didn't. Sherman was literal in a manner that was so different to any other literal type of person that I'd met. "Ah, now. I was just asking how you are and if anything was going on with you."

"Fine, fine," said Sherman. He grinned. "All that's going on is talking to you, at the moment."

The two men snickered and I couldn't help but smile at them.

Skye glanced over at them. "These are two Osage friends of ours. Jimmy Redcorn and Charles Lone Bear."

I nodded to them. Behind them a shadow flickered, unattached. I frowned, deciding to ignore it. Beside me Raven muttered "iktomi" and chuckled.

I turned my attention to the men. They were maybe in their thirties with black hair worn in a single plait down their backs. Jimmy was slim and under a beaded and embroidered vest wore a button down shirt tidily tucked in a pair of jeans. Charles, on the other hand, wore a baseball cap, glasses and was heavier set, with a slight paunch under his dark T-shirt and jeans.

"This one here's a real riot," said Jimmy, indicating Sherman.

"I know," I said.

Charles grunted. "He's just got too much going on in his head."

Skye smiled benignly at Sherman. "There's much he has to tell us, if we listen."

Again with the cryptic. But I decided I liked it. Sure, didn't it add an extra spice and kept my mind busy with things other than what I was trying to avoid?

"He does, he does," I said. "I'm still working out exactly what he meant when I first met him. I'll have to record you, Sherman. So I won't forget."

"We don't remember enough that's important," said Charles.

"Isn't it the truth," said Raven. He nudged Jimmy. "And there's a lot of important things going on here, aren't there? Anything new?"

Jimmy looked at me and cocked his head. "Not especially new, except the vulture is back in his nest."

Raven gave a shout of laughter. "Oh, that's good. Vulture. Putting it in language I speak very well."

Now, I felt as though I was coming in the middle of a conversation in a foreign language where I only understood every third word. And that shadow flickered again, melding to Jimmy's own shadow.

"Any more evidence found?" asked Raven. "I thought I noticed more wind turbines built, too. That wasn't Osage approved was it?"

Charles shook his head. "No. There's someone new now who's going through the old records to see if there's more evidence to link the deaths to the vulture and his cronies. But the oil leases may be sidelined. There's much more at play now."

I looked at Charles, trying to figure out the implication of what he'd just said and the little flicker of unease that was beginning to grow inside me, an unease triggered by the word "oil".

A small group of middle aged Native American women came up to us. They touched Skye's arms tentatively, grabbing her attention.

"Skye," the tallest one said. "We're so grateful for your presence here and that you want to help." She nodded at Raven and Sherman warily, not meeting their eyes. "And both of you too."

Raven winked at them, his eyes twinkling. I narrowed my eyes. Was he flirting? Seeing him flirt with them hinted that his flirtation with me maybe hadn't been as personal as I'd thought. That his "I am so handsome" come thither looks and actions weren't to impress me specifically. It was just Raven being Raven.

I tried to mentally step back, to find a place where I could view a fine specimen of a man and have a fun time with that specimen while only appreciating his assets in the physical sense. Sure, what else would I want? Specimen appreciation was who I was.

Skye patted the hand of the tall woman. "Of course."

The tall woman gave her a shy smile. "Can we talk with you a moment?"

Skye glanced at the others. Jimmy and Charles shrugged, Sherman gave a puzzled look and Raven just smiled enigmatically.

"They probably want to give you a heaping plate of cookies," said Jimmy with a laugh.

Raven was the one who would be glad to receive cookies from them, and probably more.

Skye moved off with the women, and began to talk with them, a few of the women casting anxious glances towards Raven.

"How long has the vulture been back?" asked Raven, frowning.

"Not long, but he has some others with him this time," said Jimmy.

"Others?" asked Sherman, glancing at Raven, with an "I told you so" expression. He did a little hoppity dance with his feet, his arms flapping, his eyes dancing. "Other vultures?"

"What are you doing, man?" asked Jimmy, as I asked the very same question in my head.

"The vulture dance," said Sherman.

"Vulture dance?" I asked.

"Good," said Raven. "We need that dance."

I looked at Raven, his face turned solemn. Charles's own expression mirrored his and Jimmy's held a satisfied grin. "Yeah, you're the biz, man. Vulture dance."

"Sorry, now," I said. "Is that a special dance you do here?"

"It could be," said Raven.

"It should be," said Charles. He nodded, the solemnity still present in his face.

"Does the vulture dance signify anything?" I asked.

I was doing my damnedest to avoid leprechaun territory, but I was curious. I was trying to make sense of this exchange. The words were English, so they were, but the meaning was beyond me. Or was I fighting the idea, the feeling that was creeping in? That feeling the echoes of "ancient" and "mysterious" were attached to? The drum beat sounded inside me, memories of what I'd heard earlier. Ah, feck off, I thought. Cowgirl bliss, that's what I wanted.

"It's intentional," said Sherman.

"As in it has intention," said Skye, joining us. The women were walking away now, their manner ebullient, a little bounce to their steps. Had she kept one ear on our conversation while she talked with the women?

"What's the intention?" I asked, trying not to show my unease.

I could feel Raven beside me, possessing a raw energy that sent my own into overdrive and left me tense, but the tension was a complicated mix of need and want and...fear. It was a tension in which I found no comfort.

"To get rid of the vultures," said Sherman.

"A good intention," said Jimmy.

"A noble intention," said Skye.

"The best intention," Raven said, grinning. He shook his head. "You should teach us all this dance."

"Your dance will be good," said Sherman. "You're a bird. A very big bird who can feed on the waste."

Raven shrugged. "It's one kind of dance."

"It's a dance that's needed here now."

"But I do like your vulture dance. Any bird dance is a good dance."

"Are we really talking about dancing?" I asked.

"We're talking about vultures," said Raven. "And getting rid of them."

"These would be the oil vultures," I said hazarding a guess.

"Exactly," said Charles.

"We have similar vultures in Ireland. Some of them own energy companies. One of them I particularly loathe. He runs an energy company. Has a headquarters here in America too. You might have heard of his company. Balor Energies."

I was throwing out guesses everywhere, so many that there was more guessing than anything approaching a solid idea and it was all hazarding. But the stunned looks I received told me they hadn't fallen into a lake of nothingness. At least one of them had hit a target.

"Yeah," said Charles. "We've heard of Balor Energies."

"Son of a bitch vulture," said Jimmy.

"Did you say you knew him?" asked Raven.

Sherman laughed and resumed his hoppity flap dance to ward off vultures.

I POPPED out of the SUV, shutting the door with purpose and a small wave to Raven. He took off into the traffic quickly, heading who knew where. I still knew little about him. The drive back had been quiet only in that no words had been spoken, but the tension had been sky high, I felt that any word or unusual movement would have me transformed and flying before anyone could say boo. All the unease, the desire, the confusion that had filled me at the powwow still swirled around me and clouded my ability to sort through the questions and answers that battled underneath all the rest of my emotions. I needed to be alone so I could manage it all, find the rhythm and beat that was me. I needed my lads. My crows who would know me and how I ticked, how the tune that was me flowed strong and steady. They would get me on my beat, my hum, my rhythm, they would of course.

After I'd mentioned Balor Energies, the group that weren't my lads had quizzed me about this connection. It was a direction not unexpected and I'd told them who he was in Ireland, but nothing more. They'd nodded and accepted my answers as if that was that. But I knew, with a certainty that was bolstered by my inner tension and confusion, that this wasn't it. There was more. But any question about Balor Energies here in this area were met with shifting eyes, shrugs, and Raven changing the subject. They knew more. Balor was connected to this place, I was certain. And my certainty made me even more uneasy. About so many things. And the top of the list was why I was here. Why, in my strange desperate flight from my home in County Cork I ended up flying all this way and landing here, or near here on an Osage Reservation in the middle of Oklahoma.

I shook my head and turned from the street, searching my jeans pocket for my room key. Key in hand I walked to the door, my eye catching a poster in the glass window of the florists below my room. It was the shamrocks that I'd first noticed. They danced across the page along with musical notes and a little pot of gold. I read the words on the poster and barked a laugh.

Tuesday Night Music at O'Malley's
    This week:
    Irish Trad Group
    Daghda's Warriors

Well, feck, I thought. I didn't even have to guess at the names of the band members or the instruments they played. There was no confusion, and maybe even more things were clear.

13

LUKE

Luke sank back against the chair and sniffed. The hotel room was stuffy, stale air from poor ventilation making his nose itch and his jet lag worse. He'd only been here a day and already he hated the heat and the dry dusty feel of the city. No sign of the sea, let alone the feel of the salt water hanging in the air, or the gentle light at the end of the day. None of that. This was the opposite, the paradox, at least for him. He glanced out of the window to the streets below where people passed each other, some ambling, some in a hurry, but no sign of "how's things", "how are yous" or even a nod. No salute of any kind, let alone an exchange on the intricacies of the weather. Sure, what could you expect when there was no weather? Only hot, dry and dusty. At least that's what he'd observed since he'd arrived. Who knew what the others thought? He'd been avoiding them as much as he could since they'd checked into this motel the day before.

At least he had a room to himself, Smithy and Finn opting to be the ones to share, leaving Saoirse and Luke to have their own. It surprised him, really. He had assumed that Smithy and Saoirse would share a room and he would have to share with

Finn. Still he wasn't complaining. The room wasn't large, just enough to fit in the basics, plus a small table and the chair in which he now sat. But having his own room eased some of the pressure he felt from all of them, especially now, with his laptop in front of him, trying to figure out Balor's movements. He'd hoped he might gain some information from local news sites at the very least, but there was nothing mentioning Balor specifically. Now, he was trying once again to get information about Balor's headquarters and his house. He was perusing lists of old property sales going a few years back and then he planned to search building permits. It was a long shot.

After a while, he stood, stretching. His cup of coffee had long since gone cold. Time for another. But he would do this final search of the local building permits. He was just about to click on the search when a soft tap came at the door. He walked over and looked through the peep hole. Saoirse.

He opened the door, giving her a nod. "How's things?"

She shrugged. "Thought you might want to get something to eat."

"Eat? What's the time?"

She smirked at him. "Gone one."

"One o'clock?"

"The very same."

"Ah, sure, I've been so caught up in...you know."

"Yeah. That's why I thought you might want a break."

"I was just getting to that idea," he said with a laugh. "Come in a moment, I need to finish up this search and then I'm fit to go."

She followed him into the room and he hovered over his laptop and clicked on the search button. He looked up at her.

"Have you had a look around, so?"

"Around the city, you mean?"

He nodded.

She shrugged. "A little. It's different, I'll say that much. What I expected but then again, not."

"I'd say it's all I expected."

She poked his arm. "You haven't been outside this motel, so how would you know?"

"I've seen enough."

"You've seen TV, is what you mean."

"Ah, you can learn plenty from the TV."

"Plenty of shite."

He smiled. "Yeah, you're right. I've not seen much. I've been working on this and my jet lag."

"Food, Luke. That will help. And fresh air along with a bit of exercise."

"Is that so, Dr Saoirse?"

"It's a perfect prescription."

"I always obey doctor's orders."

"Good."

He looked down at his laptop, feeling a bit better after the banter. Sure, it was silly and stupid, but it lightened the spirit and wasn't that important? His eyes snagged on one of the results that had just popped up. A request for permission to build an extension. The name attached to it caught his attention. Eithne Howard. He had no idea where the Howard came from, but it was an easy bet that there weren't many Eithnes in this area. Only one, in fact. And he knew her.

He pointed to the result. "Look at this."

Saoirse peered over his shoulder and down at the laptop screen. "Feck. You think that's her?"

"I know it's her."

"And it's a request for an extension?"

"It is. And there are blueprints attached."

Saoirse squeezed Luke's shoulder. "You found him."

"I found them."

"Tell the others. We can all go out and celebrate."

His stomach tightened. Was it the word "celebrate" that made him feel uncomfortable, or telling Finn and Smithy about his discovery? He stifled the feeling.

"Let have a quick look at the blueprints, see what they look like. It could all be nothing."

She nodded. "Fine, so. But I think it's something. A big something."

He pulled up the attachments that were filed with the request and loaded the images. He glanced at them one by one. Elevations, blueprints with room dimensions and other helpful details, and even the exact location. It was just what they needed.

He looked up at Saoirse and nodded. "It's all there."

Saoirse held up a hand to him. Ironic high five. He slapped it upside down, the irony confused, small. She held a fist, he slapped it once on either side. She bumped his hip. He gave her a bow. Yeah they were too ironic for their own good. But there was no triumph there. Not for him. Not even ironic triumph.

"Food, so," said Saoirse. "Celebratory meal. Let's go get Smithy and Finn."

He nodded and closed down his laptop.

LUKE SHOVED the food around his plate. He was thankful for a plate and not some polystyrene box shite, or wrapping, that were some of the options in this city. Saoirse had chosen the place from some app she had on her phone. It was Italian and he supposed that it was good and more authentic than you might get in the likes of some towns in Ireland. But he wasn't a pasta man, if he was honest. It was clear the others were, though, so he let it be and toyed with the meat ball that topped the spaghetti before him.

"Do you want to try my pasta?" asked Saoirse. "Or maybe Smithy's calzone?"

Smithy looked up from his meal in surprise. "Hey!"

Luke shook his head. "No, I'm grand."

The restaurant was a good size with plenty of tables. On the walls hung faded pictures of Italian landmarks, draped in plastic grapes and other symbols of Italy. It wasn't that crowded, though, the lunchtime rush petering out, which allowed them to talk without having to lean over and shout at each other. A positive that added to the retro charm he knew he was supposed to feel, or was it ironic? Who knew? Maybe it was what it was. He knew Kayla would appreciate the description when he told her, so it had its charm in that way. He thought a moment what Mon would have made of it. How they would both have great craic critiquing the place. And the city too. Mon could be a real gas man if he was on form. Luke frowned. He'd doubted that he would encounter Mon on form any more. He pushed the thought aside. Best to leave it. Give it space. Give Mon space. Luke didn't feel there was anything to forgive, just because he'd had a relationship with Mon's ex, especially when he didn't even know that's who she was, but Mon clearly did. Leave it, Luke, he thought. Toss it into that bottomless lake. Best place for it. Sunk deeply.

"So, what were the blueprints like?" asked Finn.

"I'll show you when we get back," said Luke. "But there's potential there. The house is large, of course."

"Of course," said Smithy drily.

Smithy shook his head dolefully and ran a hand through his hair. Luke thought he looked a bit rough, a "not sleeping well" rough, but at least he was present. That was a marked improvement on just a physical body with the rest somewhere out in the ether.

"It's large and flashy," said Luke. "At least from I can tell from the blueprints. So security is bound to be sophisticated."

"Have you managed to tap into the security system?" asked Finn. He was looking pale, but his eyes were clear and at least he appeared well rested.

"No," said Luke.

"How about the headquarters?" asked Smithy.

"Not there either. But I might have a greater chance of hacking that system than his house, because there are more opportunities, more avenues to do it."

"It wouldn't be more sophisticated?" asked Saoirse.

"You would think so. From what I've looked at so far, it isn't." Luke frowned. "On a hunch I had a little look at his financial records and found a payment to a security company. It was dated two days ago."

"Was that for his company or for his house?" Finn asked.

The question was there, but Luke knew the answer was already in their minds.

"His house," said Saoirse flatly. "So does that mean the treasures are there?"

Luke shrugged. "A likely conclusion. But we don't know that for certain."

"So what next?" said Finn.

Luke sighed. He'd been thinking about this from the moment he'd discovered the payment record this morning. It was in part why he'd decided to go through all the tedious lists of planning permissions and house sales.

"I think we should still look into the headquarters first," he said.

"You do, why?" said Smithy, his tone sharp. "Isn't that just extra risk? Why not work on the house first, given that the best guess is that the spear and slingshot are there?"

Luke gave Smithy a sidelong glance. Yeah, Smithy was back, but so was his belligerence.

"Because, Smithy my man, I don't know the security of the house yet. And there's no harm in at least looking around the headquarters and their security, since the two systems are similar."

"We don't have to break in, Smithy," said Finn, his tone a study in reason. "First we can have a look around. In the daytime, like. Make some fake deliveries, hand in a fake CV, or other things. Each of us could target a floor, get an idea of it and report back."

Luke shrugged. "Fine, so. Why not. It's a start. We should at least walk by the building, see what we're dealing with."

"Can't we drive out to his home? Smithy asked. "See what that looks like as well?"

"We can of course," said Luke, trying to match Finn's reasoned tone.

"Grand, fine. Let's do that now," said Smithy.

"Maybe it would be better if we leave the house until tomorrow, when we're more rested," said Saoirse, eyeing Luke. "We can just walk by the headquarters, now, when we're done here."

"We have the gig tomorrow night. We should rehearse," said Smithy.

"Rehearse?" Luke said with a laugh. "Do we really need to?"

"We should at least agree on the tunes we're playing," Smithy said, his tone and expression stubborn.

Saoirse cast Smithy a glance. "It might not be a bad thing to rehearse, Luke. Make sure we agree on the sets and how we want to handle them."

"You'll do the talking, of course," said Smithy, looking at Luke, his eyes narrowed.

"Or maybe Finn?" said Saoirse.

Finn shook his head. "No, I'm grand, Luke can do it."

Luke raised his eyes toward the ceiling. "Finn, it's your thing. You do it."

"Ah, no, no. It's all yours."

"For feck's sake," said Saoirse. "I'll do it."

"Fine, so," said Luke. He sighed again. This was so much fun. He rose. "Come on, then. Let's go have a look at this man's place of work. It won't take long." He looked at Smithy. "And then we can discuss the gig."

14

SAOIRSE

Saoirse fought her way through the door, the others trailing behind her. The pub was crowded. Creatively named O'Malley's Irish Pub, it was more or less true to form of any wannabe Irish pub and was better than the real thing. The bar, the trim, and floor were all highly polished wood and brass, the taps lined up neatly with all the discs facing in the right direction and the optics behind hung with precision. Guinness held its place of prominence and was reverently and patiently poured and let stand on the towel mats provided. Behind the bar was a freckle faced red haired woman whose freckles were probably real, but not much else by the look of what was poured into her clothes. The other bartender was an older man who seemed more Italian than Irish, but what did Saoirse know?

People stood at the bar or against the walls, avoiding the mirrored pictures with pithy Irish sayings and the framed photos of famous Irish men like Michael Collins and Eamon de Valera. Other people crowded the tables scattered around the large room. At the back, where bodhrans and old fiddles hung from the ceiling, was the space for the musicians, the chairs and mike stands already laid out.

They were relying on the sound system provided by the pub, so Saoirse hoped that it was good enough to overcome the din in the place. Her session experience told her that people wouldn't always quieten down to listen to the music, if the lure of their own conversation and craic proved too compelling in comparison. Who knew what it would be like here, in America, where long held traditions about trad music didn't hold sway?

She looked down at the purple skirt and fuchsia top she was wearing, paired with her Doc Martens. Her hair was in its usual crown of braids on her head, out of the way while she played the flute. She wondered what this audience would make of her outfit. It was what she was used to, but was it who she was anymore? That was a thought to keep for another time. For tonight, she was Saoirse the flute player. Saoirse, member of a trad band. Bríd would have to be in the background.

Saoirse glanced at Smithy. He was wearing the usual men's dark clothes of most trad bands. Dark jeans and a black button down shirt, sleeves rolled up to show his muscular smith's forearms. Finn had conceded a little on the dark front and was wearing a pale grey T-shirt with his dark jeans. The spotlight caught his auburn curls, relaxed and long in this dry climate. They framed his face, giving him an angelic quality that she knew would make him grin if she told him.

Luke was in a black T-shirt, a faded logo on the front, his jeans slung low with a "surfer dude" slouch. Sure, he'd be the best at coping with all this tonight, she thought. He was so strong in all his musical talents and he'd had enough experience, as well. But Luke seemed lost in his own thoughts, and had been since they'd walked by the headquarters yesterday when they hadn't even been able to take a peek through a window, let alone gain entry there. The only view in was via a heavy door accessed by swipe card and an intercom system. They'd waited for at least an hour before someone had emerged and they'd taken advantage of the opportunity to have a quick look inside.

There hadn't been much to see, according to Luke who'd been at the front. A security desk and a row of lifts behind him. There was a security camera over the door and by the desk. Presumably there was a separate security room elsewhere that housed the monitors for the whole building's CCTV cameras. Luke had explained all this dispassionately, but Saoirse knew he was disappointed. He'd been quiet the rest of the evening, even when they'd sat down and talked about the set list for the gig. He'd agreed to all the suggestions without any comment, only a nod or a shrug. Saoirse had been anxious to include tunes she knew Smithy had down, so there was no risk of him failing. She was surprised at Finn's eagerness to support her suggestions, his own glances at Smithy telling her that she wasn't the only one who understood Smithy's limitations. Well, good. That was grand. He needed to have someone on his side. Someone like Finn. He might make better headway with the stubborn git.

They unpacked their instruments after the manager had checked in with them and explained the set up. There was nothing unusual. They'd be more or less left to manage themselves, but drinks were on the house. Finn's eyes lit up at that announcement and Smithy managed a smile. Luke was the only one who seemed unmoved.

"Well it's good to hear that some things are the same here," said Finn.

Saoirse grinned at him, glad to see his mood had shifted to a more positive one. Hopefully, Smithy would follow. Luke, she knew, if the past was anything to go by, would get his joy from the music and soon loosen up. She was determined to enjoy herself, too. Get the flow, the flying that music gave her.

Her flute assembled and ready to go, she blew through it a few times just to be certain it hadn't suffered from the change in climate. Hearing a few notes, she twisted the two pieces a fraction to sharpen the sound. The few little ditties she'd dared to play in her room had told her that this would be a constant need while the wood of the flute adjusted. She could only imagine what the others' instruments were going through and suddenly understood why Luke was reluctant to bring his uilleann pipes tonight.

She glanced over and watched him tune his bouzouki. His hair was still short enough, but more settled looking after the strange porcupine look he'd been sporting when she'd first saw him on the Beara. There was a bit of the "surfer dude" there, but mostly he was all brooding musician. She scanned the crowd and saw that some were beginning to look this way. And some of those curious eyes belonged to women looking at Luke, with more than polite interest in their expressions. Luke was oblivious. Intent on his tuning. This was a new Luke. The observation made her giggle and Luke looked up and gave her a puzzled frown.

"All right?"

She nodded. "Just thinking at the irony of all of this. Never imagined I'd be playing a gig in America, let alone with you, Smithy and Finn."

"Ah, yeah. A big haha." He gave her a smile to show his comment was meant as fun.

"So, you going to dazzle them with your 'I can switch instruments mid strum?'"

He snorted. "I will be my usual brilliant self."

"Give him a bodhran," said Finn. "See what he does with that."

"I can think of plenty of uses for the tipper stick," said Smithy.

Saoirse laughed and nudged Smithy. "Careful, it might be a place you wouldn't enjoy."

"Oh, I can handle a bodhran," said Luke. "Especially the tipper stick. I can work marvels with the tipper stick."

Saoirse laughed again, glad that there was some good energy there now. She could work with that. She checked that everyone had their instruments tuned at a reasonable level. There would always be the little tweaks as they went along. She stepped up to the main microphone and gave a short introduction before they zipped off into a lively reel set. The set was packed with well known favourites like *The Kesh.* She tripped and skipped along with the tune, feeling herself relax and the music take her. She could hear the ease in Luke's playing, the tune just running through his fingers as though they conjured the notes. Finn's guitar gave the driving beat, strong yet lively and all grin. A grin that was wide and full of fun and she felt the joy of it lift her own playing and reached further for it. And underneath it all was Smithy, his fiddle sound tentative at first, but then came an idle didle, fiddly slide and a decoration, a sly double stop. She wanted to whoop with the thrill of it all, the way they meshed at that moment, the pure, pure drop of what was going on with them all. She let it swell inside her, reached for the threads that were woven together in this perfect set of tunes. The reels that sent her reeling. She hardly dared glance at any of them, no it was better to just speak through the music. They would feel it just like she did.

They ended on a whoop from Finn, the joy plastered on his face, his guitar still vibrating with the force of his playing. Saoirse laughed, Smithy looked stunned and Luke smirked and raised his brows at Saoirse. He was holding his mandolin, having switched mid stride. Ah yes, you are a feckin' brilliant musician, she thought. She shook her head and laughed again. Laughing, it was good and she would do it the rest of the night.

The audience applauded loudly and Saoirse was pleased to see that most people were facing towards her and the group, their attention fully given and "good craic to be had here" looks on their faces.

Saoirse waited for the applause to die down before she introduced the group, just briefly mentioning their names and where in Ireland they hailed from. She put Luke in Dublin, but he gave her a dark look, so she amended it to the Beara Peninsula and he nodded. He received loud applause and she chuckled, wondering if she detected a feminine touch to that applause. She put herself, Smithy and Finn from Cork and was surprised when a loud "go rebels" was shouted. The audience laughed and Saoirse exchanged a grin with Finn and Smithy.

She leaned down at spoke into the mike. "Ah now, you can't go anywhere without running into someone from Cork."

There was more laughter and clapping too. A "Mayo" and "Meath" was tossed out. It was all good. "Oh, well they always tag along, so," she said, throwing out the first thing that came to her mind.

More laughter and claps and then she was explaining the next set, a group of tunes that were a mixture of familiar jigs, slides and polkas with their own little twist. She explained it as a twist, but in truth it was a fragment Finn had shared with herself and Smithy and then Luke. An Otherworld fragment. She hoped Smithy would manage it well enough, because it had an off tune beat that she thought she, too, might even make a haimes of. It was a mad tune, a fragment that went "ta da" on its own, announcing itself as a kooky sly thing that popped out and waved at you. It was a twist and double stop rolled into a decoration that Finn somehow managed on his guitar that Smithy could only shake his head at and Luke thought was feck off awesome.

But they would try it. Now, early enough in the night when

the hum was on them but they weren't feeling tired at all. Early, so that Smithy's concentration and memory would be razor sharp, as would anything else that was affecting who he was and his ability to perform. At least she hoped so. She pushed this piece up the list from its original place near the middle because she felt the "now is the time" moment.

She didn't look at the lads as she announced the set, just grinned at the audience and took up her flute. Then she glanced at the others, heard a bit of the old tweak and twist of the pegs as the lads tuned their strings, Luke now back on the bouzouki, for the first part at least. She just gave a mental headshake at the notion he might switch back to mandolin again. Beside her, Finn began tapping his foot, setting the beat for the countdown. Luke nodded his head along to it and then began his finger play riff, striking up the rhythm, the support and framework for the melody that she and Smithy would play. She glanced at Smithy. He gave her a slight nod and the two of them took off into the tune, his bow strokes confident and sure. She smiled at him and he returned it. It was a smile that reached his eyes and one she felt sink deep into her. She let herself hope, let herself ride the smile and the tune that danced to it. It was a jig that jigged all giggly and flirty, a tune you could jump for joy with and so she was. Her notes blended with his in a mosh pit kind of jam that let her be concert high.

They played on and the key shifted along with the tune and they all went with it, the jig turned polka and on they sailed, mosh pit abandoned for the whirling dervish feel of the mad fun that shook everything loose, full of ahhs and whoops.

She was filled with these notes, these rhythms and beats. They were all she was at this time and when that twisty cheeky fragment came, it was all part of the craic. It surprised her how it jumped up with the grace and skill of an expert as it found its place, slotted in like it belonged, only better. It was the frame, the structure, the beat and the tune all at once. It was the essence. Luke filled it in, mandolin in hand (how had he done that?) shaking out the magic of it, giving it depth, while Smithy put down his own layer on top of it, challenging Saoirse to do the same. She took its hand, her notes and his, and they shimmied it, rolls and decorations bouncing off one another, like partners holding both hands and spinning.

The set lasted longer than any she'd ever played before. It was a set that was beyond an extended LP, a marathon that held her captive. It was a ride she didn't want to get off. But end it did. Luke found the wind down notes, Finn followed along and the tune eased its way to finish, a few notes lingering, reluctant to let go.

When the lingering sounds of their instruments had ended, silenced greeted them. Saoirse opened her eyes, slowly coming to her surroundings. Applause burst out, loud and insistent. It took her breath away, or was that what had just happened? She stole a look at Smithy, like she used to do after a tune at a session. Always Smithy. He looked a little stunned, but he smiled, a true, loving smile that brought tears to her eyes. "Magic" she mouthed to him.

Finn nudged her and leaned over. "Feck me, that was brilliant."

She nodded in agreement and looked over at Luke. His eyes were alight, an appreciative smile on his face. "Brilliant."

"Not just you," she said, her tone teasing.

He snorted. "No."

The applause died down eventually and Saoirse thanked the audience and announced the next set on the list. They began the tune, all of them relaxed and on form. The set went off well, Luke adding in a few flourishes, picking out the tune. Smithy even added his own little twist at the end of the set that had

Luke raising an appreciative brow and Saoirse grinning. It was fun. It was great craic.

They wound up the first part of their performance after two more sets, both of which went off flying before they barely struck the tune. It was all so good.

Just before the first part ended, Luke leaned over to Saoirse and told her to sing a song.

She frowned. "What song?"

She hadn't planned on singing anything until the second part, when she had more confidence. She didn't have that many songs to sing that she would feel at ease singing here.

He shrugged. "Any one."

She looked at Smithy. He mouthed, "go on, so. You're brilliant."

She reddened. And so she did. She sang. She told the lads the song, and Smithy started her off, his subtle fiddle notes laying down her foundation, setting a tempo that would melt into hers once she started. She sang *An Bínsín Luachra*. She hadn't planned on this one, but the words came to her without thinking and she could just exist inside them. It was done.

It was nerve racking, but she sang and Smithy was there with her the whole way, giving her a hand with his notes, played softly under her voice, a wooing that gave her an understanding of him, as much as the words she sang. When she'd finished, she held the notes inside her, wanting to savour and cherish them for the pure love that it was.

The group rose and bowed briefly, their instruments down, and she announced the break. She stood there a moment, wondering what she would do, before she collected herself, glanced at Smithy and was surprised to see a woman talking to him. She was Native American, doe eyed and slim with long silky black hair that hung down her back, her simple short sleeved top and skirt a golden yellow that accentuated her beauty. Saoirse caught her breath at the sight of her, though it was perhaps that she was resting her hand on Smithy's arm and he was listening to her attentively. Saoirse couldn't hear what she was saying, but her meaning seemed to be addressed in that hand that now clasped Smithy's arm.

15

SAOIRSE

Saoirse took a deep drink from the pint glass. It was Guinness, not her choice at the moment when the heat from the crowded room and playing music had her in a sweat. She wiped her hand across her brow and looked around the large room. Some people had made their way outside, but Saoirse didn't think she would fare any better there. Instead, she leaned back against the bar and tried to avoid the corner where Smithy was still talking to the woman. Finn had joined them a while after she'd left and that gave her some bit of reassurance. Whether Finn was still there was something she didn't want to know. Luke was outside, phoning Kayla, a thought that caused her to grin when she saw the disappointed women scanning the room for signs of him.

"You've a very striking voice," said a man coming up next to her.

She turned to him. He was striking in himself, she thought, his shaggy dark hair, dark eyes and copper skin. He tipped back his cowboy hat and she saw the face. It was so distinctive. Mygod, she thought. Sure, there he is, straight out of a film.

She blinked. "Thanks," she said. "Though it's not really professional."

"Oh, I think so," said the man, his eyes twinkling. "And I've heard many voices over the years."

"You hear voices?" she asked, her tone lightly teasing.

"Only voices with something to say."

She laughed. "Ah, sure, they're the only ones to listen to."

"You've something to say," he said.

It was a statement. A "I'm just making an observation" kind of statement. No question that it was a fact. It just was.

"Oh, thanks."

He shrugged. "There's nothing to say thanks to."

"Will you tell me your name? I'd like to know who it is that thinks I have things to say."

He held out his hand. "Raven."

"Raven? Like the bird?"

"There are other kinds?"

She laughed. "Are there?"

"There's only one."

Saoirse liked the humour in him. The almost cackle caw like his namesake that was his laugh, his air. "I have a friend who would like you," she said. "Pity she isn't here."

"It is a pity," said Raven. "I'm sure I would like your friend. She likes birds, I take it."

"Oh, she does," said Saoirse.

"And your friend, she's Irish I take it?"

"Oh she is, all right. A rare bird."

"And why isn't your rare bird here with you? Doesn't she play music?"

"She does. She has a beat all her own."

"But her beat didn't bring her here."

Saoirse shrugged. "You could say that."

"But you're here."

"Music takes me many places."

He nodded. "And only music?"

"Music has a lot of power."

Raven laughed. "Oh, I wouldn't dispute that. But there are other kinds of power."

Saoirse gave him careful look. Whatever were they talking about? Suddenly she wasn't certain. Suddenly things felt "more". More than this moment having a banter in between playing. She glanced over where Smithy had been. He was staring at her, the woman gone, his face cryptic. She couldn't see Finn.

"While you're here you should check out this bar a few blocks over from here. Murphy's. It's a place I think you'll find captures the essence of Bartlesville."

She laughed. "In what way?"

"Oh, there are a lot of currents and undercurrents in this city. Call it a crossroads of history of those undercurrents and currents."

"What currents?"

He winked at her. "Ah, but wouldn't it be more interesting to go there and see if you can figure it out? And if you don't I'll be there to help. Bring your friends, too."

"Sounds tempting. I'll ask them."

"Why don't we meet there, say day after tomorrow?"

She had no clear idea about their plans for then. "Right, fine. Do you want to give me your mobile number in case we can't make it?"

"No need. If you're there you're there. Any time after eight is cool."

She nodded, still uncertain what the conversation had really been about. Or what he was about.

She felt a hand on her arm. She turned and saw Smithy, a quizzical expression on his face.

"Time for the next set," he said. He glanced at Raven.

She nodded. "Smithy, meet Raven. He was just talking about a bar he thought we'd like. A place he called a crossroads of history and currents."

Smithy raised his brow. "Really?" It was a polite inquiry, one that held all the suspicion Saoirse had felt a moment ago, but now seemed ridiculous."

"Ah, no, Smithy, it's grand. It's a reflection of Bartlesville. Full of characters I bet. We should go."

"You should," said Raven, his voice all lazy and full of laid back charm. He grinned at Smithy. "There's no harm in it, man, just a lot of interest."

"Interest. Yeah. I can see that," said Smithy. "There was mention of interest just now when I was talking to this woman, Skye. She's Mohawk, she said. Like you."

Raven placed a hand on his heart. "Not Mohawk, but I'm flattered. I'd more likely be found in the Alaskan region."

Smithy raised his brows in surprise. "Alaska?"

"Yep," said Raven.

"You're some distance from home, then."

Raven shrugged. "It is what it is."

Smithy laughed. "It is what it is." He looked down at Saoirse, his eyes holding a touch of humour. "Come on, so. The others are waiting."

Saoirse went then with a heart lighter than it'd had been for a while, trailing Smithy, noting his shoulders had lost their droop, that his step might have just held a trace of a bounce.

She held that feeling, that warmth and wrapped herself up in it as she took up her flute and played the first set. It was after that, when it came time to announce the next set, that her world took a spin and Smithy spoke before she could and announced that the next piece would be a song that he would sing called *Eleanor na Rún*. Eleanor my darling.

She'd only ever heard him sing a little and it was mostly accompanying a piece that they were listening to on her phone or his, or on one occasion when they were all singing in the car, a diddle diddle biteen song that was now taught in national school. But now, he sang out deep and resonant, his rich baritone nearly bass with the key he used. The song, filled with a man's love for a woman, a love that would last the ages, touched her deeply. It spoke of things that hadn't been spoken, it was a love song that told her so much and some of it was maybe. It was hope. It was his hope and hers. She would keep that hope, then, see where it went, but keep it quiet all the same. That was the best kind of hope, one that wouldn't be noticed, but could be carefully nurtured, in secret.

16

MAURA

I wiped down the surface of the bartop. It was a "something to do" wipe, made with little effort and not much effect. It kept me from looking at the door, wondering for the tenth time where Raven was. I was nearly cross-eyed with the effort to resist it, myself and I arguing like it was a contest with no runners up, "myself" putting forward all the points that had words like "hot body" "good company" and "great craic". "Hot body" kept topping the list and was pointed to as though it weren't obvious, but "I" kept swiping that little item aside in favour of "feck off out of it you never want to have anyone have a hold on you". I couldn't say who was winning this contest, only that I was annoyed with it all.

I hadn't seen Raven since the powwow a few days ago. I was still unnerved by the conversation I'd witnessed there and full of curiosity, mixed with some apprehension, over Raven's part in it all. Not to mention the "feck me" who is this man, that myself found so incredibly hot and attractive. That I couldn't find a way to channel that attraction, that I was nearly beside myself with girlish flusters and strange feelings that were all wrapped up in this man, raised my anxiety and apprehension to nerve racking levels.

There'd been no sign of Skye or Sherman either. They seemed an inseparable threesome some days, another aspect that had me wondering.

A newcomer took my attention, asking for a refill. I'd already gone through the "where are you from are you Irish" conversation with him, something that was losing its humour, which meant I was less inclined to give them answers to amuse myself. The "are you Australian" question I'd had the day before had been a change and I managed to find some humour in trying on an Australian accent that had Lenny choking on his water.

The door opened and I refused my cross-eyed self to look and kept talking to the refill man, suddenly interested in where he was from. He gave an answer but I no more could tell anyone what he'd said than explain the complexities of calculus, because I was so aware of the figure approaching.

I handed the man his change and turned to Raven.

"How's things?" I asked.

My tone was casual. I was "cowgirl casual". My new boots told that story, right down to the feckin' blisters on my little toes. My T-shirt, said it all too, worn ironically with all of Lenny's assets listed under his Murphy's logo. Raven's grin was casual as was his wink, once he'd reviewed every asset on my chest.

"Good," he said. "All good."

I nodded. "Can I get you anything?" Casual, casual.

"I'll have a beer and maybe some company, if you have the time."

I glanced at Lenny who was chatting to someone down at the end of the bar. It was a slow night. I looked back at Raven. His brows were raised, amusement clear in his eyes. I laughed. "Fine. There's time."

I busied myself getting his beer, conscious that he was

watching me. After indicating the opposite end of the bar from Lenny's position, I set down his beer and a glass beside it. He ambled down there, a half smile on his face. I settled on a stool behind the bar, up against the wall.

"So, stranger, were you still recovering from the powwow?" I asked. "Was it too much pow and wow?"

"Pow and wow?" he said, giving a wry smile. "No, no you don't."

I gave him an innocent look. "I don't? I have plenty 'I don'ts', but this one might be new."

"And how many 'do's' are there?"

I cocked my head. "I don't do 'I do'." I let that rest a moment. "There's plenty of 'will' though."

Raven laughed and took a sip of his beer, ignoring the glass. "I have a 'will I' myself."

"Oh, and what's that?"

"Will I ever figure you out?"

Now, that was my language. "No, never. It's my charm."

"Charm? Is that what you call it?"

"What would you call it?"

"I call it an enigma."

He took a deep drink of his beer, set the bottle on the bar and tapped one of the rings on my fingers. It was a large silver one, shaped like a talon and it wrapped around my index finger with the tip upwards, ready to hook someone. I'd had Smithy design it for me to my specifications and I'd worn it the day I'd taken flight, wanting its reassurance and statement of who I was.

"Why are you here?" he said softly.

I looked into his dark eyes, trying not to fall into their questions, the promise of things I didn't even understand. All I wanted was to objectify and have fun. Enjoy the beauty of his smooth skin and all that went with it. But his eyes made me think of things that mattered. The tap on my ring, the talon that would claw through difficulties. It was my world. But I wanted "cowgirl happy". I had the boots and I deserved it. Forget the pow or the wow, the deep beat of the earth reaching up into me. I wasn't that. It wasn't me. The talon was to get me out of there. To here. To my place of fun, and little bits of tease and scratch, a little irritation and fun.

"I'm here to work," I said, my tone deliberately light. I ran my finger along his arm. "And play."

He shook his head, emitting a soft chuckle. "What brought you to Bartlesville, really?"

I looked away from him and his too deep eyes. Eyes that seemed to see beyond my black clothes that shouted their "stay away" and "danger" message to most people who tried to get too near. No I wouldn't look at them. I settled for his chin, well jaw, that square "hoo boy" jaw. Maybe a finger along that would do me some good. My finger lifted to follow the thought, but Raven caught it and held it a moment, and there were the eyes again, pulling my own towards his.

"Who are you?" I asked, my voice a whisper.

"Raven," he said, in an even tone.

"Raven? Just Raven?"

"The Raven," he said, the eyes twinkling now.

"And what does Raven do?"

"Raven is a creator."

"A creator? Like an artist?"

"A trickster artist."

"Grand, so. Does that mean Raven's art form is tricks?"

"Artful tricks."

This was wordplay, the kind that told you so much but so very little. It was frustrating and clever and it stirred things inside me that I only found confusing.

"Where does Raven exhibit? A gallery?" I found myself continuing to refer to himself in the third person, just like he was. He spoke as if it was him and not him, and it was his way of showing and telling me so much I didn't understand.

"Oh, it's free form. Kind of pops up in unexpected places."

"And does Raven suffer for his art or does someone else?"

"It varies."

"Is Raven working on a trick now?" I asked, thinking this whole conversation seemed one big private trick and I had no clue what the goal or result would be.

"Raven always has something underway, something going on. It's who he is."

I laughed. "It's who you are."

He shrugged, grinned and added a wink in with it.

"Am I able to be in on this trick?" I asked.

His expression suddenly became serious. "I think you might be. That's what I'm trying to discover."

I blinked at him. "Grand, so," I said eventually. I plastered a smile on my face, determined to be that "cowgirl happy". "I'm here to make a new start. Find a new place to be me. So it would be fab to be part of your trick. Tell me, what is it?"

He gave her a slow speculative smile. He tapped my ring again. "I think it's best to let time tell you what the trick is. And we'll see how we weave together."

My "cowgirl happy" self captured his finger this time. I took it and placed it in my mouth and gave little suck. "I think we would weave together well."

Raven withdrew his finger from my mouth and gave my hand a squeeze. "Patience darlin' patience," he said in a real cowboy drawl. I grinned. Hoo boy.

17

LUKE

L uke stood outside the motel staring at the phone, willing the time to be earlier. He knew it was late to be phoning Kayla, but he wanted to hear her voice. It was a sign that all was well enough with her, with Bláthín, Nana, with the world, and if he were to be honest, with himself. Himself was having the most problems lately, he was barely finding the self that was Lugh, the warrior, king's champion and all things heroic. There was no hero here now, just a mess of a washed out surfer and a somewhat competent musician. Though last night had something more than competent. It had been a rare unicorn of a music evening, when they were all tuned to each other and that inner world well of music magic. A magic that he knew they'd conjured from the parts of themselves that were really not of this world. He'd savoured it, let the tunes inhabit him long after they'd left the pub and he was lying in bed, thinking of Kayla.

But now, after sleep had finally seeped in with the dawn, he was thinking only of Kayla. Kayla and tonight's plans. Was he cut out for this, now? Any of it? He ran a hand through his hair and tugged at it, remembering its length was anything but cooperative for such a gesture. Yeah, those plaits that had bound him to more than a woman, but to a bitterness and revenge he wanted no part of. Except it was his bitterness that had him caught in the first place. And his bitterness and anger that was dragging him through this mire of plotting to retrieve two items that were to lead him on to the next step to bring him up against his grandfather. Only for Kayla and her daughter and mother would he do it. Those three women, the land, the Beara, all of it. Only for them. They called to him, always, now. Even in the middle of this dusty and hot city.

His mobile rang, right there in his hand, startling him out of his reverie. Kayla's name flashed up on the screen. He smiled and answered it.

"How are you?" he asked.

"Fine, so," she said.

Though he'd only talked to her early this morning, he still felt relieved to hear the words and the calm in her voice. "And Nana and Bláthín?"

"The same." He heard the smile in her voice. "How are you?"

It wasn't the words so much as the manner in which she said it that told him she understood what he needed.

"Fine for hearing your voice," he said.

"What are your plans, now, Luke?"

He bit his lip. He hadn't told her that he was going to try and get into the headquarters today. That he hoped to even find a way up to Balor's offices. It was a wing and a prayer plan – more wing than prayer – that he'd suggested casually and told the others required no help from them.

"Nothing special," he told her.

She laughed. "Ah, no you don't."

He smiled. "No, I don't."

"You'll be fine," she said. "You're bound, now, woven in, so that I'm with you Luke. I'm with you."

His breath caught at the words. That's what he felt with her. Woven in. "Woven in," he said. "No thread unloose."

"Not one," she said. "Now, take care, but know that you have our strength and we have yours."

He nodded, though he knew she couldn't see it, but he understood that she could feel it. Like she felt everything about him, now.

HE STOOD OUTSIDE THE BUILDING, assessing it and his "wing and a prayer" plan. He took a deep breath and was just about to go inside when he felt a hand on his shoulder. He turned to find Smithy beside him.

"I don't deny you can charm the state secrets out of a spy, but I can pick locks and gain access to a secure room better than any professional."

Luke looked at him, too surprised at first to say anything.

"You distract, I'll go in," Smithy said.

Luke started to shake his head, but Smithy held up his hand. "Let me do something," he said. "Be useful in some way, at least."

The unspoken words about the way in which he wasn't useful hung between them. Luke forced himself to ease the tension from his face. "Fine, so. Be useful."

Luke gave a small smile and pushed his way through the entrance, heading towards the reception desk, Smithy in tow. A young woman sat there, her hair short, pixie like, studs in her ear and a stud in her nose. Perfect. Luke sauntered up to her and gave her a lazy smile.

"How's things?" He looked at the name tag on her shoulder. "Darla."

She bit her lip, her eyes lighting. "Hi," she said. "Did you want something?"

"Oh, there's so much I want," he said, leaning on the desk. He could hear Smithy give a soft snort behind him.

She giggled and tapped a blue fingernail against her lip. "Hmm. Maybe I can help?"

"I was wondering if my uncle is around."

She raised her barely there brows. "Your uncle?"

"My uncle, Padraig Balor?"

She flushed. "He's your uncle? Of course he is. I can see the resemblance and you've got that sexy accent, too."

Luke forced himself to flash her a smile, the one that had the dimples, his sure winner one, even though his first urge was to glare at her and deny all resemblance to Balor. He tapped his finger slowly on the counter, giving himself a beat, a rhythm to help him make this work. Surfer dude beat. It followed the waves, enjoyed what was thrown at him. He could do that.

"You think my accent's sexy, do you?"

She ran the nail along her lip and sucked it. "Oh, I think all of you is sexy. Every last bit." She looked behind him. "And your friend isn't bad either."

"And you're not saying that because Mr Balor is my uncle?"

She shook her head slowly. "No, that's all your own."

He winked at her. "Don't worry, I won't tell him you think he isn't sexy."

She laughed. "I didn't say that."

"No," he said slowly. "But I liked what you did say."

"Mmm. I'm happy to oblige."

"That's sounds good. Maybe after I see my uncle."

"That sounds great. You can bring your friend too." Then she gave him a guilty look. "Oh, wait. I meant to say. Your uncle's not here. He's out of town."

Luke assembled a disappointed expression but the grin

inside broke into a whoop. "Oh, I thought he said he would be here. I'm doing a gig nearby and thought I would stop in and arrange a catch up."

"Oh, that's a shame," she said. "Wait. You're playing a gig? A gig like in music?"

He nodded. "Yeah. I'm in an Irish trad band." He pointed to Smithy. "He is too."

"Oooh. Wow. Musicians. I love musicians."

He nodded, tapping out the surfer dude beat on the counter again. "Glad to hear it." He flashed the grin again, trying to lean into that beat, that mode.

"Tell you what," said Darla. "Let me just call up to Mr Balor's PA and find out if she knows when he's back. Maybe she can schedule a meeting for you."

He leaned over, looking deep into her eyes. "That sounds fab, Darla. Will we just go on up and talk to her, make my own arrangement to see him?"

She bit her lip. "Why not? But make sure you check in with me when you go."

He flashed her a big smile. "Count on it Darla."

18

SMITHY

Smithy tried to calm his nerves as he followed Luke out of the lift. He wiped his clammy hands on his jeans. He was useful. That was him, all right. And he would be now. Let Luke do the charm and he would do the trick.

He could see the glass door and partition at the end of the hall, the company logo and Balor's title inscribed on the door. They made their way down the hall, Smithy noting the doors on either side. Offices? Meeting rooms? Toilets? All were locked, so who knew. He'd never had any desire to be a part of this kind of world, so his ignorance showed with a big "I haven't a clue".

They opened the outer door of Balor's office and a lounge area greeted them, with the PA's desk just around the corner, the edge of it in sight. Beyond that lay another glass door which presumably was Balor's private office. Smithy motioned to Luke that he would linger in the lounge area, out of sight of the PA, while Luke did his "Jack the lad".

Luke sauntered on ahead, his demeanour changing, the lazy, slouchy, persona appearing and Smithy nearly laughed with it all – could almost see the board shorts, the sun bleached shaggy hair, the leather bracelet filled wrists that were in truth gone except for one. He was once again the person in that photo he'd taken from Luke's house of him and Mon, two dudes catching waves.

That dude approached the PA, asked her name and began the chat. The banter. She was older than the receptionist downstairs. Smithy didn't have to see the woman to conclude that. He could hear it in her voice, her manner and her words. Professional, but with a touch of the friendly that increased once Luke told her he was Balor's nephew. Nephew. Ha. Smithy supposed he would put what distance he could from Balor and still have some impact. And nephew Luke certainly was getting somewhere. Nephew Luke was having her check his schedule. He was asking her if he could stay here and do a little work handling fan mail, while he waited for his fellow "band members" to finish sorting the car rental for their next gig. It was a slick pitch and Smithy found space to admire this lad, your man. He was such a lad, all get and go go. Though a sense of wariness still lingered in Smithy, because charm was charm and could be used on anyone, in any situation, with such a one.

The PA (now Nancy to Luke), woven into the fabric of Luke's story, a story that became more musician than surfer, the wave taking him to that story, where a band member was writing lyrics and she became the centre of songs after a "did you know" that took him through several old ballads that had fair haired and blue-eyed Nancy at their centre. That same Nancy offered him a cup of coffee, a muffin and the use of Balor's office and your man with the proper bashful refusal, eventually agreed. Smithy finally was able to put Nancy's name to her face when she walked through the lounge and out the door and found that blond meant, dirty blond and blue eyes were hard to see behind the glasses, but a neat trim figure in a suit gave the poet some credence. It was a brief glimpse only, because he was tucked in an alcove and once she'd disappeared through the door he was at the entrance to Balor's private office. Luke was already inside, scanning the room.

"You were determined to have no use of me," said Smithy in a low, joking voice.

"Ah, you know. Your one was easy enough."

"You just got lucky with her."

"Luck has nothing to do with it. Still, with two of us, we can make fast work of it."

Smithy shrugged and made his way to the window, besides which a locked press stood. It was modern in design with pale blond wood that matched the press on the other side of the window. Beside this press was a low long drinks table which contained bottles of Jameson's and other specialty brand whiskeys from Ireland, as well as a few other types of spirits, and some Waterford crystal glasses. Smithy focused on the locked press and drew out his tools, working quickly. The press opened. There was nothing of interest at first glance. Some local artefacts that looked like arrow heads, a clay pot, some silver jewellery. Did Balor have an interest in Native American culture?

He closed the press and relocked it when he could find nothing else of interest. Luke was going through the rest of the room, which mainly comprised plush chairs, a sofa, bookcase and a desk. The desk, though modern, had a few drawers and that's where Luke focused his attention. Smithy turned to the other press and made quick work of the lock. Once opened he reached for the files that were piled there, wondering if any of them would shed a clue on the location of the spear and sling-shot. He flicked through them quickly, noticing once again that Native Americans were the subject. He saw "Osage" on one of the labels and "oil licences", "wind turbines" on the other two. Looking inside, he found photocopies of wills, deeds, and photos of people and places. It looked strange and wrong and something in Smithy made him lay these files down and quickly take photos of the first few pages of each with his phone. He glanced at Luke. He was working on the computer, quickly reviewing its contents.

"Anything?" Smithy asked as he shoved the files back in the press.

Luke shook his head. "Not really. Except I have a better idea of the security system at his house. He has the contract and specs on here." With a shake of his head, he tapped on the keyboard a bit longer, slammed down the lid and nodded to Smithy. "If there's nothing more, you should go before she gets back."

Smithy nodded, gave the room one last glance before he slipped out and made his way through the outer door and headed towards the stairwell, out of sight from Nancy when she returned. He sat on the steps, waiting for Luke, took out his phone, pulled up the photos and began to study them. There were private emails, old ones and then some notations on the side. He would bet they were Balor's notations. He studied the documents more closely. It took him a little while to piece together what he was reading. They were fragments of a story. A story that was dark and evil. A story perfect for Balor. Nothing like a seanchie tale, here. There was no hero that fought battles, no little laugh, or twist or nod to the justice of someone's downfall. This was dark. Dark like famine, dark like greed, dark like murder with no consequence.

The darkness made Smithy look up, take a breath, a breath so deep it made him wonder that he had the lungs to manage it. Holy feck and then some. But what to do with this knowledge? It gave him more reasons to want to kill Balor. But was that enough? He sighed and put his phone away. He would have to think on it. Because now that he found he'd been useful, he wanted that usefulness to matter more than just being a lock pick.

19

MAURA

I was looking forward to tonight. Last night when Raven had stopped by the bar promises had been made and I was lighting up at the thought of those promises. Hoo boy. On,e hour and I finished work. My cowgirl boots were ready to go knocking, a phrase, an idea, I'd learned and now was determined to explore. Knocking boots, hoo boy. My dreams made true and Raven would be mine. That was what I'd read in his veiled words, the tease and the weave, but I could tease and weave just as well and now the web was woven and we would close in, I was sure. Certain sure. I had the lingo, I had the boots. Sure, I'd knock it out of the park.

Eventually, the door opened and I looked up. Sherman walked in, followed by Skye. I looked for Raven but he wasn't there. My disappointment was there, though, heart sinking down to those boots who had no one to knock against, at least not at the moment. Still, there was time, and with it, hope. And Sherman and Skye were company that passed the time.

I gave them a nod. Sherman gave me a big grin and Skye sketched a wave. They made their way over to me. Skye had on skinny jeans and a light coloured top that would have been nondescript on anyone else, but she gave it all the description to make it striking. Her hair swayed loose, its lustre catching the light in a way that said, "flowing river".

"Hiya," I said. "Didn't know you were coming tonight."

"It's the place to be," said Sherman.

Skye laughed. "We wanted to be here."

I nodded. "Have you been out at the reservation until now?"

Skye nodded, her face turned solemn. "There's much to do there."

"I can imagine," I said.

"Can you?" asked Sherman. He studied me. "Yeah, maybe."

For some reason that pleased me. "Sounds like they're having some trouble there," I said. I thought of what I'd overheard and what I'd pushed aside at the reservation. I tried to push it aside again, along with the beat, the rhythm, the all the sounds of the earth that I'd felt there. That was too much feeling, too much of my past wrapped up in threads that were too tangled into my old ones. No and no. I was going for the new me. The cowgirl happy. The one who wore the boots. The knocking boots.

"Will you two have anything to drink?" I asked.

They both nodded. Skye asked for a hot water and two beers. When I asked her why two, she told me the other one was for me. Sherman also surprised me, asking for a glass of wine. Wine? But then he was a person of surprises.

"What kind?" I asked. "Red or white?"

"What do you think?" he said.

"Oh, right," I said. "What else but red."

Nearby, Lenny laughed. "Yeah, 'cause you're red on the inside and outside."

Sherman raised his brow. "That's who I am. That can't change."

"No," I said. "And why should it?"

"Exactly," he said, nodding, more to himself than me, it seemed.

"Hey," said Lenny. "You go ahead and sit down with your friends, I got this. I'll bring them over to your table."

I gave Lenny a genuine smile at the unexpected generosity. "Thanks a million," I said.

I grabbed my phone from under the bar, tucked it in my jeans and lifted the partitioned section to join Skye and Sherman on the other side.

"Will we go over to one of the booths?" I asked. I was happy that I was staying, marking time a while, the "while" that would give Raven a chance to show, to fill those promises.

"Yeah, let's," said Sherman.

He led the way, his dark T-shirt and flannel shirt he wore this night, in its usual backwards, inside out position. The skirt this time was short and worn over a pair of jeans that looked to have no front or back, or inside and outside. He had his laptop bag slung over his shoulder, facing front so that it banged his legs. It was a situation that didn't bear thinking about. At least not my thinking. Those thoughts were heading elsewhere, along with the boots, should a certain person finally get his arse in this bar.

We took our seats in the booth, Skye sliding in next to me and Sherman opposite us, his laptop at his side. We were a curious threesome, and from the glances I could see some had that curiosity, giving us a few side eyes and raised brows. Sherman was oblivious, as was Skye. Lenny brought over our orders a few minutes later and placed them on the table. After a nod he was gone.

I looked at Skye. "What's the hot water for?"

She tilted her head. "For you."

"Me?"

She nodded and pulled out a small packet from her jeans

pocket. She tapped the contents in the hot water. I looked at them swirling in the water.

"Special herbs," she said. "For you."

"Why? What are the herbs?"

"Herbs to calm, herbs to know, to understand."

"Cannabis?" I'd not heard of cannabis tea, but then again anything was possible.

She laughed and shook her head. "No, these are my herbs, specially blended for you from my plants. They include osha, lavender, mugwort and sweetgrass."

I nodded, looking at the liquid. The tea was a kind of a golden colour. The aroma wasn't offputting. I pulled it towards me. "Thank you." My manners, I had them, I did. They were part of me.

I took a small sip. The taste was faintly mint, faintly flowery, soft. A soft taste? I could discern nothing more specific.

"You think I need to calm down, to understand?" I asked. My tone was only half teasing.

She put a hand over mine. "There's so much we all need to understand. Taking time to drink, to sip, is half way to calm. You'll get there. And calm helps understanding."

It was metaphor, cryptic in a way that left me more puzzled than frustrated. She was telling me something and nothing, but a nothing that wasn't full of hot air. It was a nothing that could fit into my something. But I had put that something away. Tossed it behind me. My something didn't fit with "cowgirl happy".

I drank more of my hot drink and Sherman sipped his wine. Skye watched us both, chatting about the various plants she felt were important, throwing out names. The names hung in the air for a moment before they weaved in and around us, creating a world of possibilities of healing, health and goodness. One in particular caught my attention. Sweetgrass. I knew the words, "sweet" and "grass", but together they sounded perfect, a match that was inseparable and stood for so much that could only be good.

"Have you ever smelled it?" asked Skye.

"I've never even seen it," I said. "What does it look like? What does it feel like?"

"It smells of wonder, and joy and all things fresh."

"A powerful scent," said Sherman.

Skye nodded. "Sweetgrass is powerful."

Somehow, this woman who defined "babe" in her skinny jeans and flowing hair at one moment, now became something more. That "scritch, scritch, scritch" was back. Something that was part of the powerful sweetgrass.

"Braiding sweetgrass connects you to the natural world, reminds you that you're woven into the fabric of that natural world."

"Braiding sweetgrass?" I said. This was a thread that was taking me on a path that had no cowgirls following. I knew it, but I couldn't help myself. "How do you braid sweetgrass?"

"Like you braid hair. Weaving, weaving."

She lifted her hair, divided into three sections and began to weave the sections, over, under, over, under. I watched her, mesmerised, her fingers working deftly, all those strands of hair winding and curving. I touched the braid, felt its silkiness, its strength. A plait so thick and strong I could Rapunzel my way down from a tower with it.

"You try it," she said.

She loosed the braid, shaking out the weave until all the sections were gone. Without thinking about it, I slowly divided her hair into three sections and started to weave them together, just as she'd done. When I'd reached the end, she pulled out a strip of leather from her pocket and wrapped the strip around it.

"There," she said, smiling. "You've braided sweetgrass, you've woven yourself into the fabric of the earth."

I looked up at her, my eyes widening. "I've feckin' done what?"

Just then the door opened I lifted my eyes, looking for the cowgirl that owned these boots I was wearing. Wanting her to come skipping back. Raven stepped through the door and behind him was a familiar face, followed by three others. Feckandfeckandfeck. Suddenly my little toes began to feel a strong pinch from the boots.

I KNEW the moment they saw me, their stunned expressions making them appear like they were briefly frozen in time. My own surprise and other things I didn't want to examine, were mainly focused on Raven. Surprise that he knew them. Surprise that he would bring them here. Surprise that he hadn't mentioned them to me, because, sure, why wouldn't he tell me he met with other Irish in that "all fellow expats would surely want to connect in a strange country" assumption people made.

Raven made his way toward me, the others following like he had a flute and was piping out a Hamelin tune. They stopped at our table, Raven nodding to me. The others stared at me, still too stunned and uncollected in thoughts or expressions.

"Raven," I said. "I see you've acquired more friends."

"I have, sunshine," he said.

I raised a brow. "Sunshine?"

"Irony?" he replied.

Sherman laughed. "Hey. Pull up a few chairs, squeeze in here."

I looked at Sherman, frowning.

"I'm not sure they want to stay."

"Why are you here?" said Finn, the shocked expression on his face replaced by a decidedly stormy one.

I looked at him, holding his gaze. I saw the fury, along with other things that were best left unacknowledged. "It's where the wind took me."

"The answer is blowing in the wind," sang Sherman off key.

I gave him a "not now" look.

"Does your friend know his clothes are on inside out?" said Smithy, looking at Raven. "And backwards?"

"It's who he is," I said.

Smithy shrugged. "Oh. Grand, so."

Saoirse leaned over and put her hand on my shoulder, a silent greeting, gentle, kind. I let it rest there, but said nothing.

Raven grinned at me and then sat next to Sherman, shoving him over to the edge and making room for one more person. Taking his cue, Skye did the same with me. Saoirse sat down next to her and Finn took the seat next to Raven. All the better to glare at me, I supposed. That left Luke and Smithy to sit in the chairs they pulled up, at the end of the table. A tight squeeze, one that reflected my feet and my emotions.

Lenny came over, scanned our group and shook his head, muttering, "yeah this'll be a story", before he asked for our order. There were shrugs and then the old Budweiser fall back of an Irish person's idea of American beer came out of everyone but Raven, of course. He ordered a specialty beer, just to be contrary, I thought, thinking that maybe he and Sherman had more in common than I'd first realised.

I looked at Raven. "Is this a trick?"

Raven laughed, long and hard. "Life is all tricks and twists, Maura."

"And some are yours," said Sherman.

Raven nodded. "Some are mine."

"Right, so," I said. "You're saying you tricked me."

Raven blinked at her. "No."

The others watched the exchange, curiosity, puzzlement and a mixture of emotions on their faces. Except for Finn. Finn's face held anger and so much else that indicated he had no interest in Raven's tricks, but other possibilities that Raven represented.

"No? No, what?" I said. I took a deep breath. "What is this, Raven? A coincidence? You thought, 'ah grand, some more Irish, let's have a get together. A céili even'. But let me tell you now, that's not a tune I'll be dancing to."

Raven laughed again. "Oh yeah, that's good." He took a sip of his specialty beer that Lenny had just delivered with a shaking head a few minutes before when they were all staring at each other.

"Oh, it's clear you dance to your own tune, Maura." He looked at the others. "Most times. But, no, I wasn't thinking that. I was thinking that we all had things to talk about. Matters to discuss."

I looked at Skye for her reaction because Sherman's would only confuse me. She gave me a compassionate look. "No harm was or is intended, to you or your friends. We met them last night. Saw who they were and thought, yes. We must talk."

I studied her face. Calm, reassuring. Genuine. "Who are you?" I asked, feeling uneasy despite her expression. "Who are the three of you?"

Skye gave me an easy smile. "I'm Skye. Truly. Skye Woman if you want the all of it. And Raven is Raven."

"Can't change that," said Sherman with a giggle.

"And you're Sherman, I suppose," I said sighing.

"Why makes you think they're someone else?" asked Luke quietly. He was studying Raven, his expression speculative.

"How did you meet them?" I asked Luke.

Luke shrugged. "Raven was talking to Saoirse and Skye chatted to Smithy in the break."

I looked at Saoirse, raising my brow. "Raven just came up to you?"

"Raven's right here," said Raven. "Look, it's not important how or why we met. What's important is the now. And why all of you are here."

I opened my mouth to speak, but Raven held up his hand. "Don't waste your breath repeating what you'd said before."

"Maybe I should ask you why you're here," I said, my tone belligerent. "You're not from this area. You're not Osage." I was annoyed. With him, with all of them.

Raven shrugged. "I thought that was obvious. All three of us want to help our people. We don't have to be Osage to do that."

I bit my lip. I knew there was something more. It was in the beat of that drum at the powwow, something in Raven's eyes and Skye's voice. That triple scritch.

"I think it's obvious why we're here," said Luke. "To play music."

"And sing," said Saoirse with a small laugh.

"And see America," said Smithy, his face determined. "There's so much to see."

"You wanted to see Oklahoma?" asked Raven, his tone sceptical.

"It's different," said Saoirse. "So different to Ireland."

"You came here because it's different," said Raven in a flat tone.

"And to play music," said Finn, finally shifting his eyes from me to Raven. "A new experience with a new audience. We had the opportunity given to us to play a few gigs and get to see a part of America. Sure, why wouldn't you?"

"Oh, I surely wouldn't," said Raven. "But then again, I'm me."

"You are you," said Sherman. "Nah, it's not half bad here. I'm liking the company for one." He looked at all of us. "Yeah, interesting."

"Why don't we just enjoy an evening with our new friends?" said Skye giving everyone a generous smile.

Raven looked at Skye and sighed. "Maybe you're right. For now."

It was a stalemate. For all of us. An uneasy peace after a minor conflict, with nothing to show for it but my suspicions and a raging anger that I was no longer alone, unencumbered in my cowgirl happy place.

20

MAURA

The beer flowed and I managed to recover some good humour, found it tucked away in my box of ironic things. Ironic how the more I tried to get rid of my old life, it kept finding me. Ironic how the more Finn glared at me, the more I found it funny. Ironic that Raven suddenly found all this hilarious and kept joking with Sherman, attempting to wind me up. Ironic that underneath the table, though, Raven started playing footsie with me, creating more confusion in me and that large bundle of confusion that was becoming too big to handle. And it was ironic that when I got up to go to the bathroom Finn followed me and stopped me outside it.

"What's going on?" Finn said, his voice tight.

I laughed, the irony box overflowing. "You think I know?"

He gave a frustrated snort. "What are you doing here, in Oklahoma?"

I tried to recover some of the calm from earlier. When I was with Skye, plaiting her hair, drinking her tea. "Working at a bar." Keep it simple, I thought. No confusion, no irony, just simple truth.

But Finn wasn't going to settle for simple truths. No irony

there either. "Why did you come to Oklahoma? Were you hoping to meet with Balor? Make a deal with him?"

I gave him a shocked look, too stunned to speak. "What?" I croaked out eventually. "Feck me, Finn, what do you think I am?"

"I don't know, Maura. You told me I didn't know you, isn't that right? So maybe the Maura I didn't know has decided to work with Balor and is here to coordinate some plan."

I blinked at him, fighting the tears that came to my eyes. Tears? What did I want with those? Not one thing. I tried to shove them in the box of ironies but there was no stuffing allowed. One slipped down my cheek. I brushed it aside.

"Oh, feck off, will you," I said darkly. I walked past him and flung open the bathroom door. It slammed with a bang and closed behind me.

IT WAS JUST the two of us left. Raven and myself. The others had cleared off to their respective beds, drinks finished, stalemate achieved on many fronts. We were all enlightened by not very much. Linked by our determination to say as little as possible in the most entertaining or cryptic manner possible. Outdoing Sherman. All of us amused and all of us suspicious. Except Finn, who could add fury and disgust to his armoury of emotions. Ah, and myself of course. I had the run of the emotions playing up and down like some beginner on a violin playing scales, complete with all the screeches.

But now I looked up from my beer, or no, it was whiskey now, obtained by someone in the course of the night when we were all jolly palsy and bantering away, determined to get something out of the evening, since no answers were to be got. Except for Finn. Oh, and myself, who stared morosely in my drink one moment and the other was determined to joke away with Sherman. Or Raven. Whoeverwhatever mode. Looking into Raven's eyes, now, though, I saw something I hadn't expected. Compassion.

Oh. Oh. And another oh. Feck. I pasted on the grand smile, the one that says "not a bother" because it wasn't. Nothing was.

I leaned forward, tilted my head. "Hey cowboy. You hoping for a good time?" It was my best cowgirl accent, crafted from the very best of TV and bar talk.

Raven laughed, the compassion gone, and I leaned back, satisfied, the whiskey feeling good inside me. Underneath the table, I initiated the footsie game again that he'd abandoned after I'd returned from the bathroom.

Raven winked at me. "You're some woman, aren't you?"

"I am, so."

He nodded. "Worth knowing."

An answer that would get high points for banter rose to my lips, but I hesitated. A slow smile formed. "Thanks," I said eventually.

He shrugged. "You're a woman to reckon with. And I reckon I should get to know you better."

I laughed. "I wouldn't mind that."

We drank on, me with my whiskey, he with his specialty beer and banter to be had on all subjects that meant nothing. When we'd had our fill, my vision narrowed and full only of our footsies and his face, he leaned toward me.

"Why don't we go to your room?"

I laughed. "Why don't we?"

He smiled. "We should."

"We should."

And so we rose, he took my hand and led me out of the bar, and we eventually landed at my room door and then inside. Will I make tea or coffee, was uttered, I think, but my head was somewhere else and my confusion smothered under a blanket of whiskey and Budweiser. My boots were there, on my feet, but really not in charge. We sat on the sofa, mugs in hand, our tea/coffee steaming our faces.

"I can help," said Raven. "I think. Maybe. Give me a chance."

"Help what?" I said, wondering if I'd missed something.

I sorted through the box of ironies in my mind, reviewing all that had been piled in there that evening and came up blank. There was plenty of confusion all around too and this statement could easily be knitted on to its edges.

"You. Your friends. The reason you're all here."

I narrowed my eyes, studying him. "The reason we're all here? I'm here for me."

"Are you? Are you really? I don't think your friends feel that way."

"They're not my friends," I muttered. I sipped my mug, hoping the steam would provide some camouflage.

"Sure they are. You're just having a rough patch with them."

I snorted at this. "Rough patch. Ah, I like that. But no. It's an 'I'm finished with them' patch. Only the patch is huge, uncrossable, never ending in size."

He laughed and I sniggered, taken by my own wit.

"I'm sure they still care about you, no matter what's happened. And I think you still have some sort of connection with them."

I shrugged. "It can take a while for some connections to fade. But it will happen."

"I think they'd prefer to keep the connections. They're here, aren't they?"

I frowned. "They didn't know I was here. Couldn't you tell that? Or didn't Finn's 'why are you here' not clue you in?"

"I think some of them thought you might be here."

"I don't see how. Their presence is a complete coincidence."

Raven raised his brow. "Is it?"

I looked at him and pursed my lips, anger growing. "You think it wasn't? You think I planned to come here? Or they knew I planned to come here? You think I'm working with Balor like Finn said, is that it?"

He placed a hand on my face, looked me deep in the eyes and shook his head. "No, I don't. And I don't believe your friend does either."

"He's not my friend," I muttered again.

But the words, even as they poured out of my mouth, I knew they weren't ironic, a repetition of my earlier statement. Nothing cutesy or banter like. It was just what came to me. Stupid and childish, and deep down I knew the words for the untruth they were. No. I thought. I didn't want this.

"But they're here for Balor. So, since you're not with them, they think you're against them and working with Balor. I can see why they might conclude that, but it's not true."

I shook my head stubbornly. "It's not true. I'm here for me. A new start."

"But the question is, why choose here for the new start? A place where Balor is?"

I sighed. "Feck me, if I know. It's just where the wind blew me."

"Hmmm," said Balor. "The wind chose an odd place. And now you're here. And they're here. And they have a task to do."

"They can do it without me."

"Maybe. But then, maybe, together we can help them a little."

I looked at him, narrowed my eyes. "What do you mean?"

"Gather your friends. Tell them we'll meet them at the coffee shop tomorrow afternoon, before your shift. Discuss things. You know that there's stuff we know about Balor."

"We?" Suddenly I was off balance. How had we ended up

talking about Balor and his misdeeds? How had Raven done that? What had I said? Feckityfeck. What? Confusion rose up around the box of ironies, tossing it around, emptying it in a dance of such power I nearly spun with it. As it was, I held my hand to my head and rubbed it hard.

"A feckin' trickster. That's what you are, Raven. A feckin' trickster.

He laughed at me. "I did say, didn't I? My name is Raven, after all."

I shook my head, even more confused.

21

———

SMITHY

Smithy stared out of the motel window. The skies were sunny, but he could see big clouds rolling in from the distance. It held the promise of a break in the hot weather, and for that Smithy was glad, but the air also held a charge and the clouds looked anything but friendly. With the hairs on his arm nearly standing at attention, he hoped that the clouds and thundery weather didn't mean something serious like a tornado. Was it a tornado region? He thought of *The Wizard of Oz* and Dorothy. She lived around here, didn't she? Or was that Kansas? Kansas, he decided. Though lately, he felt like he was in the middle of some weird Oz tale, and instead of the Munchkins, there were Your Ones, the Watchers. But there was no doubt that the Wicked Witch of the West – with the letter of each word capitalised, of course – was Balor. They definitely needed to ding dong him. The question was, who was the man behind the curtain?

That man behind the curtain was certainly creating illusions and fantasmical events. Fantasmical. He liked the word. Rolled off the tongue and said exactly how it felt. How it felt at the gig, with the music spinning round him until it tugged at his sleeve, took his hand, drew him into the circle dance with the rest of the group while keeping fast to his hand. He didn't know how, or why, but it was as if a huge beam of light shone down on him, warming him through, making his bow light across the strings, making his fingers fly. It was a feeling that stayed with him, bolstered him and grew even more. While he talked to Skye, that feeling grew and his blood sang, giving him an insight to all possibilities. Those possibilities had bloomed when he found himself stepping forward after the break to sing that song *Eleanor na Rún*. Eleanor my secret, my darling. The translation of *rún* with its double meaning worked so well for all he felt, just as the other words told of Eleanor's beauty and power. "She would sing the birds off the trees" was one of the phrases that made him smile as he sang it.

It had surprised him, when he sang it. It had surprised the others too, but a quizzical glance from Luke, an affirming nod from Finn were the only indications that they'd noticed. It was Saoirse who stared at him, her eyes glittering with emotion. He'd had to look away, because he didn't want to promise her more than he had in him. But at that moment he would have promised her eternity and felt it possible.

He'd avoided being alone with Saoirse since then, but he'd felt her eyes following him, along with the questions that hung in the air between them. But it was all too fragile. Not yet, he thought. Not yet. Maybe. It was hope he dared not even voice to himself. Would he go to Diancecht's daughter, Airmed, when they returned? Her herbal knowledge and understanding of ailments exceeded her father's, though few dared to mention it. Maybe.

But for now, he tended this feeling, the power that he felt within him, like a tiny tender shoot, afraid that one strong wind would kill it. He just hoped that any wind that would threaten it would be nothing like the winds in Kansas. He wasn't certain he wanted to meet his wizard.

He turned from the window of his room at the sound of his door opening, gave a small nod when he saw it was Finn. Finn nodded back, a cardboard tray holding two cups of coffee in his hand. His T-shirt was rumpled, his hair in disarray, though that wasn't unusual, but his face told the full story. Haggard, dark bruising under his eyes from little sleep, it was filled with suppressed anger, confusion and worry. Smithy could sympathise.

"Thanks," said Smithy, taking the proffered coffee cup. "Not sure I'd make much sense of the next few hours without it."

Finn grunted. "No sleep for the weary. The room is feckin' stuffy, for a start."

"Yeah. Stuffy, all right."

"And the air conditioner. On, off, on, all night with a racket that could wake your granny from the dead."

"Not my granny," said Smithy with a grin.

Finn gave a small laugh. "Yeah, guess not. Nor mine, really."

Finn moved over to the window and stood next to Smithy. "Time to be going, really. Get this over with and go home."

"Not your kind of place, America? Or at least Oklahoma."

Finn sighed. "No. I don't know. It—it's different. Not what I expected."

"Not what you expected." Smithy wasn't certain if he was really talking about Oklahoma, America, or something else. Someone else.

"I'm not sure, Smithy. It's all...complicated. I'm trying to sort it all through. That's what I've been doing all night, going over things."

"What things?" asked Smithy.

Finn shuffled in his place and ran a hand through his tangled hair. "What do you think? Is she working with Balor?"

Smithy pulled back a little, surprised at the blunt words. Not Finn's style. He'd be reasoned, diplomatic in presenting the issue. Explain both sides, before leading you to the proper conclusion. Or he'd be all wit, cajoling you to the best possible outcome before you knew you were there. Smithy shook his head and tried to assemble his thoughts.

"I doubt she'd spend so much time helping us, only to turn around and help Balor."

Finn looked at me, his eyes troubled. "But you don't know what she was like just before she left, how angry she was."

"What was she angry about so much? She'd said that she was fed up with us and that Anu only wanted her when she was useful. But that was in the heat of the moment. We all were useful in some way. We had to be."

"I think it was something more than that. Something deeper."

Smithy turned to Finn. "What do you mean?"

Finn shrugged. "Just from what she said to me, just before she left. And things she didn't say."

"Like what?"

Finn sighed. "She said I didn't know her. That's not true. I've known her for ages."

"Ages?" said Smithy archly.

Finn gave a small laugh. "Ages. For many ages. We go way back. I remember her well before the Battle of Magh Tuireadh. Searching her out for Daghda. Talking with her. And then when she'd come to see Daghda, she always chatted with me, had a few laughs."

Smithy snorted. "Well Daghda certainly had use for her back then."

Finn gave Smithy a dark look. "Yes. He did. And maybe he took that usefulness for granted."

Smithy blinked at him. "Is that what this is? Anger at Daghda?"

Finn shrugged and leaned his head against the window pane. "Feck me, I don't know." He took a deep breath. "She was angry. So angry. But there was something else. Something I can't quite figure out. Maura is who she is, anger, war and a lover of a good fight. And that's her passion, but she's more." He'd said the last phrase as if it were a question, as if he was asking the question of himself.

Smithy considered Finn's words carefully, testing them out, thinking about Maura. "You're right. She's more than just a warrior bird. The crow. Feeding off a battlefield."

"She plays music," said Finn.

"She certainly has her own beat, her own rhythm."

Finn smiled wryly. "She certainly does."

"I know you care for her, Finn. You just have to find a way to let her know." The words seemed safe as he said them. He didn't think his friend was ready to hear anything more than that. And sure, wasn't he just as much an ostrich sticking his own head in the sand? He only hoped they both didn't choke to death on all that sand.

Smithy, Finn and Saoirse stood around Luke, who was seated at the table, the laptop before him. Luke was pointing out all the details of the blueprint of Balor's Oklahoma home, looking for possibilities and giving the outlines of a plan. It was sketchy at best, and Smithy knew it. But they had to start somewhere.

"Is there any sign of a safe at the house?" asked Finn.

He looked a little better than he did earlier, Smithy thought, though he could still see the tightness around Finn's eyes and mouth, as if he was willing himself into calm.

"I'm still trying to access the cameras. It seems there's some kind of extra password. I've tried a few things, but I'm no expert."

"Still," said Saoirse, indicating the screen. "We have the blueprints. That's something."

Smithy nodded, started to speak and then shut his mouth again. All morning he'd been wondering if he should say something to the others about the images of the documents on his phone. He hadn't had a chance to tell Luke when they first left the headquarters and were returning to the motel. Luke had filled the conversation with the blueprints and his initial impressions. And what they didn't find. Luke was convinced that Balor had both items at his house. Smithy had wondered at his strong insistence initially, and now the thought returned to him. It made sense, but something about the dark expression on Luke's face when he said it made Smithy think there was more to it than just common sense.

"I think we need to go there and just see what it looks like," said Luke. "You can see from the elevations that it's modern, open in plan with large floor-to-ceiling windows. We can see if there's anything obvious, especially with a pair of binoculars."

"We could ask Maura," said Saoirse. "She could do it herself. Both floors."

Smithy glanced at Finn, saw the dark look on his eyes and the trace of hope that lay behind it.

"No," said Luke. "We probably shouldn't trust her."

"You think she's working with Balor?" said Finn, an edge to his voice.

Luke shrugged. "We can't be sure either way. Best to be safe. And now those others she's with. I don't know."

Smithy started to say something, but Saoirse got there first. "Maura wouldn't work with Balor. Sure, she hates him just like we do."

"Does she?" said Luke, his tone dispassionate. "Or did it suit her to show hatred for him?"

"Stop," said Finn. "You don't know her at all."

"And you do?" said Luke, one brow raised.

Finn gave him a steady look. "I do, of course."

Luke looked as if he was going to challenge that statement, but he fell silent and shrugged. "Ah, she probably wouldn't want to help out anyway. You saw what she was like at Murphy's."

"We weren't exactly trying to understand or build bridges," said Saoirse.

"She was the one who went off in a huff," said Luke. "We've managed well enough without her so far."

"We've struggled. We're struggling," said Saoirse.

Luke sighed. "We can manage. And there's this Raven fella. Who's he, then, when he's at home?"

"He's a strange character, all right," said Smithy. He thought of his conversation with Skye. "Though his friend Skye seemed okay. Genuine."

"Genuine?" said Saoirse, giving him a look of scepticism and something else.

He gave a little laugh. "Yes. I mean, talking to her, she was interested and interesting."

"Oh?" said Saoirse.

"Interested in all of us. That's what we discussed. She wanted to know where we were all from and how we became involved in music."

"Did she?" said Finn, looking thoughtful.

Smithy glanced away from him and fixed his eyes on Saoirse once again. Surely she didn't suspect that he was flirting with Skye. The thought left him amused initially, until he noticed the trace of hurt in her eyes. His smile faded.

"Yes," said Smithy. "It wasn't me specifically she was interested in. Just us as a group and the music and Ireland, I suppose.

You know how it is. The myths, magic and music thing. The *céad míle fáilte* thing."

"Sure it wasn't the 'sexy Irishman' thing?" said Saoirse, her brow arched.

"Me? Sexy?" Smithy said, grinning. "Aww. Thanks." He gave her a warm smile, a smile that he hoped conveyed there wasn't anything to be worried about. He felt the warmth at the thought that she would need reassuring. The meaning behind that need. But slow, now. Slow, slow as slow. He would just hold that and go carefully.

"What exactly did Skye ask you?" said Finn, frowning a little. "Did she mention Raven at all?"

"Raven?" said Smithy. "No. I didn't realise they knew each other until later."

Finn nodded, frowning. "Oh, right."

"What are you thinking?" asked Luke.

Finn shrugged. "I don't know. There's something off there. The pair of them. Or really, the three of them."

"Oh, I think it's obvious that there's something off with Sherman," said Smithy wryly.

"Are you sure your distrust isn't down to Maura?" asked Saoirse. Her tone was quiet.

"What? No."

"Finn's right to be cautious with them. Raven in particular seemed to be digging for information last night. And cute out with it."

"I don't know," said Smithy. "I can see why you would be a little suspicious. But I don't think they mean us any harm. He seemed to want to help. That's the feeling I got from him and from Skye."

"Maybe, but we can't take the risk," said Luke.

Smithy took a deep breath, pulled out his phone. "When I was in Balor's office looking in one of the presses, I found a bundle of documents. They were about the Osage, land rights, oil rights and some fraudulent practices. They imply Balor has been involved in illegal activities here, possibly even murder."

Smithy pulled up the images and handed the phone to Luke, who skimmed the documents silently, his face grim, while the others looked on. When he was finished he handed the phone to Finn. Finn examined them cursorily, muttering under his breath. Finally, Saoirse looked at them, the outrage plain on her face when she'd done.

"Do you think Raven and Skye know about this?" said Luke.

"We can ask them," said Smithy.

"I don't know," said Luke.

Finn's phoned signalled a text message. He frowned, shrugged, pulled out his phone. "It's Maura," he said eventually. "She says Raven wants to meet with us at a coffee shop near here."

"Funny that," said Luke.

"Funny, indeed," said Finn flatly.

22

———

LUKE

Luke stared at his phone, watching it ring Kayla's number. It was the second time he'd done it since the others had left his room an hour ago. He didn't have much time left before they'd be going to meet Maura and her friends and he wanted to make sure he'd checked in with Kayla before he left the room. Again there was no answer and it went to voicemail. He left a message, tried to sound casual, but even he could hear the worry in his voice. He ended the message and his finger scrolled down the contacts and found Anu and pressed. He hardly knew the finger's intent before it was done, but he had no quibble with the result. Except it kept ringing too, that relentless double buzz or beep or whatever the feck description you wanted to assign the noise that kept going in his ear until another AI voice interrupted and told him to leave a message, thankyouverymuch. That voice didn't want to hear the message he had for it/him/her.

With a frustrated sigh he threw the phone on the table and stared at it. A moment later he picked it up, typed out and sent two texts; one to Kayla and one to Anu. That completed, he slipped the phone back into his pocket and was left once again with the various "what ifs" playing through his mind. The "what ifs" played ping pong with the "should I's" and the "what ifs" were too feckin' good at batting back the old ball. "Ah don't be going there," says the lone spectator, your man who has no bets and little interest in the outcome. Of course he'd gone there with all the scenarios his team of "what ifs" came up with and a few of them not so much half baked, but more like "extremely possible get your arse back to Ireland" types of "what ifs".

Frustrated beyond words as that ping pong took on a higher level, he opened his phone and began to search again for any news items that might give an idea if his worst "what if" might have happened. He scoured the Irish news sites – RTE, *Examiner, Irish Times* and all the rest he could think of, including the tabloid news – for anything that might indicate an increased threat to Kayla or Anu. He came up empty, until he found a piece in *The Southern Star.* It was just a small clip in the local news about the Bantry area and the oil storage tanks on Whiddy Island. A leak had been discovered in one of the tanks and it was seeping oil. They weren't certain how long it had been leaking, but "steps were being taken to address it". Steps. Whatever that meant. In the meantime, the oil that had already spilled had made its way down to the sea, he would bet. It was more than soil, more than wildlife. It was a whole ecosystem so inter-twined. He knew this. And the knowledge was so deep inside him now it was part of his core self. He was Kayla's champion, wedded to the land just as much as the king was in times past. As he was across the water. And now, here he was, across a different kind of water. How could he champion his lady here?

The full depth of his thoughts kicked out the teams of "what ifs" and "should I's" into the ether, because he had no use for them now. Because he was twined with Kayla, woven into her fabric and the Beara's fabric in ways those yokes could never understand. And no banging or kicking against that mental door of "I should be there" would help. He was here and the helping he could do, would do, was centred here for the moment.

He looked at the time on his phone. And just because his moment was here, didn't mean he couldn't rush that moment and do what needed as soon as possible. Get the meeting over. Go to Balor's house and find the spear and the slingshot. Done and done.

THE COFFEE SHOP was fairly empty for a weekday afternoon, though there were a few mothers with infants in pushchairs and a smattering of teens clustered around a table. The only thing trendy about the place was that it served up lattes and cappuccinos with some side pastries and croissants to go along with the doughnuts and bagels. That was fine with Luke. He followed the others up to the counter and placed an order while the others decided. He wasn't bothered. Coffee how it came would suit him.

While he waited he scanned the room more thoroughly, but saw no trace of Maura or her friends. He sighed. He and the others weren't exactly on time, as one or the other of them hadn't really managed to collect themselves quickly enough to make it on time. No one had the sense of urgency he had. An urgency that seemed to find his foot and make it tap, and then his finger when it drew near the counter. It was a "hurry up" beat that was universal enough to draw glances from a few strangers and frowns from Saoirse and Finn. Smithy just gave Luke a wry glance, but for once, Luke felt no animosity there. Small miracles.

Coffees in hand, and in Finn and Smithy's cases, doughnuts too, the group sought out a table and sat down. Luke's chair was wobbly, but it suited his mood and gave the tapping an extra syncopation that pleased him. Foot tap, chair leg, foot tap, chair leg, finger tap. The beat drew him in, his head giving a short bob and he continued on until Saoirse slapped her hand over his finger and placed her other hand on his leg.

"For feck's sake, Luke," she said.

Luke shrugged and tried to halt his tapping, the beat still in him and giving voice to the emotions that were spilling over. Concern, impatience. The "get the show on the road and get it done".

"I know," said Saoirse. "I get it. We're doing the best we can, though."

Luke nodded. Sure, what could he say? Let's just go now. Go to the house, get the items and go back to Ireland. Tomorrow. Yeah, he could say that, but would it happen? He sighed.

The door opened and Luke looked over. Feck. Not them. He glanced at Finn. "Will you text Maura and ask where they are?"

Finn looked at Luke, objection written all over his face along with so much else. He sighed and nodded, took out his phone and began to type in the text. A moment later the door opened and there they were, Maura in front, wearing a light T-shirt with her dark jeans and what looked like a pair of cowboy boots. Luke hadn't noticed her clothes at the bar, primarily because she was sitting down most of the time, but now they stood out strongly, a signal. He glanced at Finn, saw his pained look, his tight mouth and the eyes, fixed on Maura. Behind Maura, Raven, Skye and Sherman followed, Sherman with a laptop bag slung over his shoulder.

Saoirse rose and began to move another table to join theirs, Smithy jumping up a moment later to help. Finn followed Maura and the others, who nodded to them and gestured to the counter. Clear enough. Once coffees and whatever else they bought were in hand, they made their way to the tables, grabbing chairs and sitting down. Maura sat next to Raven, who had

Sherman on his other side, leaving Skye to sit in the chair next to Smithy. Saoirse drew her chair closer, next to Smithy. It was only a small shift that could be mistaken as an adjustment for comfort rather than a point being made. But Luke saw it and grinned inwardly. Ah, Saoirse.

Maura leaned forward, placing her arms on the table. A stance. "I'm here because Raven asked. This isn't me being General Maura. This is me being obliging. Amenable, like."

"Amenable?" said Finn, brow raised. His expression was neutral. A tightly controlled neutral, to be fair.

Maura shrugged.

"It was my suggestion," said Raven. "To explore winds that blow and why they blow in certain directions."

Luke groaned inwardly, glancing at the others, who looked as impatient as he felt. Did they have to cut through a mire of mud and cobwebs to get some answers and find out why they were here?

"No metaphors or tricks, Raven," said Maura. "Just ask them what you want to know and tell us how it figures into what your concerns are." It seemed Maura was sharing Luke's feelings.

She looked at Luke. "They're having problems with Balor too."

The others stared at her along with Luke and then, almost in concert, looked at Raven.

"You know Balor?" said Finn, his tone suspicious.

"I don't know him personally, no," said Raven, his tone reasonable. "But his energy company has many dealings with the Osage here. And some other tribes in various places across the country."

Luke studied Raven while he explained, trying to read him. The truth of him. There was something there. A big something. But he just didn't know what it was. Finn was still suspicious of Raven. That was obvious. But Luke wasn't certain there was reason for it. Maura on the other hand, well, you could never be sure with her. Luke looked beyond Raven, first to Sherman and then Skye. Sherman was odd in an obvious way, but something underneath that, beyond that, said something like "wise". Wise in old way, despite the youthfulness of his face, wise in a way that was important.

When his glance rested on Skye the feeling of "more" increased, as did the sense of wisdom and oldness. He wanted to take her hand, to feel her rhythm, because he felt once he'd done that, known the beat of her heart, he would know what that "more" was. And that knowing would be possibly overwhelming. He wasn't certain he wanted that knowing.

Luke studied Maura, wondered if he sensed what he did about Raven, Sherman and Skye. There was nothing in her manner that suggested it. Still, it would be wise to take care.

"What kind of dealings does Balor's energy company have with the Osage?" said Luke. He could feel Smithy's attention on him.

Raven looked over at Skye, then Sherman, exchanging some kind of silent communication. He took a deep breath, a sober expression on his face. "Balor has been acquiring oil leases, land and other things of the Osage. He's part of a number of men who have done this over the years, by fair means and foul. Even the fair means seem questionable. But on the surface, on paper, it all seems proper. Legal."

"How?" asked Saoirse. "How have he and others managed to do this?"

Raven shrugged. "Manipulating the system. Finding the loopholes in the law and creating opportunities when they could. Planting judges, lawyers, lawmakers to twist things in their favour."

It was vague, it was suggestive and also unnerving, this

explanation that wasn't one. He gave Raven a puzzled look. "Exactly what do you mean?"

Skye rested a hand on Raven's arm. A "let me" gesture that Raven conceded to with a wry grin and a shrug. She turned to the others and if she'd been Irish "*fadó, fadó, fadó*" would have been the first phrase out of her mouth. A story, a tale, but one with meaning.

"When the Osage were forced to move for the second time in the nineteenth century, they bought land that turned out to be full of oil. They earned millions and became the target for anyone anxious to exploit their wealth. Some would stop at nothing, even murder. But that's the past. Maybe."

"And what's the present?" asked Smithy.

"The present is murky," said Raven. "There are so many dangers around. Balor's company is only one. He exploits the people and the area in subtle ways. Advising the government on green washing and other methods to appear to be environmentally sound in the extraction of oil and other resources. Huge, massive wind turbines were erected on Osage lands, constructed with his men, his supplies. Faulty supplies, faulty construction. He's built up many of the old oil refineries and is supposed to be re-purposing them, but he's used them to store chemicals and other effluents from factories that are supposed to be green now. And he's also secretly dumping toxic waste all over the area, including Osage lands. We just don't have the proof."

"And you're trying to help get that proof?" asked Luke. He gave Smithy a look, hoping it would signal him to keep quiet for the moment.

"What proof do you need?" cut in Smithy. He started to pull out his phone, refusing to look at Luke.

Raven shrugged. "Anything that links him without a doubt to any of these activities."

"And you haven't been able to so far?" asked Smithy.

"Nothing concrete," said Raven. "And that's why I came and offered to help. And Skye and Sherman."

"It's important," said Sherman. "This land, it's speaking out. We need to listen."

"It's important that everyone listens," said Skye.

"Right, so," said Maura. "You both have common interests. Maybe it makes sense that you all work together."

Luke nodded. "It does appear to make sense."

Smithy held out his phone to Raven. Finn leaned forward, frowning, but after a moment leaned back. "I did find these in his office," said Smithy. "I don't know if they help."

Raven took the phone and looked at the screen. Carefully, he scanned the images and finally, when he'd finished, he grinned and passed the phone on to Skye. He saw that Maura watched them carefully, her expression curious. Was it a risk to show these in front of Maura, he wondered? Maybe.

"We need to search his home," said Luke, finally. Finn gave him a dark look. "Is that something you can help us with?"

"What kind of help?" asked Raven.

"Do you know anything about the layout of his house? Or his security system?"

Raven glanced at Sherman, who shrugged and nodded. "Maybe. Let me see what can be done."

"Tonight. We need to know by tonight," said Luke. Feck if he would let this be dragged out.

Raven gave him a speculative look. "What happens tonight?"

"Tonight we're going to have a look inside."

Finn, Saoirse and Smithy all gave him a surprised look.

"We are?" said Saoirse.

"We are," said Luke.

"And just what is it you want from his house?" asked Raven, his brow arched.

Finn crossed his arms, a stubborn look on his face. Smithy was looking doubtful.

"Some things of mine that he has," said Luke, carefully.

Raven nodded slowly. "I see."

Sherman cocked his head. "A thief."

Luke stiffened. "No. Just retrieving what's mine."

"Ah, no," said Finn. "Luke is many things. But he's not a thief."

"Balor," said Sherman. "He's the thief."

"Oh, right," said Luke, relaxing. "He's a thief."

"There's plenty of words along those lines to describe Balor," said Smithy. "Rogue, villain, conniving fecker. I could go on."

"No need," said Raven. "We'll help. We'll go to his home with you. I'll tell you what I find out."

"Maura," said Finn. "Where do you fit in all of this now, then?"

Maura looked at him and shrugged. "Wherever the wind blows me."

23

***

MAURA

The knock was loud. But sure, I was only staring at the wall, my thoughts all over the place. That meeting at the coffee shop, that was all over the place, too. What had been said, what hadn't. Luke, very cagey altogether. I couldn't blame him, really. Why would you trust three people you'd only just met, no you wouldn't. And he clearly didn't trust me. The thought of that made me laugh and it also made me want to cry. Why? Another why there, to lay against the other whys that were starting to crowd in on me. Finn, now. He'd been a bag of emotions. That was new, new in a way that made me angry, frustrated and again, that weird need to cry. Feck the weeping willow act, I told myself. That wasn't me, sure it wasn't. Not me at all. But Finn thoughts returned again, sneaking in like some little lad trying to get into an 18 certificate film at the cinema. You kick him out, but he's back again a while later, trying it on.

My world was on its end. Yes, I knew that. I wanted that. It was a different end up, with me ending up here, cowgirl happy. Yes, that was it. Just a little wobble on those boots. I would be grand. New friends, new times.

I rose from the sofa and opened the door, the smile on my face filled with my latest resolution. It's all good. My smile turned sultry and Raven grinned at the sight, a small laugh escaping.

"Come for a little cosy before you venture out tonight?" I asked.

"Sure. Exactly. Cosy chat, just you and me."

I opened the door wider to allow him entry and he passed through to the middle of the room.

"Sit, sit," I said, gesturing to the sofa. "Unless you'd rather somewhere more amenable to reclining."

Raven laughed hard this time. "No, the sofa's good. I'll do the sofa."

He strolled over there and took a seat, draped his arms across the back of the sofa, one leg crossed over the other. Relaxed, cool, calm.

"Coffee?"

He shook his head. "Nah, I'm good."

I shrugged. Cup of tea for me, I thought. If only to give me something to do, because suddenly I was nervous. Me? No, no, sure that wasn't me, not me at all. I slammed on the kettle, found a mug and a tea bag (awful yokes this brand) and poured the water once it boiled into the mug. After a splash of milk I was done and yet my head was still in a shed, or some feckin' place I couldn't find it.

I sat beside Raven on the sofa and turned to him, a determined phrasing of cowgirl happy, with a good country rhythm with it, making a determined loop through my mind.

"When do you head out?" came out of my mouth. Sip of tea, stop the gob, I thought and held the cup to my lips.

"That's what I wanted to talk to you about."

"Talk?" I said. That's what he wanted.

He rested a hand on my arm and began to rub it. I looked down at the hand, puzzled. Was this some kind of innuendo?

"I'm happy to talk," I said. Was that a good response? Or should it be "happy talk". I had no clue.

Raven leaned closer. I leaned closer, my eyes on his. His said nothing and everything. What was I to do with that? I leaned even closer, my lips inches from his. Finn's face flashed through mine. Feck off, I told it and kissed Raven. A light kiss. A kiss that said things could get better. There was more. Raven rubbed my arm, kissed me back. Pulled away a moment later and leaned his forehead on mine.

"You're a lovely woman, Maura from Ireland. A woman of power."

I pulled away, confusion drowning out the cowgirl happy beat, beating hard. "What do you mean by that?"

"Just that," he said.

His dark eyes, so difficult to read sometimes, were now filled with sincerity and maybe a little amusement. I stiffened when I saw it. Amusement was definitely not among my feelings at this moment.

I crossed my arms. "What is it you want, Raven?"

He squeezed my arm. "Nothing for myself. Just your company. And the wit that goes along with it."

My expression eased, my arms uncrossed and I gave him an inquisitive look. He leaned forward, kissed me on the mouth and brushed the hair away from my face. A caress?

"You have my company," I said, trying to keep my voice even. "You have my wit, well as much of it that's around, because for some reason half of it seems to have flown away."

Raven chuckled. "There you go. So, so clever."

I shrugged. "No, not really."

"Flown away. I like that."

Another puzzled frown came to my face. Sure, those puzzlement muscles were well exercised now. Raven still had his hand on my arm and I looked at it now. Seeing my glance he rubbed it a bit again and let his hand drop.

"Balor's home," he said finally. "Do you know it?"

I narrowed my eyes. Was this it? The reason for wanting my company and my so-called wit? "No."

"But you knew they were looking at it."

I didn't need him to explain who "they" were. "I knew it was one place they were interested in. But that was a while ago."

He nodded. "They didn't say what their interest is in Balor. I mean I know he's Irish, and has a headquarters there in Ireland, so it makes me wonder that maybe he's committed some illegal practices there. And that you and the others were trying to get proof to put him out of commission, or behind bars. Or something that might stop him from continuing."

"Yeah, you could conclude that," I said.

Part of me wanted to trust him. The "cowgirl happy" part, but that "cowgirl happy" also wanted nothing to do with anything connected to Balor. And the part that might still be Maura, goddess of war, ally of the Tuatha de Danann knew I shouldn't trust him. So either way, it was the "say nothings" that held the day. They joined from both sides of the aisle and made me sigh.

"Balor is an evil man," said Raven.

"He is," I said. Sure, that was safe enough.

"That's why I think you and I should work together on this. We both want the same thing. Put Balor out of action."

"Haven't you got enough from the documents Smithy photographed?"

Raven shrugged. "Yes, probably. But the more we have, the better. Once they lawyer up, his kind get away with just about anything. There might be more inside the house."

I nodded slowly. I could understand his interest. Of course I could.

"What do you want from me?"

"Come with me. Tonight. I know they won't trust me enough to be involved. But maybe if we went earlier, had a look around. At least see if it's possible anything is hidden there."

"What about Skye and Sherman?"

Raven grinned. "Sherman? He's working on getting into the security system. He'll be along later. As for Skye, this doesn't really suit her, not really."

"NOT REALLY, NO" I said, slowly. I could understand. Regal, stately, Skye. She certainly didn't say, "sneaky job at night". I sighed. "Right, so. Fine. I'll help you."

He leaned over and kissed me again. Brief, without passion, "thank you" written all over it. I sighed again. Tried to drag those wits of mine from all the scattered places they were hiding. Including the shed. Feck me, what was I like?

IT WAS STILL WARM, the early evening air still carrying the heat from the sun. I had on a long sleeved black T-shirt, that I'd managed to find at a local Walmart a few days before and it felt too hot. Or maybe it was me. We stepped out of Raven's SUV and shut the doors. We were near the automatic gate that was an entrance to a landscaped drive that led up to the house. Raven approached the gate, gave it a little shake and then, noticing the CCTV camera overlooking the entrance, walked away back to the SUV where I stood, out of its range.

"You wait here," he said. "I'm just going to have a look around. See if I can climb a wall or a hedge."

I shrugged. Fine, if he wanted to try and find a way to climb the impossible,so be it. I could see that the walls stretched down both sides and presumably along the area around the corner from where we parked. I had my own ideas. Why, I don't know. But curiosity was strong.

I watched Raven disappear around the corner, his step jaunty, not a care in the world. When he'd gone, I stepped away from the car and took flight, changing in an instant. I wasn't about to let walls and height keep me out.

I landed on a balcony terrace and shifted back again. Something I deemed safe enough from random CCTV cameras. I shook myself out, rolled up the arms of my T-shirt and was about to try the sliding door to the balcony when I heard a ruffling behind me. I turned and there was Raven, standing beside me. He grinned and gave a sharp laugh when he saw me and shook his head.

My mouth opened and shut. Opened again but before I could utter a word his finger pressed against my mouth.

"Later," he said.

I was about to argue, but then held back, because he was right. We didn't have the time for arguments, discussions or any of the million and one items that crowded my mind. The "who-the-feck-what-why-how" of this man. Raven. Of course. No irony there. I snorted. Feckin' raven all right. And I'm feckin' raven mad to think I hadn't known. Hadn't suspected, forget about hadn't been told.

My wits were all scattered to the wind again, so it took a force of will from who knows where that had me turn and start to peer into the window. It was a bedroom. Large, spacious and with the outrageous gaudy roundness to the bed and the mirror on the ceiling above it, I didn't need two guesses to know whose it was. Even one guess would be too much, because who wanted to spare any thoughts imagining Balor in that bed doing anything?

The room was tidy, full of streamlined modern furniture making statements all over the place, but suggesting nothing other than itself and sparing no room for storage, or files or anything of that nature.

Raven turned to me. "You take the upstairs windows. I'll look downstairs. We'll meet back at the car."

I nodded. "Right, fine."

At this point what I did seemed immaterial. Just getting beyond it and back to the car might be the biggest challenge for me. I paused a moment, uncertain if I wanted to shift into my crow form in front of him, until I got angry with myself and just huffed off in a flap of wings. His soft laughter followed me for a moment.

Later, back at the SUV, I toed the ground while I waited for him. I hadn't seen anything that would suggest a potential place for either slingshot and spear or files. It had been only bedrooms and a few frosted windows I presumed meant bathrooms. It was down to Raven to see if there was any possible chance that what we were searching for was here.

I tried not to think about all the implications of Raven. Raven with a first letter capitalised and small case raven. Or his knowledge of me, now. All that on top of the "who-the-feck-what-why-how". Where didn't matter. That was something.

"Hey," came a voice.

Startled, I looked up and Raven was standing beside me. Not a whoosh of a wing. Just there he was. I thought of the times people had complained when I'd done that. Paid back now in spades.

"Any luck?" I managed.

Raven nodded thoughtfully. "I think. Maybe. There's a room that looks to be a study and off of it is another room, I think. At least it seems so from the outside layout of the house and the door going into that section from the room. A storage area that maybe contains a safe, or something like that. The study is possible too. In any case it's worth taking a closer look."

I nodded. I had no words.

"You avoided the CCTV cameras, yeah?" asked Raven.

I gave him a "feck off" look.

He raised his hands and grinned. "Sorry, sorry. Just checking. I meant to say it before we split up."

I nodded and got in the SUV, Raven following suit.

"When do you meet the others?" I asked.

"About a half hour."

"You don't have much time. Where are you meeting them?"

That grin came out again. "Here."

"Here?" I thought and then knew what had to be. "Fine, so. I'll wait with you. But then you knew that, didn't you."

"Let's say I hoped."

I nodded and fought the urge to put a hand over his mouth so I couldn't see that feckin' grin.

24

MAURA

When the others did come, all piled into a hire car and Luke driving, I was still attempting to retrieve the head from the shed and gather all the bits of myself into a semblance of a functioning self. That self tried its best, "you know yourself" could never be applied because, the "know" and "self" were still wide apart. And yet. But still. I kept coming back to the raven. The Raven raven. Who he was. All this going around in my head while we sat there in silence. Didn't he have any questions, the fecker? Or was it all worked out and waiting for me to catch up, like some slow git not quite able to figure out the equation thrown out by a teacher? Who knew? What I knew was that Raven was a raven. A shifter. A shifter like me. And that thought hit me, just as the others parked behind us and got out of their car.

By the time they reached us and I'd got out of the SUV there was a smile on my face. I could even manage a grin as I glanced at the five of them, standing there, determined. Yeah, five. Somehow Sherman had found his way into the SUV.

And there was Luke with the warrior expression, Smithy solid and especially determined, almost matching Saoirse, and then Finn. I would label Finn's expression fierce. Warrior fierce, but also something else. It was the eyes that gave it the "something else", and they stopped me for a minute, made my smile slip, until I felt Raven's hand at my back. Raven, who was like me. The same. Corvids with purpose. Corvids with power. Sure, hadn't he called me a woman with power?

"You're here, too?" said Luke, his manner cool.

I looked down at my body, pinched myself in matching cool while still trying to find that shed that held my head. "I am."

"I have to say I didn't expect it," said Luke.

"But I'm sure you're glad she is," said Raven, a grin on his face. Feck off with the grinning, I thought.

It seemed to help, though, defuse the situation to some degree. Saoirse gave me a genuine smile and I nodded back. Feck the others.

"We've had a look and narrowed down possibilities to a room at the back," I said. "It seems to also have another room off of it that we think might be a storage space of some sort." I shrugged. "It has potential, in any case."

"Had a look around, did you?" Luke said, studying me, his eyes narrowed.

I gave another shrug. Let him make of it what he wanted. "Just through the windows."

"Oh that's brilliant, Maura," Saoirse said. "Sure, you've saved us bags of time."

After glancing at Saoirse with a frown, Luke crossed his arms. "Did you take care for the CCTV cameras?"

I tried not to bristle but my tone was sharp. "Of course."

"Do you want Sherman to disable them?" asked Raven.

Luke looked at Sherman, obviously weighing the benefits of that option.

"You could do that?" his tone was sceptical.

Sherman nodded.

"You couldn't hack it?" I asked. It hadn't occurred to me that was a problem for Luke, superhero. I smirked at him. I had no choice, the emotion rushed in and plastered itself all over my face.

"Feck off, Maura," he said calmly. "No, I couldn't. I'm not a tech whizz."

"You mean, a tech whizz like I am?" The smirk was still there, just wouldn't leave.

Was it pride, glee and more of that smirky need to show him up that drove me remind him that I could hack, even though I knew Sherman had done the job? "You know yourself what it's like" came to my mind, but then at this moment "self" was still out there somewhere looking for that shed. Or something. Still, that part of me did take pleasure in his grunt of assent and the laptop he handed me eventually. I watched Sherman place his laptop on the bonnet of the SUV and go to work.

It took a bit of time, but eventually he had a convincing loop going through all the security cameras so that anyone watching them would see nothing unusual. He also had a look at the alarm system and temporarily disabled it. When he'd finished I looked over at Luke and the smirk slid right back on my face. Luke raised a brow and gave a grudging nod of approval.

"Well, that will make things simpler," said Smithy.

Smithy had watched the whole exchange in interested silence, glancing back and forth between me, Luke and Sherman. I looked over at Finn. There was a hint of laughter in his eyes. Sure, he'd appreciate a bit of piss taking when it came to Luke. And that I'd bested him, or at least showed him up as less than perfect. I grinned at Finn, and he gave me a small smile. That smile eased something inside me for a moment, made me want to secretly pinch his arm, nudge him. Acknowledge the shared joke? Something. I pushed the thought aside, putting it down to those scattered wits and lost head.

"Right, so," said Luke. "Will we focus on that back room first? See what we can find. If nothing's there, we'll check the rest of the house."

There was no question it was the best approach so we all nodded. Luke took the lead up to the front door, the rest of us following. Once at the door he stepped aside for Smithy to perform his own wonders with the lock. It didn't take him long, and with the alarm disabled we all walked into the house after him as if we were invited.

"We should be quick," I said. "You don't want to give them time to realise that the alarm is off and the cameras are on a loop."

The others nodded. "Where to?" asked Luke, looking at me.

I gestured in the direction of the study and started to make my way towards it, moving through the spacious entrance area heading to a small hall that took us to the back of the house. Raven was right behind me, taking in the surroundings. The modern look that had been upstairs was equally matched down here, statement furniture and artwork dotting the floor space and the walls. Some of it was tasteful, at least to me, and some of it not, though they all had one thing in common. Large. I could nearly feel Luke's rolling eyes, behind me. I chuckled.

"Do I detect some overcompensation?" said Finn, mirroring my thoughts. It prompted me to turn and catch his glance. We exchanged brief amused looks, until his fell and he looked away. I sighed softly.

We entered the room, me taking the lead and the others following close behind. Once inside, Luke assigned us different areas to search, then took Smithy with him to pick the lock to the door in question. I began to search my assigned area of the spacious room. There were so many big statements scattered around, you couldn't help but wonder. Wonder a host of things. In fact you could have a party with all the wondering you could do with this room. I snorted and sought out Finn again, sure he'd feel the same. He was on the same side of the room, studying one particularly heinous large piece of art that stood against the wall. Made of bronze with a phallic shape, it had a barely visible narrow plinth underneath so that it appeared to be sitting on the floor. Finn bent down to examine it closer.

"It's a thumb," he said in a low voice, straightening.

"A thumb?" I said. "Why?"

Finn shrugged. "Feck me if I know the why of any of this art."

"But a thumb?"

I studied the piece again. I could see horizontal lines etched in what had seemed random places. I drew closer and could see the outline of a nail bed.

"Tom Thumb?" I said. "Thumbs up?"

"Thumb in your eye?" said Finn, humour clear in his voice.

I laughed. "Thumb in your eye? What is that?"

He shrugged. I started to laugh and couldn't stop. Feck if I knew why it was suddenly the funniest thing I'd ever heard.

Saoirse came over. "What's so funny?"

I pointed at the thumb, but was laughing so hard I couldn't say a word.

"It's a thumb," said Finn.

Saoirse cocked her head. "Really? Why?"

I laughed harder.

"Thumb's the word," said Finn. He held a straight face for a moment, but Saoirse's snort, started him off and the three of us were laughing.

"What?" said Raven, moving toward us, Sherman following.

They'd been on the other side, checking a few drawers of two small chests that stood there. The desk was modern glass without a trace of a computer, let alone drawers.

I pointed at the source of humour. "Thumb."

He looked at it. "Fucking awful. You call that art?"

Sherman laughed. "It sucks."

"I call it a thumb," said Finn. He started to laugh again.

"Or not," I said, gasping.

Raven shook his head. "You lot are crazy."

"Nah," said Saoirse. "Just all thumbs."

The three of us pealed out more laughter.

From the other room I heard Smithy give a cry. "Feck! Luke, come here."

Our laughter stopped and I stared at the open doorway. Luke moved in front of it, blocking my view, but not before I saw him pocket a piece of paper. Curious, I moved forward, the others already ahead of me. I felt strangely nervous. Was this it then? Had they found the spear and slingshot? I glanced at Finn and he caught my look, raised his brows. I would know soon enough.

Once inside, we gathered around a long rectangular locked glass case. A cloth had covered it, but it was pulled up and draped on top. Inside the case, laid out on velvet, was a spearhead and a slingshot, along with a few other items. But those two held my attention.

I hadn't taken much notice of the spear and the slingshot when they'd been in Luke's possession so long ago. They were tools of war and that was it. Tools that would be noted for quality of materials, balance and other subtleties that would make it a good tool or a bad tool. The spearhead looked dull, darkened with age, the shaft missing. The leather of the slingshot was stiff, the oil long gone. Old tools of war. But now, knowing that these tools represented Luke's battle with his grandfather, the means by which he thought he'd killed him, and also the last great battle across the water, made them seem more and filled me with unease.

And it wasn't just the battle they represented that made me pause. It was the thought that the search was over. This was it.

The next steps would be entirely different. The next steps were focused on war. Battle. My blood should have sung at that knowledge. My body should be humming with the prospect.

Raven moved alongside Luke, staring at him curiously. "Is this old?"

Luke nodded. "You could say that," he said drily.

"Ancient," said Raven, looking down at the objects. It was a statement, not a question.

"Yes," said Luke.

"Irish," said Raven.

"Irish," said Luke.

Raven looked back at Luke again. "Yours, then?"

Luke gave him a steady look. "Mine."

Raven nodded and I looked from him and to Luke. Was I reading too much into that exchange?

"We need to get a move on," said Luke. "The case is locked. Smithy, can you pick the lock?"

Smithy moved forward, tools in hand, but Luke held an arm out to stop him. "Wait, not so fast. It seems too easy."

"Too easy?" said Smithy. "We've been searching for ages, in multiple places and you're calling that easy?"

Luke shrugged. "I don't know. It's just a feeling. We'll take it slowly. Smithy, you pick the lock, but let me open it. The rest of you stand back."

"You think it's booby trapped?" asked Raven.

"I don't know," said Luke. "It's as I said. I have a feeling and this seems too easy."

Raven nodded, appeared to accept his words. I looked at the others, discomfort and unease plain on their faces. Silently, we all stepped back while Smithy got to work on the lock. It only took a minute or two before we heard the click of the lock releasing. Luke gestured to Smithy to step back and he did, joining us about a metre behind Luke, watching him. Carefully, Luke eased the lid open and after a moment I heard a low hiss. Luke shut the case quickly, and the case filled with a gas that obscured the contents.

"What the feck kind of gas is that?" I asked in horror.

"My guess is a very bad kind," muttered Finn.

Smithy glanced around the room and pointed to a window. "Take the case to the window and we can open the window and let the gas out there."

"Or we can take the case out of here," said Raven. "It shouldn't be too difficult with all of us to help."

"We'll do that," said Luke. "Just to be safe. Then we'll bring it back in here. I want him to think all is well until he sees that empty case."

"Makes sense," said Raven.

Without wasting any more time, Luke, Finn, Raven and Smithy lifted the case and carried it from the house, shouldering it like a coffin. Not a portent, I told myself. Once the case was placed on the ground, Luke lifted the lid and stepped away to join the rest of us who instinctively had pulled our shirts up over our noses.

When it appeared the gas had dispelled, Luke pulled out a pair of thick leather gloves from his pocket, slipped them on and lifted out first the spear and then the slingshot from the case. He laughed, held them up in triumph. "Gotcha, you fecker."

25

SMITHY

It was coming up for midnight. They were all crowded into Luke's motel room, Raven included. Skye and Sherman would be here soon, too, according to Raven. Smithy wished they could just get it over and done with so they could be on their way, back to Ireland. He could feel Luke's jumpy energy from where he sat at that small table, in front of Smithy. The spearhead and slingshot lay on the bed, wrapped in a cloth, the centre of everyone's attention while they waited for Sherman who'd gone to fetch Skye.

Smithy leaned back against the wall, trying to relax but conscious of Saoirse beside him. He could feel the comfort of her presence even now, with the distance he'd tried to put between them. A distance that was now a joke, because since the song, since the gig, he couldn't suppress the desire he felt or the compulsion to touch her, be with her, even though he made himself walk the other way, talk to someone else, or be in a different room. The need to refuse all promises to her, even by a gesture or a look, was still there, but it warred deeply with all the other opposing desires. And now that they had the spearhead and slingshot there were no more distractions. Back home. And though he knew it meant the next stage would begin, the preparation for battle, he still wanted to go. Find Airmed, see if she could help him so he could do his part in full. Make the swords, the spearheads and anything else he might be called upon to do.

His fingers tingled with the thought of it. He knew it was the combination of hope and all that might be possible if that hope became real that was causing it. He flexed his fingers, feeling for the first time a real desire to hold metal. To work it, to shape it. He glanced at Saoirse, suddenly alarmed at what he was feeling. She was staring at him, her eyes quizzical, cautious. Her hand moved towards him, her finger touching his and he felt the hum of that touch, a current now complete, full circle, looping through him and back towards her. He folded his hand around hers, their palms pressing against one another and a strong rush of desire washed over him with such force it caught his breath. Saoirse's face was flushed, her mouth forming a small "o" and Smithy knew that at this moment he wanted more than his hand pressed against hers.

A knock sounded on the door. Finn moved to open it and Smithy managed to drag his attention away from Saoirse to see Skye and Sherman walk in, smiling with delight.

"You were successful?" said Skye.

Luke glared at Raven, who grinned back at him and shrugged. Raven turned to Skye and Sherman. "They were successful." He nodded towards the bed. "They found the items they were looking for."

"But nothing to help our cause?"

Raven shook his head. "Not really. There wasn't a laptop. He must take it with him, or he brings home the one from his headquarters. And no files, at least none that I could see." He looked over at Luke. "Did you see anything in the storage room?"

Luke shook his head. "Nothing like that. Just the items in the glass case."

"What items?" asked Skye, her eyes bright. She glanced at Sherman, who shrugged.

It was the first time Smithy had noticed that Sherman's clothes were surprisingly muted in style and colour, giving him a more sober presence. The T-shirt was dark and on inside out, but not backwards and he wore dark jeans as they were designed to be worn.

Skye moved over to the bed, ran her hand along the cloth wrapped spearhead and slingshot and looked over at Luke. "What items?"

"Sure, Raven could tell you more about that," said Finn, his manner genial, though his eyes betrayed a caution that was mirrored in Luke's eyes.

As if prompted by Finn's words, Maura, who'd been standing apart from all of them over by the far wall, moved towards Raven, her expression closed. Curiosity, maybe, thought Smithy, but there was definitely something off about Maura.

Raven gave Skye a thoughtful look. "Besides the things that belonged to Luke, there were a few other items. I can tell you that they were items belonging to our people. Or at least they appeared to be."

Skye gave him a puzzled look. "What do you mean?" asked Skye, an edge to her tone.

Raven ran a hand through his hair and sighed. "There was a small pot and some arrowheads. The pot had markings that might be Cado. Or Mandan. The arrowheads, well they looked old but..."

"But what?" said Skye, her tone curious.

Raven shook his head. "No. They're fake, I think. Or tourist stuff made to look authentic, old."

"Why do you say that?" asked Luke.

Raven shrugged. "The markings on the pot weren't quite right. The arrowheads, well they didn't look the right shape."

Luke nodded. "I didn't really notice, to be honest." He turned to Smithy. "Did you?"

Smithy shook his head. "I was more concerned with the spearhead and slingshot."

"Did you leave the other items behind?" asked Skye, frowning.

Finn gave a wry grin. "Ah, no. Couldn't resist them. Didn't seem fair to leave those behind for Balor. Or anything he might consider valuable. So I took them. Put them in a bag in the car. They're still there."

Raven looked at him and laughed, shaking his head.

"Will I go get them?" asked Finn.

"Yeah," said Sherman, frowning. "I wouldn't mind a closer look."

Skye gave Sherman a concerned look. "Is everything all right?"

Sherman considered her words. "Backwards, forwards, man. Backwards, forwards."

Raven nodded, seemingly satisfied. "Isn't it always?"

"Do you think we have enough evidence with the documents Smithy took photos of?" asked Skye.

Raven shrugged. "Yeah. I do. But it doesn't hurt to have more. I'll take it to the lawyers as soon as I can."

"Let's hope," said Skye.

"Yeah," said Raven. "Let's hope. We still have much to do, though. Balor's only one man. Only one company."

Maura placed a hand on his shoulder. "But he's very powerful. In a way you don't realise."

Raven looked at her. "He is?"

Maura nodded. "He is." She gave a small laugh. "Or maybe you can imagine." She gave him an intent look and a slow smile spread across his face.

"Are the rest of us missing something?" asked Luke, studying the two of them.

Maura raised her brow, a hint of mischief in her eyes. "Ask Raven."

A knock sounded on the door. Finn. Smithy moved to open it, Luke and the others too focused on the exchange with Raven. Finn walked in, a plastic bag in his hand. Seeing the others, his eyes narrowed.

"What's going on?" he asked, his voice tense. He surveyed the room. His gaze finally resting on Maura.

"We were just asking Raven if he can imagine how powerful Balor is."

Finn gave her a startled look. "Really?" He glanced at Luke, then Smithy and then back to Maura. Maura grinned at him and his expression darkened. "What?"

Raven laughed and all heads turned to him. He pointed to himself. "Corvid born and bred."

Silence filled the room as everyone digested what he'd said.

"He's Raven," said Sherman, finally giving everyone a puzzled look. "Of course he's corvid."

"Raven," said Luke flatly.

Smithy stared at Raven thoughtfully for a moment then pulled out his phone. A few minutes tapping and searching, until he found what he was looking for. He scanned the page and then raised his head.

"Raven, as in the myths of the Tlingit, Tsimshian, Haida and other peoples of Northwest America? Trickster and so much else?"

"That's me," said Raven, still smiling.

Luke, Smithy and Finn exchanged glances and in unison turned to Maura.

"Did you know this?" asked Luke.

Maura's face was pale. Her eyes were a storm of emotions,

anger, frustration and a little bit of joy that struck Smithy as odd. "The corvid part."

"It's the 'so much else' that interests me," said Luke. "You're a god?"

Sherman laughed. "Our people are different. He's Raven. Creator, trickster, bringer of light to the people. He is who he is."

"I'm who I am."

"And who are you?" asked Finn, looking at Sherman.

"I'm Sherman."

"Heyoka," said Maura. "That's who he is. A person who tells and shows truths." She looked at Skye. "Am I right? Isn't that what you said?"

Skye gave her a kind smile. "Something like that. He helps expose falsehoods and assists in healing ailing hearts and minds."

"And you are....?" asked Luke.

"Skye."

"Sky Woman," said Maura. "You told me that once. Sky Woman. Haudensaunee. You said you were Haudensaunee. But what does being Sky Woman mean?"

"She's first woman" said Sherman. "The creator of Turtle Island."

"Like Kayla," said Luke softly.

"Kayla?" said Skye, her eyes alight.

"*An Cailleach*. That's her name in our language. She's part of the land, she is the land, the mountains, trees, sky, water. All of it."

Skye nodded. "Yes, maybe."

"You're here for the Osage then," said Smithy.

"No," said Luke moving forward towards Raven. He placed his hand on Raven's shoulder. "They're all here for a much bigger purpose. To save this land, because the land is part of the people."

Smithy regarded Luke, seeing for the first time what Luke had become. Perhaps it had been in him all along, but it was recently with Kayla that who he fully was had come to light. Lugh the shining one, the hero warrior, leader and now wed to the land in the way it had been in the ancient past.

"The land and The People are one," said Sherman, his tone serious. "One cannot live without the other."

And Smithy knew. Sherman's pronouncement was truth in a manner that made the word "people" larger than a general group of humans.

"We are all related," said Skye.

"So we are," said Finn carefully. "So we are." He looked at Maura, a hint of a smile on his face. "And you knew none of this?"

She shook her head, her arms crossed defensively. "No. But it doesn't change anything."

"It changes everything," said Luke. "Now that we know."

"Know?" asked Raven.

"That we can count on you to help."

"And who are we helping?" asked Raven. "A group who were anxious to retrieve an ancient spearhead and a slingshot?" He gave Maura a pointed look, an amused expression on his face. "A group with a corvid among them?"

Luke smiled. "A group who isn't so very different from you, in some ways. A smith of great power."

"Two smiths," corrected Saoirse.

"Two smiths, one who is also a poet and healer."

"Was," said Saoirse. "Maybe."

Raven laughed. "Don't you know?"

"She is," said Smithy firmly.

"And Finn, here, is a warrior, a man of great charm and erudition."

"He means Finn can charm the leaves off the trees with his words," said Smithy.

"He seems a man of few words now," said Raven.

Finn frowned at him. "My words are gold, so I don't spread them around like dust."

Raven and Sherman both laughed.

"I like him," said Sherman.

"I'm not so sure he likes me, though," said Raven.

"Don't mind him," said Maura. "He's all bark, no bite."

"Oh, I can bite," said Finn.

"No biting now," said Saoirse. "What all these allusions mean is that we are the ancients, the direct children of Anu, our mother."

"Anu. That is your Sky Woman?" asked Sherman.

"Ah, maybe."

"Trying to understand our people with the eyes of your Irish culture won't bring true understanding," said Raven. "So I imagine the reverse is true. It is what it is."

"It is what it is," said Luke.

"And the spearhead and slingshot?" asked Raven.

"Mine. Sacred, especially the spearhead. An ancient treasure of my people and one that I used in battle."

Raven nodded. "And now?"

Luke took a deep breath. "And now we're taking those treasures back to Ireland, across the water to fight another battle."

Raven raised his brow. "A battle with Balor?"

Luke nodded. "Yes."

Raven nodded. "It's as I thought." He looked at Skye and Sherman. "As we thought." Raven pointed to Luke. "Balor's one of you?"

"No," said Luke sharply.

"He's Fomorian," interjected Finn. "Not one of Anu's people."

"Oh," said Raven. "Is that why he feels he can kill the land? He has no connection?"

"Partly," said Finn. "It's complicated, but suffice to say he has no scruples on that front and we intend to stop him. Permanently."

"And you have to stop him in a battle?" asked Raven. "Why not here?"

"I suspect you understand that it isn't that simple in this world," said Luke.

Raven sighed. "Yes. We certainly do. And for that reason we're trying to pursue it through the law. A frustrating and often fruitless process."

"And that's one reason why we're battling him in a place where we can end him for good," said Finn.

"Kill him, you mean," said Raven.

"Fine, so," said Finn. He glanced at Luke. "Kill him."

Raven nodded. "I'm glad we were able to help in some way. After all, you did find those documents for us." Raven turned to Smithy. "Thanks for that."

Smithy shrugged. "Happy that it was some help."

Finn put the plastic bag on the bed. "Now, so. The artefacts. Do you want to have a look?"

Raven went to the bed and pulled out the items one by one. From Smithy's perch against the wall he could see what appeared to be two elongated arrowheads dark with age and a black bowl painted with decorative white jagged lines.

"They're not quite like anything I've seen," said Raven.

"And that's saying a lot," said Sherman, snickering.

Raven gave a snort. Smithy drew closer, always interested in anything metal. He picked up one of the arrowheads suspiciously and realised it wasn't an arrowhead, but a spearhead. He rubbed the metal and black paint flaked off. Underneath the paint he saw a glint of bright metal. Silver. With his nail he scraped off the rest. When most of the paint was removed, he felt the warmth of the metal in his hand. Its familiarity. He folded it in his palm and a surge of emotions rushed through him.

"Feck me," he said. "This is mine. I made this."

"What?" said Luke. "When?"

"A long time ago," said Smithy.

"Oh, that narrows it down," said Saoirse.

He gave her a weak laugh. "After the battles, after the Milesians. After we left across the water. I made it for a man who followed the old ways. Our ways. He came to me, half knowing what I was and asked for these spearheads to help keep his family safe from a new set of invaders."

"New invaders?" asked Saoirse.

"The Normans," said Smithy with a snort. "Or that's what they're labelled now."

"How the feck did Balor end up with them?" asked Luke.

Smithy shook his head. "I haven't a clue. The last time I saw them was the twelfth century." He picked up the bowl. Studied it carefully, then ran his nail across a small patch underneath. Again, paint scraped away, revealing a glint of metal. His metal. He scratched a bit more, instinctively, until a larger patch was revealed. He polished it a bit with his sleeve, to give him time to process what he was seeing, feeling.

He looked up over at Saoirse, his eyes wide. She came towards him, her eyes questioning.

"What?" she said.

"This bowl. It's one I made."

She nodded, smiling. "You remember that, too."

He nodded, understanding why she was encouraging. He was remembering, though she might think that it was another event in this world that he was remembering.

"It's more than you think, Saoirse," Smithy said. "I made this bowl for you."

"Me?" she said, eyes wide.

"For your medicinal herbs. To blend them."

She took the pot from his hand, her eyes narrowed. She studied it slowly, unblinking and looked up at him. "Feck."

26

MAURA

"I don't know," I told Raven looking up at him from my perch on my room sofa. "I haven't a clue."

I took another sip of whiskey, still trying to process what had happened a mere few hours ago. Too many revelations for me, thank you very much. That meeting had raised more questions than posing any kind of solutions or closure. And I didn't want to know. I was more ostrich than crow at this point, looking for the nearest sand dune to bury my head, forget the shed. So, when Luke shut down the meeting after Smithy dropped that bit of "can you believe it" *Ripley Believe it or Not* moment, I was more than happy to make my exit. Raven, however, was far from happy. There was enough connection to him and his people in this present mystery of bowl and spearheads to make him pushy to know every detail and speculation. But Luke had decided no, this wasn't going to be discussed in front of people he considered strangers. Well, not quite people. Or maybe.

I looked up at Raven. He'd cornered me after Luke had dispersed us and suggested we two go back to my room. I agreed, for more reasons than even I could admit to myself. Not quite "twa corbies" hanging out. And it was all the "not quite" parts that were joining all the rest of the questions in my head.

It didn't stop Raven from asking for answers to whats and whys I didn't know.

"Who are you, Maura?" asked Raven.

A question I could answer. I took a drink from my whiskey. Sip, sip, pause, pause. I shrugged. "You know," I said. "I'm like you."

Raven laughed. "You're not like me."

I frowned and then formed a grin on my face. "I am. The Irish crow to your native raven."

He slowly shook his head back and forth. "Didn't I tell all of you earlier that you can't compare us?"

I sighed. Where would I go from here? "Fine, so. Whatever I am, I still can't explain the bowl and spearheads."

Raven nodded. "I accept that."

"Ah, now," I said, my tone sarcastic. "That's good of you."

He sighed. "I'm not being difficult. I just want to understand as much of what's going on as I can. For my people."

I nodded. Fair enough. "There's not much more to know, not really. Balor's their enemy and they want to get rid of him."

He raised a brow. "Their enemy? Not yours?"

I shrugged. "I left all that behind. I'm here now. Here is where I want to be."

"You can't run from who you are."

"I'm not," I said, trying to keep the defensiveness out of my tone. "I came here, I like it here."

Raven gave a wry smile. "What do you like here so much? The weather?"

I gave a laugh. "Sure, the weather's grand."

"Grand? Maybe in a large way. Lots of heat in summer. And then there's the snow in winter. You'd like that too."

"Snow?" I said, delighted. "I can make a snowman?"

Raven laughed and shook his head. "Oh, Maura."

"What?"

"Who is Balor?"

The question took me by surprise, even though I knew it was Raven here before me. "Balor is Balor."

"An enemy of your people."

I frowned. "Not my people."

He gave me a puzzled look. "Who are your people, then?"

I gave him a tight lipped smile. "Me. My lads."

"Your lads?"

"Corvids. Like you."

He shook his head. "Not like me."

I sighed. He was playing that game again. Will he ever give it a rest? He knew it wasn't true. We were alike. So alike.

"But Balor is from your world."

It was a statement and not a question. How to explain it to him? Did I want to explain it to him? Would he understand me, then? Understand what I was trying to explain?

"Balor isn't one of Anu's people."

Raven nodded. "I gathered that. But he's from your world, isn't he."

I nodded. "A powerful enemy we killed a long long time ago."

Raven gave me a startled look. "Killed?"

"Yes."

Raven studied me for a few moments. "He had that kind of power, then."

I considered his words. "I'm not sure if it's his power that brought him back to life. I think it might be that he took advantage of the power of something else. A well that can bring the dead to life again."

"And that well is in your world?"

I nodded and bit my lip. "He's still dangerous, though. In this world, especially."

Raven's eyes darkened. "I can see that. And is the goal to capture him and kill him with the spear and slingshot? Do they have some power to ensure he remains dead?"

"No, at least I don't think they do." I looked away. "Raven, I don't know. I told you, I'm not involved anymore."

Raven sat down beside me and placed his hand over mine. "Maura, you're involved, whether you want to be or not. It's the way it is. Instead of avoiding it, take hold of it and be who you are."

"Why did you ask me who I am if you already knew?"

Raven chuckled, shaking his head. "Because it's what I am."

I looked at the dimples, the dark hair that was falling over his forehead into his dark eyes and saw and felt all the charm and magnetism that was Raven. It drew out my smile that became a grin.

"If you know me so much, then you can see how we are alike. That the two of us could be good together."

I believed those words, desperately. I wasn't an eejit. I knew that his trickster self could just as easily trick me out of my sense, even if he wasn't trying, but there you are. I could take joy from the conflict of fighting that trick. We'd have fun, sure we would.

"I am a destroyer, creator, trickster, Maura. In this world. This is where I belong, where I'm needed. You are who you are in your world, where you're needed."

"A few may need me, but I'm not wanted. I'm a destroyer. A maker of conflict, not unlike you so much."

I'd learned from my own conflicts and how people use others, especially Daghda. Maybe I was playing with fire here. But I wanted it. Wanted this cowgirl life. I would hold on to it with a tight fist and a big grin.

"No, Maura, you think you want this, but you don't, because it isn't you."

"You're telling me I should leave? Go back, fight this battle that's coming?"

"You have to, Maura. For your people and for mine. We need to ensure that Balor no longer is a threat. That his life is ended. And they need you to do that."

"Because I'm Morrigan," I said flatly.

He stared a moment. "Morrigan."

"War," I said. "The goddess of war."

He nodded slowly, his eyes fixed on me. "Because you're Morrigan. And you are wanted."

I shook my head, banged my cowgirl boots together. He placed his hand under my chin and lifted it. Slowly he leaned down and kissed my lips. It was deep, sensual and full of promise. The promise, though wasn't a trick. It was a promise that said all would be well. And it was something else, I think. A goodbye.

27

SAOIRSE

Saoirse sat on the bed in her motel room, staring at the bowl she held. She'd not even asked Raven, Luke, or anyone else if she could have the bowl, why would she? Sure, it was hers, and she wanted it. She'd held this bowl, used this bowl in that time before. That "before time" when she'd been different – a different personality, even a different name to this time. and had fully known herself. This bowl had been part of that self and Saoirse wanted that self now, wanted all of it. She rubbed it slowly, trying to feel what it had been to her, but the black paint was dark, dead, and the white jagged lines painted on it led it into another self that had nothing to do with her.

She needed this bowl. She knew that in ways she didn't understand. And she had to do something to keep her mind off Anu. Anu who still couldn't be contacted. Who was back in Ireland in a state Saoirse could only imagine. Her mind reached out for Anu, for home and all that it meant to her, but she met only darkness. But the bowl was tangible. It was a bowl she used for healing. Healing was what was needed now. Healing for Anu, for Smithy and for Kayla. And all that went with healing them.

On impulse she rose from the bed and went to the bathroom

and her toiletry bag. Inside, she dug out her nail clippers, flipped out the small metal nail file and took it back with her to the bed. Picking up the bowl again, she slowly began to scrape off the paint.

It was tedious task that required more delicacy than a scratch card, though the paint had the same quality. She just hoped that her reward was more than three slot machines lined up or bunch of cherries. This was her own jackpot, private and necessary. She scraped away and, slowly, Smithy's delicate and intricate craftsmanship was revealed, the twirling, interlocking etched patterns that seemed beyond any human possibility but were part of his magic. The sight of the design made her scrape faster, a strong desire to reveal all its beauty, as soon as possible.

It took about an hour, and it was an hour she filled by humming and singing the tunes that came to her. They weren't tunes she usually played and there was nothing like them in her playlist, or anyone's playlist she could name. And no, she'd not heard them at sessions. These were tunes that came from some-where else – that felt they should be here, now, for this moment to be part of the revelation. The tunes grew inside her, coming out as more than a hum, greater than any didly dee foot tapping jig or reel or polka, bigger than an air, growing large. They were tunes that came out in full blast, in her mind and then through her mouth, mouth music at its most grand.

When the bowl was clean of all its paint and dubious mark-ings, Saoirse took it in both hands and cupped it, staring at the inside. Black flecks of paint still clung to there – Saoirse had found it more difficult to scrape at the awkward angle the inside required – but the silver glinted dully in the light from the window. She rubbed the side with one hand, her own genie lamp, and tried to unleash the power that she instinctively knew it held for her.

The tunes still soared within her, but she was no longer

humming them aloud. And maybe it was because she no longer hummed the tunes and that now they were contained inside, they grew ever louder and swirled within her, twining with every part of her. This bowl that had held her healing herbs was reaching out; the metal, so magical in its etched designs, in its fashioning, was connecting with her. It was as if Smithy's creation, so beautifully and lovingly produced, his magic, his power was reaching out to her. She opened herself up to all of it, let it pour inside her. And the music embraced it. She embraced it.

Smithy, she thought. Goibhniu. She could nearly feel him here now, through this bowl. The man who had created it. His warm touch, his loving attention, as he worked the metal, the etchings he inscribed. This man. It all poured into her and the thoughts and emotions that blended with hers and settled into place. This healing bowl was hers. Bríd's. And Saoirse's. Both of them.

"Smithy," she called softly. "Goibhniu."

Saoirse tapped on Smithy and Finn's room. A few moments later Finn opened the door. His eyes were tired and bloodshot and his hair was all over the place, but he assembled a smile on his face and his eyes grew softer.

"Ah, Saoirse, how's things?" He looked down at the bowl in her hands. His mouth quirked. "You want some more? I'm afraid Oliver Twist ate the last of it."

Saoirse laughed. Ah, Finn. "No, I've had enough, thanks. It's Smithy I'm after. Is he here?"

Finn shook his head. "He's gone off for a walk, I think." He gestured down to the bowl. "I see you've taken a stab at restoration there. Did you find out anything from the bowl?"

Saoirse looked down at the bowl. "It's mine, all right. And Smithy's work." She held it up for him.

"Oh, I can see that. I've known only one person who can create something that beautiful," he said thoughtfully. "And now it's restored to you."

"Yes, it's restored to me." And restored me, she thought silently.

"How do you think it came to be covered in that feckin' awful paint and designs?"

She bit her lip, considering. "Balor obviously came across it somewhere, maybe some dig, and thought it best to disguise it."

"Ah, yeah. That's probably what happened," said Finn. He looked at her, a wry smile on his face. "You could text him, if it's important."

"What?"

"Smithy. You could text him."

"Oh, yeah. Of course. I will, so."

Text. How funny that it hadn't occurred to her. Or not funny. Or not unusual, because Bríd was so much a part of her right now, she hardly knew where she was. Phone. She pulled out her phone, giving Finn a wave before he shut the door, and then she ambled down the corridor back to her room.

She typed out a quick message and sent it. Waiting at her door to hear the familiar signal of a returned message. She stood in the corridor waiting, hardly breathing. It took a few minutes but the ping came and her breath released. Hastily she opened the text and the flutter came a moment later. A flutter that mixed hope with desire and all the emotions she'd held down for too long now. A flutter that said Smithy was coming.

When he arrived and she let him in, she hardly knew what to do with herself. Open the door, allow him to enter, offer a drink – the words came to her head and she tried to act on them, ah but she did, but somehow the words got lost, the gestures

swallowed into a tidal wave of emotion. So she stood at the doorway, her eyes wide, staring as she took him in. Smithy. Goibhniu.

Lines of tension were etched on his face and he held her
gaze. Searched her wide eyes as if he was looking for a clue, or
an answer to the question that hung over them as it had for so
long. The question was in parts and had many threads but they
all fitted into the bigger whole that asked who they were.

"Goibhniu," Saoirse said softly.

Smithy frowned at her, cocked his head. She had no words,
but she did manage to hold out the bowl that was still in her
hands because she'd been unable to release its comfort, its
knowledge. The fear of losing what she'd so recently gained was
too great. But to Smithy, for Smithy, she would hold out the
bowl.

He took it from her gently, studied it and looked up at her.
"Is this the bowl from the glass case?" he asked softly.

She nodded. It was all she could manage.

He traced his finger over the design, a slow smile emerging
on his face. He looked up at her.

"I remember working this," he said. "In my workshop. It was
a surprise for you."

"And it was the most wonderful surprise anyone ever gave
me," Saoirse said.

He looked up at her, stunned. "You remember?"

"And you remember." There was wonder and hope in her
voice.

Smithy nodded slowly, his face puzzled. "I remember this
bowl. I—I remember making it, giving it to you, the joy on your
face." He bit his lip. "And the love," he said softly.

"Given in love, received in love," said Saoirse. She placed a
hand on his arm. "Anything else?"

He looked at her hand, placed his own on top. "I think so. I do. That's why I went out. I needed air just to clear what seemed like fog in my head. But it seems that it was memories, crowding back in." He took a deep breath. "I don't know what it means, sure I don't."

"It means," said Saoirse carefully. "That there's so much possibility out there. For you. For us."

"For us," said Smithy. He took his hand from covering hers and placed it on her cheek. "Let there be an us."

She leaned up to him and kissed him slowly, her mouth covering his, sending him all her possibilities. He took her possibilities in and deepened the kiss, added his own and they twined together, blended, bigger.

"Smithy, there will always be an us," she said when the kiss had ended. "It's who we are."

He gave her a gentle smile. "It's who we are?"

She gave him a nod filled with conviction. He looked at her and took her in his arms, buried his face in her neck and showered light kisses there, moving along towards her jaw and then back to her lips. She burrowed deeper into his embrace, wanting to touch every part of his body with her own. His lips on hers, tasting, sensing, enveloping. The hum began, those tunes that had been so loud before and had sent her feet tapping, now filled her again, only this time it was an ocean of sound, taste and emotion. She opened up to them and poured out their magnitude of their sound into the kiss that was more than a kiss.

Suddenly the "more than a kiss" was "more to be shared" tunes all played out on each other's bodies, clothes gone and only bare skin. His touch for her alone and her touch for him alone. Smithy laid her gently on the bed, stroking her face, her shoulder and kissing the hollow of her neck, all touches sending tunes into the fullest of sounds. Kissing, tasting, his scent so full of the earth, the heat and metal that was of him. Her smith, her

Goibhniu, her god. The tunes played him, played her, set them both on fire, a forge of such power, such creation potential. He entered her and it was then the fire became greater, flamed more, consuming them both. Two were now one. One and only. Only one.

28

LUKE

Luke stared out of the window, the morning sun pouring in, his phone against his ear, listening to the continual ringing. It was like deja feckin' vu, trying to contact her over and over again, even though he knew, deep down, it was pointless. Missing its point. Or he was missing the point? But he wasn't, not really. The point was that he should be there, not here. Feck it all. He would leave, the others could linger, if they wanted. Wait another day. Or they could all feck off into the wild yonder of this country for all he cared. He was leaving now. The flight was booked.

He ended the ringing and scrolled down for another contact.

"Saoirse," he said when the call connected.

"Luke? What's wrong?" she said.

"I'm leaving. The next flight is in a few hours and I'm going to be on it. Will you tell the others?"

"Of course, I will. But why the sudden hurry?"

"Not sudden. I told you I haven't been able to contact Kayla."

"Still?" There was real concern in her voice.

"Still. Something is definitely wrong. I need to go back. Now."

"Of course. Yes. Let me talk to Smithy. We'll come with you."

Despite his worry, Luke registered her words and allowed a chuckle. "Will you take long?"

"Uh, no," she said and then laughed. "Right, fine. He's right here." A muffled exchange took place for a few moments until Saoirse spoke. "No worries. It's set. We'll come with you, providing we can get on the flight."

He was just about to end the call when Saoirse spoke again. "I'm sure Finn will come, too." She paused. "And maybe Maura."

Luke snorted. "Maura? I doubt it. She seems happy to remain here, from what I've observed. That Raven fella has caught her attention."

"Maybe. Maybe not. But I'll ask her just the same. I'll let you know."

"Grand," said Luke.

The call ended. Luke put his phone on the table, forcing himself not to try Kayla again. Or Anu, because it would only increase his anxiety. For a moment he wished he had his ship from the Otherworld. The ship that would speed across any sea and ocean. But that was long ago. A long ago that was gone. Too long that even *fadó fadó fadó* wasn't enough to tell listeners how long. And Mon. His foster brother, Manannan's son. With the ship and Mon's help he would be there in almost an instant. Or at least less time than his flight that involved changing twice. Feckin' awful journey. But Mon wasn't here, his ship wasn't here.

He went to the motel wardrobe, drew out his suitcase and starting stuffing clothes inside. He packed his whistles, still wrapped in their cloth case, inside the pocket of the inner compartment. The mandolin and bouzouki were all ready to go in their cases on the floor next to the wardrobe.

A knock sounded on the door. Luke moved towards it and looked through the peephole, surprised at who was there.

"Finn," he said, opening it.

Finn was ragged, weary and nothing like the Finn he knew, a faint shadow of Ogma, the King's champion, the warrior and the charmer with words.

Finn nodded and entered the room after Luke, who moved back over to the bed and resumed his packing.

"You really are going now?" asked Finn.

Luke nodded. "Saoirse told you, right?"

"Yes. She told me. Said you can't get hold of Kayla?"

"Or Anu," said Luke.

Finn shook his head. "It does sound serious, so. I know Anu would never willingly allow us to worry."

Luke stiffened. "Neither would Kayla."

"No, no, of course not. I didn't mean it like that."

Luke relaxed. "Sorry, sorry. I'm just all over the place. Worry. The need to do something."

"Well, you're leaving, so that's something."

Luke gave a weak smile. "Yes. Feck, if only I could get there sooner. If only I hadn't left, I should say, if we're doing the 'if onlys'."

"Forget the 'if onlys'. It's a bad path to travel, take it from me," said Finn said in a wry tone.

Luke paused, studied Finn. "Yes. I guess you would know something about that. And I wish that part of your experience hadn't been down to me usurping that experience. But, if it's any comfort, it wasn't something you could change with 'if onlys'. And the role I took on led me in a direction that gave rise to many, many 'if onlys'."

Finn laughed, his eyes showing a trace of sadness. "Any 'if onlys' from that time are now officially banished."

"Good. So they should."

"And your present ones should go with them. Exiled, gone. Just focus on going there."

"I will. My flight is booked and I'm just finishing up here

before I head to the airport. Are you coming?"

Finn paused, looked away. "I don't know. I might follow in a day or so. It depends."

"Depends?"

Finn sighed. "On Maura."

Luke felt a surge of compassion. "You should prepare yourself, dude."

Finn looked at him, a trace of humour in his expression. "Dude? Really?"

Luke shrugged. "It just came out. Too much time hanging around Mon."

Finn nodded. "And how is Mon?"

It was Luke's turn to look away. "Fecked if I know. He's not speaking to me."

"No? Why not? You two were inseparable. Closer than brothers."

"Foster brothers. The best combination," said Luke. "And like you said, more than brothers."

"And?"

"And nothing. Crossed wires and complications. That's it. No longer close."

Finn shook his head. "You should fix that, Luke. It's not something you want to lose."

Luke stared down at his overstuffed case. "You're right." He eyed Finn. "I think you might have something to fix, too. Something you don't want to lose."

Finn nodded slowly. "I know. I know."

He turned then, heading towards the door. "Good luck, Luke, if I don't make the flight. I hope all the worrying turns out to be something trivial."

"Thanks," said Luke. "I hope."

"Hope is good."

The words echoed in Luke's mind as the door closed and

Finn was gone. A moment later his phone buzzed with a message. He looked at it. Anu. He opened it quickly, scanning the words. Feckfeckfeckfeck. He punched the phone and waited for the ringing. Answer, answer! It took only two rings before the phone connected.

"Anu?"

"Yes."

"What do you mean she's gone?"

"Just that, Luke. I travelled to Kayla's home myself after that friend of hers, Seán Óg, I think, contacted me to say that when he went to check on all of them and she was gone."

"But Bláthín and Nana are still there?"

"Yes, but they're both unconscious. Or rather in some type of deep sleep."

"What?" Luke's mind raged, and he fought for control. "Are they in hospital?"

"No, no," said Anu. "I'm here with them. But I don't want to leave them. I'm not sure where Kayla's been taken. I'm trying to contact Daghda to see what he can discover."

"She's been taken? Are you certain?"

Anu sighed. "I'm sorry, Luke. I should have made that clear. Balor's taken her."

"No." Luke cursed himself with every word that came to mind. "There's no doubt about it? She hasn't gone to another part of the Beara? Or gone to Killarney, or somewhere?"

"No, Luke. There's a note. It's addressed to you."

Luke's breath caught. "Me?"

"Yes. I took the liberty of opening it. It says, 'come and get her'."

Luke banged his fist against the wall. "Feckin' gobshite. I'll kill him."

"Yes," said Anu. "That's the plan. But first we must find Kayla and get her back."

29

MAURA

I scanned Lenny's bar, taking in the motley crew of drinkers and talkers whose lazy gazes gave me the once over check before resuming their business of sinking sorrows, avoiding life, and or looking for a chat. There were a lot of "and ors" here this afternoon, the Friday afternoon crowd working its way up to the Friday night fun.

I didn't expect to find Raven here, let alone Skye and Sherman, but it was a last ditch hope. Hope born of desperation that came from scouring every one of his haunts I could think of in this city. Except the main haunt. His place. I had no idea where that was, and for the first time I stopped to wonder why. What had seemed convenient and lazy for me when he'd come to my room either on his own, or with the others, now seemed to signal another difference. Or hint at the reasons why it was impossible for us to be us. He was here and he was nowhere. Nowhere in this city except when he wanted to be. Or needed to be. And now, no text, no responses from my phone. He was gone.

To the reservation? Maybe there? But inside, way down deep in my corvid sense, I knew that was just mist and mirrors too.

Sure, he'd blown smoke in my face the whole time. I was a right eejit to think or believe anything different, because I'd known right from the start that Raven was something more, hadn't I? That what I took to be his "Indian-ness" was actually peculiar to Raven himself. The feckin' powwow should have told me that.

I stood there in the bar and all the other "should have known" points when Raven had been in my company came flooding back. Well, didn't he tell me he was a trickster on more than one occasion? Yeah. Eejit.

And with him went Skye. Sky Woman. And Sherman.

The reservation, though. Maybe. His work wasn't done. Their work wasn't done. Could I help? I shoved aside the night before, the messages he'd sent that even now I refused to receive.

I went over to the bar where Lenny was serving up a beer. "Lenny."

Lenny nodded to me. "Hey. What's up? You're not on until six."

"Right, fine. I know. I just was looking for Raven. Have you seen him?"

Lenny shook his head. "Naw. Not since he was with you. But he don't come in that often. Usually when you're on. So he may be in tonight, you never know."

"Would you know where he lives?"

Lenny laughed. "Yeah, check with my social secretary."

I shrugged. "Sorry, it was just the off chance."

I turned away and headed out the door, pausing at the entrance. Where to next? The door opened, and would have banged my face if not for my cowgirl boots. Those boots. I jolted back and an auburn head popped into view. Tight curls, hanging longer than they used to. I caught my breath. Surprise. Good or bad, it wasn't who I expected and, I told myself, who I wanted.

"Maura," said Finn, a relieved look on his face. "I'm glad I found you here."

I stepped back further so he could enter. "Why?"

"Why?" he said. "Because here is the only place I know that you might be found."

His words suddenly seemed too much more than idle responses or quick banter. I could hear the undercurrents going strong, and I didn't want them to pull me with them, words wooing me down that river, into that sea.

"I'm just leaving, sorry," I said.

Finn caught my arm. "Wait, Maura. Please."

The currents swirled around me, tugging at me. It was his power, his words, him. I tried to shake them off, but his grip was firm.

"Can we talk?" he said softly. "Let me get you a drink."

I found myself saying yes, just as part of me wailed at the thought of that yes, where it would take me and what it would mean.

"I can't stay long," I bit out.

"Fine," he said. "A quick drink."

He pulled me along, his hand on my arm and led me to a booth at the back, away from the light of the window. My boots clattered across the floor, their noise trying to knock some sense into me, keep me straight, keep me on that horse named "cowgirl times".

He'd ordered two beers from Lenny as we passed by and they came soon after he'd planted me in the booth across from him, our knees nearly touching, my boots knocking his with a click.

I took up the beer bottle in my hand, noting it was Lenny's attempt at stocking a craft beer. I took a sip, hardly tasting it, and watched Finn do the same. Copper stubble glinted on his chin and his eyes were lined and revealed a weariness I'd never seen before in him. His expression was both pained and cautious and so unlike the Finn I knew. My Finn. I scrubbed the thought and waited for him to play the opening gambit. It was enough to have the currents swirling, I needed all my energy to resist the rest. This was seanchie time, the tale teller who would weave spells with words was stepping up. I could see his expression change and watched him reach within himself, drawing on that well of words that would invoke so much emotion in a listener they'd be full to the brim with it. I knocked my boots together once, bracing myself.

"Maura," he said.

"Ah, no," I said, cutting in. "I think you mean Morrigan. Because that's who you want. That's what this is about."

Suddenly I was off, taking this bull by the horns before it took me. It was a plan, the one that found me and I would take it, because it was all I had.

"You want the warrior, the goddess of war, the one who can help you defeat Balor," I said in a low menacing voice. "That would be Morrigan."

"No," Finn cut in. "I'm not here for Morrigan." His words were firm, direct and his gaze fixed mine into place. His eyes darkened and then flared, his own emotions surfacing to mix with mine.

"What?" I said. The plan seem to crack and fall apart then, leaving me standing, bare and unprotected.

Finn looked down at his hands which were clasped around his beer bottle. He took a sip. Ran his tongue along his lips and feck me if I didn't follow that tongue and imagine it travelling along other places. I flushed with the thought and looked away.

He placed a hand on my arm briefly and took it back. I felt its heat, even after he removed it. I took a deep breath and forced myself to look back at him.

"Maura," he began again. "I'm here because I care. Because I wanted to understand what it is that drew you here and if it's enough to keep you here."

"What drew me here?" I said, echoing him. It was an echo that repeated again and again inside me, the great question that I'd only ever answer with my own smoke and mirrors.

"The wind," I whispered. I looked up at him. "The wind?"

"Some wind," he said. "An east wind?"

"Winds of change," I said without thinking.

"Winds of time," he said, his voice low.

"A changing wind," I said. It was banter and yet it wasn't. It was a game of exploration of possibilities, a search for answers and only Finn could play this game with me.

He reached out for my hand and squeezed it. I held on to it tightly. This exploration of possibilities was taking me to places that were unfamiliar. It was unnerving. I felt off balance.

"Another side of Maura discovered?" he asked.

I blinked and gave him a faint smile. "Maybe. Cowgirl Maura?"

Finn laughed. "Cowgirl Maura. I like the sound of that. I'd like to get to know cowgirl Maura."

"Got the boots to match." I said with my best American accent. I clicked my boots together, the sound echoing. "She's a real hardass, that Maura."

"Always," said Finn. "Just like all the other Mauras."

"Feck yes," I said. "She can do line dancing."

Finn's brows lifted. "Line dancing? Is that so?"

"She can of course."

"She also made some interesting friends. Learned about powwows."

"Cowgirl Maura is really amazing," said Finn. "She's someone I'd be proud to know."

"You like cowgirl Maura, eh?"

Finn nodded. "Very much. Just as much as I like the other Maura."

I sighed. "And who is that other Maura?"

He was still holding my hand and he took it now, brought it up to his lips and kissed my knuckles. I blinked back the tears that came to my eyes.

"A person who is witty, brave, beautiful, loyal and even occasionally kind."

"Kind?" I said, my voice ragged. I attempted a laugh. "I'll have to fix that."

He kissed my knuckles once again. "No, don't fix anything. You're perfect as you are."

"Am I?" I asked, looking into his eyes. They were a sea of emotions of kindness, compassion and love. I felt them envelop me with all their warmth, embrace me with their strength.

"You are."

"And who is that?" I said.

"You are who you are," he said. "Maura. My Maura is a warrior goddess and so much more."

"Your Maura?" I gave a wry smile.

He said nothing, just kissed my knuckles one more time. Three times the charm. And that charm pulled me to him and I kissed him briefly on the lips.

"Come home, Maura," he said softly. He stroked my hair. "Come back to Ireland."

I clicked my boots again, trying to fend off the tidal wave of emotions, but that click, being third and like that charm, could only take me one place. Home.

PART III

THE FINAL BATTLE

30

———————

MAURA

I stared at the weathered wooden door, unsure if I wanted to enter. Inside, I could hear talking, or rather jumbled voices, because they were all speaking at once, voicing their opinions, everyone wanting to be heard. Except Anu. Through Kayla's kitchen window I could see her sitting silent in one of the chairs, her drawn face, sunken cheeks and hollowed eyes giving evidence to the very danger that was around us. In the time since I'd seen her last, Anu had fallen ill. Seriously ill – and it didn't take much speculation to know what was behind it. Or rather who. At least at the moment. What had Balor done now?

Seeing Anu in that condition set a rush of emotions through me that I didn't want to feel. It was more than I had bargained for when I'd told Finn I would come. Let him lure me into agreeing to his request. I'd allowed my emotions to overcome my better judgement and even now I berated myself for doing it. That kiss. Why did I give him that kiss? And all the other whys crowded in now. At least I had the presence of mind to tell him I would follow after them, take a different flight. I didn't dare fly myself. Couldn't trust what the winds would do, where they would take me. Would I ever trust them again?

Still, the flight I'd taken the next day had been brutal, shifting constantly in my seat while my cowgirl boots pinched me into all modes of foot agony and the in-flight entertainment bludgeoned my mind. All my cowgirl happy left behind, a dream left behind in the dust and heat.

Inside, Finn moved in front of Anu and caught sight of me. My breath hitched. Was I ready for this? I straightened, pulled my leather jacket armour in place, shoved my hands in my pockets and pushed the door open.

They were all there. Saoirse and Smithy sitting at the table, near Anu, and Luke leaning against the cooker, arms crossed, his expression tense, no idle surfer there. Sure, that surfer was gone, replaced by a panther-like menace that signalled all sorts of trouble.

Saoirse saw me right away. "She's here! The one and only." She gave me a grin and a quick hug. "I'm glad you came."

I gave her a wry grin. "Sure, what else could I do after the golden tongued man summoned me?"

"Golden tongue? Do tell," said Saoirse.

I forced a laugh, hoping my face betrayed nothing. I gestured towards Finn. "Ask your man over there. He's the one with all the words."

"Words?" said Finn, a little of the old twinkle in his eyes. "I'm knocked speechless, now."

He was leaning back against the wall, hands in the pockets of his hoodie, elbows out, very casual altogether, but the muscles were still there, visible underneath the arms of the hoodie and through the legs of his jeans. The warrior, latent, but still there. Elegant grace, elegant tongue. Too elegant. I drew my eyes away and looked at Anu.

"How are you? Not so well by the look of things," I said.

"You answered your own question," said Anu with a tired smile.

"Where's Kayla?" I asked, regarding Luke. "Is she okay? And her daughter and mother?"

His ravaged face gave me the answer before he did. "She's missing. Bláthín and Nana are upstairs in a type of coma."

"Missing?" I said, stunned. "Coma?"

"Balor," said Luke, anger straining his voice. "So far Bláthín and Nana are ok, I guess. I'm keeping an eye on them." He glanced over at Anu. "And Anu is as well."

"Feck," I said.

This wasn't what I'd expected, but knowing Balor, it should have been. We all should have known. I caught myself. Was I ready to be included into this band of merry men again? I glanced at Finn, who was giving me his own tentative friendly looks as if he heard my musings. I grimaced at him and he grinned back. He cocked his head and I widened my eyes. A conversation that only we could have in those expressions. A "will you—won't I—maybe—please" exchange with no resolution but a sigh from me. A sigh of resignation. Not even a golden tongue in play in any form got that concession. The pity of it. A thought that gave me a jolt and sent my eyes back to Luke.

"The why of it is obvious, but the where isn't," I said finally. "Do you know?"

"No," said Luke curtly.

"The where. That's what we're discussing," said Smithy. His tone was reserved, cautious. No *céad míle fáilte* from him, then.

"Any conclusions?" I looked at Luke.

"Not yet," he said. The frown was on his mouth, in his tone and in his stance and they all screamed "let me kill this man now".

"I don't think she could have left the Beara," said Anu softly.

"Well that narrows it down," said Smithy. There was no sarcasm there, just fact.

"She could be at his house," said Luke. "I'll check there now."

"Luke," said Saoirse, kindness in her voice. "Like Smithy said before, it could be a trap. It could be just what Balor wants."

"Why don't you think she's left the Beara?" I asked Anu.

"Because of who she is. Because she's *An Cailleach*."

"But where? Where on the Beara would he take her?" asked Luke, his frustration clear. "Do you think he'd hire a house, or take a room in a B&B? Stay in that hotel just outside Castletown-bere? Feck, no. It makes sense he would take her to his house, where he has security, where he can keep her confined and under surveillance."

Anu nodded. "It does make sense when you present it that way, but I still stand by my words. My instincts."

Anu's instincts weren't to be disregarded lightly, even I knew that, but I could understand Luke's reasoned argument. I'd be inclined to check there, too.

Luke straightened. "Right, so. I'm off then. I'll be back as soon as I can."

"Wait," said Finn. "Smithy and Saoirse are right. It could be a trap."

He looked across at me and resumed our silent conversation. It only took that look – I knew what he wanted – I didn't need the woeful, pleading eyes, with the glimmer of humour behind it that told me he knew he was playing it up and poking me with it.

The sigh. Yes, I heard it come out of me. Again not even a sign of the golden tongue. Sure, I was a pushover. One tap, one little glance from his blue eyes, a slight grin that showed the old cheekbones and I was toppled over, flat.

I pursed my mouth. "Fine, fine. I'll go."

All heads turned towards me, surprise written on all their faces except one. Well there were no guesses for that person because, ah sure, he knew me. Knew me like anyone and no one never ever had.

"Will I drive you nearby, save you exhausting yourself?" asked Finn, a barely repressed smirk lurking on his face.

"You brought your car?" I asked.

He nodded. "I did."

I didn't want to explore that revelation and assured myself with the thought that it was too crowded in Luke's SUV. Or maybe Smithy used his motorbike, or something.

I shrugged. "Grand."

"I'll come too," said Luke. "So if she's there I can get her out."

"We should all go, in that case," said Smithy.

"Are you well enough to look after Bláthín and Nana?" asked Luke, looking at Anu.

Anu nodded. "I'll be grand enough. You go. Do what you must and then return here."

It was a dismissal of sorts. I headed towards the door.

"Will we all squeeze in Luke's SUV and let him drive, then?" said Finn. "Give him something to do so he doesn't punch things that weren't meant to be punched?"

Smithy laughed and shook his head, but Luke didn't seem to find the humour in the remark.

"It'll be grand, Luke," said Saoirse, patting his arm. "We'll find her."

We made our way out through the door, Finn waiting for me. He squeezed my arm and told me thanks in a low voice.

"You know your levity is really inappropriate in so many ways," I said to him.

"Ah, now, there's the Maura I know and love," he said.

I raised my brow at that remark. "Again with the golden tongue."

"You love my tongue," he said. "Admit it."

I gave a non-committal grunt, unwilling to risk any comment, or even to open my mouth for fear of what might come out of it.

IT WASN'T LIKE old times in so many ways. We'd never all ridden in the SUV at the same time, all of us. Somehow Smithy had ended up in the front, nominated by the fact of his bulk and long legs, leaving Saoirse, me and Finn that after some strange musical chair juggle had put me in the middle, Finn's body spreading itself far beyond the borders of his space into mine. Not old times there.

Not old times in the tension that seemed to hang between Finn and me. Not old times when he raised his arm and draped it over the back of the seat. Not old times when he leaned down and whispered in my ear his gratitude for my return and willingness to help. That feckin' golden tongue, right by my ear. Feckin' ridiculous, that's what it was. I was. The state of me. Not a state to be in. Impossible state, in a huge state of impossibilities all of them were mine because there were no possibilities that had Finn's name on them.

I was Morrigan. That large "m" was written and shouted so large, it heralded my presence well before I appeared. I was trouble. I was conflict. I was anger. I was all of that, no matter what Finn said. No matter. I told this to myself, over and over, sitting under his draped arm that somehow slipped off the edge of the seat and onto my shoulder. I should give him a "what the feck" look right now, I told myself. But no one was listening, my mantra of war gone off to a different beat of someone else's drum, leaving my heart the only beating thing behind and that was going so rat-a-tat fast no warriors would come. Only dancers, those yokes that jump up and down so fast with joy, so taken away with the music you think they're mad. That was me. Mad.

"Did you see Raven before you left?" asked Saoirse next to me.

"Sorry, what?" I'd heard her voice and it was only now that the meaning sunk in. "Raven. Yes. Yes, he, uh, came over."

Saoirse waggled her brows. "Really?"

I looked away, hoping that would avoid the flush on my face. Raven. What to say? Sure I didn't know myself what happened, not really. Except the result.

"Yeah. He said goodbye. Said to tell you the same."

I'd added the last part for good measure. To save face. In more ways than one. The face that still held the flush wasn't saved and I felt Finn frowning next to me, listening attentively.

I fashioned a shrug, but it only led me to feel Finn's arm around my shoulder even more and that face that was looking desperately to be saved, I knew would fail on another count.

"It was nothing. It was more a 'pleasure to do business with you, pleasure to know you' conversation," I said.

Thank feck Saoirse's waggling brows unwaggled and settled into a more neutral position and she nodded.

"Oh, grand. Nice of him. But then he was. Nice. They all were."

"Hmm," I managed to say.

"And considering he was...well, Raven, he was nice. Not much trickster about him." She turned keen eyes on me. "Well, that I observed."

"No, not much trickster about him," I muttered. Beside me, Finn shifted and his thigh pressed against me even more.

Saoirse let the conversation drop, my tone and lack of conversation hopefully telling her all that she needed to know.

As we journeyed on, with only the occasional exchange

between Smithy and Saoirse, I almost wished for Saoirse's questions because that "not like old times" feeling grew between Finn and me.

By the time we arrived at Balor's road I could hear little of any conversation for the sound of my own heartbeat drowning out everything, including my thoughts.

Luke pulled up in the layby they'd used before. Briefly, he explained to me the house's layout and all the points and places to avoid. He drew out his laptop and began to disable the cameras and the security system while the others watched. Finn squeezed my arm, leaned over again and wished me luck.

The luck stayed in my ear, echoing through my mind. His golden tongue, his golden voice. Coated caramel, I would have said, rather than golden if I was describing it accurately. But that was too mental for words and I needed my sanity right now and caramel, coated or not, could go take a hike with malted chocolate and all the rest of them and leave me the feck alone.

I got out of the SUV and walked down the road a bit, trying to get hold of myself, then get over myself. Deep breaths, deep breaths. Full of all those deep breaths I took flight, shifting quickly, the final way to get beyond myself. By the time I landed on the patio outside of the large sliding doors that led off of the kitchen I felt better.

I peered in, trying to make out the interior. It was filled with contemporary this and that, all stationary, no figures at all. I both flew and hopped to all the windows, upstairs and down, but could see no trace of a movement. It wasn't until I arrived at the one of the upstairs windows – presumably the main bedroom, his bedroom – that I saw lying on a table, underneath the window I was looking through, a piece of paper. And on that paper was a great big smiley face.

I stared at the image for a few seconds and took off. No need to search further.

31

LUKE

"He's playing with you," said Maura as she slid into Luke's SUV.

Luke knew from the look on her face that Kayla hadn't been there. No, there'd been too much annoyance for that to have been the case.

Luke gripped his hands into fists. "What do you mean?" Suddenly there seemed too many occupants in this vehicle. Too little air.

"I mean I just checked all the rooms and in his bedroom – well I presume it was his because of the hideous bed and his awful decor. There, on a table under the window he had a piece of paper with a huge smiley face on it. He knew we were coming. Or at least he knew I would be checking out his place."

Luke stared at Maura, processing the words, while around him the rest of them muttered their own displeasure and curses. But his rage couldn't be contained in muttered displeasure and curses, his rage was too big for that.

"Hey," said Saoirse leaning forward and placing her hand on Luke's shoulder. "Calm down, think it through. You don't want to play into his hands."

"Add 'any more than you already have' to that sentence," said Maura.

Luke frowned at Maura. Back to herself, she was. But she was right. He forced himself to unclasp his hands.

"What now?" asked Smithy.

"Is that a nice way of saying 'I told you so'?" Luke said icily.

Smithy held up his hands. "No 'I told you sos', here."

Luke nodded. "Right, so. Yes, we go back to the Beara. Hopefully Anu will have had some word or indication from Daghda about Kayla's location. Or some information that's helpful."

Luke's imagination took flight during the return journey, the kilometres and road eaten up by visions of Kayla, ill, untended somewhere, slowly dying. Why would Balor take her though, when he had already found the quickest method to eliminate her? But Luke knew. It was because Balor understood how taking Kayla exploited so many of his weaknesses and demonstrated to the world that Luke was no hero, no golden warrior and certainly not cunning enough to prevent Balor from taking Kayla while Luke was off chasing his hero toys. The note in the case with a smiley face. He was an eejit through and through. The feckin' smiley face said it all. He hadn't even bothered to ask Maura if it had been a laughing smiley face in this instance. There was no need.

Eventually, and after too many loops through the visions and harsh verbal self-flagellations, Luke pulled up the SUV outside Kayla's house. It looked no different from when he'd left. He could hear the sheep bleating in the distance and the ground was muddy with the latest rainfall of the day before. There was a hint of saltwater in the air, a tang that reminded him of another self. A self that seemed so long ago, and not time that was most accurately measured in weeks. He shook himself out of his thoughts and got out of the SUV, the others already at the kitchen door, Saoirse opening it.

He followed them, tried to focus on next steps and entered the kitchen to the sound of Saoirse's voice relaying what had occurred to Anu. Anu hadn't moved from her chair at the table, it seemed, though she did reassure Luke that she'd checked on Bláthín and Nana and had no change to report.

"Any news from Daghda?" Luke asked as soon as Anu had told him about Bláthín and Nana.

Anu nodded slowly. "He did say that he'd heard nothing of any use, except to mention that he was certain she hadn't left the Beara Peninsula."

Luke noted there were no 'I told you so' words in her statement either. He was grateful to her and Smithy for that omission, but a small bit of him found it annoying. He sighed, nodded and thanked Anu.

"Will we start searching the Beara?" said Saoirse. "We could split up. Take different sections."

"Do you have any idea where the best place to look would be?" asked Finn.

Luke glanced at Finn, an ease on his face that hadn't been there for a good while. No temper tantrums for now, thank feck for that, thought Luke.

"No, but Saoirse's idea sound good."

"Maura and I can take the west."

Maura frowned and gave Finn a look that told him in no uncertain terms he shouldn't speak for her.

"Do you want to go with Saoirse?" Luke asked her. "You can take Kayla's car. Smithy can go with Finn."

Maura reddened, a sight that surprised Luke. "Or whatever you want. Fly, I don't know," he added.

"No, she can come with me," said Finn. "She just likes to remind me that she's boss. She's done that just now, so it's grand."

Maura opened her mouth, the outrage on her face plain, but

she shut it after a moment and shrugged. "Right, fine. But I'm driving."

Finn laughed and bowed. "As the boss commands."

"Will we search Bere Island and Dursey?" asked Maura, ignoring Finn.

"There's nothing on Dursey," said Smithy.

Luke frowned. "That's not true."

"Well," conceded Smithy. "Just a few houses."

"Still," said Finn. "We should check there."

"Definitely," said Luke. "It's Balor. Who the feck knows what he's decided to do?"

"Smithy and I will take the other side of the peninsula," said Saoirse. She looked at Smithy. "Is that okay with you?"

Smithy nodded, his smile tentative. "No worries. That suits."

"Grand. That's sorted," said Luke. "I'll take this side, since I know it best. I'll give you all a list of places to check, though, so it's not so much a needle in a haystack."

"More like a button, then," said Maura, her tone flat. "Is this all your plan is, then? Search? Do you have specific places in mind?"

Luke looked at Maura, tried to judge her mood. He took a deep breath. "We can narrow the scope by eliminating some of the obvious possibilities. Clusters of holiday homes, for example.

"Oh, that won't take long," said Maura drily.

Luke frowned. "It's something. It's a strategy."

"What would Balor expect you to do?" asked Maura impatiently.

Luke paused, looked at Anu, her eyes expectant.

"She makes a good point," Anu said quietly.

Guilt flooded through him as he realised the truth of Maura's words. And Anu's. He sighed. "You're right. I should take a step back, think this through."

"Would he expect you to go haring off, scattering us around, expending your energy?" asked Maura.

Luke snorted. "He would enjoy that, all right."

Maura nodded. "Exactly."

A knock sounded at the back door and then it opened. A head peered around the door. Feckin' Seán Óg.

"Ah, lad. Glad to see you're back. Is Kayla here, too?"

Luke gave him a tight lipped smile. "No, not yet."

Seán Óg entered, surveying the group. "Got the posse out, then?"

Luke crossed his arms. "These are my friends. And Kayla's." Luke didn't know how much more pointed he could be than to actually state "feck off". "She's fine," he added for good measure. "A friend of mine collected her and he's bringing her back here tomorrow." It was the first thing that came to mind, and he hoped it would provide enough of a "feck off" signal for the man.

Seán Óg smiled, but the disbelief was written all over his face. He nodded to the others. "You're friends of Kayla's too?" His gaze rested on Anu. "Ah, Annie. I'm glad you're still here. How's things upstairs? Any better?"

"It's good of you to call in, Seán Óg," said Anu, her tone pleasant. "How are you keeping?"

"Grand, so." He said. His eyes brightened. "Have you heard the news?"

Always with the feckin' *sceal,* thought Luke. Normally he would have the patience. Would have even been amused, well for the most part. But now Luke fought a desire to take the wellie drooping over by the door and stuff it in Seán Óg's mouth.

"No," said Anu mildly. "What news?"

"I'm only after finding out myself. There's chaos all over the peninsula. Rock falls and landslides west of here are making the roads impassable. The cable for the Dursey cable car has snapped. The ferry going over to Bere Island has run aground and the waters are too treacherous to get any other boats out there."

"The cable has snapped?" said Luke. "Rock slides?"

It was obvious Balor was behind this. Balor and his men. It had to be. He glanced over at Finn who gave a hint of a nod, then Smithy, who raised his brows. Saoirse's confirmation was in the set of her mouth. And Maura? Maura's face was all fury.

"Crazy," said Seán Óg. "The fairies certainly had a field day." He gave a hearty laugh, looking to the rest of them to share it.

Maura sniggered. "Oh, those fairies. They're real chancers, so they are."

Finn laughed and Smithy joined him a moment later. Saoirse shook her head, glanced at Luke and gave him a sympathetic look. Luke just rolled his eyes. Sure, the man was an eejit.

Seán Óg glanced around the room again, straightened and gave a final nod. "I'll be off then, so. I've the animals to see to."

The news had been delivered, and, not quite meeting the reception he hoped for, he left to seek better craic. That's how to deliver the "feck off" message to this fella, thought Luke.

"Obviously, she's somewhere in the west," said Maura.

Luke nodded. He'd heard that message loud and clear.

"What's the best guess?" asked Smithy.

"I'd go with Bere Island," said Finn. "Can't get there, by the sound of it."

"Dursey is unreachable, too," said Luke. "The tidal race is impossible in the Dursey Sound and we can't be certain that the seas aren't turbulent there." He looked at Maura. "Would you be able to check the situation?"

Maura looked at him, her eyes flat, her expression dour. "I would be able to. Of course."

The emphasis she'd put on the word "able" Luke knew it was

done deliberately. He studied her, saw the tension in her face and he thought back to America. And before.

"I'm sorry," said Luke. "I'm asking for your help. I'm not assuming it."

Maura gave him a curt nod, her expression easing a little. "Grand. Okay. Yes. I'll do it."

Finn placed a hand on her shoulder. "Will I drive you as far as possible?"

She gave him a tight smile. "No, thanks. I'll be grand."

32

MAURA

I took flight in a whirl of confusion and shoved it aside. I couldn't think about it, not a bit of it. I needed to focus. Feel the wind, the lift under my wings, survey the ground below. The sea stretched out to my right and the bogs and hills of the land were to my left. Head west. That was the goal. Head west, but not too far west, I chided. Feel the wind swell, take it and don't let it rule.

I kept that centre, pushing down and out all other emotions that might take over. Too far west wasn't where I wanted to be at this moment, and emotion could very well take me there. Looking down, I sought familiar landmarks, using them to fix my thoughts. I noted the blocked roads, shaking my head at the fecker who contrived it.

By the time I reached the outskirts of Castletownbere, I was the corbie in charge, beak ready, battle prepped. Yes, oh yes. I scanned the hotel for Balor's vehicle or anything that might indicate he was there, landing on window ledges, peeping in hotel rooms, until they all seemed to look the same. I knew it was unlikely, but still, it was best to be thorough.

Eventually, having ruled out the hotel, I took flight and

resumed my search, finally heading towards Bere Island. There was little enough there that offered possibilities, but still, I knew it had to be done and thankfully it didn't take too long to rule it out.

I headed west again, my instincts telling me the cable car was the biggest key to her location. And when I arrived there, the toll of my efforts starting to become evident, it was if I could feel the poison hanging in the air and the agony of the land. While I rested there, near the stop for the cable car, I listened intently.

My heartbeat slowed and as it did I felt the beat of something more. The land. Sluggish and faint. She had to be here. I could hear her. It was a question of where.

I was conscious of gathering clouds overhead. Rain soon and not just a light shower. It was storm season and the clouds were very much aware of it. And the sea below was answering, the churning waters of the Dursey Sound threatening.

I took off, suddenly desperate to find where Balor was keeping Kayla. There were so many things that seemed off. Unnatural. And it was that feeling, and the faint heartbeat that pulled me on, sight keen and ear on alert. The pulling took me towards the other side of the island, away from the walkers, to a small place, off on its own, abandoned and half obscured under the ivy and moss. It seemed unlikely, but likely for Balor. And once I landed, it was all I thought and all I feared. Kayla, inside a tent pitched within the ruin, lying unconscious in a sleeping bag. And tending her was Eithne.

Fury caught me by surprise. Of course that fecker would have his daughter out here while, in the safety of his little hideaway, he pulled the strings in this macabre theatre piece of his.

I flew off. I'd seen enough.

"EITHNE IS THERE?" said Luke, the anger evident in his face and tone.

I was back in the kitchen, standing before the others who were staging a wake-like vigil with tea, sandwiches and whiskey cluttering the table.

Luke stared at me as if I might deny the words I'd said. I only wish. Anger had filled my wings on the flight back and no thoughts disturbed my mind but how to outwit that fecker. He turned away and left the room. A moment later footsteps sounded on the stairs.

Finn squeezed my arm and gave me a nudge in the ribs with his elbow. "Aren't you a star," he said in a low voice. "You and your beady eyes found her."

I raised my brows. "Beady?"

"Beady. Beady is good."

I smiled. "Okay." Giddiness hit me and I wanted to hit it back. Giddy, me? Feck no. I managed to half swallow the giggle that threatened to escape, but a gurgle emerged and it had Finn pounding me on my back lightly.

"Sorry, sorry," he said. "I should have warned you before I gave you a compliment."

"That's never a compliment," I said.

"Keen-eyed, Finn," said Saoirse. She looked at me. "He meant keen-eyed."

I snorted. "Ah now, in that case."

Smithy offered me a glass of whiskey. "Restorative," he said.

I nodded and took it gratefully. Overhead, I heard footsteps heading towards the stair landing and then descend. A moment later Luke arrived, sword in hand.

"Right," he said. "I'm ready. Who's coming with me?"

"Now?" asked Smithy.

"Luke, give yourself a moment to calm down," said Anu. "We'll discuss and decide how best to approach it."

"What needs discussing?" said Luke. "We know where she is. We can head out now. We can find someone who has a boat who can take us to Dursey."

I shook my head. "It's not that easy, Luke. You know that. There's a storm about to break, the currents and tide are against us. You'll be hard pressed to find someone willing to take his boat out in these conditions."

Luke bit his lip, frustration clear on his face. "If we can get a boat, I can get us there."

Finn shook his head slowly. "You don't want to go out in a storm. Besides, waiting it out will give us time to plan, as Anu says."

"Sit," said Anu, her voice firm. "Let's go through everything Maura discovered."

Reluctantly, Luke took the chair Smithy gave over to him and poured himself a small whiskey. Finn took my now empty glass and handed it to Smithy for a refill. Once done, I leaned back against the sink, glass in hand and prepared to recount every detail I could. Finn was beside me, his quiet strength somehow a comfort.

When I was finished, Luke nodded quietly and thanked me.

"We should wait until the weather has calmed," said Finn. "Then we can find a boat and get Kayla."

I glanced at Luke. He was staring out of the window, his expression tight. He peered out, studying the sky. After a few moments he drew back and shook his head.

"The winds are strange," he muttered. He looked over at me. "How did it seem to you?"

I nodded slowly. "Different. The scent in the air, the wind direction. I don't know. Not right. And the sea..." I shook my head.

Luke looked over at Anu. "What do you think?"

Anu gave him a sympathetic smile. "I think you could be right, Lugh."

"Balor's persuaded Manannán to create stormy seas?" said Finn, disbelief in his voice.

"Why would he do that?" asked Smithy. "He'd never side with Balor."

Luke paled. "Mon," he said.

"Mon?" said Smithy.

Luke ran his hand through his hair, his expression filled with anguish. "It's Mon. Lately, he's been able to control sections of the sea."

"Again," said Smithy. "Why? He's your foster brother, sure he'd never do that to you."

Luke looked away. "He would now."

"So these stormy seas could continue for a long time," said Saoirse quietly.

"Until Manannán finds out," said Smithy. "He won't be best pleased."

"That could be a while," said Finn.

Luke placed fisted hands on his head. "Feck! This is my fault."

"Why would you blame yourself?" asked Saoirse quietly. She placed her hand on his arm, but he shook it off.

"Because he thinks I betrayed him."

"What?" said Smithy.

Luke sighed. "Clíodhna. He thinks I betrayed him with Clíodhna. She trapped me into a relationship and I didn't even know that's who she was. I'd never met her when Mon was involved with her."

It was an ancient tale. Everyone knew of it. Mon angry at Clíodhna spurning him for her mortal lover and Manannán killing her lover and washing her back into the sea to take her place among the Tuatha de Danann. Even I knew of Mon's pain and remorse that his father had used his love of Clíodhna to reclaim her for the Tuatha de Danann.

"What should we do?" I asked, startled that I'd slipped into the use of "we". I looked at Anu. "Would you be able to contact Daghda to let him know? He could pass it on to Manannán."

"No," said Luke. "This is my fault. So I'll fix it."

"What will you do?" asked Saoirse.

"I'm going to find Mon."

33

LUKE

He was all cold determination as he started his SUV. All the "ah sure it's only Mon" words had long since gone out of his vocabulary for tricks and pranks that had been part of their relationship since they were young lads. The "ah sures" that had made him laugh and take the joke, finding ways to have an even bigger joke on Mon that was all part of the craic. No, those "ah sures" had left him the moment Mon had turned away, refused to accept his denials and apologies for things he hadn't known he'd done. Feckin' Clíodhna. But really, he knew it wasn't her fault. It all came back to Balor. Balor had recruited her to entrap him.

And now Mon. It was hard to imagine, but it seemed like Mon was helping Balor. And that knowledge gutted him just as much as it made him angry. He had to face Mon, though, just to confirm that the man who'd been the brother of his heart had betrayed him. On one level he could understand Mon's pain, and that it had blinded him, but still. Still and all, he thought his bond with Mon had been more.

As Luke drove, the gut wrenching emotion that had seized

him from the moment he'd realised Mon's betrayal started to settle just enough for him to conclude that a guns blazing approach was out of the question. Kayla mattered most. She mattered above everything, even Mon. And the irony of the words struck him. Ruefully, he acknowledged it and his anger subsided a little more, so that eventually, it was a sigh that he emitted. A sigh that reflected more sadness than anything else. That their relationship, their connection had resulted in this awful act of revenge.

By the time he reached Clonakilty he had the framework of a plan. It was simple enough, he just hoped that it would work, because he had few other ideas at the moment other than get Mon's father involved. And he knew that having Manannán step in would most likely alienate Mon further, if not permanently. At the moment, he had the hope that Mon taking such a drastic step, to allow Kayla to be held captive by Balor, was also a way that Mon would get Luke to come to him. If Luke was right, than he was more than ready to plead for Kayla, to show Mon how much Mon's actions had hurt him and to try and make amends. He just hoped he could find the right words. Finn would have been better at this, he thought. He seemed to have somehow managed to get Maura to return and help them.

He was able to find a spot to park the SUV and walked the rest of the way to Mon's flat above the shop. It was a gamble that he'd find Mon here, but Luke knew that trying to ring Mon was useless. After a few knocks, a press of the buzzer and a few more knocks, it seemed a lost cause. He had no idea what the tides were, or if Mon was still here to surf, but instinct told Luke he was. The instinct that also told him that Mon wanted him to come.

Luke turned away and returned to his SUV. A few moments later he was heading out the road to Incheydoney, across the small bridge and along the road until he reached the main carpark. He could see some surfboards and paddle boards strapped to roofs and people changing into and out of gear, but a quick scan told him Mon wasn't among them. The carpark was crowded enough, but it only took him a few minutes before he spotted Mon's car. Encouraged, he got out of the SUV and headed down the steps to the main beach, where he could see surfers swimming out to meet waves. He scanned them, looking for that familiar shock of white blond hair, but it was too difficult. He moved his gaze to the beach and it was there, among a group of surfers walking towards him, that Luke spied Mon. Beside him was Mud, the Australian surfer Luke had come to know this past summer, along with a few others that Mon had hung around with. *Na laddaí*, Luke had called them privately. The lads. There were new lads there now, the others he'd presumed had moved on. Wilder shores, wilder rides. But Mon had stayed. And that told him something too. Despite Clíodhna, he was here. Or maybe it was the reason. Because in nearby Glanmore she'd been washed in a great wave into the sea to the Tuatha once more, but never more the same and never ever to be Mon's, as he'd so desperately hoped.

This was a place of mourning for Mon, and now for him. But, he resolved, it was time to make it a place of making amends, or at least an acknowledgement that some kind of restitution had been made.

Luke approached Mon at an even pace, no hesitancy, and he knew the moment that Mon saw him. A hitch in the step, barely detectable. A sneer started to form on Mon's face. He spoke to his companions, veered off from them and headed directly for Luke, his stride more purposeful. It didn't take long before he was standing before Luke, his arms crossed along his chest.

Luke nodded. "Mon."

He returned the nod. "Dude. Didn't think it would take you this long. I overestimated your attachment."

Luke stiffened, the anger suddenly present again. But no, no, he told himself. Your man was just trying to make him angry. Mon, the younger son. Mon the purposeless, ignored, younger son. Mon who had nowhere else to put his anger, his loss. Mon, whose father was all powerful in the seas, who favoured no one but his whims. Mon, the brother of his heart.

"I was away," said Luke. "I've only just returned."

"Is that what you're saying? Fine, so. I guess that explains the ease with which Balor was able to swoop down and take your woman. But then, you never give much thought to any woman do you? Sure, there's always another one to come along."

"If that was the case, then why am I here?" asked Luke, trying to keep his tone reasonable. Trying to keep all of himself reasonable. Despite the words, despite the repeated use of "dude" which Luke had found amusing back in the summer but now found irritating. Mon knew all his buttons and could push them with glee at the best of times. Now, though, he was slamming them, all fingers to the ready and pressing with the fullest force possible.

Mon shrugged. "I don't know, dude. You don't like your toys being taken?"

"She's not a toy," Luke bit out. "She does mean a lot to me. More than you can know."

"Feck me, dude. You do move on quickly don't you? It wasn't all that long ago you were saying the same thing about Clíodhna. Or should I say Clio. The name doesn't matter, though, does it, because they're all the same, yeah?" He was adding a bit of an American street drawl to his tone now. Cool, cucumber cool was the intent, but the mottled red face said something else entirely.

"This is different."

"Different, is it? How?" The sneer was back again, cool gone.

"This time I get it, Mon. I get it. I didn't really before, but I do now."

Hurt flashed across Mon's face. "What do you get?"

"All of it. The fear of losing someone you love, the fear that they will never be with you again, and the pain it brings. The agony of worry. And most of all, the guilt because you know it's your own fault that she's suffering."

Mon stared at him, a range of emotions warring in his expression. Grief, pain, anger and, at the last, the guilt. He turned away. "Try experiencing it for as long as I have, man," he said quietly.

Luke ventured a hand on Mon's arm. Mon flinched at his touch but he didn't shrug it off.

"That I would hate to imagine, Mon. The agony of it. And I can only offer you my words, my sympathy." He paused a moment. "And my love," he whispered. "You're still my brother, Mon. No matter what."

Mon, still turned away, looked down at Luke's hand. "My brother?" He shook his head. "I don't know."

"Please," said Luke. "Forgive me. I am truly sorry. Let me make amends."

Mon turned back to him, his face inscrutable, all emotion gone. "I need to change, man. Come back to my place for a beer. We'll talk more."

He left, striding on, running to catch up with his companions, leaving Luke to stand there watching his retreating figure.

LUKE PRESSED THE BUZZER, uncertain of the type of welcome he might receive. He'd taken his time driving to Mon's, reflecting on their encounter. Back at the beach he'd felt that he'd reached

Mon for at least a few moments there, but now he wasn't so sure. The "come back for a beer" invitation had been voiced in a tone that had no invitation in it at all, the dismissal afterwards even more uninviting. It was the dead flat tone of "more things to discuss that aren't pleasant" and after some consideration Luke entertained the possibility it might even be that Mon wanted somewhere private to really put the knife in, a thousand cuts death of their friendship, their brotherhood.

He heard the clatter of footsteps down the stairs and a moment later the door opened and Mon stood there. He nodded and turned, retraced his steps upwards, leaving Luke to follow.

Once inside, Luke glanced around. The state of the place spoke to Luke in ways he wouldn't have expected. Tossed clothes, odd cups, plates and flatware, empty takeaway bags, a couple of empty whiskey bottles and glasses and other bits of detritus cluttered the room. The PlayStation was on the floor as if it had been tossed there angrily. Stale food and dirty washing odours hung in the air.

Mon took a seat on the sofa and Luke headed over to the lone battered armchair, shoving some clothes off to the floor before he sat down. He looked across at Mon.

Mon sprang up. "Feck. Beer. I said a beer, didn't I?"

Mon crossed the room to the small kitchen area off the sitting room and opened the fridge, retrieving a beer. One beer. After taking off the lid, he made his way over to Luke and handed him the beer. Luke took it, giving Mon a puzzled look.

Mon shrugged. "A whiskey for me, I think. You need a clear head."

What the feckityfeck? Thought Luke. He was getting no sense of things now.

Mon made his way back to the kitchen area, opened up one of the presses and retrieved the half full whiskey bottle. He poured a hefty amount into one of the used glasses that cluttered the worktop. Once he was satisfied, he took up the glass and bottle and made his way back to the sofa, where he resumed his seat. He made a place for the bottle on the coffee table, before he leaned back along the sofa, glass in hand. He drank deeply and draped his other arm along the back of the sofa. Back to cucumber cool.

"Right, so," he said. "This is your 'sorry' visit, then, is it?"

"It's me coming to you, head bowed and a heartfelt expression of remorse and real sense of understanding."

"Awfully big of you." The tone remained flat, the expression unreadable. There was effort there, though. Underneath, Luke could feel a little give.

"What did Balor promise you?" Luke asked.

It was the burning question for Luke, part of the "how could he" and "why would he", because deep down he couldn't believe it of Mon. Not unless it was something huge, something heartfelt, a train of thought that led him to one word. One name.

"Have you seen Clíodhna?"

Mon's face twisted in pain and he looked down, shaking his head slightly.

"What did Balor promise you?" Luke asked softly. "Was it Clíodhna?"

Mon lifted his head, his expression forming into something like resignation. "Yes."

"How?" Luke asked, choking on the words. "What did he say?"

Mon took a deep breath. "He said that if I helped him, defied my father and took hold of the waves, that Clíodhna would be impressed. That she would admire me and it wouldn't be long before I could win her over. If I continued to defy Manannán. Be my own man." He frowned. "Be a man."

Luke shook his head, all the anger, the resentment leaking away. "Feck, Mon."

"I know, I know. Feck it, do I know." He looked at Luke wryly, but the pain was there underneath. "I'm a full-fledged eejit. A gombeen of the first rank, sure I am."

Luke shook his head. "Desperate, man. You were desperate."

"Oh, desperate, all right. It was all desperate, in all the levels of meaning." He shook his head. "What the feck was I thinking to believe that gobshite?"

"You weren't thinking," said Luke in a low voice.

Mon gave a bitter laugh. "I never do when it comes to her."

"She's working for him."

Mon nodded sadly. "Yeah, I know. And maybe it was because of that I had this thought, this idea she might, well, she might look at me again if I was helping him, too. To show that I wasn't happy with Manannán's actions."

"But you were happy with it. At the time."

Mon studied him, the war going on in his mind, clear on his face. "Was I?" he whispered. "Was I? Or was I being a stupid desperate prick, asking my father to help, not understanding that it was an opportunity he'd been waiting for. An opportunity that he fostered, nurtured. 'Oh, Mongan, my lad, you can't let her get away with it. Be a man, take your woman'." Mon gave a noise of disgust. "As if you could take Clíodhna."

"You tried explaining it to her, long ago, she wouldn't listen."

"She wouldn't listen."

"She was heartbroken. She lost the one she loved," said Luke, his voice kind. "She probably still is heartbroken if she's working for Balor to get back at Manannán. And you." Luke uttered the last words softly.

Mon nodded slowly. "Yeah she was heartbroken. We both were."

"It's past, Mon. That time is gone, for better or worse. You have to find it in you to take a different path, leave behind the mourning shite."

Mon frowned at Luke. "It's not something I like doing. I've tried. You know I've tried. For so feckin' long I'm tired of it. Tired of myself."

Luke nodded slowly. "Yeah, feck me, I know you've tried. And we've had some good times with your trying."

Mon smiled weakly. "Yeah, we have, so."

"We will again."

Mon sighed. "You promise?"

Luke put his hand to his heart. "On my honour. Mon, you're my brother, of course we'll continue to have fun."

"Honour?" Mon raised his brows, humour present in his expression now.

Luke grinned. "I have all the honour in the world."

"Shall I ask all the ladies that?"

Luke laughed. "Ah, no, no." He sobered. "But that's past now. You know that, don't you?"

Mon studied him. "That's past, is it? But wasn't that where we had fun?"

Luke shook his head. "No, no. Not all. Not the best parts. The best parts are just us." He pulled out an imaginary sword from its scabbard and wielded it with all the swash and buckle of a stage actor.

Mon laughed. "Fine, fine. I believe you."

"Good. And now, I need your help."

Mon snorted. "I suppose you do."

"Will you?"

"Will I what, bro?" asked Mon, his eyes wide with innocence.

"You want me to beg?"

"Of course."

Luke got on his knees before Mon and held his hands up in a supplicatory fashion. "Will you help me get Kayla?"

Mon made a shooing motion. "Not so close to the genitals, dude." There was a twinkle in his eye.

"Feck off," said Luke.

"What?"

"Feck off, but I need your help first."

Mon laughed, swatted Luke across the back of the head. "Let's go, then."

34

SMITHY

S mithy studied Saoirse through the kitchen window. She was standing outside, hands poked in her leather jacket, her dark jeans and Doc Martens looking a little at odds with the rural idyll picture of the small stone shed she was leaning against. Her posture was one that said "laid back, ready for a smoke" until she leaned her head against the shed and looked skywards. The thick waves of her hair were caught up in a plait that hung over her shoulder, though wayward tendrils danced in the light early autumn wind.

The storm that had threatened a few hours earlier seemed to have receded, the approaching dusk appearing to have smothered it with the promise of night that would fall shortly.

The waiting was killing Smithy and he wasn't sure why. He was concerned about Kayla, he was of course, but there was an underriding anxiety that pressed on him and signalled something, he just hadn't identified it yet. Looking at Saoirse, though, soothed him. Sure, she was the honey and he was the bee, eager to be sated, drugged so that all his worries drained away.

And maybe that was the cause of his anxiety. There had

been no honey, a thought that drew a wry smile from him. No honey since America. They'd hardly had the chance to talk, let alone spend the night, or even make love. Here in this little house it was a kip on the sofa or floor situation, a squeeze into a cramped caravan. They were soldiers on campaign. Warriors waiting for battle. No opportunity for even a short conversation. And he understood, he did. But the need, the desire was there, always with him. Especially since America.

He could still feel her lips and the joy of their connection, his body responding in the ways he could now recall, the ways that it had in the long ago. Their long ago. And more than anything he wanted to make that long ago their present. He wanted to preserve their twining, reinforce it so that its fragility would be made firm. He never wanted to lose it or her again. The force of their energy together, he needed that, too, because he knew it was his very life and key to who they were, what they were. Two faces of the one. He needed that. He wanted that.

As if she heard his thoughts, Saoirse lifted her head and stared in his direction. No words were needed, but the message was clear. He set his cup down on the worktop, muttered an excuse to the others, Anu with her endless cup of milk, Maura and Finn in their strange conversation dance, a bewildering mix of coded phrases and words that only they could decipher. Feck's sake, he thought, grinning. Well he had his own conversation, and then some, to have. Hopefully then some.

He excused himself and went outside, making his way to Saoirse, her eyes on his the moment he was in her view. She straightened, her expression curious.

"Is there news?" she asked.

He shook his head, suddenly nervous. "No. Just wanted to get some air, like you."

She raised her brows, a small smile forming on her face. "Air, is it?"

He grinned. "Maybe a bit more than air."

He took up a place beside her, his fingers brushing hers. The hum was still there, the sense of deep connection that lit him up and sent all the music they'd shared in the past through his body like a current that was complete, spinning and whirling in the dance between them. It reassured him, gave him courage to say what he had to say.

"I'm sorry." The words, now he uttered them seemed easy.

"Sorry?"

He gave her a rueful smile. "You're going to make me spell it out, aren't you?"

"It's only fair," she said, her tone light.

"Fair. Fine, so. I suppose it is." He took a deep breath, because it seemed the best way to begin. "I'm sorry for my behaviour, that I've been...."

"So awful?" said Saoirse in a helpful tone.

He laughed. "Ok, yes. I suppose that's the best way to describe it."

"I think so. You were getting really tiresome."

"Sure, I was sick of myself as well."

She laughed. "I would hope so. It was becoming a chore. You were a chore."

"Some chores need to be done, though."

She nodded thoughtfully. "I suppose."

"Thanks for doing this chore."

She laughed. "Well, Smithy, 'doing you' isn't always a chore."

His eyes lit at that and he took her hand in full, traced his thumb across her wrist in a lazy manner, relishing the small shudder his touch arose in her. Her eyes darkened, she licked her lips.

"We've had no time to ourselves," Smithy said. He stared at her mouth, marvelling at its fullness.

"No time."

"Did you want to check the shed? See if we can find anything that might be helpful?"

She nodded. "I think we need to find anything that might help. Wherever possible."

He took her hand and led her into the stone shed, shutting the door behind him. It was small enough, storing tools and other small farming equipment. A narrow window at the back provided some light. But the light was unnecessary at the moment, which required instinct only to draw her into his arms. He lowered his mouth on hers, kissing her first softly, tasting her, exploring her for what seemed like the first time, but what he knew now deep inside him was countless. Their lips together, it was where they were meant to be. Where he was meant to be.

He deepened the kiss and could feel her response quicken, and as they pressed their bodies close it was more than two together, it was melding, two metals become one, her quickfire and his, igniting a flame until they were combusting, melting, moulding themselves into one.

He groaned, stroking first her hair, tangling his fingers in her plait, moving his lips to her throat, drinking in her scent of air, breath and all things musical. He found the inside of her jacket and the bare skin under her shirt, stroking it gently. She ran her hands under his leather jacket, and along the curves of his chest. Her touch spread the flame, the heat rising and the joy of it all and the feel of its perfection that was more than just a memory now, overflowed and wrapped them both in its warmth. The perfection carried her leg to wrap around his, and he to press closer, both wanting and needing actual union.

He stepped backwards, pulling her with him, but his foot caught a rake and it slammed into him, catching him off balance. He grunted with surprise and the pain of it. Saoirse pulled away, her face filled with concern.

"Are you okay?"

He gave a wry laugh. "Feckin' rake. Popped up and caught me."

Saoirse giggled. "Rake? Is that what you're calling it now?"

He gave her a good natured shove. "Were you complaining?"

She shook her head. "Never." She put a hand on his chest. "But you are okay, aren't you?"

He knew she meant more than a hit with a rake. He put his hand over hers. "I think so. I don't know."

"You remember though."

"I remember."

"Your leg, your strength, is it back?"

"As far as I know. I haven't really tested it. I'm not sure about everything." He stroked her face gently. "I can hear the music again. Not all the time, but sometimes."

"When? Any time specifically?"

He kissed her lightly. "Now. With you."

"With me?" Her tone was tentative. "Just me?"

"Not always. There was a time without you. But I had the bowl. Your bowl. It started then."

"My bowl you made?"

"Yes."

He'd given her the bowl again and he knew that she had it near, in her bag inside the house.

"I was thinking I might try and find Airmed. Ask her if she knows anything about what's happening."

"Not Diancecht?"

He snorted in disgust. "He already voiced his opinion. No, I thought maybe Airmed might have some thoughts. I would rather be sure in the days to come. Sure about myself, so that when the battle is here, I'll know what I'm capable of."

"I'm sure you'll be grand. But yes, I understand."

He squeezed the hand that still rested on his chest. "Thanks."

"For?"

"Everything."

"Exactly what things?"

He grinned. "You're going to make me say this as well, aren't you?"

"You should know this by now."

"Fine, so. Thanks for being there. Being supportive and all that you did for me. Saving my life." He kissed her softly. "And for now. For understanding."

"Will I go with you?"

The words were simple and he knew she meant to see Airmed, but underneath those words there was a larger, deeper meaning.

"Always," he said.

"Always," she said.

It was the sound of a car pulling into the yard that drew Smithy reluctantly away from Saoirse this time. He knew who it was, before confirmation came at the sight of Luke's SUV when Smithy opened the shed door. Luke was just getting out of the driver's side and, to Smithy's surprise, someone else starting climbing out of the front passenger side. Mon.

The sight of Mon caused Smithy to stop in his tracks. He looked over at Luke, saw the bright expression filled with hope and also the tension of a battle ready body.

He gave a mental shrug, a "fine, so" thought that still left him curious and led him to the house, his hand still holding Saoirse's. She'd made her own little, "oh wow" noise and followed without complaint or further word.

Once inside, Smithy and Saoirse stood together, off to the side, curious onlookers to the spectacle of the two men, looking very much in their surfer dude attitudes, and except for Luke's short hair, they could have been the double take of the photo that Smithy had removed from Luke's house months ago.

Anu, who had risen and embraced Mon, pulled back and patted him on the cheek like a naughty child.

"Ah, Mongan, it's good to see you," she said, but her eyes were full of mild reproach.

"Thanks," said Mon and he had the grace to seem contrite, though Smithy did wonder.

"He's come to help me," said Luke.

"He will of course," said Anu, nodding. She took a seat again, tired, but managed a smile for Mon. "You're a good brother, Mongan. I know that."

Mon looked away and gave a slight nod. Anu resumed her seat at the table and patted the now empty chair that had been Saoirse's earlier. Mon took it, but he seemed uncomfortable so near to Anu and her close scrutiny.

Luke moved over by Mon and leaned against the wall behind him. "We've formed a general plan."

"Do tell," said Maura drily. "I'm sure it's grand."

Luke gave her a cool look. "It's the best that's possible, given the circumstances."

"It is of course," said Finn, his brows raised.

Smithy smiled inwardly, amused at Maura and Finn's pairing. They were standing beside each other now, both of them with their arms crossed, expressions sceptical. He fought the urge to nudge Saoirse and nearly laughed a moment later when he felt a small poke of her finger in his side. There was no need for further clarification. She'd seen it too.

"And the plan is?" said Maura.

"Mon and I will cross in a boat. At night. A stealth approach."

"A stealth approach?" asked Finn, humour in his voice. "Ah, sure, I forgot, you're a special forces team."

Luke gave him a dark look. "Mon and I know the sea. Together we can make a safe crossing."

"Just the two of you?" asked Maura.

Smithy stood quietly, enjoying the dynamics. Sure, Maura and Finn were doing fine, asking all the relevant questions. All he had to do was listen. So far, there was no need for his comments.

"Yes," said Luke. "Just the two of us. It will be more efficient and effective."

"Efficient and effective," echoed Maura. "And what of Balor's people? Will just the two of you be more efficient and effective if there are a large crew of them?"

Luke looked at Mon. "We work well together. We fight well together."

Maura exchanged disbelieving looks with Finn. She laughed. "Do you hear that? If we ever doubted he was a hero, there's no need to now, because he doesn't need us. He can do it on his own."

Luke frowned. "I'm not doing it on my own. Mon will be with me."

"Mon, who helped create the situation in the first place," said Finn, his tone flat, containing no accusation. It was a statement of fact.

Mon flinched, looked down at the table, remaining silent.

"Anu has faith in Mon," said Saoirse stepping forward. "She just said that."

"No she didn't," said Maura curtly.

"Not in those words," said Anu. "But Saoirse understood correctly the meaning of the words I did speak." She stood up and moved to Maura, resting a hand on her shoulder. "As do you, Maura."

The annoyance and anger that filled Maura's expression died away and she gave a sigh. "I suppose you're right."

"Do you want our help at all?" asked Finn. He'd moved closer to Maura, their shoulders touching. "You have it if you need it."

Luke paused a moment. "Come to the end of the peninsula with us. And wait. Just in case."

"In case?" asked Maura. "Any specific 'in case'?"

Luke tensed and shook his head. "Nothing specific."

Saoirse put a hand on his arm. "Will you be all right with Eithne?" she asked softly.

He pursed his lips, glanced at Mon. "I think so." He straightened slightly. "Kayla will be there, it'll be grand."

"Bring her back, Luke," said Anu in a low voice.

"Kayla?" Luke asked.

"Eithne."

Luke and the others stared at Anu. Finn began to nod slowly. "Yes. That's it all right."

Maura nodded. "The only way, really."

Luke frowned. "No."

"Yes," said Anu. "It must be done."

Smithy who'd understood almost immediately the moment Anu mentioned it that taking Eithne as a hostage was the perfect way to lure Balor, just as he no doubt had planned for Luke with Kayla. Instead of an island off the coast of the Beara, they would take Eithne back to the Otherworld. There, she would lure Balor across, because everyone here knew there was at least one Tuatha de Danann who could take him and any warriors not already there across. Clíodhna.

"You have to," said Smithy, lending his own voice.

"Yes," said Saoirse. "It has to be done."

The words hung in the air, the doubt leaking out of them like a slow drip on a tap. Smithy heard it, nearly felt it.

"We'll all go, so we will," he said. "Keep vigil."

Saoirse looked down at Anu. "But not Anu. She can keep vigil here. With Bláthín and Nana."

35

LUKE

Luke could see the lights of Kayla's car in the rear view mirror, pulling up behind them in the small area where he parked his SUV. It was the best place he knew that would offer shelter to launch the small boat that Mon had obtained from a friend of a friend of a friend. Luke could see the friend waiting, his body hunched against the wind, the boat nearby.

The wind was unfortunate, but he trusted Mon. He did.

Mon's expression was solemn as he studied the sky a moment before looking at Luke. "Right, fine. We're doing this."

Luke gave a nod. "We're doing this."

Luke reached into the back seat of the SUV for his sword and dagger, while Mon did the same as if it was choreographed, part of some costume drama, only minus the medieval clothes, the armour and most of the swash and buckle. In his dark jeans, boots and jacket, Luke felt more like the SWAT team member Maura had inferred, or even a Ninja warrior, rather than some errant knight out to save his lady. But Kayla was so much more than some simpering female and so must he be. More. All that was needed.

They both exited the SUV and made their way over to the friend, Luke giving a small wave to acknowledge the other four waiting in Kayla's car. He knew they were anxious, mistrusting of Mon, and maybe even himself. Sure, could he even he trust himself? He knew that he was determined to get Kayla back, but he couldn't predict what would happen with his mother involved. Or how he would deal with her. He knew what he should do, what the others wanted him to do. But he was just as likely to kill her as take the trouble to bring her along. His relationship with Eithne was the contradiction to the collection of mammy jokes and any other collection of ideas regarding the mammy and her son. The original helicopter parent and full of so many in-jokes, comedy shows and books had made huge profits on the concept since so many related to it. For him, though, it was alien, foreign, but, the thought came to him, so was he. His relationship with his mother was the stuff of Greek myth, only his was Tuatha de Danann. Or Fomorian. And there you have it, he thought. There he had it. And what twist would this myth take now? The dark humour of it made him smile sourly.

The boat, once they launched it, proved sound enough, he knew Mon wouldn't have selected it otherwise. Mon handled the boat and the launching with a manner so capable the friend of a friend of a friend seemed reassured and stopped insisting he go with them. There was a small light on the boat and Mon turned it on only for form's sake, until the friend was out of sight. After that it was all instinct and Mon. Mon feeling the waves, talking to the waves and the elements that governed every aspect of the water. His strength, his power, him. Luke could sense Mon's connection, the joy he felt at this connection, how it soothed him just as it emboldened him. There was a song there, rising up as the sea itself thrilled under Mon's steady hand at the helm, governing it with a firm but sensitive hold to be smooth, gentle and persuasive. For the current to push just enough to move the boat along, no matter that the engine pretended it had control, or the rudder gave it direction. Its north was the north of the sea and where it chose to make it, where the current sent it. All this Luke could feel under his feet and up through his body. It was a song. Mon's song. A hymn to his own joy and connection.

They'd decided to try to land in a small cove with only a spit of a beach. They had some ropes to climb the small cliff and from there they would make their way to the abandoned place where Eithne held Kayla. The thought of Eithne camping out seemed unimaginable. The woman he was familiar with enjoyed luxury, but again, he reminded himself, he really didn't know her. Just as she had no interest in him, he had none in her. So she might have been camping for years, joined a group, trekked mountains. Who the feck knew?

He made an effort to calm himself as the cove drew in sight. Mon's focus was tight, so many aspects to navigate, to control. The rocks were there, hidden most times and ready to rip great holes in the boat. Mon was a master at navigating waters, even though he'd run aground in his personal life.

Any tiny doubts Luke might have had about Mon and his willingness to help were slowly dissipating, because Luke knew that Mon could have easily contrived to have Luke thrown overboard and lost in a wave. But there'd not been the slightest hint, not even a joke of an attempt, nothing. It was all serious intent. And though it was unlike Mon, forever joking Mon, Luke felt some of his tension pertaining to Mon ease.

And now, as they prepared to ascend the cliff, unfurling ropes and preparing the other equipment, Luke tried to push any other reservations aside. If this was a trap, he didn't think

Mon was leading him, or even guiding him into it. At least he hoped not.

They ascended silently, Luke leading, the rope anchored safely above them, and once again, Luke felt like a Special Forces team or a Ninja warrior. But the tension in his body wasn't anything mythical or storylike. When they reached the top, he suppressed any inclination to joke with Mon, and it was only in one brief moment, when Mon was unfastening himself from the rope, and he'd looked up briefly at Luke with such humour in his face, that Luke knew they'd shared similar thoughts about the situation. But still, he'd said nothing and the moment had passed, the humour faded and Mon looked away. Whether it was Luke's doing or Mon's, it was unclear.

They stowed the equipment under a nearby gorse bush, marked it with some stones and set off at a light jog, the swords slung across their backs, daggers at their hips. Luke had dithered about bringing Retaliator but had decided this was not the task for that sword. He'd left his shield behind and wondered now if that was the best decision, but shields were something more easily noticed should they come across anyone. Sure, a shield would provide little protection against guns. Because guns were a possibility. Guns were always a possibility in this world. Across the water it was different altogether.

As they drew near the ruins, the two of them separated to make a wide circle around the house. No words had been spoken before or now, it was just there, the knowing between them, that bond. The bond he'd never thought would be broken. And now it was retied, but he wasn't sure how firm that knot would hold. But he'd go with it now, enjoy the seamless way they worked together and use it. "Now" was what he had in so many ways. He would stay with that.

He made his way across the stony ground, careful of the boggy areas and jutting outcrops of rock but always on the lookout for any unnatural shadows or movements. There was no sign of any animal or human as far as he could see. In the distance, though, he could hear a sheep bleating. Looking for its lamb, he supposed. Or was that past now? Feck, he'd really lost that touch, hadn't he. Too long living the surfer dude/metro life.

Off to his right he thought he heard a noise. He scanned the area, eyes straining to focus in the dark. The sky was black, any trace of stars obscured by the clouds that had filled the sky earlier. Rain still threatened, hanging in the air but not quite making it to drops. But it was enough to muffle the sound that he'd heard. He moved slowly, his hand on his dagger, ready to draw it. There, he thought, when he heard it again. Below, he could see a faint light. It took him a moment to realise that the ruined farmhouse and outbuildings were there and the light was most likely coming from the place Eithne and Kayla occupied. He stopped to study it, squatting low, looking for any signs of movement. Was that where the muffled sounds had come from? He didn't think so. Both times it had sounded like a grunt, as if someone had stumbled.

He scanned behind him one more time, but there was nothing. Carefully he rose and moved forward, taking extra care where he placed his feet, but also alert for any more sounds or indications that there was someone or something nearby.

Luke was nearly half way around when he saw the figure up ahead. At first he thought it was Mon, the circuit for both of them nearly complete, but there was something about the height, the way the figure carried himself, that told Luke it wasn't Mon.

He drew up short, squatted behind a small outcrop of rock and studied the approaching figure, uncertain if he'd been seen. It wasn't until the figure was less than a metre away that Luke knew who it was. And it wasn't because the figure approached him with purpose or had a drawn sword, suddenly evident. No, it was an instinct.

"Ah, now," the figure said in Irish. "I thought you'd be bolder than this, Lugh. King's champion. Sneaking up like some shameful little secret."

Luke rose, straightened and drew the sword from his back. "Ah, sure, Eithne. I can be as bold as you please."

He held his sword aloft, showing her, showing himself. They were enemies, not to be trusted. That much was true. It was, sure it was.

In the gloom Eithne approached slowly. "You don't want to do this here, in the gloom, do you?"

"I can see well enough. You can stop right there. You're grand where you are."

"You're not afraid of me, are you?" There was a slight sneer there.

Luke snorted. "Why would I be?"

"Because of all the time that's passed, since I saw you," she said in a dark tone, though something underlying it made him pause. Wonder. "Who knows what power I have now? What my dear father has taught me?"

"Sure, you only saw me the other day."

He'd kept the tone flippant, for his own sake, because she was right, it had been a long time since they'd seen each other. They both had made certain of that. Or so it seemed.

She gave a brief laugh, but it hit a sour note. "Oh, that. Well, I suppose that did count, since I knew to expect you, only I wasn't certain about the when. Just as I knew to expect you in America. Did you find the message with the little gifts I left for you?"

Luke struggled to keep his tone even. "To be fair the little gifts were more for Goibhniu and Bríd, than me."

She smiled at him. "Ah, now, my oh so clever Lugh discovered the secret."

Luke shook his head. "No, not me."

"My father found them, in a small store in America that sold Native American artefacts, but he knew immediately that they were something else. Something from a time not here."

"He did of course," muttered Luke. "How does he feel about the slingshot and spear?" Perversity made him ask the question, along with a desire to needle.

Eithne glanced down at the ruined farmhouse for a moment. "Don't be bold, now. That's not a question, because you know the answer."

And he did. Suddenly the desire to spar verbally with this woman left him. "I do indeed," he said coldly. He lifted the sword and moved towards her.

She stepped back a little, her stance taking on a more war like posture, her sword raised to meet his.

"You would fight your own mother?" she asked. "This isn't a Greek tragedy."

"You would fight your own son?" he said.

She spat to the side. "That son is a traitor to his people."

Luke stiffened. "His people are the Tuatha de Danann. He is no traitor. And up to now I'd stayed out of all affairs, until your father made it impossible for me to do that."

"No," she said, her voice cold. "No, you were always wanting to be something you're not. I'm Fomorian. You are therefore Fomorian."

"You can state that all you want, Eithne, but you cared nothing for me, Fomorian or de Danann."

"You're just like your father," she said, her voice rough.

"I wish I knew," he said simply. "But I don't. So I can only be Lugh. King's champion. Oh, and a kickass musician and surfer. Ask Mon."

Eithne snorted. "I wouldn't ask that boy anything. Or his family. They're worse than any of those others you now call companions."

"Fine, so," he said.

He'd heard enough. More than enough. Nothing had changed and he didn't know why he thought it might have changed. He moved slowly to the side, advancing on her at an angle. She moved towards the other side, her dark trousers disappearing against the landscape behind her. Her shoulder length dark hair flew out, caught by the wind. It whipped into her face and Lugh moved in quickly, taking advantage of her obscured vision and swung his sword, hitting hers with a hard thwack that sent it spinning from her hand and flying across the ground. A moment later there was a clang as it hit a rock.

A figure moved behind her, rising up from the lower ground and seizing her arms. Mon. Luke felt some of his tension ease.

"Now, so," said Mon. "You think I'm worse than any of Lugh's other companions, is it, Eithne?"

Even in the dark Luke could see her glare. Mon just laughed.

LUKE MADE his way down the slope of the hill with care, and with Mon's help, leading a gagged and bound Eithne between them. It was heavy going, and the lighting poor, but Luke was still reluctant to put on any kind of torch until he could be sure there was no one else besides Eithne guarding Kayla. He hadn't bothered asking Eithne, not only because he wouldn't trust her answer, but also because he'd had enough of her – and himself for wanting something he knew wasn't available. Feck off with yourself, he thought, not clear if the words were directed at his mother or himself. Himself, he decided, especially that he even thought the word "mother" in regard to this woman before him.

She made it easy to gag her, to tie her hands tightly, and even twisting the rope that little more so that it bit into her skin. Petty, so petty, but there you are.

They reached the bottom of the incline and moved towards the ruins, the dim glow from the tent inside them becoming more visible. Luke tensed, surveying the grounds around him as they came closer. It wasn't until they were nearly at the clearing that used to be the yard that a figure jumped out at them from behind a half ruined wall, knocking them all down with the force of it. Luke rolled with the fall, regaining his footing as soon as possible, before launching himself on the figure that had attacked. Eithne broke away and started to run for the tent, but Mon tackled her, bringing her down once again. Luke meanwhile wrestled with the figure and felt the sting of a dagger against his hand, cutting him.

For a moment the thought came that it might be Balor he was fighting and he thrilled at the possibility of ending it here, no matter that Anu had said it must be in the Otherworld. He would kill him now, make his threefold death across this water. He would find a way to make it so. The thoughts and the joy that went with it lasted no more than a few moments, because the wiry agility of this person he fought was nothing like Balor's looming bulk. Anger surged through him and with a frustrated thwack, Luke shoved the knife out of the person's hand and pinned him to the ground. A dark knit hat was pulled down low over his head, to his eyes. Luke drew back the hat. Colm, the man who'd stolen Retaliator.

"You, you fecker," said Luke. "How the feck did you escape Daghda?"

Colm fought to regain the knife but Luke gripped harder, feeling the man squirm under his efforts. The anger was back. "This time there will be no returning," he said, and plunged the dagger in Colm's side, angling it upwards towards the heart. A moment later the struggling stopped and Colm's limbs went limp. He was dead.

Panting, Luke checked the pulse at his neck and, satisfied Colm was dead, he rose. There was no sign of Mon or Eithne, and he could only presume they were inside the tent.

He moved to the entrance. It was large enough, so that he only had to duck a little to go through the opening. Once inside, he blinked against the light of the two lanterns that hung from hooks on either side of the curved roof pole. There was a cot on each side, sleeping bags laid out on top. Kayla was on the one at the right side, lying in one of the sleeping bags, her eyes shut. He was glad to note the small rise and fall of her chest, but still, he rushed to her side, kneeling beside her and placing his fingers against her neck. A weak pulse beat there. He nearly moaned aloud to find her in such a state.

He pressed his lips on hers. "Soon," he told her softly. "We'll get you home and then all will be well soon after that. I promise, my love. On my life I promise."

Across the tent he heard a snort from Eithne. Kayla didn't move her mouth, or utter a sound but the phrase "ignore her" echoed through his mind and it contained all Kayla's intonations and her loving coaxing. It made him smile. He kissed her forehead and stood up.

"I'll carry Kayla. You take Eithne," he said to Mon.

"What about your man outside?"

Luke shrugged. "He's dead. He can wait."

Mon nodded. "Good enough. We can make arrangements for him later." He glanced around them. "Will we pack this up?"

Luke shook his head. "No. We won't bother. Leave it."

Mon shrugged. "Right, so."

Carefully, Luke lifted Kayla into his arms. She weighed nothing. The wind would take her away, she was so light. He knew such little weight would make it easier for him, but his concern washed away any positive aspect because of what it really meant. They had little time. And it didn't take the dead and dying grass, the stagnant and acrid smelling pools of water scattered across the peninsula, or the volatile weather to tell him that the Beara was on the edge. Kayla was on the edge.

Time was running out.

36

MAURA

It was late, after midnight. Finn was leaning up against the wall beside me. We seemed to be doing a lot of leaning against walls lately in a "not enough chairs" kind of way, but really it felt like we were at a party, or a club, intimate but not, together for a chat. Him next to me. Me next to him. There was chat all right and it was noisy and raucous, only I was trying not to. Chat. Trying really hard. What was going on between us I couldn't control and I found it unnerving. I did. Him next to me, me next to him, the chat. Unspoken of course, but it was chat and I didn't know what to do with it.

Conversation went on around us and over us, or at least over me, and my head all over the place, unable to hear it, or concentrate for the chat between us. Him next to me, me next to him. I didn't even venture a glance or a look, it would have been too much, sent me over the edge. I knew that. And knowing that, I tried to focus, tried to grab my head and put it firmly in the attentive space for the conversation at the table, the one where we're all discussing purpose and intent. The one I should be paying attention to.

Eithne had been a surprise. Even though I knew she had

been at the ruins, guarding Kayla, I had presumed Luke would leave her there dead, or disabled and unable to give chase, at the very least. But, according to Luke, Mon had agreed to deal with her struggling as he rappelled down the cliff face, and in the boat. Fair play to the man for managing it. With Kayla safely tucked in her bed now, Luke was ready to explain himself. Was explaining himself. And it became clear, in fact it was clever. And now the woman was locked in the shed. I smiled at the thought of all her designer clothes having to make contact with rusty old farm equipment. And the ground. Yes, I'd noticed the pricey gear and the glam make up. Feck, the woman even had hair extensions, or at least that's what it seemed. Every bit of glam available. Everything but Botox, but then why would she? I tried to picture her wielding a sword with menace as Luke had inferred. Ah stop. It was too funny.

"She tried to kill you," said Smithy. "A perfect lure for Balor, but dangerous. She'll need constant watching."

I blinked, trying to make sense of that image.

"It's what we intended," said Anu.

"Was it now?" asked Smithy. "You wanted to kidnap that woman?"

"As Luke said, it's the best way to lure Balor across the water."

"Sure he'll know it's a trap," said Smithy. "He'll just send a few of the men he has there already and try to get her back. One of the traitors will be perfect."

"I'm not so sure," said Luke. "It's a risk for him to do that, because if they fail, he knows we'll interrogate them."

"Knowing Balor, he'll probably send people who have been given false information," said Finn, speaking up for the first time.

I looked at him then. His expression was difficult to read, at least to me. He seemed intent on the conversation, his tone engaged, his words making sense. But then there was the chat. It was still going on. Him next to me. Me next to him. I found it disorienting still. I clenched my fists.

"Ah, he'll go across the water, all right. He wouldn't be able to resist it."

Anu nodded carefully. "Yes, that's what I think."

"So we'll bet on that, is it?" asked Smithy. He sighed. "Fine, so. I'm sure you're right."

Saoirse placed a hand on his shoulder. His posture eased a bit and his expression cleared. He gave a slight nod, acknowledging her gesture.

"Where will we hold her?" asked Finn. "Tara? That seems the best place."

"We'll take her to Tara, yes," said Anu. "At least initially. We'll talk with Daghda."

"Not Magh Tuireadh?" asked Mon.

Luke looked up at Mon, a slow smile spreading on his face. The others regarded Mon, Smithy with a careful look, Finn interested and Saoirse curiously. All except Anu. She nodded knowingly.

"Exactly," she said. "We must check with Daghda about that. The terrain, the battle placements, and if that's where it's best held."

"And other things," said Luke, his tone dark. He shook his head. "Would there be other elements involved in this that would compel the battle to take place there, or somewhere else?"

Mon moved next to Luke. It was a gesture of support, acknowledgement that no matter the difficulties each faced for the battle, Luke's role was the most dangerous and the most important.

"I'd say the signs point to Magh Tuireadh," said Anu her voice turned reedy, nearly disappearing. She cleared her throat.

"I'm sorry. It's getting late." She cleared her throat again. "We must check with Daghda, but I think, yes. It's the best place, for all considerations."

None of them spoke the details of those considerations, but I knew everyone thought of them at that moment.

"Considerations?" asked Mon softly.

Of course. Mon didn't know that detail. I looked at Luke, as did the others, to see if he was going to answer Mon.

"A threefold death," Luke said, looking down.

Mon nodded. "Threefold. And you're the one who must give it to him?"

Luke nodded. Mon gave a short intake of breath, the not quite gasp, the not quite sniff so commonly used locally but, here, now, from Mon, who gripped Luke's shoulder, it spoke volumes of the strength needed for Luke to complete such a task on Balor. His grandfather.

That I could read so much in that intake of breath and Mon's gesture made me wonder of its impact on Luke. That bond between them, it was almost tangible and as Luke looked into Mon's eyes, the conversation there, silent but full of so much power and emotion, nearly knocked me over. And then Finn, his own hand rested on my arm, a chat turned serious, a calming and support that spoke volumes to me. And only me, I hoped.

I wanted it private, this chat. I wanted… him next to me. Me next to him. But I couldn't. Could I? Could I not?

"If that's decided then," said Smithy, breaking into the silent conversations being had by all, "Saoirse and I will head off. Go across the water. We've much to do, much to prepare."

Anu nodded. "A good choice."

"Sound out," said Finn. "We'll follow when we can."

Luke nodded and Mon shrugged his assent.

"Fine, so," I said, determined to use my voice. Show I was a part of this conversation.

"Do you have everything you need to head across the water?" asked Finn.

We were standing outside, a mug of tea in hand, the early morning mist starting to clear off the mountains. The day was dull and only a slight breeze stirred the air, but it felt fresh, new, just the same. Or maybe it was me. My resolve.

I shrugged. "Sure, my sword is there back at the house, but I can always find one to use over there."

"No, no, you're grand. I'm going to call home, collect a few things before heading over. You can come with me."

I straightened, took a deep drink from my mug. "Ah, there's no need. No need it all."

"It's fine. It's on the way, so. No bother at all."

I snorted. "On the way?" I raised my brow.

He laughed. "Figure of speech. You know yourself."

If only, I thought. I don't. That's the problem. The conversation had gone on all night while I'd attempted to sleep in the hugely uncomfortable sofa turned bed in the caravan. The crick in my neck reminded me even now this was never going to occur again. Like the chat. I'd resolved that too, just before I'd risen and left the caravan to go find something to eat. And the cup of tea. Which she held now and Finn trying to convince her to go with him.

Go with him. At the moment the "going with" seemed more than just a spin in a car. And I couldn't. I could not. It wouldn't end well. I didn't want to lose Finn and the "going with" seemed to guarantee that.

"I can't, Finn," I said quietly.

He stilled. "You can, of course. Why can't you?"

"I can't." My voice came out strangled. "I'm not like you. I'm.... Sure we're friends, are we not?"

"We are of course."

He reached for me, but I moved away.

"What's wrong?" he asked.

"Nothing," I said. My voice was stronger now, firm. "It's all good. I'm your friend, you're my friend. Friends. Always."

He moved again, clasped my shoulder. "I'll always be your friend, Maura," he said softly. "I'll always be Morrigan's friend, too."

I choked at those words, a half strangled laugh, half sob. "You're a fool to be friends with Morrigan. Though she is grateful."

He laughed and even the sound of that hearty laugh was enough to make me blush. Oh feck me, but this was awfully pathetic. It had to stop.

"Friends," I said feigning brightness. "Good, so. I'm glad to hear it. It's what I want. What I need."

"What you need?" he said, his tone neutral.

"Of course. I need you, Finn. There, I've said it, though I'm sure you know that by now. Didn't I make a fool of myself there in America because I told you I didn't?"

He rubbed my shoulder, his hand creating a heat I really could do without. But I let it be, my one little treat that I'd allow, because it would be the last time. All friends and nothing more. Just the nod, the smile and laugh for friends. I couldn't be having the touch of his skin, or the feel of him even. The feel of him.

I sighed. "Sure, we'll always be friends. We will, so. Forever."

He laughed. "So you'll let me take you to your house so you can collect your things?"

I inhaled. "No, Finn, best not. I'll be grand. I'll cross over here and use what I can find over there."

I took a sip of tea, refusing to look at him, to move in his direction. I felt his hand withdraw, I felt all of him withdraw, confusion and hurt hanging in the air.

"Fair enough," he said. "I'll go now, shall I?"

I couldn't even manage a nod, but I felt him go, heard the movement that went with it. It was for the best. When all was said and done I was Morrigan. Didn't I learn that in America, if nothing else? War goddess extraordinaire, no matter what Finn had tried to tell me, what he'd tried to finesse me into believing so I'd come back. It was for the best. I told myself that, knowing I'd be saying it every day, and every hour of that day and nearly every minute of that hour. Feck me—it was. For the best.

37

SAOIRSE

Saoirse and Smithy travelled in silence and had for some time, both jogging lightly across the rough bog of the Otherworld terrain, swords and round shields at their back, daggers at their sides, avoiding the forest. It was a strategy they'd adopted by unspoken consent the moment they'd arrived on the Otherworld banks, crossing over just past noon that morning. But now, the dark forest which was nearly a kilometre away, still seemed to rise up in front of them, along with the question. The question that now hung in the air, that question Saoirse knew had to be answered sooner or later. She would just rather have it later. Later would be best. It was the risk they took coming now, earlier than the others. But there was much to do, much to prepare for, and Airmed to see.

They could have made the swords back in Gort na Tubrid, at Smithy's forge there, but the carrying of them, that was it, the carrying of them would have been too much. That's what Saoirse told herself. And sure, they probably hadn't enough materials there for fashioning who knows how many swords. For they needed the count from Daghda. Your ones who didn't have magic swords, because they were lost, gone, stolen, as well as your ones who'd never had a sword in the first place types of statistics that would give Smithy and her a goal. She hoped that was the reasoning, in any case. Sure, it was a sound reasoning. Smithy was better now, maybe a little wobbly with it, but he could do it, they could do it. Together they would create the swords, fashion them out of the silver, steel and magic. And the swords they made would be the best that had ever been forged, Retaliator aside. These swords would battle until every enemy was down. That she knew, deep inside her. Sure, Smithy knew it, didn't he? Couldn't he feel it?

Smithy started to slow down and she drew in her pace as well when she saw the approaching mounted figure ahead.

"Do you know who it is?" she asked.

Smithy shook his head. "He doesn't seem familiar, no."

She studied him. His horse was nothing of note, a pony that functioned well on the rough terrain. He wore a thick cloak that obscured the rest of his clothes, though it wasn't that cold, or at least it didn't feel so to Saoirse. His boots, dark and scuffed with age, were tucked securely into the stirrups. On his head he wore a stocking cap that seemed out of place and only accentuated the long beak like nose and the bushy beard that adorned his chin.

As Saoirse and Smithy closed in on the man, he looked up, smiled and raised his hand in greeting. It was then that Saoirse noticed his humped back under the cloak, and it was sympathy that overwhelmed her rather than caution.

He spoke quickly, his words tumbling into each other, gesturing expressively with his hands and at first Saoirse just didn't bother listening. Sure, she had no clue about Irish, let alone the old language most commonly spoken here. Why would she understand? So it was only gradually, after he'd spoken for a few minutes and more, that she realised she did understand him. He was asking if they were stopping soon, if he could share their fire and their fare and he would return the favour with a tale.

Smithy looked surprised, rather than wary, or even confused. It took a moment for her to realise that they both understood the man. And not because he was speaking English. No, it wasn't that strange. Well, it was strange enough, because it was the old language the man spoke and the strange part was that they both understood him. At least it appeared so.

"You're welcome of course," said Smithy.

She needed no other confirmation before the joy, the amazement washed through her and it was all she could do not to shove Smithy as hard as she could with all the "would you feckin' believe it" strength in the motion. What is this? What the feck? And all of it. All of the words of disbelief poured out in one big shoving match of joy But she didn't because all of the Bríd, the Bríd that was her swelled forth and uttered the formal words of hospitality that told the world and Smithy "Bríd has returned".

It seemed impossible that, for this moment, she was wearing jeans, T-shirt and a leather jacket, when she felt she was wearing a shimmery flowing gown with long billowing sleeves, hair cascading, not in some plait tucked tidily underneath her jacket. A Saoirse thought, but derived from Bríd. Her two selves. Herselves.

Smithy grinned at her, as if sensing her feelings. "We will break our journey here, and as my companion said, we'd be happy to have your company."

It was a good place to break the journey. There was no doubt, she thought as she spied a sheltered outcropping nearby and thought of the food in their packs. Dusk was approaching. All the ingredients, those elements were. She glanced over at Smithy, just to check, only from habit. Yes, habit, and also because it seemed right. No reassurance needed, that hadn't prompted her, no it hadn't indeed. Still, when Smithy's answering warm smile came, she felt a bit of easing. The man was harmless, hunched back or no. In fact more harmless, with that to burden his body, it must be a crippling disease to cause such a back, sure it had to be.

"Turlough," the man said, giving a graceful bow.

"Turlough?" She glanced at Smithy and smiled. "Like the blind harper?"

"Exactly like him," he said. "Only not blind. Not here."

The remark was cryptic but Saoirse shrugged it off and grinned. "Only not blind and not a harper with it."

He chuckled. "Ah, no." He started to remove his cloak, like some magician in his "abracadabra" moment and there on his back was not a hump but a leather bag. Harp shaped.

Saoirse laughed. "A harper then. But not blind."

He grinned at her. "Not blind."

"So we've stories and music to look forward to after the meal," said Smithy.

"Oh certainly."

Joy rushed through Saoirse at the prospect. An evening's respite from the tension and sense of imminent battle, of testing her strength and the dilemma of who she was.

The joy carried her through helping to establish the camp and spreading out the fare for all of them. Smithy had introduced the two of them to Turlough as Saoirse and Smithy, thankfully going for the simple approach that required no extra explanation or potential demands. Poetry might be the least of them, and sure she would be happy to offer some, but that would now be only if the moment moved her to do so.

Darkness had fallen by the time they'd settled into that mode, that frame of mind that said "I'm comfortable, ready and listening just for the love of it, the wonder of it". And whether there was good craic to be had or not, she was certainly ready and comfortable.

The small fire they'd lit gave a soft glow to their faces. Smithy leaned against a large rock, Saoirse reclining against his chest, as if she was a puzzle piece interlocking with his. A perfect fit.

Turlough took the harp in hand and rested it on his lap. Twenty-six strings gave it enough of a range, each one ringing out purely as he tested them for tuning. Saoirse marvelled at it, until she reminded herself where she was. Still, she felt the beauty and clarity of the sound, allowing it to envelop her, cloaking her in the fullness of the sound of each string as Turlough plucked it.

Tuning complete, he struck up a chord. It was a "get your attention" chord and completely unnecessary in Saoirse's case. She was already riveted, drawn to him, her eyes following every movement and her ears alert and receptive. Smithy's arms came around her then, pulling her closer, feeling the connection, too.

It was a tale, the language's *fadó, fadó, fadó* beginning it, signalling the long ago that started every old tale. It made her smile and gave even more warmth to the words and the atmosphere. A warrior and his lady, he told them, which made her smile even more. Sure weren't they all a warrior and his lady, a knight and his damsel? She could feel Smithy's amusement and enjoyment as much as her own.

The tale took them to a king's hall where the warrior was one of his men. The lady, treasured by all, most especially her father, the wise and great leader of the land, and worshiped afar by the warrior, a fierce and noble fighter who had a way with swords.

Smithy's hand absently stroked her shoulder, a gesture both reassuring and loving. She leaned her head against his chest as a response.

"The warrior's skill with the sword," continued Turlough, plucking and strumming the harp to create sounds that illustrated and enhanced the story, "was such that he began to fashion them, because in his hands the sword took on different properties, a finer edge, a better balance. Metal became his strength, his power, and all admired it. Especially the lady, for she found herself drawn to metal just as she was drawn to him."

Smithy's hand froze on her arm and Saoirse stiffened. What was this, who was this man? Surely a coincidence, surely it was just a tale that had grown and twisted in the multiple tellings to somehow sound like their tale.

She reached up and took Smithy's hand in hers needing his touch so that she could continue to look at this harper and pretend that all was well. Just a tale. *Fadó, fadó* and all that.

"It came to be that everyone wanted this warrior's swords and his place in the hall became so elevated that few preceded him. Even the king's champion carried one of his swords, demonstrating how well wrought they were, how perfect they were. And in the time, when war seemed to be on the horizon, such an honour was important. All these accolades gave the warrior cause to hope. Hope that the lady who favoured him with her visits, her conversation, and he had even cause to think, admiring glances, might somehow indicate that she would someday look upon him as more than a warrior, or even friend. But her gifts were many. Beyond her incomparable beauty, was her skill at healing, music, poetry. She was the pearl of the hall, the shining star. But still the warrior hoped. He made her a bowl to mix her healing herbs and plants, a special bowl that would lend its own power to the mixture, and she received the gift with an abundance of gratitude that fed the hope even more. Later, when he was fashioning a sword, the lady appeared, wanting to watch, to learn, and even to take part in the fashioning that so intrigued her. He welcomed her, thrilled to her touch when he guided her there, and helped her forge a small piece, just a little dagger that would be hers.

"It was after that meeting, when they'd fashioned the dagger together, and a small delicate handle worked in silver to go with it, that he dared to kiss her. And she responded. The joy that filled him made his hopes soar. He was certain then. The two of them would be together. They were meant to be. In that moment they both understood that.

"They parted on the understanding that he would approach her father and ask that they be wed, forever a couple. Nothing would separate them. His certainty carried him to her father's presence and there he made his case known. Her father nodded solemnly, said he understood, but that it was impossible. She was newly promised elsewhere. To the king."

Smithy's arms tightened around her. She could feel the tension in his body, the deep emotion held in check, even as she struggled with her own. The rage, the grief that suddenly rose up as the memories flooded her mind. The awful, awful memories, but also the joy of that first kiss, his lips on hers, all the love that had poured out in that one kiss.

"This is a sad tale, harper," said Smithy, his voice tight.

"It's full of trials and tribulations assuredly," said the harper. "As is any good tale. To test the two lovers. To see if they're worthy of a happy ending."

"A happy ending," murmured Smithy. "Are you saying there's a happy ending?"

A clatter interrupted their conversation and the tale. The harper struck a few dissonant chords. A group of figures appeared in front of them shadowed in the low flames. One stepped forward, the light playing off the planes of his face, the angry expression, the dark eyes, dark hair. There was no height on him, but he carried a spear.

The Hunters had found them.

38

SMITHY

It was a staring contest, and one he had no problem participating in because, feck it, his wits were scattered. The story, the pattern of it, Jaysus tonight, it was unnerving. And he knew the tale well, remembered it as though he'd only just lived it, something he didn't want to do, thank you very much. He'd been thinking "who the feck was this harper" when the tale unfolded and it became clear it was no make believe. If only. He could feel Saoirse's unease, too, the tightened grip on his hand, the breathing gone shallow, as if she remembered too. As if she remembered too. It was that thought that had scattered his wits further. And then the bit with the happy ending. If they deserved it. What the absolute feckin' enormous hell did that mean? Call me stupid, he thought, but what seanchie, what harper, even says that? If they deserve it. If anyone deserved it after all he and Saoirse had been through, they did. And just when this strange retelling of their ancient lives might show the way, might tell them of their happy ending, these gobshites show up and ruin it. And him, standing like some gombeen staring at them, stunned beyond words.

And angry.

He rode the anger for a small while, showing the glare on his face, just until he could straighten out his head, shove the wits into place. Then it was time to put the anger aside and summon up all the cunning he could. The Hunters and their demands for spears and swords. Not a hope or a prayer for them, no. Not a happy ending either. For the Hunters. He would make certain of that.

He removed the glare and put up the grin. Yeah, the grin was best.

The grin put your man the main Hunter on the back foot. But only for a few moments. Well less than a few and more like one. But he'd go with that.

"You haven't kept your promise," he said. "You must face the consequences."

The spear inched forward, towards Smithy's throat. Smithy kept the grin in place and crossed his arms for added effect. Go on try, he thought.

"Time is relative, lads," said Smithy.

Saoirse moved closer to Smithy and put her hand on his shoulder. The harper looked up curiously at the three of them, his harp still in hand. Another tale in the making. His eyes told that truth and Smithy nearly rolled his eyes. A tale that would grow with the telling. Or perhaps not, judging by the one he'd just heard, for there was every truth and no elaboration.

"Time is relative?" asked Your Man, the lead Hunter. His eye twitched. "What does that mean, exactly?"

Smithy gave a patient sigh, as if he was about to instruct a toddler. "It means, my lad, that just because I haven't made the spearheads and sword yet, it doesn't mean I haven't kept my promise. Did you hear the key word here? It's 'yet'. Now that shows you that I still can. The potential is there."

"So, you will make them," said the leader, Your Man.

What was his name? Though Smithy remembered everything about the deal they'd made, thank all that was holy for that, but he couldn't remember this littler fecker's name.

"I will make them most definitely as promised," said Smithy. "As we agreed. And witnessed by Morrigan, I do believe."

Your man's eyes narrowed, but he nodded slowly. "Yes."

Smithy nodded. "Good. Right, so. No better time like the present. Will we go to my forge?"

"No," said Your Man, curtly. "We will go to ours. One that has been set up specifically for this."

Smithy hesitated, unsure if this would lead to more trouble. He looked towards the other men, the spears now visible, their anger palpable. Saoirse squeezed his arm, but said nothing, but her concern was there, hanging between them. He should insist they go to his forge, in the midst of Tara, with Daghda and others to help if need be, but he knew he would never be able to persuade them. Not again. It had been force that had persuaded them before, with Daghda's might giving it the strength to make it convincing. This time it was he and Saoirse against these angry men who may be short, but their trickster twists with words and spears and the promise of the rest of all the Fir Bolg that might be waiting in the wings, gave him great pause.

"Fine, so," he said with a sigh. "Your forge it is. But I hope you have all the proper materials."

"There's no need to worry about that. We took them from your forge."

He had no doubt they had. The feckers.

THE FORGE WAS a little cramped for the two of them and the horde of people who gathered around Smithy and Saoirse, ready for the show as it were. Some show, he thought, suddenly nervous. Suddenly wondering if he would end up making some godawful haimes of the whole thing. But at least the fellas here, all lined up to ensure no tricks were made, would see he'd tried. He had to at least appear like he was trying.

Saoirse gave his finger a reassuring squeeze, a little signal that told him she knew what he was thinking. But then she always did, didn't she. They'd never needed to speak to know each other's thoughts. Not really.

And with those unspoken thoughts he told her he didn't want her involved, didn't want the Hunters to know that there was any possibility that if he failed, she might complete the bargain for them. Because he wouldn't allow that, there was too many outrageous possibilities that might follow that and put her in danger. And he wouldn't do that willingly, if he could help it.

Smithy conjured up a sigh and a slow reluctance in his movements, to add to the theatre of it all as he took the first bar of silver steel in his hand. He could feel the magic whispering through it, confirming that they had indeed raided his store, but also confirming that the power was in him, latent and ready to be used. He hoped. It was all good. Not a bother.

Saoirse gave him a worried look, but as soon as she saw his eyes on her, she pasted on a reassuring smile.

"You're grand, Smithy, so you are," she said in English.

No need for them to know she understood the old language now, no need at all. He was glad she understood that, but of course, she understood it all and she knew his thoughts with this understanding.

Beside him the heat of the forge became strong as the flames within it came up to temperature. He knew the time, the moment when it was perfect, as clearly as if the flames told him. The metal hummed in response, ready to take on its transforma-tion. For a moment he wished for Bríd's hand on his, her body next to him, but it wasn't safe and he quashed the thought just as he realised he'd thought of her as Bríd. It made him smile and his heart swelled with the notion, just as he picked up the tongs, gripped the steel with them and inserted them into the heart of the flames.

The heat was fierce, but he revelled in it, as the humming grew louder, the rhythms of the flame, the metal changing shape, each formed their own melodious tune that resonated inside of him. A perfect melody, shifting and shaping itself around the metal bar, even as he withdrew it and added his own harmony in support with his hammer. He rang out the changes, shaping, flattening, and imbuing the metal with its own special tune, in its own key.

When he was satisfied that the metal before him had found its shape, the tune complete, Smithy plunged the blade into the vat of water nearby. He was panting and dripping with sweat, something he hadn't realised until that moment. He'd been so caught up in the shaping and shifting that everything else had vanished from him. The thrill of that experience rushed through him and he could only look at Saoirse and grin with the joy of it. Her eyes lit in response and he could see the tiniest jump from her and nearly heard the internal squeal that accompanied it. He laughed.

"Is something amusing?" said Your Man, the leader.

Smithy glanced over at him, gave a shrug. "I'm always amused."

Your Man frowned and gestured to the heavy table where the now completed sword blade rested. "Get on with it."

Smithy regarded the blade. A bit of polishing, and a hilt to slip onto it and it would be ready to go. Perfect. A pity such a blade held a dismal future. But there was no help for it, no help for it at all. He gave it a final stroke of affection and turned to the next small bar of silver metal to be used for the spearhead. This wouldn't take long, he could feel it and he was glad of that. The sooner he could be away from these feckers, the better.

He went to work on the metal, waiting first for the hum, and then inserting it into the heart of the fire at the right moment. It felt good to listen out and hear that tune, a small enough one this time, but with a nifty little lift to it. A fine thing, but he tried not to become too attached, because again, the dismal future.

He made short work of the finish, getting it as close to apparently perfect as he could manage. Apparently being the important word, the best illusion, because, it was a "you never know" situation. Things could go wrong. How well he knew that.

There was no laugh this time, but the joy was real, as was the satisfied grin he exchanged with Saoirse. He'd felt her presence this past time, strong and curious, almost entwining herself with him and that tune. Another reason to have cut it short. Too, too risky by far. But it felt good. It felt exciting.

He placed the completed spearhead on the work table beside the blade and turned to Your Man, regarding him solemnly.

"There. I have fulfilled our bargain," he said.

Your Man crossed his arms, his expression dark. "Two spearheads. That was the agreement, not one."

"Yes," said Smithy. "Two spear heads. I made the other one already. You witnessed it. So I have completed the bargain. I agreed to make you two spear heads and one sword blade."

"Where is the other spearhead?" asked Your Man. "Give that and these two and we'll call the bargain complete."

Smithy shook his head. "The first spearhead is across the water, I'm afraid. But you can't dispute I made it."

Your Man shifted his feet, his face reddening. "I cannot dispute the making of it, no. But it does us no good across the water, or where ever it is. We must have that spearhead as well as those two items before we can call the bargain complete."

Smithy shook his head. "No, I'm afraid you're wrong. The bargain was that I agreed to make you two spearheads and one sword, which I have done. There was no statement that said I must give them to you. If you have any doubts I'm sure Morrigan would be happy to verify it."

Your Man opened his mouth, rage clouding his eyes. "You tricked us!"

"No, old man, I didn't trick you. I've just fulfilled the bargain to the exact wording. Words you stated, not me. You can't argue with that. And you can't go against it, or the punishment is banishment. As you well know."

The Hunters stepped forward, crowding around Your Man, casting furious glances in Smithy's direction. Smithy pulled Saoirse to his side, a "you never know" move that gave him a little reassurance. He could feel her tension, and the small inward amusement at what he'd just done.

"You remembered the wording of the bargain," she whispered.

He nodded slightly. They both knew it was more than just remembering a bargain. It was so much more.

Your Man stepped forward, poking him in the chest with the tip of his spear. "We will agree that this was the bargain and that you are free to go. But this won't be the last you will hear of us. You and your cheating kind."

Smithy raised his brow. "My kind awaits your revenge," he said, maintaining the bravado, but a small kernel of worry lodged inside him. Daghda wouldn't be pleased at this turn of events.

LUKE

Frowning, Luke stared across the sitting room to the sofa where Anu was reclining. She'd collapsed after the others had left, Saoirse and Smithy to go immediately across the water and Finn and Maura to, well, do something before they went across. Or not. Finn had left on his own and Maura had shifted, to fly in the same direction. Mon had departed with a promise. A promise Luke hoped he would keep.

In the background, the radio provided a low murmur. The news was on and half of him wanted to stride over and switch it off, until its words caught his attention. As the newsreader continued, Luke's frown deepened. Gorse fires, toxic waste in waterways, and a threatening bad storm. All seeming accidents and natural disasters, but Luke knew better.

"It's time, Lugh," said Anu, stirring from her place on the sofa.

"Shhh," he said. "Get some rest."

"You must go, now. There can be no more delay."

He thought of Kayla above. And Bláthín and Nana in the bedroom next door. It was difficult to bring himself to leave them. It wasn't safe. But he knew that the longer Eithne stayed locked in the shed outside it became even more dangerous for everyone. He nodded to Anu and walked past her to the stairs, ascending them quietly.

He hovered outside Bláthín's room, looking in. She was lying there, staring up at the ceiling. He put stars up there a while ago, formed constellations and told her the stories associated with them. Back when she was less ill, before all of this had really started and he'd left for America. Now he could see her eyes roaming them, no doubt thinking of the stories, or creating new ones. Probably creating new ones.

He smiled and she looked over at him, sensing his regard. She gave him a weak nod and beamed. She was so much better now than when he'd first returned and found her unconscious. It was as if his presence gave her that bit more strength, something that gladdened him more than he could say. She was so much a part of his heart, now, and if this improvement hadn't shown that, he didn't know what would.

He moved inside the room, careful not to wake Nana, who had improved a little as well, but not quite as much as Bláthín. She was eating, or rather taking broth and some tea, but her waking periods were short.

Luke knelt beside Bláthín's bed. "Are you looking at your stars?"

"I am," she said.

He leaned over and kissed her cheek. "Any particular ones?"

"The ones that people wish on."

"Oh," he said, his heart lurching just a little. "And what are you wishing for? A pony?"

She snorted. "No, why would I? I already have a pony."

"Oh, so you do. Let me see, a great huge cake, then."

"Ugh, no. I couldn't manage a cake. No, I'm wishing for all of us."

"All of us?"

"Me, Mammy, Nana and you, of course."

The "of course" hit him with such power. "Me?"

She turned her head to look at him. "Silly, you're one of us. Don't you know that by now? Of course I would wish for you, too."

He nodded. "I suppose it was a silly question," he said, trying to keep his voice level. "And what's that wish?"

She pursed her lips. "I don't think I'm supposed to say. But since it's you, I'll tell you. I wished for it to be finished. For the balance to come back. For all to be well for us."

He took her hand and squeezed it. "That's a really, really good wish, oh wise one."

She slapped his hand lightly. "Don't make fun."

He shook his head solemnly, put his hand over his heart. "I'm not, on my honour."

"Well, if it's on your honour," she said, her eyes twinkling, "I believe you, because I know you have loads of honour. More than anyone I know."

Luke gave a harsh laugh. "I hope so."

"I know so," she said, her voice determined.

"With such faith I can be no other way." He rose. "And now I must go and help make that wish come true."

She held his hand, looked at him. Those golden eyes bordering on hazel, so like her mother's, stared into his, searching.

"Come back," she said. "Please."

"I'll do my best, little one."

"Not that little," she muttered.

He gave a small laugh and stroked her hair. "Not so little and so very wise."

SHE WAS WAITING for him when he entered, sitting up, her hair loose and hanging about her shoulders, the smile wide, the eyes bright, but the skin, so pale and translucent, vulnerable. He was still taken by her beauty. It sung to him, held him speechless.

"I heard you next door," she said.

She lifted her hand towards him and he moved forward, drawn by the hand, by her. He sat down by her side, took the hand and kissed the back of it, tenderly. They'd not had enough of these moments since they'd come together, too much had come between them. But he resolved that they would soon. He would make everything all right. Set it to order. He leaned over and kissed her mouth, feeling her lips give under his, and the flame that sparked between them. It gave him hope, that spark, a desire that still kindled at the lightest touch, the merest look.

He deepened the kiss, brushed his hand along the curve of her jaw, down her neck to cup her breast through the thin material of her nightgown. He loved that she wore something so old fashioned as a nightgown, loved the way it draped her shoulders and her breasts. He caressed her nipple lightly and enjoyed its immediate response to his touch. He bent his head to kiss and suck it and revelled in the soft sounds she made.

He moved his hand under the covers, caressing each curve of her softly, tenderly. He looked into her eyes, saw the matching desire and made a decision. It was a decision that was reflected in her own expression, a mutual consent born of so much knowledge, understanding and want.

And as he shed his clothes and joined her in the bed, removing her nightgown with one swift movement, he suddenly knew that this was more than just a simple coupling, this was a ritual, sacred and important to what they were and what he must do. He felt it in her skin, the heat of her body, the way it met his. He kissed her, tasted her, every possible place he could place his lips, just as she tasted him, each moment more arousing than the previous, each fulfilling the other's desire in myriad ways, until the final joining, when it didn't seem possible they weren't fused forever, two made one. The hero king joined to the land.

And when they were sated, but still twined, she lay in his arms and spoke.

"You must go," she said.

It wasn't a question. She was telling him it was time. Past time. That this union between them had been the last piece in the preparation for what was to come. The final battle.

LUKE SHOVED the woman into the boat. That's what he'd decided to think of Eithne. The woman. He didn't want to name her in his thoughts, and certainly didn't want to think of her biological relationship to him. Never that. As "the woman" she could remain anonymous, or even better, an enemy woman. That described her perfectly.

The enemy woman glared at him, nearly tripping as she tried to gain purchase in the boat. It was a little larger than he would have liked, this boat, but it was what had arrived after he summoned it, by the Glengarriff River north of Glengarriff, in the nature reserve. It was the nearest point he knew that would best serve his needs. He wanted to be away from the peninsula, instinct told him that. Too much opportunity for ambush, if Balor should choose that moment to try and rescue...the enemy woman.

Luke pushed her down against the seat, toying for a moment with tying her to it, anything to ensure she'd stayed put. For a moment he wished Mon were here to help keep watch, to hold her firmly while he navigated across the water. If he could reach the Time Between Time he thought he would be safe, but even then, there were possibilities.

He wore Retaliator strapped to his back, the spearhead and slingshot in a pouch tied to his jeans and a dagger sheathed next to the pouch. It was a risk, that dagger, but a necessity, also.

She was still gagged, and he was thankful for that as he took up an oar and pushed away from the bank, because her glances could set a forest afire in no time. He grinned at the thought of her discomfort and frustration, resisting the urge to smirk. That was too childish altogether, he told himself. Still, a half quirk of the lips escaped and her eyes snapped. He felt a little thrill of enjoyment. Sure, a little one couldn't hurt. He'd stop now.

He turned his mind away from little tortures and focused on the enchantment he was weaving through thought and whispered words. He hadn't uttered these words in so long he wasn't certain he would remember them all. There were several twisty turns to manage to find the right currents to reach the Time Between Time from this remote location, and Anu, being in such poor health, made the land slow to respond to him, to help him reach that special place and beyond it, to the other side.

The words trickled out, the old language falling from his lips easily, at least at first. When he reached the middle part he stumbled a little, felt for the next phrase, suddenly uncertain, until the breath of wind told him the rest, a breath that smelled of Kayla, her faint voice so familiar, so much a part of him. He spoke the words and the rest followed, his confidence gaining as he reached the final section.

The boat floated, seemingly indifferent to the current, until one particular eddy caught it up and took it, a steady movement, determined. He sighed. The Time Between Time.

The woman's eyes stared at him furiously. She struggled in her seat and he reached out to grip her arm, to hold her still. Suddenly she rose up and flung herself overboard.

"Feck!" he shouted.

His anger rose and burst forth in an unstoppable rage. He plunged into the water, the current taking him and her along. She disappeared underneath, her dark hair floating up, before it, too, was swallowed into the depths. Cursing again, Luke dived under, but it was difficult to see in the dark murky depths. His mind raced through the implications of a "will I just let her drown" scenario, but he knew there were so many reasons why he shouldn't – and one reason, which angered him even more, why he couldn't. It would give him great pleasure for Balor to feel the pain of the loss of his daughter, but the subsequent consequences of this pain couldn't be risked. He knew that, and certainly it was why Eithne had taken this last resort. And, he told himself, that was what was propelling him to swim fiercely through the water, searching as much as the water allowed, until he saw a limb, grabbed it and held on, dragging it towards him until he could see the rest of her, her hands still bound, the gag in place. He locked his arm around her waist and kicked to the surface.

The water broke over his head with a burst of noise. Eithne was unconscious in his arms, her limp form heavy, but not impossible. He scanned the water for the boat, pushing aside the nagging concern about the implications of this turn of events in the middle of Time Between Time. He felt more hopeful when he located the boat. At least it hadn't disappeared, forcing him to summon another one, wondering if he could.

Luke began to swim, bracing Eithne against him on one side and stroking the water with his free arm. The boat floated just beyond his reach. He stroked the water faster, and more firmly, but it seemed as though the boat was always just out of reach. Feck. Would he summon another? On impulse, he took a deep breath and dived once again. It was a risk, but he had no other ideas at the moment, except the bigger risk of summoning another boat. He moved quickly under the water, dragging Eithne behind him. After a few moments he burst through the water once again, pulling Eithne's head above as he did so, and shook the water from his face. A shape loomed in front of him and he reached his hand out and hit solid wood. He allowed the relief to fill him as he hoisted Eithne into the boat first and then himself.

He panted heavily, unable to move from his recent exertion for a moment, until he recovered enough to tend Eithne. He removed the gag, unbound her hands and felt for a pulse at her neck. He frowned, unable to detect anything, until finally, he felt a faint, thready pulse. He sighed, glad that at least his efforts had been worth it. At least so far. There was still much to be done with her. Feckin' Eithne, he said to himself. If he could he would take her by the ankles and turn her upside down to get the water out of her. Maybe shake more than water out of her at the same time. He smiled at the thought. She was his prisoner still, and he could take satisfaction from that. Sure, there was great satisfaction to be had in that, all right.

He rolled her on her side and began to pound her back, to get the water out of her. This was the next best thing, he told himself. He'd enjoy this, the rest could wait.

40

MAURA

I glanced around the spacious practice yard of Tara, watching some of Daghda's men working on their battle skills. Swords rang out in the crisp autumn air as they clashed against each other, along with the thud and clang of metal hitting either wooden or metal shields.

I stared at the sword in my hand that I had been using on my own, working through positions and strengthening exercises. The sword felt wrong. I moved it back and forth from left to right hand, trying to find the balance point and sense the thread of energy, the connection that would make it mine and enable me to wield it with a deadly and accurate force. Not for the first time I mentally cursed that I hadn't retrieved my own sword and other gear before going across the water. My sword was me. It knew me, it was a part of me during any battle. Sure, I'd known that. But still I had to be stubborn, and stubborn for the worst of the "what the feck" reasons I could possibly imagine. What would it have hurt me to go with Finn? And, the little voice inside of me added, if I had I would know where he was, now. Because he wasn't here at Tara and hadn't been the past two days since I'd arrived.

I scanned the practice group again, looking for the familiar figure among the forty or so men using the time and space to prepare for battle. There was no sign of him. I frowned, wondering for a moment if I should go back across the water to check. Something might have happened to him. He could have been in a car accident, or another kind of accident. Or...my mind trailed through different possibilities that might account for his delay. His car breaking down on the way to his place. Something at his house. A friend delaying him? Or, an unthinkable possibility, something happened on the journey across? I knew that was always a possibility, but a rare occurrence and I tried to take comfort in that.

I waved my sword around again half-heartedly, trying to distract myself. I needed a different sword, there was no doubt about it. It wasn't one of Smithy's. I'd known that from the start, because even the look of it said "make do" and that's what I was doing here. But I wasn't a "make do" person in battle. "Make" was always coupled with "fierce" or "happen", not "do". "Make do" would get anyone in trouble.

As I took a look around at the warriors, some women among them, I could see a few signs of the same struggle I was having. Smithy really needed to get going on the sword making if they were to have enough in time for the battle. There was no specific time set for it, because as far as I knew, Balor didn't yet know that Eithne was captured and she was here. Or would be here, when Luke came. Luke still hadn't appeared with her in tow. So no one knew if she was here, in this world. It was worrying that Luke wasn't here, but not alarming. I knew he wanted to spend time with Kayla before he left. That much had been obvious, but still. Daghda had been wearing a frown that was only getting deeper as the hours and days wore on.

Daghda. That fecker. I pushed the thought of him away. I wasn't here for Daghda, who'd only used me for a night and then for a battle. I was here for...me. It made sense, so it did. Perfect sense, no one would doubt that. I was here because I wanted to. Because I'd been asked nicely by Saoirse. And when she was asking, she was asking me, a friend, not Morrigan, war goddess. And Finn I supposed. I was here because he was a friend, too. And friends helped friends.

I lifted the sword again and it was like a dead weight. No feel to it, just metal and weight. I suppressed the urge to throw it across the yard in disgust, and instead, headed to the entrance to the fortress. Inside, the smoke and warmth greeted me like a smothering wave after the fresh air and the sweat I'd worked up outside. I made my way past a few of the smaller chambers, towards the hall.

It was his voice that caught my attention. All too familiar – and the resulting swell of happiness at its sound, was becoming too familiar as well. I stopped, deliberating if I would peek inside or go in all guns blazing, taking him off guard with a friendly shove and a suggestive "where have you been". Just for a laugh. Wasn't it the way we were, teasing and eager to get a fun jab in whenever possible? The way friends were. I grinned, savouring the prospect just as the door opened further and Finn stood there, holding it wide to allow someone to pass through. A woman. A woman dressed in a blue silk gown, her long blond hair plaited and draped becomingly across her shoulder. Oh, the sway on her, as she moved past him, all hips and "feck me" arse. Then the eyes, turned up towards his face, lips slightly parted. Her name escaped me, but her type didn't and I stiffened at the sight of them. Her laugh. His amused eyes looking down at her.

Before I could turn around, retrace my steps, Finn caught sight of me. He smiled, but there was surprise and hesitancy and it was the hesitancy that was my undoing. And brought tears to my eyes. I turned quickly, before he could see them. Feck if he was going to see that. Or anyone.

I walked quickly, hearing him call my name, but I quickened my pace, still clutching the sword, determined to reclaim my place in the yard. Best to leave when I had a sword in my hand, because at the moment another use of it was definitely in my mind.

No one noticed me as I moved around the group, looking for a space to resume my exercises. The place I'd occupied before was thankfully still vacant and I headed there, already running the paces through my mind. Anything but the image I'd just seen, sure, it was nothing, anyway. Why would I mind? He could talk to anyone he chose. Do whatever he wanted. It was nothing to me. I frowned as I swung the sword, annoyed even more by the leaden feel it had. Feckin' thing. I suppressed the urge to throw it across the yard. Where the feck was Smithy anyway? Off somewhere having the feckin' time of his life, no doubt, shagging Saoirse or some feckin' thing.

"Do you want a partner, or someone to murder with that thing?" came a voice behind me.

I turned to see Finn, a smirk on his face. "Feck off, yourself."

"Ah, I see murder is the answer. But that sword doesn't look capable of much beyond holding up plants."

He'd spoken in English, a conversation meant only for ourselves, and I couldn't help but smile at his choice of words and their meaning.

"I think the plants would object." I tossed the sword to him. "I would murder you, only you'll have to wait until I can get a sword that knows its use."

He arched his brow. "I'm flattered that you would need a sword."

"I suppose poison might be a consideration, but it wouldn't be a satisfying. You know. The blows, the actual physical act of stabbing, hitting and anything else like that."

Finn nodded, a grin breaking out on his face. "Violent, then.

I see. Is it just me, or is it anyone who might present an opportunity?"

I crossed my arms. "Oh, the honour's all yours."

He nodded again, slower this time. "Right, so. Should I give you my sword and find another for me?"

I sighed, suddenly tired of this game. "Oh, feck off, Finn. Just go and leave me be."

Finn moved towards me and I started to back away, glancing at the others around us. They'd hardly noticed us and I took a bit of comfort from that. Why, I didn't know. I felt there was a lot I didn't know at the moment and it annoyed me. Finn annoyed me.

He folded his arm around the edge of my shoulder, his face so close to mine. "Maura," he said softly. "What's wrong?"

I wouldn't be that person. I wouldn't be that woman. I'd throw that woman across the room if I met her, silly gobshite. I straightened.

"Ah, it's grand, Finn." I shrugged off his hand, slapped up a smile. "It's all grand. Just having a bit of craic."

I lifted the sword, tapped him on the head with it lightly. "I think I may have found a use for this sword after all." I walked past him, swatting him on the backside and headed back into the hall. "I'm just going in search of Smithy, or see if anyone knows where he is."

There, I'd done it, not sign of any green monster to be seen, not even a leprechaun sized one. Because sure, why would there be?

41

SAOIRSE

We found Airmed in her herb garden. The herbs had grown up on her brother's grave. Miach, who could heal any illness. And with these herbs she was able to continue her brother's work. Maybe. Saoirse knew the stories around her, knew from what Smithy had said, and what she now remembered. But it wasn't that simple. That "maybe" was still up there, in view, awaiting attention. Because the "maybe" was linked to Diancecht, their father, a complication and cause all in one. He'd killed his own son and ruined beyond recognition the herbs that had grown there. Airmed's painstaking care had given the "maybe" its possibilities when she'd rescued what she could, and over time had learned their potential and purpose. And in that was the core of the "maybe". Maybe she would know what was happening with Smithy and maybe what she knew would confirm or complete a cure for him. Airmed's gifts were beyond herbs, were indefinable. And she had compassion, where her father had bitterness and sarcasm.

Airmed gave the two of them a warm smile when she lifted her gaze from the herbs she was tending. The scents of lavender, thyme, sage, meadowsweet and so much else that Saoirse had no name for, greeted her with their own welcome. The scent promised much.

"Goibhniu, Bríd."

Saoirse nodded to her, suddenly tongue tied. She looked over at Smithy, who wore a tentative expression, his eyes clouded with uncertainty. She took his hand and squeezed it. He looked over at her, his eyes lit up and Saoirse felt her own response, a spark kindled, a tune begun. A little slip jig, with a skip hop that was so sweet and filled with all those scents of the garden. Saoirse gave him a smile filled with all those scents, with the tune. His nod was only a fraction, so slight, but it said it all and affirmed the connection between them.

"You look well, Goibhniu," Airmed said. "I'm glad to see you've recovered from your...injuries."

Smithy nodded slowly. "The injuries. Yes, right." He took a deep breath. "I'm not sure what my injuries were, not afterwards. Tricky."

Airmed gave him a puzzled look. "Do you need some help? Have you come for my assistance?"

"In a sense," said Smithy, gathering speed. "I have had some problems since...the well. The renewal."

Renewal. Saoirse admired his choice of word. It said something about how he felt now, how his thoughts, his mind had created a positive word. A hope word. Saoirse squeezed his hand again, loving this hope word. Renewal.

"What problems?" asked Airmed.

And so Smithy told her, named the parts, the ills, but stated it with an objective tone, separated it from himself. It was apart now. The ills were outside of him, no longer his.

Airmed nodded slowly as he spoke and when he'd completed the explanation, she tilted her head. "And?"

"And?" he asked.

"And where are these ills now?"

He studied her a moment. "Well, they're gone, I think. I don't know."

"It's the 'don't know' we're here about," said Saoirse.

Airmed gave a light laugh.

Smithy smiled. "Ah, well, you know yourself. It's not the easiest thing to explain." He took a deep breath. "I feel sound now. Good. But I need to be certain. I have to know I can count on myself. That others can count on me."

Airmed studied him a moment. "Have others ever not been able to count on you, Goibhniu?"

Smithy stood silently a moment. He looked over at Saoirse. She gave him an encouraging look, a look that spoke the tune. The tune that still hummed between them. The slip jig moved into a tune that had solid rhythms, rhythms that said they were something, that they had a reputation.

"They haven't," said Saoirse. "He's never failed them. Or me." The last few words came to her because she knew this was the heart of it all. The heart of him. There was nothing ever in him that had failed her. She'd failed herself and others had helped. Her former fate was wrapped up in all those events that had shaped her people. She'd agreed to have that failure of a king, Bres, as a husband and all the events that had come with that choice. Because she'd known. She'd known that such a choice would lead to her undoing. Bríd's undoing. But now, here with Smithy and all her experiences as Saoirse, she understood that this journey had brought her to the possibility of being with him, at one with him, joined in a way that wouldn't have been possible until now. Because he was Smithy as well as Goibhniu and she was Saoirse as well as Bríd.

"If what Bríd says is true, Goibhniu," said Airmed. "Then I would say that you have your answer."

Saoirse clutched Smithy's hand as they made their way to his forge. The desire to keep his hand in hers was both the need to have some part of him touch her and reassure her, and also to share the buzz, hum and tune of the excitement that was coursing through her. To know that he felt it too, even though she could sense the waves of rhythm, the faint melody that was in him. It was all raging energy and heat, a wild mad jig danced at full speed in the climax of a night's playing, everyone's instruments in perfect sync and flying. Following where the music took them.

She seated that thought deep in her and it made her smile, because she knew this was how it was meant to be. It would all be grand. It would be perfect. The music would be there, the metal would transform and they would fly with it.

When they arrived at the forge, she could see that it had been prepared ahead of time, though the workshop was empty of people. All the metals, the magic humming from them, were laid out, ready for them. There were two leather aprons. Two. She loved that number.

Smithy grinned at her and handed her the smaller apron. His eyes lit as she took it. Suddenly she knew exactly what he was thinking. She gave him a shove.

"Ah, no. Not a chance. I'm not risking a branding or a flying spark just to give into a moment's lust."

He laughed. "Oh, there would be plenty of sparks flying. And that would be before we even started forging the metal."

She kissed his cheek. "Mind on the job, Smithy. Mind on the job. There will be loads of time for that later."

His eyes turned suddenly serious. "I hope so."

It was a sobering thought, but she pulled away from it. "Ah, there will be. How can there not?"

He nodded, the smile and light in his eyes returned, and he pulled her close to him. "There will be. But now, we must get these swords made. I just had Maura chewing off my ear demanding she have the first one because the one she has now isn't worth staking tomatoes."

Saoirse laughed. "Where's her own?"

Smithy shrugged. "She didn't stop to collect it, she says. I didn't ask why. That question had the 'don't ask' label all over it."

Saoirse nodded. She understood the prickly Maura side. A side that had appeared all too often and now made Saoirse grin. Maura was nearing the other side of that prickly journey. At least Saoirse hoped she was. The avoidance strategy told Saoirse that Maura was beginning to realise what had been obvious to Saoirse even before she'd recovered her memories. Saoirse just hoped that Maura realised it in time, and when she did, she understood the blessing it was, the wonder of it and, most of all, allowed it to come to its natural and best conclusion.

Smithy led her to the table. Two tongs lay there, ready for them both. They would act in concert, twinned in their movements, like a duet. She took up one pair and he the other, and they began their piece. She let her instincts take over, just like she would when she played the flute, when they were all in pitch, feeling the rhythm, the beat and the tune play through them.

They both took up the metal bar, not a word between them, and Smithy moved behind her, enveloping her body with his. They inserted the bar into the heart of the forge's fire. She could feel the heat of the fire blanket her front. The blue flame rose, expanded, responding to their rhythms, their magic, his front, pressing up against her back, so close she could feel his heartbeat as it matched hers.

The metal softened, reaching that malleable state perfect for the shaping. They withdrew the bar from the flame and moved it towards the anvil. Smithy took up the hammer and began the tune that would fashion the metal, tame the magic and create the perfect balance of the sword. There were no words, the sound was all in the ring of the hammer, and the shapeshifting metal speaking its new form. It was a tune they both became lost in, and time moved outside of the two of them, shaping, forming, creating, as the magic flowed before them, behind them and all around them, like a sacred prayer, a lorica so ancient, the old words were lost.

When it was finished, the metal doused in the vat of liquid beside them, they laid the sword on the worktop, ready for its polishing and a hilt to be attached. That was for later. But even without its finishing touches, Saoirse could see that the sword was special. Not just because they'd made it together, but that it was done with both of them, at the height of who they were, together. As it should be. As it was meant to be, she thought.

She could feel Smithy's pleasure radiating from him. She turned to face him and put her arms around his neck and drew him in.

"It was perfect," she said. "You're perfect."

Saoirse wiped her brow with the back of her hand. It had been hours, and though these hours had passed without her realising, she felt it now, when they'd stopped. They'd worked as tirelessly as possible, both of them somehow conscious that time was short, precious. That soon, these blades would be called to action and as many blades as possible would be needed. At the moment there were ten blades laid out before them, ready for Credne to finish, to polish and make the hilts. Credne was the other metal worker, at this moment crafting spearheads. Spearheads were their next task, too, she knew, once they'd taken a break to eat and rest a while.

Smithy brushed his hand over her hair, now coiled around her head in a plait, so much like it had been when she'd met him first as only Saoirse. It was fastened there not as a statement of eccentricity, as it had been then, but for practical reasons. And maybe just a little bit because she knew how much it stirred something in him. She smiled at the thought and turned her mouth to his, his lips salty with sweat when she tasted them. She inhaled his scent, the sweat and muskiness of too long working at the fire, but glorious for all that. And if her hair stirred something in him, his scent – the Smith God that was so much him – stirred something in her. And together they would stir something more. Perhaps this could be the later they'd promised each other. Sure, a little break would be no harm. No harm at all.

He took her hand, still warm from smithwork, and led her up the slight grass rise and across the yard to the rear entrance of the fort. A small chamber had been put aside for them to sleep and rest, and it was there they headed, the unspoken intent clear between them. They were nearly to the door when someone called them. Daghda. Saoirse's heart sank. She didn't need to hear the words, she didn't even need to see his face. She knew.

Slowly, the two of them turned towards Daghda. His face was grim, eyes sparking with fury.

"He's come," said Daghda.

"How long?" asked Smithy.

"A day. Maybe two."

"So we should leave soon," said Smithy. "If we want to choose our battleground."

"Yes."

"And do you have any place in mind?"

Daghda nodded. "It's been decided. We'll draw them towards Magh Tuireadh."

Smithy nodded. She knew he understood, that it made sense. Three. The number of the battle at that site. Three was a good number. A number of good fortune.

"Does Lugh know?" she asked.

Daghda's expression darkened. "He hasn't come, yet."

"He's not here?" Her tone held all the disbelief she felt. She was certain he would have arrived while she was making the swords with Smithy. Felt it even. Something wasn't right.

"Mongan is here, though," said Daghda. "He assured me that Lugh is on his way. That he has every intention of carrying out his task."

Saoirse nodded. She already knew that. But what she wasn't sure about was if Daghda understood that Eithne was at this moment with Luke, and all the possibilities those two together could mean.

"Where are the weapons?" asked Saoirse. "The spear, the slingshot and Retaliator? Do you know?"

Daghda shook his head. "I presume with Lugh."

Saoirse looked at Smithy. His expression was filled with worry, but a moment later he hardened it. "If it comes to it, I'll do it. I'll fashion a spearhead, a slingshot and use my own sword. It will be enough. I'll make it enough."

Daghda nodded. "We'll count on you for that, Goibhniu. But there's still time. And Finn has promised all the help he can give."

Smithy nodded and Saoirse slipped her hand into his, wanting to comfort and be comforted. She must let him do what he would. What she knew he could.

"One more thing," said Daghda, turning to go. "The Hunters.

They've joined Balor. Apparently they didn't find your little trick amusing."

Saoirse squeezed Smithy's hand. There'd been no reproach in Daghda's voice, in fact she thought there might have been a little humour. She only hoped Smithy read it that way.

A moment later she heard him chuckle. "Did they not?"

42

LUKE

The small track stretched up ahead of them, taunting and never ending. Fields lined one side, so nondescript the only clue as to whether they were just fallow at the moment or they were never farmed were all the furze bushes scattered throughout. So cattle maybe. Or sheep. Still, this conclusion was firmly put in the "ueseless speculation" category in a box full of "waste of time". The other side of the road was no better in its scattering of trees, some of which were ash, hazel and a few oak or two, for good measure, that all added up to a big fat nothing and something to be shoved into that "waste of time" box. Face it, he thought, you're feckin' lost. Lost in "feck knows where" land and in "feck knows what time".

Ever since they'd pulled themselves up from the water, or rather he'd pulled Eithne out of the water and himself at the same time, and then beat the water out of her (a small pleasure to be had) whereupon she coughed up more river water than was possible for any one person to swallow, he'd been trying to discover the answer to those two questions. But nothing doing. After Eithne had recovered enough that they'd been able to make slow progress to...well, well. He didn't know. But he was determined to find Tara. Sure, there could be no other outcome. He wouldn't even consider it. The sword, thankfully, hadn't come to any harm after its thorough dousing, and neither had the spearhead or slingshot, except for the leather pouch that held the missiles in place. That was a little stiff, as was the pouch containing the spearhead and slingshot, but it was nothing that a little grease or leather conditioning wouldn't fix. Goose grease? He couldn't remember what was used. Just like he couldn't remember the stone shed he suddenly saw in among a cluster of trees. Feck. Was it just that too much time had passed since he had been here and he didn't remember it? Or was it simply that too much time had passed? Or both. With his feckin' luck it was probably both.

He headed to the shed, pulling Eithne along with him. Once there, he looked inside, a small opening, barely window sized, provided additional light, along with the doorway, to make it possible to inspect the interior. It was bare enough, but with stray clumps of straw and a scattering of mouldy oats in evidence, the shed had obviously been used for cattle. Not recently, though. Still, it signalled a homestead close by, at least at some point in the not too far away.

He noticed a worn path just off to the side. Hopeful, he started to head in that direction, still grasping Eithne's arm, but she began to pull away. He gripped her tighter.

"Stop your struggling. It won't get you anywhere."

She glared at him and spoke, her words too muffled by her gag to make any sense.

"I've heard it all before, Eithne, so you may as well save your breath."

She grunted and shook her head, her eyes filled with desperation. Luke frowned and stared at her for a few moments, before relenting and loosening her gag.

"Well?"

"I need to relieve myself," she said. "And water. I'm thirsty."

It was a reasonable request, and objectively there was nothing wrong or suspicious about it, except that there was. A simple ruse, practised many times, at least on TV, and no doubt many other occasions that would be considered truer to life. But this was real life, his life, his mother. But all the knowledge he held about her, as well. Feck.

"Fine, so," he said.

She could scream all she wanted now, it wouldn't matter. This was reasoning he used all the way to the small bush off the path and the place behind it. She arched her brow and he arched his brow in reply. It was a conversation, acerbic and pointed. She received his answer with poor grace, stepping on his foot as she turned sideways and unfastened her trendy jeans and pulled them down awkwardly, along with her underpants, with her hands still tied together.

Awkward was the word of the moment, both in his insistence he keep watch, her obvious embarrassment and fury, and his mind trying to steer it towards obtaining pleasure from her embarrassment and not, feck all that was holy, remorse. Remorse? Really? He chastised himself, forced himself to observe every indignity she endured. Indignity, my arse, he told himself. How many indignities had she visited on others, himself included, when he was young? The internal argument continued even as she righted her clothes again and was demanding water.

It was reasonable again that he should refill his travelling flask. There was nothing left and he had no idea how long before he would reach somewhere that had a well, or at least plenty of water available.

He paused, and after a moment, headed for the direction of a stream he could hear eastwards from the worn path. Another good sign that there might still be people in the vicinity, the one said to him. But sure, there was water everywhere, the other one said to him. And he wished both of the ones would shut the feck up.

He shoved her ahead of him this time, towards the stream. Once there, he knelt down beside it and began to fill his flask. He motioned for her to take her fill, using her hands, sticking her head in the water, he didn't care.

She shook her head. "I'll wait for you to fill the flask and drink from there."

He frowned, repressing an eye roll. Would he make her drink from the stream? Impose another indignity on her? Suddenly he was tired of it all. Resigned, he finished filling the flask and was so absorbed in his own conversation and fatigue from the utter repetitiveness of it, that he was taken unawares when she kicked him hard from behind and sent him sprawling into the water.

He rose quickly, turning around in the same motion and saw Eithne scrambling away. Oh, for feck's sake, he thought. Did she really think she could outrun him? He heaved a sigh and took off after her. It didn't take him long to catch her, a few moments only. He grabbed her arm and she swung around to him and it was then he saw she had a dagger in her hand. His dagger. He swore silently again. Of course she had it.

She directed it at him, slashing at his chest, and the blade upright in her hand, aiming just below his ribcage. So, she knew what she was doing, he thought objectively, and he acted accordingly, trying to force the dagger from her hand, twisting, and turning her wrist, her arm. She was stronger than he'd imagined and in the course of the struggle the blade sent a searing pain across his hand during a quick move she'd made. His hand released its grip on her and she lunged forward, aiming for a deadly blow this time. Instinct took hold of Luke and he twisted away, avoiding the blow, just as he reached around and gripped her left forearm, thrust it upward, the other arm following, the one hand still bound to the other. He continued to bend the arm, beyond its natural position at the elbow, ignoring her howl of pain. The dagger dropped and the howling continued.

He picked up the dagger, his hand still gripping her forearm. "I suppose I should still offer you water, after that. It would be humane. But I'd say you won't die of thirst before I get you to Tara."

She looked at him, a furious expression on her face. "No. I won't die of thirst. But you had better take care of me or my father will make you pay."

"Oh, will he, so?" His expression flattened, a sudden dead calm taking over him.

"You know he will. I'm his daughter. I'm everything to him."

"Everything." Luke nodded. "Yes, I suppose. And I suppose he's everything to you. If you leave out power. Power is the key between the two of you. He loves power. He loves the power he has over you. Your affections. Or whatever you want to call it. But the thing is, *Mother*, though he might be my grandfather, he has no power over me. And nor do you."

She spat at him. "You're mistaken. But then you're like your father. A useless dreamer. Believing that nobility is a quality that will make others admire you."

"Oh, trust me, I left nobility behind a long time ago," said Luke. Months ago he would have believed that statement wholeheartedly, but now. Now, something was different. Nobility had crept in and taken up lodgings inside him again. Crept in through a window opened by Kayla. Beloved Kayla.

And suddenly he saw Eithne. Really saw her. Not the woman that inspired hatred, resentment, envy, and the other emotions that reduced him to a petulant child, a child seeking the approval and love of a parent, but a woman who was herself reduced. Reduced to a role that could only inspire pity. And the pity filled him and made him shake his head.

"Ah, Eithne," he said, sadly. "So much in your life was filled with missed opportunities."

He took her arm, more gently this time and pulled her back towards the worn path. When he reached the path and turned to replace her gag, he saw the frustrated fury on her face and also the tears that were tracking down her cheeks. Power, he thought, leaking down her face, because any power that she'd held over him was gone. And in its place was just a faint compassion, laced with the pity over the waste of her life.

IT WAS SOMETIME LATER that he found the deserted homestead. It was a disappointment for more reasons than he wanted to count. No one to answer his questions of where and when. No food to add to his own dwindling supply. Best not to enumerate further.

Eithne, thankfully, had remained silent since the stream, the gag replaced assisting with the lack of sound, but her body, her posture and her eyes had remained silent, too, as if she was shutting down all parts of herself that would communicate her inner thoughts. Just as well, thought, Luke, for there was nothing he could imagine he was interested in.

He moved beyond the homestead and found a small measure of hope when he saw the road up ahead. It was more a track than a road. A *bóthar* cows would be glad to lend their Irish *bó* to, which made it wide enough for the cows to pass through, but the condition of it wasn't particularly cart worthy. Still, it promised more and that was what he was after.

It was when that *bóthar* led to a real road, a road that had purpose and had no hint of track attached to it that Luke's strides lengthened and he was pulling Eithne behind him at a such a rate that she stumbled occasionally.

And then a mounted figure appeared, leading two horses. A figure that slowly took on a familiar shape and made him whoop when the shock of white blond hair and amused face broke into loud laughter.

"You feckin' twit, Luke, what did you go and do now?" said Mon, speaking in English.

Luke looked down at his decidedly bedraggled state. His clothes were still damp from the two dousings, his hair, he was certain had a dragged through a backward hedge look that in no fashion world would ever be seen as chic, impoverished or otherwise. His leather jacket had an awkward shrunken look that would take much working to achieve any kind of statement other than big mistake. But still he laughed. He laughed because he still had Retaliator strapped to his back, the slingshot and spearhead in the pouch tied to his jeans and most of all, his best friend, his brother in all senses of the word, was there before him with two spare horses.

"It's a long story," said Luke. "A great tale for over a few pints."

Mon grinned. "Oh, it better be, dude. And you're paying. For whiskey, because I have a feeling the story is a whiskey story."

Luke returned the grin. "A whiskey story all right. No doubt about it." He looked behind him at Eithne. "We need to get this woman to Tara, but take care, she has claws."

"Oh, I have no doubt about the claws on that one. That's why I went looking for you. Her claws are something I knew would find a way to insert themselves in you. Find the soft spot and go for it."

Luke saw Mon knew and understood. Knew him like few others did – and that knowledge had brought him here, now. His brother. Luke nodded. Nothing more to be said on that count, except one addendum.

"Not any more, Mon. The skin is thick now. No claws of hers can penetrate it now."

Mon nodded slowly. "Glad to hear it, bro. Glad to hear it. Now, get your arse up on this horse. We need to get going. There's no time to lose, there's a battle to be won."

Luke felt relief. It wasn't too late. "I'm in time?"

Mon nodded. "Only just. We have to head there, now. To Magh Tuireadh."

"Magh Tuireadh? But we have to take Eithne to Tara first. And the spearhead. Smithy needs to make a shaft for the spearhead. Or Credne."

Mon shook his head. "No time. We have to go now. The battle will most likely be underway tomorrow."

Luke looked at him in shock. "That soon? Feck." He glanced over at Eithne, saw the smug expression and that was enough to galvanise him into action. "Right, so. Off we go then. We'll just have to figure something out for the spearhead. As for Eithne, well we'll find somewhere to stuff her." He'd said it as a joke, an offhand comment, but he realised a moment later that the offhand, was exactly that. Offhand. The power was gone. She was just a minor problem, easily solved and worthy only of a little pity at this point.

43

MAURA

Finn was off to the side somewhere in the group next to ours. I wouldn't look at him. Not at all. He could stay where he was, what did I care? That was my mantra, spoken over and over in my head since I'd left him in the yard. The distance I'd been determined to maintain and hated that I hoped he wouldn't maintain, was fixed, immutable, from that time forward until now. Until, much to my disgust, I looked over in his direction and he lifted his sword to me in salute and nodded. I turned away quickly, unable to acknowledge it, fighting back the emotion that swelled inside me. Time to focus on the battle.

As of first light this morning Luke hadn't appeared. It worried the others, and to some degree it did me, but I knew deep in my gut that Balor would die. Even if I had to kill him three times myself. It would be a pleasure. A threefold death. Maybe not by slingshot, spear and sword, but I would happily garrotte him, drown him and chop his head off. The trouble he'd caused me. The way he'd upended my life. Twice.

From my place behind a tree, I flexed my shoulders, in part to ease the tension, an instinctive preparation for the fight.

Other warriors, grouped behind various outcroppings of trees and shrubs, were scattered across the expanse of grassy bog. Behind them were the mounted warriors, the few who swung their axe and sword better from the war ponies, bred to endure the grinding experience of fighting battles. This was who the Tuatha de Danann were. Who I was. Bloodcurdling cries and clever magic. A mixture of strategies that kept the enemy on the back foot.

The thought gave me a little thrill, because finally, I recognised the truth that was these people and the truth that was me. I grinned with it. Grinned widely, so widely that my teeth showed and people stepped away, thinking it was some berserker preparation. But sure, weren't we all a mixture? Myself included? Myself. Included. Yes, I was included, not marginalised out to some pedestal above, where I raised my hands and conjured up a war, or a battle. No, I was here, in the midst of it, ready to plunge in with the others. Included.

The thought, the utter simplicity of it and my blindness to it, gave me a lightness of spirit that lifted my sword above me and caused me to shout the most blood curdling cry imaginable. It was time. The battle was begun. I surged forward along with the others in my group, because even now I could see Balor's warriors approaching by stealth up the rise. There were fewer than I'd expected, a thought that made me at once suspicious and also glad. There might be more hidden somewhere, but for now this was a "no bother" type of battle, Balor aside, wherever he may be.

The first warrior I encountered had a face with blazing eyes and dark brows, his lips drawn into a sneer. I didn't even hear the words he shouted at me, his sword swinging and hitting mine with a clang. We battled on, feinting, parrying, nothing pretty about our fight, just brutal swift motions employed for their efficiency. A shove, a knee to the groin, anything. He fell, sooner than his sneering looks should have meant, and I moved on to the next one, barely conscious of those who fought near me. The battle was me. I was the battle. Sword swinging, clashing, the impact absorbed in my arm, my shoulder, my back. A cut to the face, a blow to the arm and a moment of thanks for the leather jacket and thick boots that meant stomping on a foot or any other part of my opponent that would hurt.

The sweat poured down, obscuring my vision on occasion, but only briefly, until I shook it away or wiped it off. Every so often a shout, a cry would reach my ears, but only as a muffled distant sound. On I fought, sword clashing, my hand numb for a second, but recovering enough to give a swift kick where it counted and then a swipe with the dagger in my other hand.

I paused, looking for my next combatant, taking a breath with it, a chance moment to recover, and then heard the cry. Nothing muffled about it, not to my ears. The cry seared through my body, a real and true spear in my gut, my heart. Finn.

I turned my head and a sword came crashing down on my head. I felt myself fall, and for a moment I heard myself cry his name. Feck, feck, feck. Would this be how it ended? The tragic story of the Morrigan too proud to acknowledge how she felt, who she loved beyond life itself? Was it really that awful, that clichéd that I couldn't bear to embrace it, live it? What was I losing to do that? What was I losing to not do that? I hit the ground, a foot stomped on my gut, causing me to grunt. A moment later a hand grabbed my arm and lifted me up, pulled me to my feet. I blinked, shook the hair from my face. Finn, whole and grinning, his hand still gripping my arm.

"What did I tell you about keeping your focus?" he said.

I choked, my mouth gaping. He shoved my sword back in my hand. "Focus, Maura. Focus."

And I did. I focused on his face, his mouth, the quirky way it smiled, the light in his eyes, now trained on me. His lovely,

lovely, dear self. He leaned down and kissed my forehead and I wanted to float away.

"I know, buttercup," he said. "We'll talk later."

"Buttercup?" I said, half shrieking with indignation, the other half laughter filled.

He laughed. "Got your focus then?"

I gripped my sword tighter. "Oh, feck me yes. Just wait, laddo. Just you wait until this is over. I'll give you buttercup."

I surged towards a group of Balor's men coming up the rise, Finn's laughter like music in my ears. But then a bone-shattering pain went shooting from my arm where I just realised I had been cut by a sword. I dropped my weapon, clutched my arm and fell to the ground.

44

LUKE

He could hear the sounds of battle before he saw them. The clash of swords, the cries, the grunts, the groans, the sounds of wood breaking, metal grinding against metal and the squeals of animals wounded, felled or killed. It was all there and soon visible as his horse broke through the wooded glade into the boggy outreach of the small rise, and the back end of the battle where the Tuatha de Danann had their supplies, spare ponies, men and where he now saw Daghda striding towards him, away from the battle, shouting to the small group of men clustered around a central figure. The king.

Luke approached him. Luke, a man who had been the king's champion and was no longer. A man who'd refused the honour of ruling these people out of a sense of nobility. A man who had so many talents that all had admired and envied him in the past. A warrior for the ballads, for a tale the seanchies would put in their bag of stories marked "best ones". Only Luke felt far from any of those men at the moment. His leather jacket, now dried, felt tight across his chest and back after one too many dunkings and it creaked when he moved. One of his boots had a crack across the top for the same reason and the insides were still soggy and added another creak to the almost symphonic sound he made when he moved. His jeans fitted okay, thankfully, but any semblance of cool had been lost to the gaping hole in the knee, courtesy of a thorn bush he'd had to tromp through to retrieve that feckin' likely branch to make the spear shaft. Said spear shaft now had the spearhead attached with some spare elastic bands and a bit of old twine he'd picked up at a beach near Incheydoney. A great image he made, to be sure.

Retaliator, though, was still strapped to his back, doing its best to make up for his lack of nobility and warrior image else-where, and the dagger at his side made a decent job of it too. The slingshot was prepped and stuck in the side of his belt, and if the pouch for the missiles seemed to hang a little funny, no one would notice, it still would function well enough. And the spear, to be fair, had a decent enough balance. He could envision launching it into the air and it landing true. It had managed to spear a bush with a fair amount of accuracy when he'd tried it out. And sure, wasn't the magic in the spearhead? A never fail magic that would send it faultlessly to its target? Count on it, the voice told him. He would of course. What other choice did he have?

Daghda caught sight of him, raised an arm in greeting and started to make his way over to Luke, stopping occasionally as men approached him, asked him questions and he gave his answers. Luke waited, his mind already focusing on the tasks ahead.

"Sorry," said Luke when Daghda stood before him. "Unfore-seen circumstances delayed me."

Daghda arched his brows. "Unforeseen?"

Luke sighed. "Not completely unforeseen, I suppose, in that it was due to Eithne. She jumped from the boat. And well, the rest followed."

Daghda nodded. "No need to explain any further. I understand she's here, though. Safely locked away?"

Luke nodded. "Mon is seeing to it."

Daghda smiled. "He's a good lad, your Mon."

"Yes."

There was nothing more to add to that for Luke, because it would be all words. Words that spoke much less than the look in Daghda's eyes and the feeling in Luke's heart. Daghda saw Mon's worth, even as Mon demonstrated it by showing up for this battle against Balor, because no one else in his family had ever done that before. Though Manannán had given tokens of support in the past, and had probably done so now, he didn't see the battle as his, really, though this time, he more than likely realised that there was more than just defeating Balor at stake.

"Well you're here now and the time is right. Just as it was in the last battle."

"We're beating back Balor's forces?"

"We are. It's been tough, though. There are several down and taken behind the lines to be rejuvenated by the water from the Well of Slane. But it isn't like last time."

"No?"

Daghda frowned. "He must be using something on his men's swords. The wounds, they're not natural. They're suppurating."

"Already?"

Daghda was right. It wasn't natural. Balor must have done something to the swords. It wasn't magic, though, of that he was certain, because no magic they had ever wielded would behave like that. No, this was something that smacked of a strategy from across the water. He didn't have the chemistry background to be able to pin it down, but he would stake his life on it. The thought made him pause. Sure, he might have to stake his life on it.

Daghda had been studying him carefully. "Do you know what it is?"

Luke shook his head. "Not specifically. But I can hazard a guess that it's something Balor knows from his other life. Something chemical. He's had access to some brilliant scientists, I'm sure, who would have done the work for him."

"But he wouldn't have been able to bring that kind of thing here."

"Maybe not already made up, but he could certainly bring the knowledge of it, if it wasn't too complex."

Daghda's expression darkened. He drew in his lips, the anger clear on his face. "I think it's beyond time you saw to his end."

Luke nodded. "I think so."

He took up his spear, the Red Javelin of Finias, its power that it would find its enemy, now that it had a new shaft, albeit makeshift. That the old shaft was gone, thanks to Balor, he hoped wouldn't be an issue. The hope was there, but not the guarantee. The hope was also in his slingshot, something he hadn't used since the last time. That last battle. Long ago. A seanchie's *fadó, fadó, fadó* long ago. But Retaliator was his, and held more than promise.

He strode up the rise, the sounds of battle getting louder, and when he reached the point where he had a view of the warriors fighting, mud flying in the boggy terrain, bloodied jerkins, hair plastered to heads and faces, arms swinging, blows landing, or not. In the distance he was certain he caught sight of Saoirse's hair, a crown of flames among the murky sea of bodies. Smithy wouldn't be too far away, he was certain.

He noted someone coming towards him carrying a fallen warrior away from the thick of the fighting. With a start he saw it was Finn and he was carrying Maura. Maura? The sight unsettled him and he made his way towards them.

"What happened? Is she all right?" Luke asked when Finn was in earshot.

"I don't know. She just clutched her arm and collapsed. I haven't had time to look at wound."

Luke frowned. This wasn't like Maura. No wound, major or otherwise, would have stopped her normally. But here she was barely unconscious, her arm hanging oddly from her body. And then he saw. Through the torn leather arm of her jacket, the angry looking cut.

"Get some water from the Well of Slane on her wound, now, Finn," he said. "It's Balor. He's using some kind of toxic chemical that infects the wound. The sooner you wash that shite off and use the water, the better her chance of healing." Luke caught sight of her face. "Her face, Finn. Her face."

The cut on her face, though not as serious as the one on her arm appeared to be, was already suppurating, the pus gathering at an unbelievable rate.

Finn issued a stream of curses and began striding away, towards the healing station at the foot of the rise. Luke paused to watch him go, hoping for Maura's sake that he reached it in time. Scarring at best, death at worst. Either one, he knew would make life difficult for the both of them.

Luke faced forward, suddenly angry that this fecker would have dared to violate the laws of this world, even if it was in an underhanded manner that skirted the issue. It didn't take away from its evil. Balor's evil.

He scanned the scene once again, looking for no one else but his prey. There was nothing identifiable as Balor. Would Balor have involved himself in the heart of the battle? His past action led Luke to believe he would. But the Balor now, well, that could be a different matter altogether.

Luke slowly moved forward, dodging rather than engaging in battle. Retaliator was still sheathed, but he knew he could drop the spear and draw the sword in a heartbeat, that Retaliator was already humming to him, ready for the fight, eager to find the enemy it knew was here. The thought made Luke smile, made him search even more keenly, because now he understood even more the power of that sword. He followed the hum over to a small group of fighters nearly at the bottom of the rise, where the enemy's lines were strongest. The hum grew louder, and Luke could feel it, the vibration that became a song. Luke heard the song clearly over the din of battle and he grinned.

He saw him then. Balor. Kitted out in the chicest of chic battle gear. Body armour, helmet and special Kevlar gloves. The fecker. Well, Balor needed all the help he could get. It wouldn't stop Luke, though. With an instinct he didn't question he slipped the spear into the brace holding the scabbard on his back, withdrew his slingshot from his belt and reached in his pocket for a missile. It was a special type. Lead, silver and... magic. A type of ball that he'd asked Smithy to make for him and luckily Mon had brought them from Tara.

He inserted the ball into the leather pouch of the slingshot. Balor was wielding his sword, with force, the determination in every line of his body. Two of his men flanked him on either side, all of them engaged with a group of Tuatha de Danann warriors. Luke waited a moment. And then Balor turned slightly, just enough so that Luke had a direct line to Balor's face, where the black patch across his eye stood starkly against his pale skin. Luke launched the missile, heard the satisfying thwack of his missile hitting its target. Its true target. The black patch could have been a bullseye, guiding his aim, making the hit perfect.

Balor reached up to his eye, already reeling with the impact of the missile that had passed right through the patch and out the back of his head. Just like before, thought Luke. Just like before. Only this time he would finish that gobshite for good. First death down, two to go. He started to move forward, tucking the slingshot back in his belt and reaching for the spear. The spear, with a former shaft made of an ancient and scarred ash that was now some feck all branch from a what appeared to be a willow tree (save them all) and shifted it into position. The weight seemed fair, balanced and not shouting "I am destined to end up in a bush" which reassured him to a degree. He could see Balor's collapsed body lying in an untidy heap, his men crowding now in front of them. Luke frowned, narrowed his eyes, and flung the most teeth-shattering battle cry that he could manage that pierced through the other battle sounds. He moved steadily forward in an almost walk-run and the moment everyone turned to look Luke launched the spear, his weight on his back foot and his arm arching out, following the trajectory with his hand once it had released the spear, to swing him to his other foot in the downward movement. He watched the spear fly, a whizz whizz signalling its progress to its target. Luke kept his eye focused, a "not a bush", "not a bush", underthought matching the whizz whizz, until the noise stopped, thrusting itself in its target. The enemy.

It took a moment only, a blink of an eye, but in that blink Luke's apprehension turned to complete joy as he realised the spear had found the only target possible. Balor. The spear was now embedded in his neck, the blood spurting from the carotid artery there. He let out a breath he didn't know he was holding.

The men around Balor had turned to fight the opponents closing in on them now, conscious that they needed to defend their leader who lay, Luke was certain, dying from either the great hole in his head, or the hole in his neck, if he wasn't dead already. He drew Retaliator from its sheath and headed towards Balor, determined to deal the final blow, the final death. A three-fold death. He wouldn't let Balor escape that.

His focus was narrowed, and maybe it was due to that narrowness that he didn't see the warrior coming at him from behind. If it wasn't for Retaliator's hum, that vibration that travelled along his arm and spread through his body in one flash of connection, he wouldn't have reacted in time. As it was, the initial blow struck low towards the hilt and he could barely keep the sword in hand for it, causing him to lose his balance for a moment. He righted himself, but the next blow bit him in the leg, right on that feckin' hole in his jeans and he didn't have time to parry it. Feck and feck, he thought, as he felt the slice to his skin. He needed no more preparation, he swung the sword at his opponent, the force of the swing and the blow to his opponent's sword so fierce the weapon was sent flying from the opponent's hand. Luke finished him off with the next blow, and without another moment's thought, turned to locate Balor again.

There were only two men defending Balor, now, and one was obviously tiring. Luke made his way towards them, weaving through battling figures while staying alert to any other attackers. He was just closing in on the small battling group when his leg gave way, an incapacitating pain seizing him. He glanced down and saw the open wound where the sword had cut him a few moments earlier. It was deep, the edges of skin red and raw, revealing a curd like substance in its centre. Oh feck, he thought. Not now. He struggled to rise, his sword still in hand, ready to defend himself. After a few moments he managed to stand, his leg screaming in agony, but he forced himself forward, limping badly as he headed towards Balor. No matter what, he would complete this threefold death.

He reached the battling group, his progress excruciatingly slow, the limp progressively worse. The last of Balor's guard was battling it out with two warriors and it took a few moments blinking to realise that it was Saoirse and Smithy. The sight of them, through all the pain, made him grin, especially when Saoirse, with a final little flourish, finished off Balor's man with a kick in the groin and a blow to his neck. He fell with a clunk and

Saoirse looked on for a moment before turning to see Luke. Her eyes brightened and he waggled his brow and grinned wider.

She stood back and Smithy kicked the warrior out of the way, nodding to Balor. "He's all yours."

Luke forced himself forward, his control over his leg waning to almost nothing. He stood over Balor, his weight entirely on his good foot and saw the slightest movement in Balor's chest. The eye patch was gone, half his face was caved in. The spear, still lodged in his neck, was erect, seeming triumphant, announcing a proud moment for itself. Barely alive. And even if he didn't deal this blow, Balor's time could be measured in moments.

Luke lifted his sword, knew his aim would be clear. There was no hesitation, all the agony of the past, was just that, the past. This was evil he was killing. An evil that had no hope of redemption. The sword fell, its path true, and a moment later, its purpose achieved. Balor's head was separated from his body. The third and final death was complete. Luke took a deep breath, lifted the sword and gave thanks to it, and all those who'd brought him here – and prayed that they, and everyone else, would now be safe from Balor and all the evil he'd wrought.

And that's when his leg gave out.

45

___

MAURA

I felt a hand stroking my forehead and smelled the scent of pinewood and cedar, which made no sense, since the curses, groans and grunts that accosted my ears were fit more for the battlefield than that touch and that scent. Slowly, I opened my eyes and Finn's face came into focus. A concerned face, a caring face, full of his heart.

"Am I dying?" I asked in a croaky voice. Dying of thirst at the very least. I needed water, soon.

"What? No," said Finn his voice full of alarm. "Why would you say that? Are you in pain, is there some injury we don't know about?"

"A parched throat?" I said. I tried to smile, but my face hurt. I raised my hand to my cheek and felt only a bandage.

Before I could ask the question, the one now hanging in the air, Finn raised a cup to my lips. I took a sip and then another, suddenly all I could think of was getting as much fluid down me as I could. It was water, but it wasn't, the smooth way it passed down my throat uncanny, like velvet. I sighed with the pleasure of it and finally had my fill.

I laid back against the straw pallet I was lying on and

prepared myself for the words I needed to hear. Girded my loins – wasn't that the expression?

"Finn," I began, thinking yes, begin with his name across the water. Or should it be Ogma? The indecision put me in a bit of a tailspin. Who did I want to address? Were they the same to me? Was the Ogma of the bright curls, the golden tongue, brave warrior, the darling of all, was he the same as the witty, clever musician that was Finn? They were two halves of the same whole, I knew that, in fact I'd seen it. But at this moment, the first name that came to me had been Finn. Even though all around me others had been calling me Morrigan since I'd first arrived on this side. Except Finn, Saoirse and Smithy. Luke, I hadn't seen.

"Luke?" I asked, my voice urgent, suddenly needing to know. "Did he manage it? Is the battle over?"

Finn smiled at her. "What else could a fearless, brave warrior do, but what he was destined for?"

I grinned, though it hurt my cheek. Grinned, because I knew the depth of that comment and the tone, which held no traces of bitterness or jealousy, had travelled a journey that few knew. That Finn, no, Ogma, graced with everything and not quite, had come to understand everything wasn't always enough, or satisfying, that our own "everything" could amount to very little in many people's eyes.

I also grinned because, sure, wouldn't I grin when that fecker Balor had finally been defeated?

"The battle's over, then?" I asked.

Finn nodded. "For the most part. There are a few stragglers still fighting from sheer bloodymindedness, but Balor is dead, killed three times by Luke in a threefold manner. So, I'd say our day is triumphant."

"And Luke?"

Finn looked down at his hands. "Not so grand, but we hope for the best."

"What happened?"

"Balor. All his warriors' swords were coated with some kind of toxic chemical and Luke had sustained a deep wound in his thigh. It festered quickly and now Diancecht's trying to save the leg and him."

I took a few moments to absorb all of this information. And then I knew. I touched the bandage on my cheek again. "I was cut here." The bandage felt bulky, but even as I touched it lightly, the resulting pain in my cheek made me wince.

"It'll heal," said Finn. "Airmed assures me that it will. And your arm is fine."

I gave a sour laugh and stopped when it hurt too much. "Well at least it will heal. No cheek amputation then."

Finn gave me a sympathetic smile. That smile said it all. Scarring. Suddenly, I didn't want sympathy because I knew the next step after it. Pity. I turned my head away.

"Hey, hey," he said. "At worst you can think of it like a jaunty tattoo on your face."

"You hate tattoos."

He laughed. "No, I don't. What makes you say that?"

"You hate my tattoo."

"I don't hate your tattoo."

"The way you look at it. It isn't a friendly look."

Finn was grinning now and I found it annoying.

"You think I give your tattoo unfriendly looks?"

I knew it sounded stupid, petty. Something that was childish but I couldn't help myself. "Whatever. Just know that I know how you feel. What you were thinking."

"Trust me when I say this Maura, but you don't have any idea what I was thinking, or how I felt."

I grunted. Pressed my lips together. "I'd rather not have a

mark on my face, tattoo-like or otherwise. But if I do, Mr Finn Ogma, I will own it as a scar. A battle scar."

"I wouldn't expect anything else, Miss Maura Morrigan."

He leaned over then and kissed my lips softly. "Now get some rest. We'll be travelling back to Tara soon. Daghda will have a boat ready for us, so it won't be arduous for you."

He rose then, and even though I wanted to watch him go, to get every last glimpse of him despite knowing it would only be a short while before I saw him again, my eyes closed and I fell asleep.

I STARED THROUGH THE WINDOW, watching the yard below. Finn was there, talking with Daghda. It seemed a pleasant exchange, each of them at ease. A sign that boded well. No serious discussion of bad news, something that I felt had to come. It would of course, because things had been going too well, so far. The Fomorians were gone, only a ragtag bunch left. Eithne with them, too broken by her father's death to be any real threat. Luke seemed to be on the mend, although they were saying he might have a slight limp. Though I knew him well enough now to understand that he wouldn't permit a limp. That he would fight every day to recover full use. He was the all-conquering hero and he would conquer this. To be the whole man worthy of Kayla. And the land.

The land. As far as I knew it was recovering, and that meant Kayla, her daughter and mother were too. And Anu. Hopefully. But soon I would know, because today, Finn and I were crossing the water. That would be the final test that everything had been restored. I touched my cheek. The bandage there was smaller and could probably now be removed. Airmed's ointments had gone a long way to reducing the scarring.

I went over to the polished metal that was mounted on the wall. It would be my mirror. Carefully I removed the bandage and inspected my cheek. As Airmed had predicted, it was still raw and red, taking up a much smaller portion of my cheek than it would have if not for Airmed and the water from the Well of Slane. It was a jagged patch, shaped like a kite. Or no, a crow. If I squinted at it in a certain way it was a crow, I decided. Perfect. Let everyone know who I was. What I was.

A figure came into view behind me. I forced a smile, feeling a little nervous. "So, not too hideous." I made the words a statement. I had at least that much pride.

"Not hideous at all," said Finn, placing his hands on my shoulders.

"Interesting," I said. "I've decided it's shaped like a crow."

Finn nodded slowly. "Of course you have."

We stared at the mirror, our eyes fixed on each other's and slowly Finn lowered his head and kissed my neck. "You're perfect," he said.

"You say that to all the ladies."

He gave me one half of a smile. "I do?"

"Well, at least one lady."

He looked puzzled. "One lady?"

"Oh, you mean there are more?"

"It's all news to me, Maura. What are you talking about?"

"Here, before the battle, when you first arrived. I saw you in one of the small chambers off the practice yard with..." I waved my hand..."I don't know her name, some feckin' woman."

Finn studied me a moment and then his face cleared. "Her? I didn't say anything of the kind to her. She was just asking me to give her brother some guidance on his sword skills."

"Oh, I can imagine what skills she wanted advice on."

Finn laughed really hard then and I dug at him with my elbow. "Feck off and stop laughing."

With great effort he brought his laughter under control. "I assure you, there was nothing going on with her." He turned me around to face him. "Honestly. I don't know how you can even imagine that I would be interested in any kind of flirtation with anyone else."

"Anyone else? You mean there is someone you do want to have a flirtation with?"

"Flirtation, no. Poor choice of words. A relationship. And yes there is someone else I want to have a relationship with."

"There is?" The words were faint, but the hope was strong, nearly choking me with its strength.

"Yes. And I think you know who it is."

"I do?" Those words were barely a squeak, but before I could clear my throat and say it louder, stronger, his lips descended on mine and all thoughts fled as I became lost in the kiss, his touch and all the emotions that flooded through me. The sensations, the joy, the love, the wonder that I finally could feel his body against mine, his lips exploring my face, my cheek, the hollow of my neck. And his hands, gently peeling back the light robe I wore, to feel my breasts, to caress them and travel down, caressing more and more of my body.

He led me to the bed, the robe already on the floor and his own clothes swiftly removed so that we could lie together, skin to skin, touching each other as if it was the first time, ears kissed, fingers kissed, my legs wrapped around him, my body joined to his and feeling more than wonder. Feeling the perfection of our imperfection. Two halves of a whole.

And later, as I lay in his arms, the haze of our lovemaking still enveloping us, it was then I noticed it. The tattoo. It was spread gloriously across the left side of his chest, over his heart. A crow, black with feathers subtly detailed. Beautiful. I leaned over and kissed it.

"When?" I asked.

He kissed my head. "Just before I crossed over the water. It's what delayed me."

Tears clustered in my eyes and one fell. "Oh, Finn. My Finn."

"Why wouldn't I get it?" he asked, amusement in his eyes. "You're my heart, Maura. You know that. Nothing can change it."

"And you're my heart," I whispered.

EPILOGUE

MAURA

Finn and I walked up the hill from my old farmhouse in Cúil Íarharcht to Anu's. We'd arrived just a few hours ago from across the water and we gambled that it was possible Anu might already be back in her own home, if everything had been set to rights. My phone hadn't given us reason to hope, because she hadn't answered the calls I'd made to her phone, or the texts. And Saoirse and Smithy's phones had produced equally no results. I wasn't even certain they were back here. The confirmation would all have to be done in person.

My lads were high up in the trees when we'd left the house. They'd welcomed us with a reserve that had me laughing until my main lad Rook came down and perched on my shoulder, giving me a saucy peck. And that was it. They were back to squawking and teasing and even now, as we crested the rise leading from my house, I could hear them squawking at each other.

Finn took my hand, squeezed, and I saw him grin, knowing what I was thinking. I leaned my head on his arm, still not believing I was doing that, and that it felt so natural. I inhaled him and the scents around him, feeling completely alive and—happy. Happy? Everything around me was fresh and new. Smelled fresh and new, even though it was autumn. An encouraging sign. Or maybe it was just me and my embarrassing tendency to find beauty in everything at the moment. That dear springy curl of Finn's that at this moment was flying into his face. That lovely way he caught his upper lip between his teeth when he was trying not to laugh, as he was now.

"I feel that Anu's there, at the house," I said.

He looked down at me and smiled. "I know. I feel the same, too. Though it might just be me. You know, the way I feel about you. It's overflowing into the rest of the world."

I nodded. "I know. And still."

"And still," he says.

The words were there between us. In each other, part of each other. The one who battles with words and the other who battles with swords. Two halves of a whole.

Anu's house drew into view, the white gable clearly visible through the baring tree branches. It was too early to tell, but I could feel excitement building inside me.

We breached the rise and looked into the yard, but there was nothing to indicate that she was there. I knew someone had looked after the livestock while she'd been at the Beara, Anu would have always ensured that was done. So the presence of a few cows in the lower field was no real confirmation. Just a tiny kernel added to the piles of hope that were getter higher as I drew near.

A door burst open and Saoirse came striding out, hair flying around her, boots, jeans and leather jacket looking as much a part of her as anything ever would or could. A woman come into herself. She turned to the door and broke out laughing at something someone just inside the door had said. A deep voice.

Smithy. He emerged a moment later, his stance that bit cocky, but humorously so.

"Ah, Jaysus, will you look at the two of them," said Smithy, his chin jutting in our direction. He started cooing.

"Oh, feck off out of it, Smithy," I said, grinning like a banshee at his mocking for us being love birds. Or not a banshee. There was nothing lamentable about what I was feeling.

Saoirse turned back and caught sight of us. Her eyes lit up. "Maura, Finn! You're back. Great stuff."

"Anu," Finn said. "Is she any better?"

"Come in and see for yourself," said Saoirse.

She and Smithy turned and went back inside the house, leaving the door wide for us to follow. A good sign. I made my way through the door, Finn's hand at my back, and I loved its feel there. As though it belonged. It did belong.

We went through to the kitchen and there she was, like a picture out of an old book on Ireland, leaning down over the crane to lift the kettle off its hook, a fire burning merrily in the hearth. Her long plait trailed down her back, and when she looked up and saw us approach, her cheeks were flushed a healthy colour.

"Anu," I said. "You're here. You're well?"

"I'm well enough," she said, smiling warmly. "And always ready to welcome friends and relations into my home."

"Ah, will I just go then?" I asked in a teasing tone.

"Not at all, my girl. Sit down for a cuppa. Bríd, get the biscuits from the press and the tart. I'm sure there's some apple tart."

Saoirse raised her brows. "But Anu, that's shop bought."

Anu slid me a sly look. "Morrigan won't mind. She doesn't cook herself, so she won't know the difference."

I laughed. Relieved in so many ways. The tension that had been between us, or at least it had seemed so to me, was gone.

The warmth that Anu had always given all of us, including me, was back and, it seemed, with more added.

"Sit down you two and tell me the when," Anu said. "And you too Goibhniu, no need to lurk in the background like a ghoul."

"A ghoul?" said Smithy. "I'm insulted. I thought it was a very manly lurk. Or at least deep and mysterious."

"Not a hope," I said.

Smithy looked at Finn, mock outrage on his face. Finn shrugged. "Don't look at me. I know feck all about that kind of thing. I can't even lurk properly."

"Oh, you make up for it in other ways," I told him in a low voice, feeling myself redden. It still seemed strange to have our relationship on display for everyone to see.

Saoirse came back in, bringing the biscuits and the notorious store bought apple tart. She giggled. "Ah, Smithy, I'll call you deep and mysterious if you like and you can lurk all you want with me. I like your lurking."

She placed the biscuits and tart on the table along with a small stack of plates and we all took seats around. Finn sat beside me, took my hand under the table. The need to touch him was overwhelming, and I was glad that he felt no qualms about displaying that need in public.

The tea was poured and Anu had her cup of milk in hand. The warmth, the good feeling was pouring out everywhere and I couldn't help but feel a little anxious at it.

"Luke, have you heard from him? Is Kayla ok? And the others?"

"On the mend," said Anu. "All of them. It will take some time, but they have that."

"And each other," said Saoirse. "That will go a long way towards getting them well."

"It will indeed," said Anu. "They are twined now. They have

made their pledge to each other and are bound inseparably." She looked at Smithy and Saoirse. "Like you two have."

Saoirse blushed and Smithy took her hand a kissed her knuckles. "We have of course. It's our time now."

Anu looked at me. "And so, I ask you two—when?"

I blinked at her. "When?"

"The two of you. Your binding. Your twining? You'll do it soon?"

I looked at Finn. His eyes were dancing. "She asked you a question. I hope you know the answer."

The answer was in his eyes and I hoped reflected in mine. "I will of course," I said, first to him and then turning to Anu, I said it again to her.

He squeezed my hand and I squeezed it back. A moment later I raised his hand to my lips and kissed his knuckles.

Smithy cooed again, the sound containing no mocking. But still, I stuck my tongue out at him.

Anu laughed. "I'm glad to hear it. And for now, there is a strong balance in the world. One that I hope lasts for a good while. At least until we can gather enough strength to help others who face the same peril as we had."

I thought of Raven and the ongoing fight he faced back in Oklahoma and the rest of America. And all the other places around the world who were dealing with similar challenges. Anu was right. This was an ongoing challenge, but for now, we had eliminated one element in this huge fight. And for now, we must be content with that, and I would find strength and my own contentment with this man beside me. The other to mine. Which together made the whole.

A NOTE ON THE MYTHS AND PRONUNCIATION

Some of the names and terms can appear daunting to those not used to Irish. And for those who like to know, I've put a few here in case it increases the enjoyment of the novel.

Bóthair – (road) bow (like arrow) har

Bríd – Breed

Aoife – EE fa

Anu – An New/An Na (ancient, so it varies)

Airmed – AIR med

Ban an tí –ban an tee

Bláthín – Blaw heen

Búachaill –bwuock ull

Cailín – call een

An Cailleach –an Kall ick

Céad míle fáilte (hundred thousand welcomes) Cade meela fall cha

Cían – KEE an

Cíara – Keer rah

Clíodhna – Clee nah

Daghda – DAHG duh

Daragh – Da ruh

Díarmuid – Deer mud

Diancecht –Dee an kekt

Eilís – Eye leesh

Fadó – fa dough

Gan ainim – gan eye nem

Gearóid – Geh ROAD

Goibhniu – Gub New (another ancient one)

Líam – LEE um

Lughnasagh – Loo nah sah

Mo croí – mo cree

Mo Ghile Mear (something like my shining knight) mo geela mar

Saoirse – SEER sha/ SEHR sha (kind of in between)

Seanchie — shan na kee

Siné – shin eh

Sinead – Shin aid

Sláinte –slawn tuh (Munster Irish)

Suantraí – swan tree

Tadhg –Tyg (like tie with a hard 'g' sound on end

The Myths

The myths that are explained and interwoven in this novel are from *The Book of Invasions (Leabhar Gabhala)* part of the collection of Irish myths. I have kept true to the myths, with the exception of a few interpretations and a little embellishment in the case of Bríd and Goibhniu, Clíodhna and Mon. There is nothing in the myths that say that Bríd and Goibhniu were together, but they are both smith gods, one female, one male, so it seemed natural to link them. Bríd's fate after she married Bres is true, except for the embellishment of her rape. It isn't clear but it seemed a possible interpretation. She did give birth to three sons from Tuirenn and died as a result of that birth.

Local myths are also interwoven. On the Kerry/Cork border you will find the Paps of Anu, breast shaped mountains that are always climbed on May 1. At their foot on the Kerry side, it is said by some that the Tuatha de Danann settled there. The site of St Gobnait's burial and her well is also celebrated. St Gobnait was also known as a smith and there are remains of an ancient smithy there. It is my own view that it might have also been seen as a place where Goibhniu was either venerated or an ancient smith worked and invoked him there, and later became associated with the convent of religious women that was established later, led by a doubtlessly indomitable woman who came to be known as St Gobnait, a name very close to the god's and one that has no English translation in truth. (You can see my idea of her in my novel, *In Praise of the Bees*.) Some see the translation as 'Abby' but that's more than likely just an adaptation because of the 'abbess' aspect of St Gobnait's role.

Lugh's story, even his involvement with the Cailleach, is true to the original myth, except for the part including Clíodhna. He never had a relationship with her, that's my invention. But the rest of her story is as the tales recount, though Mongan's part in Manannán's wave that washed her away when she fell asleep, isn't true to the myth. There's a site at Glandore called Clíodhna's wave to this day.

Many tales of the Cailleach, or the Hag, are found around Ireland and Scotland and particularly on the Beara Peninsula where there is a large standing stone bearing her name. The largest source of information about the Cailleach of Beara (*Cailleach Bhéarra*) came from the book, *The Book of Cailleach:Stories of the Wise-Woman Healer,* by Gearóid Ó Crualaoich. She is a complex figure with mother goddess and a supernatural female wilderness figure associations that can be linked to Indo European and Norse traditions. A force to be reckoned with.

Morrigan is the Celtic Goddess of War who did side with the

Tuatha de Danann in the battle of Magh Tuireadh after Daghda persuaded her by sleeping with her one night. My interpretation of Morrigan is my own, part feminist and entirely flawed, but likeable (at least I hope).

Native American Myths and Mythic Figures

I selected a few mythic figures to represent Native American myths who are deeply involved in the creation of earth and its peoples and also who would naturally highlight the concerns they would have over pollution and other climate change issues. Two Native American educators have gone through my depictions to ensure that I have portrayed them appropriately. They are mentioned in the acknowledgements.

Raven-- the trickster-creator and the most important figure in Northwest Coast mythology. Some stories do mention a remote Lord of the Sky who first made the world. But this first creator doesn't feature strongly in myths and ceremonies of the NW. Raven always interests himself in human affairs—too much so for comfort sometimes. His name among the Haida means; the one who is going to order things: and putting the world in order was his first task. This involved transforming the things that first existed into their current forms and establishing the laws of nature. Some NW cultures have a separate figure who did that. A major myth tells how Raven obtained light for the world, but only through his attempt to destroy it. *Native Americans*, edited by Ian and Betty Balantine. And *The Great Mystery*, by Neil Philip

Skywoman- sometimes called 'Old Woman' is an important figure in Iroquois/Haudensaunee mythology. In the myths Ancient One took Old woman to be his wife, but he was still unhappy. He fell into a deep sleep and dreamed answer was to uproot a big tree. So he did and left a great hole in the floor of the sky world. He called Old Woman to look through the hole and he pushed her through it. As she fell she grabbed seed from the tree with one hand and tobacco scented root with the other. White water birds met Skywoman as she descended onto a water turtle. She scattered the seeds that grew when a muskrat brought mud from under the sea and placed it on the turtle's shell. She released seeds and plants and they grew. Turtle and island grew to make a home for Skywoman who shortly gave birth to a daughter – the beginning of the world – *Native Americans*, edited by Ian and Betty Balantine, *The Great Mystery*, by Neil Philip and *Braiding Sweetgrass* by Robin Wall Kimmerer.

Heyoka- Divine fool, a contrary who does everything backwards — a figure among the Sioux Peoples (Lakota, Dakota, Nakota) also seen in other Plains traditions although with other names. Traditionally not allowed to marry. They embody the 'cosmic conflict in the human world: for the heyoka manifest directly into human society the perpetual conflict between the Thunderbird powers and the Great Horned Serpent below'. They have a sacred vision and share some of it with people but do it through comic actions. They are a bridge between the spiritual world and the material world and help restore equilibrium. *Sacred Earth: The Spiritual Landscape* of Native America by Arthur Versluis.

Osage/Wahzhazhe

The situation with the Osage in Oklahoma is true, in part.

In the nineteenth century the US government forced the Wahzhazhe, or Osage, as they're commonly known, to leave their original lands in Oklahoma to go to Kansas as a strategy to halt the Cherokee Osage hostilities. Later in the century they were told to move again, and with money they had acquired from leasing grasslands put in trust, they purchased the lands in Oklahoma. Then later, that land proved to be rich in oil, containing one of the largest deposits in the United States. And anyone who wanted to obtain the oil had to pay for leases and royalties to the Osage. Every registered member of the Osage tribe received quarterly checks. Eventually, the tribe collected millions of dollars and the Osage became very wealthy, the wealthiest per capita in the world in the early twentieth century. Such wealth laid them open to exploitation. Merchants charged a much higher rate for their goods, doctors supplied drugs to addicted tribe members and a guardianship the federal government set up was used as an opportunity by crooked lawyers and judges to extract wealth from the rights holders. In the 1910s and 1920s some people even resorted to murder. There were some convictions, but not all who were to blame were convicted.

I avoided using the mythic figures from the Osage culture primarily because the major figures associated with creation are called The Little Men in English. I felt that was too close to the Little People, the name given in some tales to the fairies, the sidhe, who are really the remnants of The Tuatha de Danann, the mythic figures central to the story. Since so much humour is often attached to The Little People I didn't want any such flippancy or humour to arise or be perceived in this case, so decided not to use it. The Little Men are sacred to the Osage as I understand it and I would be horrified to have anything dismissive or offensive to be perceived in any way. The closest I came was to mention Iktomi, who is the equivalent of Raven in Osage culture, in other words a trickster.

Resources

I've collected many resources over the years and consulted

them in my use of the mythic figures. For the Osage I also consulted their website. My resources included:

Killers of the Flower Moon by David Grann

Native Americans, edited by Ian and Betty Balantine

The Great Mystery, by Neil Philip.

Osage Indian: Customs and Myth by Louis F. Burns

Braiding Sweetgrass by Robin Wall Kimmerer

Plants of Power by Alfred Savinelli

The Raven and the Totem: Traditional Native Alaskan Myths and Tales collected and edited by John E. Smelcer

Various reports of the Smithsonian Institution, including 36th, 39th annual reports, 1921, 1925.

ABOUT THE AUTHOR

Originally from Philadelphia, Kristin Gleeson lives in Ireland, in the West Cork Gaeltacht, where she teaches art classes, plays harp, sings in a choir and runs two book clubs for the village library. She holds a Masters in Library Science and a Ph.D. in history and for a time was an administrator of a large archives, library and museum in America. She also served as a public librarian in America and in Ireland.

Kristin Gleeson has also published The Celtic Knot Series and The Renaissance Sojourner Series. In addition to her novels, a biography on a First Nations Canadian woman, *Anahareo, A Wilderness Spirit*, is also available.

If you have enjoyed this book please post a review. It helps so much towards getting the book noticed.

If you go to the author website and join the mailing list to receive news of forthcoming releases, special offers and events, you'll receive an e novelette *A Treasure Beyond Worth,* a FREE prequel novelette and its ebook novel *Along the Far Shores* at www.krisgleeson.com

Music is a big part of Kristin's life and many of the books have music connected to them. Listen to the music while you read—go to www.krisgleeson.com/music and download the files. Keep checking back, as more pieces will be added to the library in the course of time.

ACKNOWLEDGMENTS

As usual I owe a great debt of thanks to my alpha team of readers, especially Jean, Jane, Claire and Babs as well as Lizzie, who gave a great fresh perspective. I also had a fantastic group of beta readers, Saorlaith, Eilín, Síleann, and Eileen who kept my Ireland real and ensured the fadas were all where they should be.

I would also like to thank Rosemary Carlton, Robert Hoffman (Tlingit) and Carol Crowe (Mohawk/Algonquin) for reviewing the indigenous aspects of the novel to ensure that I depicted the indigenous people and their culture with the respect they deserve.

Also I want to thank my fantastic editor, Sandra Mangan, and my amazing cover designer, Jane Dixon-Smith whose creative genius has gone a long way to help make my books a success.

And most of all, I want to thank my brilliant readers, whose support down the years has helped to make my writing such a wonderful experience.